# THE PATRIOT'S DAUGHTER

**Also available by Brittany Butler**

**The Juliet Arroway Series**

*The Syndicate Spy*

# THE PATRIOT'S DAUGHTER

A NOVEL

BRITTANY BUTLER

CROOKED
LANE

NEW YORK

Books should be disposed of and recycled according to local requirements.
All paper materials used are FSC compliant.

This is a work of fiction. All of the names, characters, organizations, places and events portrayed in this novel are either products of the author's imagination or are used fictitiously. Any resemblance to real or actual events, locales, or persons, living or dead, is entirely coincidental.

All statements of fact, opinion, or analysis expressed are those of the author and do not reflect the official positions or views of the US Government. Nothing in the contents should be construed as asserting or implying US Government authentication of information or endorsement of the author's views.



Published in the United States by Crooked Lane Books, an imprint of The Quick Brown Fox & Company LLC.

Crooked Lane Books and its logo are trademarks of The Quick Brown Fox & Company LLC.

Library of Congress Catalog-in-Publication data available upon request.

ISBN (hardcover): 979-8-89242-388-5
ISBN (paperback): 979-8-89242-389-2
ISBN (ebook): 979-8-89242-390-8

Cover design by Emily Mahar

Printed in the United States.

www.crookedlanebooks.com

Crooked Lane Books
34 West 27th St., 10th Floor
New York, NY 10001

First Edition: April 2026

The authorized representative in the EU for product safety and compliance is eucomply OÜPärnu mnt 139b-14, 11317 Tallinn, Estonia, hello@eucompliancepartner.com, +33757690241

10 9 8 7 6 5 4 3 2 1

To the girls who were told they couldn't but did anyway. And to my sons, who remind me every day why courage matters.

# Prologue

HER MOTHER HAD vanished, yet she was everywhere eleven-year-old Ava looked.

Tonight, she was in every sound, the clattering of the washing machine, the groan of the dishwasher, within the creaks of the old house settling—all were echoes of her mother's nightly routine before she had come to hug her goodnight.

Pulling the bed sheets up to her chin, Ava tried to conjure a memory that would stop the panic from rising within her chest. But fear climbed her throat anyway. Two years. It had been two years since her mother left, and she hadn't called. And she'd always called, even on business trips abroad.

A stream of amber light pooled across Ava's butterfly-stamped bedspread, and she bolted upright. She scrambled toward the window, fingertips bracing against the sill as she searched for the glow of her aunt's headlights. But the only movement outside was from the rain streaming tears down the frosted glass. Aunt Valerie wouldn't return for hours—not from one of *those* dates. The ones that ended with her heels clattering in the hallway, her eyeliner smudged, and the sick-sweet stench of wine curling off her breath as she said, "Sorry, baby," like it fixed anything.

Ava tried to calm her breathing, but the quiet continued to press in around her, letting the questions she wasn't permitted to ask bubble in her mind. Questions about her mother, her father, the strange assurances and half-truths that had shaped her childhood. Her mom traveled often, for one month, sometimes two. But never had she felt compelled to tell Ava where she was going or what she was doing, and Ava knew better than to ask—her curt interactions with her aunt had told her that. Questions about her unknown father had been met with a similar silence, and she'd learned to bury her curiosity deep inside. Especially after her aunt's icy response one day—"He's dead"—she'd given up asking.

Ava picked up her pink journal from the bedside table and flipped open a page to stare at her messy cursive. Her journal was what she'd turned to when she was feeling sad or vulnerable—a trick her mother had taught her. It was a way of clearing out the cobwebs that made it difficult to see past her obstacles, her pain. And today, she'd written ten pages worth of prose.

Clutching her pen tightly, she strained her ears, wishing she could hear her mother's humming while she stirred a pot of homemade borscht, the fragrant smell wafting around her like a jeweled cloak. Her mom had a way of turning their tiny Pentagon City apartment into something magical, something that could withstand her habitual absence. With intricately carved Russian nesting dolls that sat perched on her nightstand to the richly patterned silks that draped the walls of her bedroom—each was a connection to her mother's other life that Ava longed to know more about.

But here, in her aunt's house, there was no borscht, no warmth, no laughter—only the stale stench of cigarettes and bitter coffee, and the sharp, metallic tang of microwave dinners. Squeezing her eyes tight, Ava willed her thoughts to drift from darkness into light. But all she was met with was the clicking of the fan overhead and her aunt's warnings echoing within her mind: *Don't turn into your mother, Ava. Pick a suitable career. Don't ruin your life with some stupid mistake.*

Inhaling deeply, Ava kicked off the covers and tried not to think too deeply about her aunt's words, words that still stung. Was she her mother's "stupid mistake"?

Leaning over the edge of her bed, she pulled out the small suitcase she'd packed earlier that afternoon. With the suitcase hugged to her side, she crept toward the door, the cold hardwood floor snapping at her bare feet. Her hand hesitated on the doorknob, and she felt darkness creep steadily toward her.

*You can do this,* she told herself. Although courage was the last thing she felt, especially when her aunt's frosty eyes had stared back at her with such indifference that morning: "I told you, I don't know why your mother hasn't called. There's no point in crying about it."

Creaking the door open, Ava tiptoed down the dimly lit hallway, her breath tight within her chest. At the front door, her green rain boots sat where she'd left them, her yellow rain jacket draped haphazardly. Her fingers trembled as she wrestled her feet into the boots. She swallowed against the lump in her throat—what if she couldn't find her mother? What if something had happened to her?

Stiffening against the fear that rippled down her spine, she approached the front door. Doing nothing, and accepting that her mother was simply gone, was the unbearable option. She gripped the doorknob, inhaled sharply, and turned it.

Outside, the cool autumn night met her with a sharp chill. The scent of decaying leaves and damp earth met her nostrils. Rain streamed in silver rivers down the worn brick doorstep, pooling near her boots and running along the uneven sidewalk in front of her aunt's house. The street shimmered with water beneath the faint glow of a distant streetlamp.

A car door creaked open, and Ava froze, her pulse skittering as she stepped back from view, hiding within the shadows.

"I wish I could let you in," Her aunt's voice floated from where she stood near her date's car, low and tired. "But my sister seems to have stuck me with her daughter for good."

"How old is she?" A man's voice murmured in reply. "And what happened to her mother?"

Ava held her breath, her blood roaring in her ears so loud she nearly missed her aunt's reply.

"She's eleven. Her mother died," her aunt admitted, her voice sharper now. "So it seems I'll be chained to the child forever."

The words struck like a slap and a deep ache bloomed within Ava's chest. She tightened her jaw, forcing her tears not to fall. She pulled her hood up over her chestnut hair, shielding herself from the night and the truth that she could no longer ignore. *It was time.* Time not just to leave the house but to shed the quiet, aching hope that someone might one day choose her. She wrapped her fingers around the handle of her suitcase as if it could anchor her. It was all she had. All she could carry.

If no one would give her answers about her mother, she'd find them herself. She slipped into the alley, the wind whispering behind her and the street swallowing her shadow, and wondered for a moment: Would anyone even come looking?

She didn't look back.

# CHAPTER

# 1

TWENTY-SIX-YEAR-OLD CIA OFFICER Ava Anderson felt the tail two blocks before she saw him.

She walked the streets of Moscow alone, her breath fogging in the air, the rhythmic crunch of her boots silenced by the hum of luxury sedans gliding past. She knew it was against protocol, that she was putting her life at risk. But it made her feel closer to the truth—closer to her mother somehow, knowing that like her mother before her, she now led a double life.

Behind her, the hulking US Embassy building loomed large, with layers of uniformed security guards, high walls, security cameras, and uniformed Russian police—their presence subtle but unmistakable, a reminder that she was always being watched. But after the encounter at the embassy earlier that night, Ava needed the cold clarity of open air. She needed to remind herself why she was here and why she had chosen *this* life.

A man lingered beneath the glow of a streetlamp ahead, pretending to scroll through his phone, and Ava adjusted her pace. She turned down Konyushkovskaya Street, the sting of the cold sharpening her senses. Moscow was beautiful in late December: the sparkling garlands, the snow blanketing the boulevards and sugar-frosted trees, beckoning memories of the stories her mother had once told.

Her mother had spoken about Moscow like a fairytale, full of nobility and elegant balls. It wasn't until Ava grew older that she'd realized that the Moscow Theresa Anderson had spoken of no longer existed.

Ava felt an itch at the base of her skull—a creeping sense like a noose that she couldn't see. The air felt heavier as she scanned the street. There was a part of her that wanted to rush into her apartment building and lock the deadbolt tightly behind her. But her training had taught her to enter a public place when followed and to try to expose the surveillant.

She turned a corner and felt someone fall into step behind her. Her gloved hand reached into her coat pocket and felt the slim outline of her burner phone—the one she could use to call embassy security if she thought her life was threatened. She spotted a café two blocks ahead and tried to breathe normally, but each step pulled regret further into her chest. Perhaps the FSB, the Russian state security service, had already caught onto her.

Perhaps it was Konstantin Morozov.

She entered a nearby café and sank into a seat next to the window, her hands and face still burning with the dry cold as she scanned the street. A man passed without hesitation, his breath steaming up the air, his phone held up to his ear. She removed her coat, the scent of expensive perfume and bourbon-laced cocktails still clinging to her. But it was the memory of Konstantin Morozov that chilled her now—the man with ice-colored eyes who had looked at her like a ghost.

*What if she had been too obvious about her interest in Konstantin, and her actions had caught the attention of the FSB?*

Her mind replayed the embassy event, two hours before, when everything had shifted.

She hadn't drunk from the champagne flute in her hand, but her fingers gripped the stem like a lifeline as she had scanned the crowd—diplomats and businessmen mostly, and the occasional spook wearing a designer suit. Her mission that night had been clear: Recruit someone from Russia's foreign intelligence agency, the SVR, to uncover the source of cyberattacks threatening US networks.

But missions like these never went according to plan.

She held the glass to her lips, pretending to take a sip, and caught a glimpse of herself in the bar's mirror. With her mother's high cheek bones, full lips, and wavy chestnut hair, Ava could pass for almost any nationality—French, Greek, German. But it was her eyes, a strange, light gray, that made her stand out.

Earlier that night, Ava had stilled her breath and focused on the familiar swirl of Russian conversations that surrounded her. The language, once foreign and tangled, now grounded her—reminding her of how far she had come and yet how far she still had to go.

That was when she'd noticed the Russian man in the corner. His shock of white hair, combed to one side, contrasted with his weather-beaten skin. Like others, he wore a dark suit that blended into the crowd, but the pin on his lapel, a Russian flag, caught the light. His glacial-colored eyes fixed on Ava like he *knew* her, and something in her gut twisted.

Her embassy coworker, Marika, had been her usual self—bold, charming, too casual about things that could get them both killed. She had sauntered toward Ava with two vodkas in hand. "Here. Relax. Drink."

Ava had accepted the glass, forcing down the sharp bite of vodka. But even as conversation hummed and glasses clinked around her, she couldn't shake the weight of the man's eyes on her. Something about him had tugged at her insides—familiar yet strange. *Had she seen him on her surveillance detection route earlier?*

"Who is that man?" Ava nodded subtly toward him.

Marika followed her gaze and took another swig of her vodka before cradling the glass. "Isn't he a little old for you, *molodyozh*?" It was what Marika called all the younger people in the office.

"It's just the way he was looking at me." Ava's gaze flickered back to the man. There was something in his face—the way his eyes roamed over her face a fraction too long, as though he recognized something in her she didn't yet know about herself.

Before she could say another word, Marika waved a hand, ushering the man over. Ava gripped Marika's arm.

"What are you doing?" she hissed.

"Introducing you," Marika said breezily. "Calm down, *molodyozh.*"

The man crossed the room, his pale gray eyes locked on Ava's. "I see you've taken to recruiting your own," he'd said to Marika in a thick Russian accent.

"Konstantin Morozov at your service," Marika announced.

"A pleasure." Ava extended her hand, keeping her face neutral.

He released Ava's hand abruptly.

Marika leaned in, although Ava could still hear her conspiratorial whisper to Konstantin. "You look like you have seen a ghost."

"I'm not entirely sure that I haven't." Ava caught his reply, in Russian. "I'm sorry," He shook his head as if trying to dislodge a memory. "It's just . . . you remind me of someone."

Marika had stepped closer so that she stood between Ava and Konstantin. "You old dog, she's young enough to be your granddaughter."

"I didn't mean . . ." Red crept up the older man's neck and Ava felt a jab of sympathy for him. "That's not at all what I meant." His eyes had flicked to Ava one last time before he'd turned and walked away.

"Vell, zat was weird," Marika said with a laugh.

But Ava didn't laugh.

There was something in the way the man had looked at her—recognition? Regret? Could he be SVR?

"Do you know Konstantin well?" Ava asked Marika, her voice steady despite the tightening within her chest.

"Not really, only zat he used to gamble with my late husband. Always lost, too." She'd swirled the remaining vodka in her glass, her tone light, but Ava's mind was miles ahead.

* * *

Now, in the café, every cell in Ava's body screamed that something had changed. She scanned the road outside, uncertain whether Konstantin was a threat or an opportunity. But one thought clung to the back of her mind like frost. He hadn't recognized *her.*

*Perhaps he had recognized her mother.*

The last time anyone had seen Ava's mother, she'd been on Russian soil, working on an operation the CIA still refused to talk about. And then—nothing. No body. No answers. Just a classified file that she'd never been allowed to read. She'd spent years digging, following dead-end leads, and questioning people who had refused to speak. And after Ava had joined the CIA, she'd hit every roadblock about accessing the "Restricted Handling" file. It was buried deep, and only the directors and a few that surrounded them knew all the details.

As she neared the café, the snow had stopped, but the cold had not. She shoved her hands inside her pockets and tried to ignore the ache in her throat. Her mission had changed. It was no longer just about the one she'd been assigned. Nor the operation she thought she understood. Because somewhere, beneath the layers of lies and buried files, the truth wasn't just resurfacing. It was coming for her.

# CHAPTER

# 2

THE CAFÉ DOOR swung open with a loud clack, and a man entered—average height and medium build with a black moustache that extended, untrimmed, beyond his mouth. He wore a bold red tie beneath a long wool coat and a grey beanie that hid most of the graying hair that curled at the nape of his neck.

It was the man Ava had spotted earlier with the phone beneath the lamplight. *Could this be FSB? Already here to arrest her?*

Her nerves seized and her chest tightened.

Then she saw the eyes. *Frank.*

Relief surged as her CIA boss sat across from her and ordered two black coffees. Like her mother, Frank had spent most of his career at the CIA in the field, chasing terrorists and recruiting spies. His salt-and-pepper hair was short, signaling his battle with middle age. But his piercing blue eyes were as sharp as ever as they raked over the café.

"I would have doubled back at Konyushkovskaya Street," he murmured. "I've been following you for almost four blocks."

"Well, I spotted you, didn't I? And now you're exposed." She exhaled, her pulse still racing as she scanned the café: families, couples, a sullen barista behind the counter.

Hopefully she and Frank looked like nothing more than two diplomats drinking coffee after an embassy function. And in

Moscow, where the FSB shadowed every whisper, sometimes the safest place was out in the open.

"I thought we were meeting tomorrow morning," she said.

"This café is a surveillance dead zone. Half the FSB avoid it because of the poor WiFi." Frank's blue eyes, lined with fatigue, flicked toward the door before he took a sip of his coffee. "How was tonight?"

"Interesting," she said, pulling herself back from the panic that FSB had been following her. "You were right. Marika seems to have access to everyone in Moscow. And I met Nathaniel Grey."

Frank blinked slowly. "*The* Nathaniel Grey?"

She nodded. "CEO of Vibrantia."

Frank sat back. "Go on."

"Marika said that he was looking for foreign investors." Ava's eyes flicked toward potential exits as she took a sip of her coffee. "The ones that don't ask too many questions. If someone wanted to inject disinformation into the US bloodstream, he's got the perfect entry point."

Frank scribbled something onto a paper napkin and moved it across the table. Ava looked down at his writing. *You think he's connected?*

Ava shrugged. "But I do know that the online chaos that we're seeing, the conspiracy loops . . . it's all exploding on Vibrantia. Nathaniel Grey's platform is either being used, or he's letting it be used."

Frank exhaled, long and low. "Walk me through tonight."

Earlier that night, Marika had nudged Ava gently with her elbow. "You seem like you're somewhere else, *molodyozh*."

Ava blinked, still recovering from the shock of Konstantin's reaction to her. "Sorry."

Marika gave her a curious look but let it drop, nodding toward a man surrounded by admirers. "Now *that* man—the one with looks and a bank account to match—he's more your speed."

Nathaniel Grey, trim and tailored in a custom Armani suit, drew a crowd wherever he went. When his eyes locked on Ava's, he smiled with confidence that carried weight.

"What's the scoop?" Ava asked, her voice low.

"Rumors are that he's looking for some new investors. He always draws a crowd."

"How is it that you know so much about everyone?" Ava asked Marika, her eyes still on Grey.

"Ah, well, I've worked at the US consulate a long time, *molodyozh*." She tilted her chin upward, eyes narrowing as she counted silently. "Almost thirty years this coming May, come to think of it." She turned patted Ava on the shoulder. "Long before you were born, I imagine."

"Not too long," Ava interjected, "I'm twenty-six."

"That's quite young for a Foreign Service officer. Are they pulling you from the cradle these days?"

Ava only shrugged, letting the question hang for a moment. The badge clipped to her blouse read *Sloane Reed, US Embassy Moscow*, and that was all Marika needed to know. As far as her embassy colleagues knew, she was just another junior Foreign Service officer pushing papers and practicing her Russian in staff meetings.

"Something like that." Ava shrugged, although her path to the CIA had been anything but easy. Her work had not been by chance, nor was her assignment to Moscow. Fluent in Russian, a skill her mother had insisted that she learn as a child, she'd sought out the CIA rather than the other way around. The name *Sloane* served well enough in this building, but the part that mattered to her most, the part that answered to Ava Anderson, belonged to a very different mission.

"Introduce me," Ava suggested.

"Of course." Marika poked her in the shoulder with one index finger. "And I agree with you. He is quite handsome."

Ava watched as Marika approached Grey and said something that made him laugh out loud, a deep, throaty laugh. He looked at Ava again, longer this time, a dark lock of hair falling on his forehead as Marika spoke to him. He nodded and walked toward Ava, his stride deliberate.

"I'm told that you're the reason this event doesn't feel like a funeral," Grey said as he reached her. His tone held a hint of admiration as his eyes roamed over her sleek dress.

Embassy functions were usually stiff, over-catered affairs—more about formality than energy. But tonight felt different: Conversations flowed more easily, and laughter wasn't forced. "I had help," she replied, her tone brisk.

"Nathaniel Grey." He extended a hand, and Ava took it.

"I know, you've got quite the following at our alma mater," she said, knowing he'd graduated from Florida State University as she had.

He lowered his eyes on her. "And where is that?"

"FSU." She smiled, close-lipped, curious whether she should have revealed that piece of information about herself. But her CIA training had taught her to stay as close to the truth as possible.

"Ah, Tallahassee, one of my favorite cities, land of the bad roads and good late-night pizza."

"Tallahassee isn't anyone's favorite city."

"How can you say that?" he asked. "The pokey sticks from Gumby's are simply divine."

"You"—she pointed at him—"have had the pokey sticks? Now that I don't believe."

Was she flirting with him? It was a fine line between flirtation and laying the groundwork for potential recruitment.

He patted his trim, athletic build. "Did a ten-mile run the next day and worth every minute." He looked toward Marika, then slid a sly glance back at Ava. "It's wonderful to meet you, Ms. . . ."

"Sloane Reed."

"Who would have thought," he said airily, "us FSU grads in the same place, same time. We've all come a long way from that little town in Florida."

"Some of us further than others," she quipped, remembering the article that listed Grey as one of *Forbes*'s richest men under thirty.

After a pause, Grey said, "I wouldn't call a US diplomat . . . nothing."

So he knew. She wasn't surprised. Someone like Grey, with his connections and resources, probably knew the names and occupations of every single person in the room. Still, hearing it aloud made her curious what else he knew about her.

"Now if you'll both excuse me," he said, tilting his head toward the cluster of men and women who looked longingly in his direction. But before he left, he smiled at Ava and stepped closer. Ava caught the scent of cologne—amber, musk, similar to the potent scent she noticed most Russian men wore. His breath warmed the shell of her ear.

"Call me sometime." He slipped her his card. "Would love to chat more about FSU, and . . . other things."

She didn't move as she watched him walk away, slicing through the crowd with the confidence of someone who knew exactly how much control he had. She stared after him, her mind racing. Why would Grey, an American golden boy turned political rising star, be inviting Russian influence into his orbit?

Russia had always known how to fracture a country from the inside. If they gained more control over Vibrantia, they wouldn't need bombs or bullets. They'd have algorithms. Targeted chaos. Lies wrapped in truth. State lines drawn by ideology and fear.

She'd placed his card inside her clutch, her fingers brushing the cool steel of the small revolver hidden inside. Ava had seen her mother's gun only once—a flash of polished metal beneath the hem of her jacket when she was nine years old. Her mother hadn't flinched when Ava noticed. Instead, Theresa Anderson had calmly said, "I carry it everywhere; it's my insurance policy."

It was a lesson Ava had never forgotten. Grey might be a gateway. Konstantin too—but either could blow open the Russian cyber plot or bury her in it. Just like her mother.

Now Ava said to Frank, her voice low, "I think Grey is a conduit, whether he's aware of it or not."

Frank edged closer, the dim lights from the coffee shop casting shadows down his weathered face. "Vibrantia has been flagged in six different cyber briefs driving state-level unrest." He adjusted his coat across his middle, gone soft from too many late-night briefings with whisky and cigars.

Ava nodded. "And he's been funding the Liberty Coalition. They're pushing antifederal rhetoric. Talks of decentralizing federal powers, isolating foreign entanglements . . ."

"It's fueling division. Just last week there was a mass protest in Texas about seceding from the union. And I can't shake the feeling there's a foreign hand stirring the pot."

A chill that had nothing to do with the Moscow winter ran through Ava. It wasn't the first time she'd considered that Nathaniel Grey's political ideals aligned more with Moscow than Washington. She'd blamed her suspicion on her training, her instincts, and maybe lingering paranoia. But the seed had been planted when she'd read the damning *Forbes* magazine article that exposed Grey's connections to a shadowy web of foreign donors with ties to the Kremlin.

"He slipped me his number," she said finally. "I think he wants to take me out."

"Excellent." Frank scrapped his grey-and-white stubble. "Then we move. Carefully." He looked down at the card she had placed on the table. "We've been playing defense too long," he muttered. "It's time we played offense."

Before she could respond, a sharp vibration against her thigh made her jump. Her phone. She glanced at it. Blocked number. A new text message lit up the screen. Her hands trembled as she read the message, her breath catching in her throat.

**She's still alive.**

# CHAPTER

# 3

THE WHITE RABBIT restaurant sat like a glass jewel atop a historic Russian building, the panoramic view framing the shimmering, snow-laden silhouette of the Kremlin. Ava's breath fogged the cool glass as she watched the world outside, its glittering skyline a stark contrast to the weight inside her chest. The air smelled of fresh fish cooked in butter and truffle oil, a scent so rich it was a reminder that she didn't belong here—not in this world of opulence, not in this game she was playing.

Across from her, Nathaniel Grey's voice flowed with practiced ease as he recounted the expansion of his business empire. Ava nodded absently, her attention elsewhere, trapped by the message that had appeared on her phone yesterday. *She's still alive.*

The text had appeared without warning. No number. No name. Just those three words. And yet she had known exactly who they referred to.

*Her mother.*

Her pulse thudded in her throat. It couldn't be true. She had buried that hope long ago—stuffed it down below the redacted files and the CIA's silence. For years she had convinced herself that it was all over, that her mother was gone. And yet *still alive* clung to her like a whisper in the dark—no one had found her mother's body.

The possibility that her mother was alive now threaded through every thought, louder than Grey's voice, like a drumbeat she couldn't silence. Someone knew what had really happened to her mother and wanted to rattle Ava. *But who had sent the message? And why now?*

Her fingers tightened on her fork, the coolness a slight balm against the fire that had burned inside her. Blocking out her past was a lie that she had told herself often. But the truth couldn't stay buried forever. And the sting of it cut too deep to forget.

The memory came again, unbidden, and she was sixteen again, climbing the narrow stairs of her aunt's townhouse, heart hammering like it might burst through her ribs.

The smell had hit Ava first, cigarette smoke that tasted like char on her tongue. Her aunt was at her desk, a cigarette balanced in the ashtray, a thin thread of smoke rising between them. Ava didn't bother with a greeting.

"What really happened to my mother?" she had asked.

Her aunt stilled, the hand reaching for the cigarette hovering in mid-air. She pursed her lips, as if weighing her next words. "It's not easy for me to tell you this, even now." She pulled out a folded letter that she handed Ava, and shook her head. "All the love she had for a country that she'd supposedly only visited only twice. I always thought that it was odd how much she'd fallen in love with Russian culture."

With chilled fingertips, Ava unfolded the paper. Her tongue swelled, making it difficult to swallow as she'd looked down at the paper her aunt had handed her. She tried to make out the words that blurred through her tears. She could not, would not believe the words that stared at her directly. A letter from the CIA director, stating that her mother had died in Russia, killed by her handler after eight years as a suspected double agent for the SVR.

Theresa Anderson, branded a traitor for selling secrets to the Russians. The evidence had been damning—encrypted messages traced to her laptop, meetings with a known SVR handler, and a bank account overseas holding unexplained deposits. But it had all been kept quiet.

And Ava had never fully accepted it. Not deep down.

A sliver of hope had remained lodged in her chest, stubborn and irrational—the child in her whispering that they had gotten it all wrong. That there had to be some other explanation. The woman who had once wrapped her daughter in love and bedtime stories could not have betrayed her country to spy for the Russians. She would have known what her lies could cost—the risk of getting caught, and the consequences of leaving Ava an orphan.

Now Grey spoke, interrupting her thoughts. "Vibrantia is really taking off as a multipurpose platform."

She straightened, nodded, and played the part, even as her past threatened to consume her. She needed to build rapport and trust with Nathaniel Grey. She needed to demonstrate her interest and empathy for the battles he sought to win. She had to focus.

"Sounds interesting." She took a swallow of red wine and let the smooth tannins flatten what she really wanted to say.

"We're combining viral short-term videos with essential daily functions like making financial transactions," he went on. "Paying parking meters and even trading stock."

Ava nodded, watching the way he spoke with measured control, the king of an empire built on algorithms and influence, and now head of a political party called the Liberty Coalition that was quickly gaining influence. She knew that a single word from him could send markets tumbling or shape the outcome of an election—all because he owned the platforms that controlled the conversation.

"But Vibrantia isn't just another social media platform," Grey said, leaning forward until his fingers grazed the top of her hand and lingered there just a beat too long, a casual gesture that felt anything but. Ava fought the urge to pull her hand back.

"It's smarter," he went on, lowering his voice as if letting her in on a secret. "It reads people, their moods, their habits, in real time. We're not just feeding them posts; we're shaping what they see, nudging them toward what they already believe. The system's always learning, always adjusting, so the message hits deeper every time."

Ava felt nausea stir, not only at the unwanted intimacy of Grey's hand on her skin but from the zeal with which he spoke of hardening people's biases, as if manipulation were a virtue. She tucked it away as evidence of the man she sought to expose.

Messaging and influencing people's thoughts was no longer about overt propaganda—it was a subtle, evolving weapon designed to fracture societies gradually. And the CIA was concerned about where things could head if Russia was permitted greater influence over Vibrantia. It could stroke the fires of discord until it evolved into something far more dangerous.

Ava inhaled deeply, breath heavy in her lungs. It was critical that she understand how this AI-driven manipulation would evolve and what Grey's plans were with the Russians.

"I'm sorry," he said suddenly, startling her. "I've been talking about my business the whole time, when really I want to know more about you."

Ava looked up from her wine glass and tried to smile her most genuine smile as the waiter served their first course: fresh oysters topped with vodka and caviar.

"Well," she said as she set the wineglass on the starch white tablecloth. "What would you like to know?"

# CHAPTER

# 4

AVA'S SECURE PHONE buzzed on her bedside table, jolting her awake. Her sheets felt damp and sticky on her warm skin from a restless night, while the air smelled of clean, soft linen and the subtle undertones of the sandalwood-scented hotel shampoo she'd used before going to bed. Despite having taken a twenty-minute shower, her meeting with Grey clung to her like a bad dream. She could not, would not let him touch her again.

She rubbed at her eyes and held the biometric reader up to her eyes. Only one person could be calling her at this hour. "Frank," she said, still groggy, sitting up in bed. "Do you know what time it is here?" She looked down at her phone.

"Ava, the cable you sent last night, do you have any idea who you met with at the embassy party?" She adjusted the phone so it showed her only from the neck up. She didn't want Frank to see the worn Def Leppard t-shirt she'd worn to bed.

"Nathaniel Grey, I told you." She clicked on the lamp on the bedside table. "I went to dinner with him last night. I can already tell . . ."

"No, I'm not talking about Grey, I'm talking about the Russian. Konstantin."

Ava froze, suddenly alert. "I figured he was SVR. He had the posture, the control. But something about him felt . . . familiar. I couldn't place it."

"He's not just any SVR agent. He's the man behind three political assassinations—all ordered by Putin himself."

Ava straightened. When Putin's power began to slip, he'd turned to the tactics of old Russia: silencing his enemies before they could rise against him.

She straightened. "That should have showed up on my initial traces."

"Not if you were using the wrong last name. I'm glad you sent a picture of him. One of our analysts ran it through our biometric databases, and we matched his irises to Konstantin Gallitzin."

A cold rush moved down her spine as she got up to insert a coffee pod into the coffee maker. She had heard about Konstantin—whispers during a training exercise about an SVR officer who had gone rogue after a botched assassination attempt in Vienna. She hadn't realized that the man had resurfaced. Or than he might be connected to the digital incursions they were tracking.

Frank's voice dropped. "I want you to stay far away from him."

"What? A direct penetration of SVR who sought me out? No way."

"I mean it, Ava. This guy is dangerous. I don't want you suddenly poisoned."

"You've got to be joking. We've been trying to connect the cyberattacks to someone in-country, and he practically walked up and handed me a lead. If he's still that plugged in—"

"He's not just plugged in, Ava, he's lethal. If he thinks you're onto him, he'll disappear. Or worse, you will."

"I think he knows which Russians are involved." What she didn't say, what she couldn't, were the thoughts that burned at the edges of her mind. What she hadn't dared put into words: that Konstantin's interest in her had felt too pointed, too personal. The way he'd looked at her last night almost felt like he knew part of her story, perhaps a part that she had yet to learn herself.

Frank hesitated. "You've only been in country for six weeks, and this is your first assignment in Russia. I don't want you putting your life at risk."

"Then don't risk me. Support me. I'm going to run with this."

Frank paused and folded his arms across his chest, leaning back away from the phone. A beat. Then another. "Fine, I'm sending someone to help you."

She frowned. "Who?"

"You remember him. He trained you at the Farm."

Ava could feel her chest tightening as she held the coffee cup up to her lips. She could hear her heart in her ears, a light, frantic sound.

"Ben Jennings."

Six months ago, Ava had been running through the dense Virginia forest, the crisp wind on the back of her neck, the gentle rustle of leaves fluttering overhead, her breath ragged, exhaustion dragging at her sore limbs. A shadow moved ahead. It was part of the CIA's training exercise, but fear had clawed within her throat. This was more than a drill. It was her future. Everything hinged on her graduating from operational training at the Farm. And she was falling behind. Late-night surveillance detection drills. Hours trekking through Virginia's backwoods. She had lost track of how many tick bites she'd gotten.

A shadow shifted up ahead, and she stopped suddenly, her pulse hammering.

Ben emerged from behind a tree, tall and broad-shouldered, with a paint gun holstered on his hip that looked far too much like the real thing. The strong lines of his back flexed as if he could sense her. He turned slowly, a smirk tugging at his mouth like he knew she was watching. His worn baseball cap sat low, but not low enough that it could hide the cocky glint in his eyes.

"You're not difficult to spot," she lied, but she was still trying to catch her breath.

"Come on," he said, flashing her a look over his shoulder. "I've outrun surveillance teams with twice their budget and ten times their training."

They walked in silence toward the mess hall, dead leaves crunching underfoot.

"If this were Moscow," he said, "you'd already be dead."

"Thanks for the pep talk," Ava gritted out.

"I aim to inspire," he replied, not missing a beat.

"I'm already aware that torture and death are distinct possibilities in this line of work."

"Only if you accept that as an outcome, which I don't." He stopped walking, turning to face her. His eyes, pale green with edges like steel, held her. "You freeze when you're unsure. Don't. Make them chase you. Be unpredictable. Make *them* sweat."

There was something in his voice, calm, commanding—a low hum of challenge under the advice. As if he wasn't coaching her, he was daring her.

"Listen," he said, low and firm, stepping closer now, close enough that she could smell the faint scent of soap and cedar. He removed his baseball cap and ran a hand through dark blond waves. "You've got instincts that most officers would kill for. You see details that others miss. But that's just a start. Confidence buys you seconds. Seconds can buy your life."

She swallowed, nodding slowly, though his words hit harder than she'd expected. She was two weeks away from her assignment in Russia and didn't feel ready. Ben had that effect on her: pulling her apart and daring her to put herself back together stronger.

Since learning that her assignment was in Moscow, Ben had devoted extra hours to her training. Late nights. Weekends. Long hours spent together running scenarios. He never said why, and she had never asked. But sometimes his fingers brushed her knuckles when passing, showing her a trick with her Glock. The air between them crackling with something unspoken as Ben pushed her to her limits—a live wire that they both knew not to touch.

Later that night, hunched over a secure terminal, their knees brushed beneath a metal desk. She didn't move hers.

"Encryption keys are everything," he explained, his voice measured, though she could feel his focus split—part of him aware of how close they were. "It's basically a string of characters used in the encryption and decryption process. When you use this key, it will unlock your messages with your sources."

He clicked on a prompt and entered his own key. The covert message converted from the ciphertext to plain text, the glow from the computer casting shadows across his face.

"Think of it as your lifeline." His jaw was tight as he turned, eyes narrowing. "Your communication with your source will be crucial for maintaining confidentiality. Only the intended recipient can decipher the information."

Ava studied the sequence of numbers, but her attention drifted to the warmth radiating off his body, the air between them humming with restraint.

"I'll teach you everything you need to know to survive in Moscow," he said without looking up. But his thigh stayed pressed against hers just a second longer than necessary.

Frank cleared his throat over the phone, bringing her abruptly back to her hotel room.

"I wish you'd consulted me before bringing him in," she said.

Frank's gaze was steady. "Ben is a professional, Ava. He's here to do a job, just like you. He doesn't need to be involved in your operational meetings. He can help run countersurveillance detection routes after your meetings to ensure you're not being followed. And he'll be armed, which gives me an extra layer of comfort with you taking this on."

Ava frowned. "I'll be armed as well. I don't need a babysitter."

"This is your second mission, and you've already stumbled onto a Russian SVR agent, one of their best assassins. You need all the help you can get."

Ava swallowed her annoyance. The last thing she needed was Ben critiquing her every move. But Frank had at least agreed that she could pursue Konstantin as a potential source.

"Fine," she said. "But the minute Ben gets in my way, I want him off this mission." But the truth was that she thought of him as a potential distraction more than a hindrance.

Frank's expression hardened. "He's the best counterintelligence officer we know. If he's hesitant about a particular source, or a certain mission, I expect you to listen. His instincts could mean the difference between life and death."

Ava decided to change the subject. "How do you propose 'bumping' into Konstantin again?"

"You said in your report that it seemed that Konstantin has a gambling problem. If you want to engineer a bump, I suggest start there."

She nodded slowly. "Perhaps Marika knows where he gambles."

"Great. We stage a bump at a casino, make sure he wins, get Konstantin to think it's his idea to talk, and feed the ego. You play curious American. Let's see what secrets fall out when he thinks he's in control."

"You're already designing the op."

"I'm protecting my officer," Frank replied. "How good are you at cards?"

"Not very." Ava sipped her coffee, eyes sharp. "The last time I played was Uno with my mom when I was five."

"I have good news for you then."

"That I seriously doubt."

Frank smiled without humor. "Ben Jennings is the best card player I know."

# CHAPTER

# 5

THE RADIATOR IN the CIA's Moscow safe house clanked like it was dragging chains, cracking through the calm interior Ava had spent hours trying to preserve. The air hung heavy with the scent of dust and secrecy, clinging to the back of her throat like the scent of mildewed towels. She sat stiffly on the couch, once a deep red but now faded into a tired, nicotine-stained rust that overpowered most of the room.

Outside, the weight of the Moscow night pressed hard against the windows, frost clinging to the edges like brittle veins. The room felt like it was shrinking with each howl of the wind as she waited. Three sharp knocks rattled the door frame, and Ava stood, her pulse thrumming within her ears. There was part of her that wondered whether she had made it all up—the intensity she'd felt when Ben was nearby, the electricity that persisted. She walked toward the door and waited for the code words.

They came low and steady from the other side of the door: "Patriot's Point."

She unlatched the top lock, and the door swung open. Ben stepped inside, brushing the snow from his broad shoulders. The cold clung to him, raising the color in his cheeks. He looked different, harder—as though being in Moscow had sharpened his edges.

"You're late," Ava said, voice flat, though her pulse thundered at the sight of him—the stubble that softened his strong jaw, the sea-glass-colored eyes that moved something inside her.

He shrugged out of his coat. "Had to make certain that I wasn't being followed."

"Do you think that someone is watching the safe house?" The question caught in her throat.

"No," he said, his gaze cutting through her. "I think someone is watching you."

She folded her arms across her chest as he stared at her, his mouth set in a tight line. "We're in Moscow; someone is always watching," she said.

Ben lifted a brow and made his way toward the window to close the blinds. "Agreed."

"Hot toddy?" she offered, already moving toward the kitchen, though she yearned to ask who he thought was watching her.

"Sure," he replied, his footsteps trailing close behind her.

She opened a cabinet, pulled out a kettle, and placed two coffee cups on the counter. "Have you been briefed by Station?"

Ben nodded and moved beside her to fill the kettle with water. She turned the knob to light the burner on the gas stove. "Then you know that Konstantin Morozov has resurfaced."

"The question is whether he will talk," Ben said.

"Why else would the SVR guard him like the last Romanov?"

Ben said nothing, his gaze steady on her face as she reached for the whisky. She poured a heavy shot into each cup.

"What else do we know about Konstantin?" she asked, trying to ignore the fluttering against her ribcage when Ben looked at her.

He folded his arms. "Since Vienna, he's kept a low profile. These days, he co-owns a string of shell companies—the kind that keep the Kremlin's dirty work funded and off the books. He's still very much on their payroll, though it looks like he's managed to rack up a fair bit of personal debt along the way."

"Dirty money?" she asked.

His jaw flexed. "Like your friend Nathaniel?"

"I wouldn't say that we're friends." She hesitated, then glanced at him. "But I went to dinner with him. Intel gathering."

Ben's jaw twitched but he remained silent. His silence said more than a comment ever could.

She looked away, focusing on the steam beginning to rise from the kettle. "Grey thinks like the Kremlin. Sovereignty over alliances. Isolationism dressed up as patriotism. He's got to be aligned with Dimitri Abramovich—I just need to figure out how."

Publicly, Abramovich had maintained the image of a neutral technocrat who, after years of service to the SVR, invested in a small AI surveillance company. He'd slowly emerged as the leader in providing cutting-edge tools to both the Kremlin and other hostile regimes around the globe. But when Russia's war in Ukraine unraveled and fractures split Putin's inner circle, Abramovich didn't just survive the fallout—he emerged as Putin's most dangerous rival.

Ben studied her face, his eyes tracing the lines of strain she tried to hide. "Why do I get the feeling that this one's personal?" he asked.

"Personal?" she repeated.

Her throat tightened when he didn't answer right away, the silence pressing heavy between them. Ava turned, retreating to the kitchen. She poured boiling water into two chipped mugs and carried them back to the kitchen island, letting the steam rise between them like a barrier.

"I'm here to do a job," she said. "That's all."

"You keep forgetting that I read your file."

She rose a brow. "And . . ."

He didn't flinch. "Your mother disappeared on Russian soil. You ran not long after that. Maybe you're not just here to stop the cyberattacks. Maybe you're looking for something else."

Ava looked up slowly, her pulse thudding in her throat. Of course he knew that much; anyone who'd read her file did. Her mother had worked at the CIA and died in Moscow. That was on record. What wasn't on record—what had been buried in the redactions, reserved only for the highest levels of CIA leadership—was that her mother had once been suspected of playing for both sides, of being a double agent for the SVR.

"I have a family," she said abruptly. "Their names are Linda and George."

Guilt swelled against her ribs. She didn't often think about her adoptive parents—not in a way that mattered. When she had run away from her aunt's house, they'd given her home, safety, even love in their quiet, measured way. But in this moment, standing on the precipice of answers about her birth mother, she felt a hollow ache for her adoptive parents.

"I don't see what any of this has to do with our mission." She took another sip from her mug.

Ben stepped around the kitchen island, his silhouette cut sharp against the kitchen's dim light. "It has everything to do with it," he said, his jaw tight. "Which is why you shouldn't be the one running it."

She didn't answer, her fingers curling around her phone. She glanced down and back at him twice as if the words might spill out on their own. But they didn't.

What she remembered instead was an envelope with her name written in looping blue ink. It had arrived not at her own home but first to her aunt's house and forwarded months later to where she lived with her adoptive parents. The postmark was Russian, the stamp smudged as if it had traveled halfway around the world before landing in her hands.

When she was a teenager, she'd spent too many nights lying awake, staring at the loops of her mother's faded handwriting as if it might reveal some hidden message about what had happened to her.

*My darling Ava,*

*If you're reading this, then the world has grown darker, and you've gone looking for truth. I want you to know I never meant to leave you with questions, only with strength. You were always so perceptive—always watching, always wondering. I saw it in your eyes, even when you were too young to understand what you were seeing. There are things that I cannot say here, but trust your instincts. The people around you may hold pieces of the truth, but not all of it. Be careful who you follow. Be careful who you love.*

*Above all, remember this: No matter how lost the world seems, no matter how deeply buried the truth, you were always braver than I was. Never let fear decide your fate.*

*Love always,*
*Momma*

"I need to show you something," Ava said to Ben. She unlocked her phone with a trembling thumb and pulled up the message. *She's alive.*

She handed her phone to Ben, the message glowing like a fresh bruise. Just two words, but a haunting, a hope that she dare not name. "My mother could still be alive," she whispered. "My real mother."

Ben didn't respond right away. He didn't ask a thousand questions like she'd half-expected. He didn't try to fill the silence. He just watched her. That made it harder somehow. The stillness, the space he gave her to feel the weight of what she hoped and prayed for.

"I know how it sounds," she added quickly. "It's probably bait. A distraction. But if there's even a chance . . ." Her fingers trembled as she squeezed the lemon into the hot water. Part of me needs to know. Why she left, or if she left. If she ever had a choice."

Ben leaned forward, brows knitted. But still he didn't speak. The silence pressed against her, heavy and intimate, like he could hear the things she didn't dare say.

"I used to hate this part of me," Ava went on, her voice dropping. "The part that wondered, the part that dared to ask. But this"—she motioned toward her phone—"this message cracked something open inside me." Now that she'd said it out loud, now that she'd given her hope breath and shape, there was no going back.

"You're allowed to want answers," Ben said finally, his voice low, almost rough. "That doesn't mean that you loved your adoptive parents any less."

He stared at her, one long, painful moment that stretched taut between them. He reached across the table and handed her back her phone. Heat curled through her chest—dangerous and uncertain.

"I'll help you," he said suddenly. The words sounded torn from him, like they cost more than he wanted to admit. "I'll ask some people I trust at headquarters if they can help track down the name and number assigned to the source of the message."

But even as the words left Ben's mouth, Ava could see the conflict raging within him, the silent war behind his eyes.

Outside the wind howled, rattling the windowpanes, and the space between them stayed thick with unspoken things. She was likely chasing a ghost, and they both knew it.

"Thank you." Her throat tightened, and she took a step toward him, refusing to be shaken. "You helped train me for this. I know what my mission is—I won't let this get in the way."

Ben exhaled and ran a hand through his hair. "This isn't training anymore."

Ava searched his face. This was exactly the kind of emotional vulnerability that got good officers compromised. "Is that really why you're here?" she asked. "Because you think I'll lose focus?"

His expression hardened. "I'm here because if this goes wrong, you'll be at the mercy of the SVR, and I'm not going to let that happen."

She blinked hard and looked away, her heart beating wildly. "Help me, then." She moved toward the kitchen table, where surveillance photos, maps, and exit routes were laid out like a puzzle. "Konstantin is staying at his dacha on the weekends, just north of the city." She dragged her index finger along the map, then pointed at recent surveillance photos. "There are two exits. One guard posted near the gate, another that stays at a distance down the road for backup." She met Ben's eyes. "Nothing I can't handle with the right team."

Ben hovered over the photos with his arms crossed. "Kidnapping isn't usually the best way to build rapport with a potential source."

"I'm not kidnapping anyone. I'm engineering a second meeting."

"Then it needs to be somewhere public. Besides, the dacha is too fortified."

"Any suggestions?" she asked.

He pulled out a diplomatic pouch and removed a secure phone. On it, he downloaded classified drone imagery in an encrypted folder. It showed Konstantin stepping out of a black car flanked by two security guards. In the background, snow-laden trees framed the stone arches of a grand estate.

"The Imperial Royal Casino," he said. "Konstantin shows up every Thursday night. He likes the back, the VIP room where no one will bother him."

"Are you kidding? That place will be crawling with the worst type of people."

"Which is why his guard will be down. Probably thinks no one will come after him in a resort crawling with oligarchs, SVR, and FSB elites.

"How do we get in?" she asked.

He pulled out two passports from the folder and slid them across the table. "You're Astrid Bergman, American heiress with dual Swiss citizenship, bored with Geneva. I'm Alexei Petrov, a Belarusian-born venture capitalist from Monaco. We make contact at the table," he added, pulling up the casino blueprints on his phone. "I'll draw him into a high stakes gambling game, make him think he's winning, then flip it. You'll give him an excuse to get a drink at the bar." He sat back in his chair, studying her. "But we're playing a dangerous game, especially if he doesn't take the bait."

She cleared her throat. "You don't think I can pull it off?"

The corner of Ben's mouth tugged into a slow smile. "That's not what I said."

# CHAPTER

# 6

On Moscow city maps, the Imperial Royal Casino didn't really exist at all. Disguised as a luxury resort estate in the forests near Zvenigorod, forty kilometers west of Moscow, it was known only to foreign diplomats, oligarchs, and high-net-worth individuals. And as one of the city's most elite private clubs, only a select few at the CIA, MI6, and Mossad knew that the casino was a meeting point for arm dealers, cybercriminals, and intelligence operatives under the guise of high-stakes gambling. Ava couldn't understand how the casino, an enormous gold dome marked with rubies and emeralds, wasn't visible from outer space. She and Ben had decided to arrive separately to give Ben time to draw Konstantin into a high-stakes game at one of the VIP tables.

When Ava exited the black sedan, she handed the armed guard her diplomatic passport, her breath tight. She tried to keep her expression perfectly neutral as she watched the guard complete a biometric ID check with AI-driven facial recognition software. She stood at the entrance, her fingers twitching at her side as people flittered past. Their looks were sharp and discerning, as if their expensive suits and sequin gowns were their credentials to judge her. She knew if her cover hadn't been input correctly, she wouldn't make it past the gate, at least not breathing.

A woman wearing a fur coat on the arm of a man twice her age glared at Ava. She turned away, her herringbone corset digging deep into her ribcage. Her pulse raced as the guard waved another over to examine her ID. She began to think of an elegant exit strategy. She was operating under a solid cover identity: Astrid Bergman, American heiress, wouldn't flinch. She needed to own the part, glide into every room with poise, and maintain her persona. Astrid was the public mask, but Sloane Reed was the blade beneath it. Tonight, she'd have to carry both identities, slipping from heiress to CIA case officer in a breath. She could feel the conflict within her, the tiny fissure when someone asked her name and she responded in fluent Russian, then switched back to English on a burner phone.

Finally, the guard nodded and stepped aside, and Ava felt the tightening in her chest subside. Forcing a calculated smile, she exhaled and stepped forward, her heels clicking against the marble stairs.

Inside the casino, an enormous Austrian crystal chandelier glowed like diamonds. She stood still for a moment and pretended to take in the opulence—the cascading waterfalls, the gold-flecked floors—while noting all the potential exits. She caught her reflection in the mirror and adjusted her long wavy hair, tendrils that whispered across her forehead and grazed her collarbone. Diamond and emerald teardrops dripped heavy from her ears, and a silver bodice hugged her small waist. The outfit was a costume, another role she had to play, and the danger suddenly felt very real.

After several moments, she moved into the VIP lounge where the gaming tables were arranged beneath massive paintings of Russian folklore. She had studied Konstantin. She knew his behavior patterns, his weaknesses, everything she would need to recruit him. But anxiety still clawed at her. The approach with him could go one of two ways, and what if she'd misjudged his interest back at the embassy? *What if he was simply being polite?*

If the approach went poorly, it could mean anything from a blown cover to her life being in danger. She tampered the fear down as best she could. She had to appear at ease and calm, even though she felt the opposite. It was as if all her training and all her efforts since joining the CIA had narrowed into a single moment. In her mind she recited the lessons she'd learned back at the Farm: She had to make the target feel seen, understood, and valued. She needed to disarm him by weaponizing her privilege as Astrid Bergman. And from what she read about Konstantin, she suspected an appeal to money and possibly ego might do the trick.

She spotted Ben at one of the VIP tables, his eyes focused on the roulette wheel in front of him as if it held answers that he'd long sought. He didn't bother to look up, not that she had expected him to, as they were both operating under aliases. They both needed to play their parts superbly if they were going to avoid SVR detection.

Ben certainly looked the part in a custom Armani suit. His blond waves were moussed back, showing off high cheekbones and a sharp jawline dusted with a light auburn stubble. He clutched a glass of bourbon on the rocks in his right hand. But by the way his left fingers tapped the table, the subtle tension in his shoulders, she knew that he was watching, waiting.

As if sensing her, he looked up, and their eyes locked. A flicker of something—recognition, regret, something deeper—passed in his eyes before he pulled down a mask of indifference. But the way his jaw tightened, the way his grip on the glass became a fraction more rigid . . .

She wasn't imagining the tension between them. He knew what that anonymous text could mean. He knew about her mother. And despite everything—the layers of deception and the stakes that surrounded them—he was still the only person she trusted enough to ask about the text message. *She's still alive.* He'd safeguarded her career, protected her secrets more than once, and that kind of loyalty was nearly extinct inside the Agency.

She forced herself toward the table as Ben's eyes collided once more with hers. Sweat sprang up beneath her bodice, and the familiar weight of nerves settled within her chest. But she forced the feeling aside as she sat in front of the golden roulette wheel, waiting for Konstantin to recognize her. She placed two bets by placing her chips on the table—an inside bet on the number eight and an outside bet on the color black. As the dealer began to spin the wheel, she overheard the rumble of a quiet conversation between Konstantin and Ben, though she kept her eyes locked on the wheel.

"It is the best game in all of gambling," Konstantin said to Ben, his eyes flicking briefly at Ava before returning to the spinning wheel.

"If you understand the odds," Ben said.

"I believe that applies in almost every game."

"But in roulette, *nyet*, there is no way to predict a pattern."

"That is why important to set budget," Konstantin added with a wry smile. "Not something I have always followed myself. I enjoy because past spins . . . they do not affect future outcomes. Everything is game of chance, *da?* What you did before . . . it does not always matter."

The dealer released a ball in the opposite direction of the spinning wheel, and a hush fell over them and the rest of the onlookers.

"Black, eight," the dealer called out.

Ava smiled widely. Both Konstantin and Ben stood at the same time and looked in her direction.

She shrugged. "Beginner's luck, I guess."

Konstantin coughed into his fist and looked at her, his gray eyes disarmingly direct. "I believe we have met before, *moya dorogaya*. How lovely you look tonight."

Ben raised a brow and took a sip of his vodka soda. "And what luck, Miss . . . ?"

"Sloane Reed," she said, giving the name she'd used when she'd met Konstantin before. She smiled at Ben, catching the humorous glimmer in his eye.

"Alexei Petrov," Ben said.

Konstantin rose from the table and walked around to shake Ben's hand, then moved toward Ava and gave a small, gallant bow. "I am happy to see you again, Ms. Reed. I did not have the pleasure of getting your name at the embassy event."

"I'm sorry, I must have been preoccupied," she said in fluent Russian.

"No apology necessary. Your Russian . . . it is excellent. Besides, I was the one preoccupied that evening." He switched back to

English. "Well, it's a happy coincidence, bumping into you again here."

"I was actually hoping I might see you here," Ava said. She caught a skeptical glance from Ben but pressed on. "It's a bit of a delicate situation, and I didn't know who else I should ask."

"We better go someplace else," Konstantin said with a half-smile. "There are . . . curious eyes about."

"Actually—" She caught the look in Ben's eyes and knew what he was thinking because she was thinking the same thing—it would be dangerous to go anywhere alone with an SVR agent. "I could use a drink; mind if we venture over to the bar?"

While Ben hung back at the bar, she and Konstantin made their way toward a small alcove across from the bar where the couches were deep blue velvet and gold, and crystal sconces cast warm pools of light overhead.

"I've been asked by a friend," Ava began once the waiter set a vodka martini and Manhattan on the table. "Marika."

"Ah, da, the one that introduced us." He took a sip of his Manhattan and set it on the glossy wooden table. "Her late husband and I were great friends. In past, we spent many nights in this very bar, too drunk on vodka to even stand."

"Yes, well—she asked if I might help her by paying off some of her husband's gambling debts so that the creditors give her some peace. I agreed to help her, but I don't know who exactly to speak with, and I didn't want those gambling debts to come to the attention of anyone who might do her harm."

Konstantin tilted his head, the ice in his glass clinking softly as he swirled the bourbon. "Ah da . . . I know who you should talk to. Though, I would beg you to leave my name out of it, hmm?" He took a slow sip, the ghost of a smile curing his lips. "I have . . . collected my own substantial debt. It is embarrassing, really. My mother raised me better."

"I won't tell a soul."

"Good," he murmured, tapping a finger against the rim of his glass. "I appreciate discretion. And please, share my condolences with Marika. I am heartily sorry for her loss."

"I will,"

"Although," he mused. "I'm not so sure that she viewed it as . . . a loss."

Ava turned back, studying him. The words were casual, but his eyes held a glint of something sharper, something dangerous. She detected a familiar current beneath Konstantin's easy talk—an intelligence officer's habit of weaponizing small talk into an assessment.

"You can be a gambler and a good person," he added, lifting his glass in a mock toast. "But that wasn't how Marika saw him."

He downed the rest of his drink.

Ava nodded but didn't reply. She didn't need to. Since the embassy event, Ava had learned about Marika's late husband's reputation as a reckless gambler and womanizer, and it didn't take much to see that hiding behind Marika's grief was relief.

"How old are you, by the way?" he asked suddenly. "People seem to be getting younger in this line of work. Or maybe it's just my perspective . . . I'm getting old." A sardonic smile flickered across his lips.

"Not that it's any of your business"—she smiled to soften the words—"but I am twenty-six."

Konstantin's brows lifted slightly. "Ah," he exhaled, setting his glass down. "So young. And yet, here you are, already playing such dangerous games."

He studied the empty glass for a moment, as if considering whether or not to refill it. Instead, he exhaled through his nose, shaking his head. "Marika, she told you about her husband. But I suspected she also mentioned my own . . . unfortunate financial obligations."

Ava shook her head, her throat tightening as she risked a glance at Ben. His eyes carried the same skepticism that had begun to crawl through her. Something about Konstantin's eagerness, his sudden openness, didn't sit right. It couldn't be this easy. She'd already flagged those debts as a pressure point the CIA might exploit; money had always been one of their most reliable tools for turning assets. And yet, a sharp thread of doubt coiled in her chest. *What if he wasn't tempted? What if he was playing them instead, drawing them closer for reasons she couldn't yet see?*

"She spoke only of her own husband," Ava lied. *It couldn't be this easy*, she thought. Unless . . . was he trying to recruit her?

Konstantin gave her a long, measured look. Then he leaned forward, his elbows resting on the table. His voice dropped just slightly, the apparent lightness in his tone laced with steel.

"I wonder," he said, "if it might be possible that we come to some sort of . . . arrangement."

The words sent a ripple of unease through her. There was something about Konstantin, something about his demeanor that drew her in. Surely there was a reason why he was considered one of the finer SVR officers. Although . . .

"I'm certain that there are people at the embassy who would be interested to know about the Russian government's dealings with Nathaniel Grey, and who is behind these cyberattacks," Konstantin said finally.

She cleared her throat and watched Konstantin's face for a fraction of a beat, searching for that moment when a man's loyalties shifted—when he decided whether to recruit you, test you, or use you as a mark.

"How very perceptive of you," she said finally, thinking of the knife strapped inside her upper thigh. He knew exactly who they really were and what they wanted. And if she had misjudged him—she'd never get close again.

But the intelligence, the potential information he held about Grey and his connections to the Russian government, far outweighed the risk.

"If I wanted to get a secure message to you," he added, with a brow raised and a finger pointed. "How would I—hypothetically—do that?"

She glanced briefly at Ben and smiled.

# CHAPTER 7

THE SOFT GLOW of the chandeliers blinked faintly behind them as Ava walked into her hotel suite, Ben close behind. She clicked the door locked behind them, shutting out the murmur of voices, the cheers and groans of gamblers who won or lost. Ava turned toward Ben, and silence fell around them like a shroud, loosening the thoughts that she'd buried deep beneath layers of focus and control.

Inhaling deeply, Ava slipped off her high heels, letting her bare feet sink into the thick carpet as she walked toward the frost-laced windows. Outside, the resort grounds dissolved into a darkened forest until it reached the Moscow River glinting in the moonlight.

Ben stepped closer, his presence steady, watchful.

Recruiting Konstantin wouldn't be like her first assignment in Paris, where a wrong hunch only meant a flight home and a bruised ego. This was Moscow, the heart of Russian power, where one misstep could mean a black bag over her head, a cell she'd never escape, and days that bled into weeks under interrogation. She needed to tread carefully—and they both knew it. Konstantin was SVR, which meant he was sure to smell a trap before it was ever set. If he suspected that she was trying to turn him, he could vanish overnight or, worse, feed them lies while remaining loyal to Moscow.

The damage that it would cause to the Agency could be catastrophic.

"Do you think Konstantin's our way in?" Ben asked, his voice low.

"I think he could be," Ava said, eyes still on the river. "If what he said about Nathaniel Grey checks out, it could connect him to a larger operation. Perhaps something coordinated, ongoing." She caught his grave reflection in the window. "The disinformation campaign might go deeper than just propaganda. It might be operational." She turned to face him.

"If we make the wrong move, it doesn't just end the mission," he said, the dim light doing nothing to soften the intensity of his green eyes. "It puts a target on both our backs."

Ava didn't flinch. "I know what's at stake."

"And . . . I'm not convinced that he's not playing you."

"Everyone is playing someone in Moscow, but that doesn't mean he's not useful."

"He could see *you* as the mark," Ben said, sharper now. "*You* as the vulnerability."

"He sees what I want him to see." Her tone was steel, but her words rang hollow, even to her. Konstantin had years of experience on her. "Any information he gives us on Grey will need to be corroborated."

"And how do you expect to do that?" he pressed.

"I'll use Nathaniel Grey to validate Konstantin. I just have to get close enough."

Ben's expression hardened. "Grey's reputation as a womanizer isn't a footnote. Be careful."

She looked away, pretending to study the icicles dripping from the balcony rail.

"Fortunately, Konstantin doesn't share Putin's nostalgia for Russian history," Ben said. "Frank must have told you that he's not operating under his real last name."

"Of course," she said, though unease uncoiled within her midsection as she thought back to that first meeting with Frank—to the measured way he'd spoken about the dangers of the job, the unblinking certainty with which he'd laid out the stakes, and his insistence that trust was a currency she could never use.

Four years ago, Ava's college roommate, Kristine, had mentioned that her father, who worked for the "foreign service," was coming for FSU homecoming that weekend between overseas assignments and wanted to go to a bar in town called Cabaret, notorious for catering to divorced men pursuing young college girls.

"Why there?" Ava had asked Kristine as she struggled with a straightening iron to smooth out her frizzy hair. It was just April in Tallahassee, but the humidity had already reached record levels, and Ava's hair sprang up into rebellious tendrils that curled around her face.

"He's divorced, Ava." Kristine stretched languorously on her twin bed across from Ava's in their dorm room. "But he just wants a drink before graduation, and they have good wine there. He's not a nickel beer kind of guy."

"I don't blame him; the last time I went to nickel beer night at Potbelly's bar, I nearly died of a hangover."

"He can be horribly boring though," Kristine sat up and moved off the bed. "All he wants to do is talk politics. Last time we were on the phone he would not stop talking about how risky it is that the United States is withdrawing from NATO, blah blah . . ."

Ava sat up. "He's right. The US is pulling back from almost all their collective security agreements. It could empower Russia." Ava inhaled deeply and let it out slowly. She had been wanting to meet Kristine's father, who she'd long suspected was in the CIA. "I'd be happy to go with you if you want," she added, her tone light. "I could use a nice glass of wine."

"Would you really?" Kristine shot up, her eyes bright. "That would be great. I never see him, and it's always awkward. I could use someone to bounce part of the conversation off." She twirled her hair around her index finger as she looked at her appearance in the mirror. "Oh, and please don't show off by speaking Russian. I hate it when I can't understand you when you're talking to someone else."

Ava raised a brow. "Your dad speaks Russian?"

"Yeah, fluently. Why?"

"No reason." Although Ava felt her heart ramp up. If Kristine's dad was in the CIA, it might be a way in—a back door into the Agency that had been responsible for her mother's disappearance and death. It could be the chance she had longed for. A personal connection could mean someone on the inside to vouch for her, get her past the red tape, and possibly even look past the black mark that her mother's disappearance had caused.

But maybe Kristine's father could change that. Maybe he knew details about her mother's case that she'd never been told or maybe his influence could open doors that had always been slammed shut. Maybe, with his help, she'd finally get the second chance no one else was willing to give her.

"His real name is Konstantin Gallitzin." Ben's voice pulled Ava back into the present. "But for the last thirty years, he's lived as Konstantin Morozov—the name SVR thinks is his own."

"Gallitzin? As in one of the old imperial families?"

Ben nodded, meeting her eyes. "They were ousted with the Romanovs. One of the most powerful aristocratic families in Russia with centuries of influence. Some even whispered that they wanted to restore the old order."

Ava let out a low whistle. "And the SVR still hired him?"

"Konstantin is very good at erasing his steps. That, and it helps that the CIA has biometric identification software that the Russians do not. He must have slipped through the cracks at the SVR, or maybe someone higher up chose to look the other way."

Ava turned from the window, her thoughts spinning as she tried to make sense of it. "So, what you're saying is that I've discovered a potential penetration of the SVR that not only has access but the right kind of motivation to work for the CIA?"

Ben gave a slow nod. "It would seem that way, yes."

"Then I'm right to pursue him."

"Yes, but . . ."

"Please don't qualify what you're about to say." Her tone was ice. She knew it was his job to be cautious, to look for holes in her plan, to challenge assumptions and anticipate threats. That's what made Ben so effective in the field at counterintelligence. But she couldn't stand how it caused him to constantly question her. And coming from him—the person who seemed to see through her tough exterior—cut deeper somehow.

"Just say it," she added, sharper than she intended. "Whatever it is, I can take the truth. I just can't stand being 'handled.'"

Ben exhaled. "Just be careful, Ava. He's hiding his money. He's hiding his identity. And he's watching *you* just as closely as you're watching him."

Ava's breath hitched, and a cold weight settled in her stomach.

Ben shifted, restless energy pulsing through him.

"What is it?" she asked.

"We have to talk about the text message."

She stilled, her pulse racing. "The one about my mother? Were you able to trace it? Who sent it?"

"It came from someone inside the SVR's old illegals directorate."

Ava's chest tightened. The message was real. *Intentional.* "Who?"

He inhaled slowly, hesitating as if carefully weighing the impact of his next words. "Dimitri Abramovich."

She stared at him, ice prickling down her spine. "The oligarch?"

He nodded, and the air between them snapped taut. For a second, she didn't move, couldn't breathe. She had read the files. Seen Dimitri Abramovich in the media. He had begun as a quiet but powerful figure. And he was untouchable, thanks to his fortune, made from a covert AI surveillance company that supplied both the Kremlin and rogue states. Publicly apolitical, privately ruthless. And when Putin's inner circle fractured over a botched war in Ukraine, Abramovich seized an opening, emerging as Russian President Vladimir Putin's primary rival.

She leaned in, her voice catching. "How the hell does Abramovich know anything about my mother?"

"I don't know, but he worked at Directorate S right around the same time she disappeared."

The room seemed to shrink around her. *Still alive.* The message had haunted her for days—a flickering ghost she couldn't put to rest. "He knew my mother?"

Ben studied her. "He mentioned her name in a conversation intercepted three days ago. He referred to her in the present tense."

Her mouth went dry, and she had to struggle to speak. "So, she is alive?"

"I don't know," he said. "But someone wants you to believe that she is."

Ava didn't speak for a moment. It couldn't be true, yet the possibility of *still alive* crawled within through the cracks of her composed exterior. She swallowed. "Why didn't Frank tell me?"

"Because he doesn't know everything," Ben said quietly. "I pulled this from a database I'm not supposed to have access to. I wasn't even supposed to be looking."

She turned to face him. "And you did anyway."

He nodded. "You deserve to know what you're up against."

Emotion flared within her chest, part fury, part gratitude—all tangled in a knot that she didn't seem to have time to untangle. Her eyes burned. *Deserve.* As if the truth were something to be earned.

"Either way I'm going to find out if she's still alive." Her face hardened, her voice clipped. But beneath it all was the ache that had never left her, the need for someone to choose her, to prove that she mattered. "I don't care how dangerous it is."

The silence stretched long enough for it to sting before he said, "True or not, that hope could be our biggest vulnerability. Or our greatest weapon."

Their eyes locked. *Our.* The single word landed like a tether, the pull of it yanking through her. She wanted to deny it, but the thread was already there between them—pulling, demanding.

"There's one more thing," she said, speaking precisely even as her pulse trembled. "If Konstantin is involved, and Abramovich is backing a campaign to destabilize the US, we don't just need him talking. We need him turned; we need him on our side. We need proof."

"That's a high-risk play, considering we're dealing with Russian intelligence."

"I'm aware of the risks." Her tone didn't waver, but inside her nerves frayed at the hope, the promise of what he was risking for her.

He let out a slow breath, stepping closer. "Just promise me something."

Her breath caught. "What?"

"Promise me you won't get so deep in the game that you forget where the lines are."

Ava grimaced. "I've been over them since I got here. There's no going back now, not for me."

His hand brushed hers—light, tentative, but it jolted through her like an answer to the question she'd been afraid to ask. "Then let's do this together."

Her pulse skittered as she angled her phone toward him. A new message from Konstantin lit the screen: **When can you meet?** One sentence, one breadcrumb, and one step closer to the truth—and potentially everything she wanted, feared, and couldn't admit.

She met his eyes, holding them as she smiled. "We'll see if you can keep up."

# CHAPTER

# 8

THE AIR IN Dubai shimmered with heat, the buildings stretching tall like they were trying to outrun it. Something old and angry lurked beneath the concrete surface, as if the city had been built too fast, too high. From the rooftop terrace bar of the Jumeriah Al Naseem, Ava sat at a table and sipped a watered-down Diet Coke on ice, watching the sun glint off the silver sail of the Burj Al Arab. She adjusted her silk headscarf and slid her phone under a napkin, its camera pointed subtly at the chair in front of her. Every instinct hummed with controlled tension. *Observation first. Interaction second.* It had been drilled into her at the Farm. You didn't just show up to a meeting like this; you studied the person, his patterns, his access—then made your move.

The UAE was an ideal place to meet with potential Russian sources, where many Russian oligarchs blended into the environment like a mirage, spending their days lounging along manicured beaches and infinity pools, taking slow drags of gold hookahs. And Dubai had the perfect mix of lawlessness and conformity—a place to make contact with Konstantin and evaluate, recruit and if she had to, manipulate.

Ava wiped the sweat from her brow and mentally rehearsed the most important rule. Not the words, but the rhythm. She'd start slow and ask Konstantin questions. She'd make him feel powerful and in control. *That* was the key to asset development. She'd gather information about who he really was—his political posture, his psychological profile, his tactical weaknesses. She knew most of it already having studied his profile. But there was a lot she could not glean from a file. And all this data had to be gathered with the main goal in mind—she needed proof, a direct line to what the Russians were doing with Vibrantia.

She spotted Konstantin at the bar's entrance, wearing a cream linen thobe. He looked like any other tourist, not an SVR agent waiting in the shadows. By the pursing of his lips, Ava saw that he'd recognized her, though his eyes remained hidden behind mirrored sunglasses as he made his way to her table, his thobe robe billowing like a cloud behind him.

"You're early," he said in Russian.

"You're predictable," she replied, also in Russian.

That earned the faintest twitch of his mouth. "You've been watching me, or your partner has."

"We have to protect our investment," she said.

"But you haven't made one yet."

The waiter arrived with two tiny cups of Arabic coffee. Ava thanked him and waited until the man left before leaning in. "That depends on you."

"I could report you to the embassy in Moscow, or here in Dubai."

"You would have done that already," Ava said calmly, though her pulse kicked up. "Besides, we both know that the SVR placed you on 'reserve' status years ago."

"Yes, my assignment is Austria did not go well." He paused as the city hummed, faint but indifferent to the intensity that pulsed between them.

"I read the Vienna file," she said finally. Konstantin didn't look up as she went on. "Officially you were a cultural attaché, but unofficially you were sent to compromise a junior liaison to the International Atomic Energy Agency, IAEA—Sophie Hartman. Only you didn't. You warned her instead."

A flicker of something, regret or pride, passed over his face. "Is that what the file says?"

"No, only that you missed your check-ins with the SVR, and you stopped reporting. I figured out the rest. SVR put you on leave after that, but we both know what really happened." She leaned forward, her voice low. "You looked at that girl, and you couldn't hollow her out the way they wanted. Not for a regime that feeds on their own rot."

He exhaled slowly, his eyes cast toward the city of glass and steel that reached for the clouds.

"You've done your homework, Ms. Sloane," he said finally with a wry smile, turning back to face her. "Although I'm certain that's not your *real* name. Nor is Astrid."

Ava ignored him. A beat of silence, dry and deliberate. "I do more than homework, I solve problems, and your country is causing a big one for us."

He sipped his coffee. "I'm not sure I'm well-equipped to help. As you said, I've been on the outs for years."

"That is what I'm looking to change. Help me expose the people who hijacked your homeland."

"Tell me, what makes you believe I would be interested at all?" Konstantin looked away again. But he wasn't brushing her off, she thought; he was thinking, remembering. He went on: "I only agreed to meet you here to get out of the cold."

"I seriously doubt that. But I'm not here to ask you to *do* anything, yet. I'm asking you to be useful. To use the knowledge and skills that you've built over the last several decades for something good, something worthy."

His brow furrowed as she went on, her voice low although they were the only ones in the bar. "You know who's funding Vibrantia. You know who is feeding unrest into the United States. You know what's coming, and I think you hate the SVR almost as much as I do." She paused, carefully weighing her next words. "You're not loyal to what Russia has become."

He studied her, then looked over the horizon, where the desert met the manmade waters. A beat. Then another until he turned to face her. "You think that you can sell me a cause?"

"No," Ava said, softening her voice. "I'm offering you a way out, a chance to move somewhere where you don't have a mark on your back, where you're not constantly looking over your shoulder. A life out of the shadows."

His features softened, though he said nothing. *That hit something.* He stood and tossed a few dirhams on the table. "I'll think about it."

Ava rose, letting him take the lead. She didn't chase, didn't pursue. This part needed to be on *his* terms. As he walked away, she slipped her sunglasses back on and let her pulse settle. There was something there with Konstantin, tentative but *real.* And she didn't need a yes today. Just the beginning of one.

That night, Ben was waiting for her when she returned to her hotel room, his back to her as he stared out the floor-to-ceiling windows. Dubai was a dazzling display of steel and glass, the Burj Khalifa rising like a luminous sail in the distance. Ava clicked the door shut and moved toward Ben, caught between a sense of triumph and dread. Konstantin had taken her bait, but the game was far from over.

On her right, a king-sized bed stood like a throne on a Persian rug. To her left, a mirrored minibar with gold fixtures and backlit marble announced luxury.

Ben closed the merlot-colored drapes, trapping the woody smell of oud perfume and orange blossom. He didn't turn to face her when he said, "You're moving too fast with him."

She dropped her purse on the ground and went to the minibar to grab a bottle of water.

"Isn't this what we're here to do?" She unscrewed the top and took a large gulp. "He's cautious. But he agreed to think about it."

"That's exactly my point," Ben said. "Men like Konstantin don't just agree. They manipulate, they calculate. They offer us bread crumbs and see how hungry we are."

"Konstantin seemed willing, but cautious. We can build on that."

He inhaled deeply, the strong lines of his back rising and falling in the dim light.

"You're not hearing me." He turned, his eyes glittering. "You made the call before we had time to assess him properly. We don't even know if he can be turned."

"And how are we expected to know that without talking to him?"

"What are you using as your basis to recruit him in the first place?" He folded his arms across his chest. "What are his motivations? Because we both know that money isn't one of them."

"He's the son of Russian royalty," she responded. "He lost everything to a regime that's now using cyber warfare to rewrite the global order. He's certainly not loyal to Putin. He's loyal to a version of Russia that no longer exists. But I can use that; I can tap into his nationalist sympathies."

"That all sounds great, in theory," he stepped closer. "But we need to do this right."

She raised a brow. "Define 'right'"

"We fly in a team—the best at Langley. Polygraphers. Psychologists. We vet him like we would any developmental, but harder. Because he's likely playing us."

"I don't think he is." She tried to hide the annoyance in her voice. "Not after what I read about his op in Vienna."

Ben's mouth twisted. "You trust him already? After one meeting? Ava—"

She hesitated. "I trust the part of him that still believes that Russia can be more than a shell of its former self."

"That's not trust, Ava, that's hope. And hope gets people killed."

The silence stretched thin between them. Outside, a call to prayer echoed faintly through the city.

"Fine," she said finally. "Call in the team. Polygraph. Shrink. Whatever helps you sleep at night. But I'm going to keep the operation moving."

Ben nodded once. "Good. Because it's not just your name on this operation."

"Is that what you're worried about? Your reputation?" She couldn't keep her voice from rising, nor the blood from rushing to her face.

"If I was, I would have done many things differently since Frank called me to help you with this op."

She stiffened, determined not to let him see how his words stabbed at her. "Then help me, instead of making me feel like I have to constantly play defense."

"I'm on your side, Ava."

"Great. Now act like it."

He nodded once and brushed past her toward the door. She watched him longer than she meant to. Not because she doubted his intentions, but because the weight of his words settled deeper than she wanted to acknowledge. Because for the first time in a long time, her instincts had gotten in the way of her reason. *And what if he was right about Konstantin?*

A knot tightened in her chest. She hated that possibility almost as much as she hated how easily Ben could cut through her defenses. He saw the parts of her she tried hardest to hide—the doubts, the second guessing—and that terrified her more than she cared to admit. Still, she couldn't abandon her plan. Whatever Ben believed, the only way to know if Konstantin could be turned was to push at the seams of his motivations, to press on his fears and exploit his hopes to see which way he bent. Only then would she know if Konstantin could ever stand on their side.

# CHAPTER

# 9

Ava's second meeting with Konstantin was at twilight, tucked in a private garden behind Emirates Palace, where the scent of jasmine thickened the air. Konstantin arrived ten minutes late, dressed in immaculate linen. His chin was low, his eyes scanning shadows in the amber haze.

She sat beneath a heavy orange tree at a wrought iron table, her kaftan sticking to her thighs like damp gauze in the thick afternoon heat. She inhaled deeply as he approached, the smell of citrus and cardamom clinging to her like a promise.

"*As-salamu'alaykum,*" he said, a traditional Arabic greeting: "peace be upon you." He slid into the seat across from her and cast a fleeting glance at the fountain at the center.

*He's either as nervous as I am, or he's already looking for potential exits.* "*Wa'alaykumu s-salam,*" she replied in flawless Arabic.

His fingers tapped once against the porcelain teacup in front of him. "You're not the first American to ask for my help, you know." His voice was quiet and dry, giving away no sign of how he felt. "But you're the first to do it over tea in a rose garden. It is . . . charming, in a doomed sort of way."

"And you're not the first Russian to betray his country, but you might be the first to do it for the right reasons."

His expression didn't change, but something flickered behind his eyes. "You assume too much."

"Ah, but I know your real name," she said. "Gallitzin."

He flinched, barely, but she noticed it.

"And I know the history behind it," she went on, pouring tea without asking. "Your family was loyal to the Tsar until the Bolsheviks made that loyalty a death sentence." She paused, letting the words settle as she took a sip of her tea.

"Your grandfather lost his birthright. His land, your family's place in Russia," she continued, her voice softening. "But I don't think you ever lost your vision for what your country *could* be."

He didn't answer, only stared into his cup as though it could offer him a way to respond. Then he wrapped his hand around the delicate porcelain and looked up, his eyes steady as stone. "I know what it means to be Russian," he said finally. "And I know what a traitor looks like. I'm not one of them. I am . . . what is the word you Americans like? A patriot."

"You call what's happening now in Russia patriotism? Putin's Kremlin is a shell of an empire, bought with money and fear. They've weaponized nostalgia and silenced dissent."

"I do not need a lecture about my own country," he replied sharply. "I live it within my bones."

*So, there's still pride,* she thought. *Good. Something he cares about, something to build upon.*

"I'm not asking you to betray it. I'm asking you to help save it. There's a difference."

He tilted his head, eyes narrowing. "And what would that look like, exactly? This 'saving my country'? More American interference? A revolution by proxy? Or perhaps saving the country with sanctions?" The sarcasm in his voice was undeniable.

Ava felt her pulse tick upward but forced her face to stay neutral.

"I'm not naïve enough to promise you a fairytale," she said. "But I can offer you a chance to carve out the rot inside your country. Starting with the SVR's cyber division. We need to know where the operations are based, how they're routing attacks, and how deep their fingers run through Vibrantia."

Konstantin's laugh reached his eyes. "You think that I have access to all this? That I keep dossiers in my sock drawer?"

"I think you know people who do," she said calmly, though she felt her eye begin to twitch. Ben's voice echoed within her mind. *Tread carefully.* "And I think if you wanted to find out, you could. You've spent the last decade investing in the very systems they're now hijacking. I don't need a whistleblower. I need a surgeon."

The silence between them thickened as she watched him absorb her words, her needs. Something trembled in his gaze. Not fear—weariness, perhaps.

"You once said Russia didn't need more strongmen, it needed caretakers. So be one."

His brow lifted slightly. "So, you've been speaking with Alexei . . ."

"Yes," she said, recognizing Ben's cover name. "We're doing this together."

"Why me?" he asked, his voice softer now.

"Because you still care. And because the people destroying your country are afraid of men like you—the ones they couldn't fully erase."

He exhaled through his nose, the tea forgotten as he lit up a cigar. A flicker passed over his face. *Regret? Hope?* Perhaps a memory.

"I'll need assurances," he said finally.

"You'll have them."

"And protection once this is over."

"That too."

Another silence passed—this time, heavy with the knowledge of what they were both about to embark upon. He gave a tight nod, then stood. "You'll have your first name in a week, but after that, I choose the pace. I won't be handled. I am not . . . how you say . . . your asset."

"Fair enough," Ava said, rising. "Just don't make me regret it."

He looked down at her, a crease forming between his thick brows. “I’m afraid regret is baked into this profession, Ms. Sloane.”

“I think you’re probably right,” she said. “I’ll be in touch.”

He held her gaze a beat longer than necessary, the corner of his mouth twitching as though he knew something she didn’t. Then he turned, walking off into the garden’s shadows, the scent of roses mingling with cigar smoke in his wake. Ava stayed rooted for a moment, listening to the gentle trickle of the fountain. She had recruited before, but this felt different. This one felt personal. As if some invisible thread connected them, tugging at her even as reason told her to walk away.

# CHAPTER 10

THE SAFE HOUSE walls were all Soviet austerity, so thick that Ben felt like he was suffocating underground. He preferred the green open space of his hometown in Montana, where the wide, blue sky went on forever and swallowed voices whole, where he could fish and ride and no one asked questions. He could still hear the echoes of his brothers' laughter, the smell of wet bark after summer rain. When they were kids, the three of them used to camp along the Clark Fork River. No cell service. No noise but the water and their own voices, arguing about which trout hole was best, whose turn it was to start the fire. But here in Moscow, even the sky felt like it was closing in. This was a concrete city meant to swallow sound and bury secrets, which Ava had yet to understand. Back in Montana, danger was a bear too close to camp, a winter blizzard accompanied by sub-zero temperatures. Now it was the woman standing across from him.

Ava stood in the kitchen, arms crossed and scanning the room like it was a threat. Yet they both knew that the threat wasn't here—it was back in DC, splintering America in real time. And if he was honest, maybe part of the danger was Ava herself, charging forward like she could outrun the consequences of a recruitment gone wrong.

His boss, Frank, sat hunched in a worn leather armchair, shadows carving deep lines on his face in a way that had nothing to do with how tired he was.

"Well." Frank's bloodshot eyes tracked Ava as she moved to sit across from Frank on the sofa, and Ben sat in the chair next to Ava, the leather squeaking beneath his legs. "Tell me about Dubai."

Ava dropped her purse on the coffee table, her mouth set in a thin line. She had been all business over the last several days, as if she'd gambled and won the bet about Konstantin. But the knot in Ben's chest persisted. None of this tracked. CIA officers didn't just stumble across direct penetrations of one of the most lethal intelligence organizations in the world. Even if Konstantin was no longer active within SVR, his betrayal would carry equal weight.

"These are the names and contact information of the SVR coders doing the work." Ava took out a flash drive where she'd recorded all Konstantin's covert communication messages and slid it across the table. Frank covered it with his hand and picked it up, examining it gently as if it would detonate. "But they're routing their messages through a stateside network," Ava added, her focus locked on Frank. "Something buried on Vibrantia's backend."

Ben picked up the thread. "Vibrantia is the weapon. The platform is feeding targeted narratives into every American fault line—race, immigration, government overreach. They're not just pushing discontent. They're manufacturing civil war."

Frank's jaw worked as he digested it. "We've suspected that for months. Do you think Konstantin can give us the location for Vibrantia's hub of operations?

"He knows that there are several coders inside Russia," Ava said. "But doesn't know precisely where. Once we verify that, we can start mapping out.the SVR's cyberattack command structure."

"We'd better move fast." Frank leaned forward, placing his elbows on his knees as he looked at Ben then Ava and back again. "Because things back home . . ." He leaned back and held his hands in a prayer-like motion. "They're breaking down faster than I can brief the director."

Frank leaned over the armchair and brought out his laptop from the bag on the floor. He sat it on the coffee table and turned the screen to face Ben and Ava. Bodycam footage rolled silently: federal agents locked in a standoff outside the Kentucky State Capitol, rifles pointed, flags waving, faces twisted in anger.

Ben felt his spine lock up. This wasn't just about digital disruption anymore. It was kinetic.

"That was yesterday," Frank said. "The governor called for federal backup after the local police department refused to enforce a national cybersecurity directive. Then this crowd shows up—fully armed, chanting about deep state surveillance. Vibrantia planned the whole thing with a series of anonymous 'leaks.'"

Ben stared at the screen and exhaled. "Jesus."

Ava leaned forward. "You think it's all directed?"

Frank didn't hesitate. "It's not chaos. It's design."

"But the Russians," she said softly.

Frank nodded. "And that's where you both come in. I need proof that shows SVR fingerprints on Vibrantia. Only then can I get operational authority to shut it down. But Ben straightened. Only Frank knew what this mission truly meant to him—and what Abramovich had stolen from his life. The thought of it burned like acid in his chest. He swallowed hard, forcing the rage back down.

"What do you suggest?" he asked, his words clipped. It wasn't strategy Ben wanted. It was the target. And this time, he intended to make Abramovich pay.

Frank looked at Ava. "You've got an in with the CEO of Vibrantia—Nathaniel Grey. Use it."

Ava shot a brief glance at Ben and lifted her chin. "He's invited me for dinner."

Frank nodded. "If you can suggest that you meet at his apartment, you could plant a listening device there."

Ben's pulse kicked up. "You want her to bug his apartment?" He stood as if the walls were seeming to close in and began to pace. "That's a huge risk. Grey's plugged in over here—Russian press, politics, tech. If he catches her, he buries her."

Frank looked at Ava. "It's your choice. But we're running out of time."

Ava's eyes didn't leave Frank's. "I'll do it."

Ben's stomach dropped. He believed in Ava but feared that Frank was asking too much of her.

Frank opened a hard case beneath the table. He pulled out a small microchip the size of a nailbed. "Directional mic. It syncs to his WiFi."

She took it and held it between her thumb and index finger. "Where should I plant it?"

"It can be anywhere. His study. His kitchen. His bedroom." Ben stopped pacing as Frank went on. "We'll pick up everything within forty feet of the device."

Ben stepped toward her, forcing his voice to remain even. "I'll be on the outside, monitoring everything."

She looked at him then. "You'll be listening?"

"I'm covering you, Ava. If anything goes sideways, I'll be there."

*But that wasn't the whole truth,* Ben thought. He was assigned to watch Ava. Frank had never said it out loud, but Ben understood the subtext of what Frank didn't, couldn't say. Ben was supposed to make sure that she stayed focused and didn't lose herself chasing ghosts from her past. If Ava slipped or veered off her mission in her search for answers about her mother and compromised the op—Ben was expected to pull her back. Or shut it down.

"Headquarters is very impressed with your work on this case so far," Frank said to Ava. "The director has asked for regular updates and briefings on your progress with Konstantin."

Ben gritted his teeth. Konstantin had delivered everything they had needed so far without resistance, without bargaining. *It was all too easy,* he thought. No recruitment flowed that easily without someone wanting it to. Ben had been in the field long enough to know that this wasn't how intelligence worked. There was more friction, more of a tug-of-war. This? This all felt rehearsed. Perhaps planned.

And yet Ava trusted it. Trusted Konstantin. This Russian who had appeared out of nowhere with all the answers that they needed—just when Ava had needed distraction. Konstantin could already be ten steps ahead. But Frank didn't see it, or maybe he didn't care.

Ava nodded once. "I'll get it done."

Ben watched her, his stomach still in knots. He believed in her, trusted her, but he also knew what getting it done might cost her, what it had cost him. And that was what he was here to stop.

# CHAPTER

# 11

AVA STOOD NEXT to Ben at the corner of Prechistenskaya Embankment, the cold gnawing through the seams in her coat, lifting strands of her hair across her face. The Gold Mile didn't reek of smoke or street exhaust like the rest of the city—it smelled like expensive cigars and polished brass. Behind them, the wrought iron fence of Nathaniel Grey's residence loomed, a tall gate armed with security cameras and a security detail that didn't wear uniforms. The two of them waited to cross Ostozhenka Street, the wind funneling down the road like a warning that had come too late.

Beside her, Ben shifted, boots planted with Marine-perfect precision, his embassy-issued coat hanging stiffly enough to sell the lie. His breath plumed white with cold as his eyes flicked to every car that glided past. He had been sent to Grey's apartment under the guise of needing to escort Ava home after embassy protests had turned violent.

But Ava hadn't needed saving.

She glanced up at him, "I still can't believe that you showed up like that."

"I went to boarding school with him," Ben said flatly.

Her head snapped up. "You, what? Why didn't he recognize you?"

"I looked a bit different back then. Half the size I am now. I didn't hit my growth spurt until I was a junior, and by the time I did, Grey had already started Vibrantia, made his first million."

Ava blinked. She couldn't imagine Ben other than he was now, six-foot-three and built like a Norse god.

"He started Vibrantia with two female students. They later accused him of sexual misconduct. He paid them off before their allegations became public."

A shiver traced her spine. "I knew there was something off about him."

Ava's mind went reeling back earlier that evening—inside Grey's penthouse.

She tapped her crystal wine glass, the sharp clink of the glass echoing within the massive walls of Nathaniel Grey's luxury penthouse. Across the sleek granite island, he seared the osso buco, the scent of rosemary and garlic curling through the air. But Ava barely noticed as she scanned the room, hunting for the ideal place to plant a listening device, something that could help her link his company with Dimitri Abramovich's mission to tear American apart.

The apartment was all sleek furniture in muted grays and blacks, their shapes angular and severe. Panoramic views and smart technology were embedded in its walls. The kitchen and family room were perfectly curated, intentional, like a performance. Like him. He was a carefully constructed figure, a man whose social media empire had turned him into a global influencer. But Ava knew the truth. Konstantin's reports had already confirmed what she had suspected: Nathaniel Grey wasn't just the face of Vibrantia—he was using it to spread dangerous misinformation under the influence of the Russian government.

Ava had read his file—the CIA kept one on any international businessman that could grant them access to the Kremlin. Nathaniel Grey had studied at the Moscow Institute of Physics and Technology and, like her, spoke fluent Russian. To her, it wasn't a question of whether he was compromised—it was how deep it went.

Nathaniel Grey reached for another garlic clove, and his gaze flickered toward her. Her black silk skirt, her V-neck cashmere sweater, the platform boots—she'd chosen them partly for comfort. But under his discerning gaze she felt like a piece of bait, a sacrificial lamb sent by the CIA dressed in cashmere. It made her skin crawl. Though she had her reasons for accepting the mission.

Her fingers skimmed the lining of her coat pocket where the tiny listening device rested, cool and weightless. If she could plant it undetected, she might obtain the corroboration for Konstantin's reports that she sought.

Nathaniel Grey wasn't just influenced by Russia; he was built by it.

The osso buco sizzled, filling the kitchen with the smell of garlic butter, dragging Ava back to her mother's kitchen. She could almost see her there again, sleeves rolled to her elbows, hands moving in quiet tandem over a cutting board. They hadn't needed words back then. The hush of shared work, the language of taste and touch, had been enough. The memory tightened her chest. Whatever it took, she would find out how Abramovich was connected to her mother.

She swallowed down the sudden grief that burned in her throat and slipped a hand beneath the table, fingers damp as they searched for an inconspicuous spot. There. A quick press. A soft click. The device was in place. Secure. Invisible. A lifeline to Grey's secrets and the truth she was chasing.

"It smells wonderful," she said, voice steady even as her pulse drummed in her ears.

"I learned from my mother. Brutal woman, brilliant cook," Grey said, turning the knife in his hand as though testing its balance. "She believed a blade should always have purpose. Even in the kitchen."

He stepped closer, close enough that she caught the faint spice of his cologne beneath the garlic. "Funny thing, knives," he murmured, tracing the flat of the blade along his own forearm, a whisper of metal on fabric. "They're tools . . . until they're not."

Ava's stomach dropped. His eyes lingered on her too long, like he was cataloging something she couldn't see. Then, without warning, he reached toward her, brushing a stray hair from her shoulder with the back of his knuckles. The touch was featherlight, almost polite, but it sent a chill straight through her.

"Do you trust easily?" he asked, voice low and too close to her ear.

She forced a breath, every instinct screaming to move, to leave. Three feet separated her from the blade, but it felt like less. The bug was planted. Her job here was done. He seemed to sense her hesitation, the tension building within her, and stepped backward.

"Are you Italian?" she asked, forcing a casualness in her tone but keeping her eyes on the knife that he had set down next to the cutting board.

"Corsican." He jingled the ice in his glass of bourbon, eyes wolfish. "My mother is one hundred percent Corsican."

She forced a smile. "Well, that explains your coloring." His lips curled as he rolled up his shirt sleeves. He was a strong build, average height, with dark wavy hair brown eyes, and a noticeable amount of body hair on his arms. "I thought I saw a Mediterranean edge."

"And what about you?" His voice dropped, and Ava noticed an intimacy in his voice that made gooseflesh ripple down her arms as he poured her another glass of wine. "With that long chestnut hair and gray eyes . . . you look as though you might have some Mediterranean roots yourself."

Her fingers tightened on her wine glass. "Irish and Scottish, which I suppose is what accounts for my short temper."

He arched a brow. "You . . . with a temper?" His eyes lingered on her for a moment longer, and she felt his gaze had turned into something greedy. "I seriously doubt that."

He poured himself a vodka. "You know, I didn't expect to like you."

Ava laughed lightly. "Why is that?"

"I assume you were one of them. The federal class. Bureaucrats with a Messiah complex."

She tilted her glass. "You haven't known me very long."

He shrugged. "You're not like any of the other diplomats I've met. You're charming, even-tempered."

Her heartbeat spiked as he moved around the island. He was getting too close—his presence suddenly suffocating. She desperately wanted to escape from his predatory gaze. But to do so would be too alerting.

"Do you know a lot of diplomats?" she asked.

"I make it my business to know everyone," he said smoothly. He rotated the meat in the Dutch oven, closed the lid and adjusted the stove to a simmer. "It's how I've gotten as far as I have in business."

The tension coiled tighter. "Maybe I'm full of surprises?" *Time to bring up business.* "So what's next for you? You must have plans to expand Vibrantia's footprint. Are you looking to expand here in Russia?"

He hesitated, and Ava caught a flicker of uncertainty in his eyes. Perhaps he was hiding something.

When he spoke, there was scratchy quality of his voice that reminded her of nails drawing down a chalkboard. "I know it's not very popular for me to say, but I admire the Kremlin for not trying to control free speech. Putin doesn't try to place federal restrictions on social media like we do in America."

*So, he is a sympathizer,* she thought to herself. She swallowed down the urge to tell him that he was fueling an entire movement that sought to rip American apart.

"I know what you mean," she said softly. *Make him feel safe. Make him feel seen.*

"Beautiful, smart and capable," he murmured. "Sloane Reed. Quite the irresistible combination." He moved closer still, his eyes dark and his long fingers tapping idly on the marble countertop. "I never realized before how beautiful you are." He tried to cover her hand with his, but she moved it to take a sip of her wine. She couldn't tell if he was intentionally trying to unnerve her or if he was really attracted to her—either way, it was unsettling.

She forced a smile. "Excuse me, I need to use the restroom."

He shifted away, and his hands dropped to his sides. But the side of his mouth twitched. He viewed her as a challenge—not a bad thing in these circumstances. But she would need to placate him if she was going to have any success in getting additional information.

"Your bathroom? Can you show me where it is?"

"Second door to the left."

Ava nodded, forcing a grateful smile. As she turned, she felt his eyes linger on her back just a beat too long and the fingers of her right hand twitched, longing to feel the cool metal of her Glock. Her heeled boots clicked down the hallway like gunshots. The second she shut the bathroom door, she locked it, pressed a second bug beneath the bathroom counter, and leaned her back against the cold wall tile. The two bugs were in place, but something was off. Grey's vibe had shifted—from inquisitive to creepy in a matter of minutes. She needed to find an exit strategy, a reason—anything to cut the night short.

She splashed cold water on her face and used a fancy towel to dab it dry. *Think, Ava. Think.*

Her heartbeat felt visible in her throat as she walked outside the bathroom and down the hallway. But the air had somehow thickened. Like it knew something she didn't. She entered the kitchen, and her blood turned to ice. Grey was no longer leaning casually against the counter. He stood upright, his posture rigid as he held the listening device. Her blood froze.

"Care to explain this, Ms. Sloane?"

Ava's mind raced, the edges of panic flaring up behind her eyes.

She threw her hands up, almost laughing. "I know. They're all over my apartment too. So annoying how the Russians keep tabs on everything we do." She shrugged, forcing her tone to remain light and prayed he didn't discover the second bug. "But that's life in Moscow, right?"

Grey didn't laugh. He looked at her like he wanted to peel her open. Silence swelled between them—the hum of the traffic outside suddenly buzzing louder than it should. Then, a knock at the door.

Grey rose a brow. "Expecting someone?"

"No," she said, truthfully.

He moved toward the front door and Ava's breath caught. *What now?*

Standing in the doorway was a tall man dressed as an embassy guard—long navy wool coat, tactical boots, a sidearm holstered at his side. "Apologies, sir. Ambassador's office sent me."

Grey hesitated just long enough for Ava to recognize the glint in the guard's eyes. *Ben.*

Ben took hold of her hand as they crossed the street, jolting her abruptly from the memory. He leaned toward her, murmuring low. "Two tails. Eleven o'clock. One's got FSB posture, the other could be private security."

The icy air off the Moskva River glinted on the polished department storefront of Petrovka Street. Designer lights twinkled behind the frosted glass, showcasing the latest fashion. But Ava's instincts prickled, dread clawing at her even as she savored the heat of his hand still intertwined with hers. She loved the feel of his callused fingers on hers, the strength of his grip—and cursed herself for loving it. Her training screamed at her to keep her distance, to wall off anything that might compromise their mission. She knew Ben doubted Konstantin, thought he was feeding her just enough information until the FSB or SVR closed in. And that gnawed at her, because Konstantin had passed every evaluation, the polygraphs, the psychological tests—every CIA asset validation technique available. Though her heart, her gut whispered something different. That Ben might be right.

When she spotted the surveillants again, Ben let go of her hand but kept walking, his eyes fixed straight ahead.

"I saw them," she said in a low voice, shoving her hands deep into her pockets as if it could anchor her to the ground. She was acutely aware that she didn't have a weapon.

But Ben was surely armed.

"They were outside the Bulgari boutique when we left Grey's apartment," Ava said.

He edged closer, and she caught the smell of the soap he'd used that morning—grapefruit and rosemary. "How do you want to play this?" Ben's hand slid to the small of her back. "They're watching us," he murmured, his voice barely above a whisper.

"Soft exit. No panic."

They moved in sync as if they were a wealthy couple walking home after dinner. She hooked her arm through his as the snow began to fall, causing a hush to fall in delicate flurries. Ava caught a flash of movement in a mirrored window, too close, a twitch in the man's step behind them that said *trained.*

Ben's gaze tracked the same movement, a shadow slicing between rows of sleek, luxury cars. His jaw tightened. "Hard exit?"

"Hard exit."

Ben grabbed her hand once more, and together they pivoted sharply down a narrow alleyway. Behind them, boots shuffled against the cold stone, echoing within the walls, and Ava's heart revved up. Ben's fingers tightened through hers as they weaved past parked sedans, her coat billowing up behind them.

Suddenly, Ben yanked her into a recessed service doorway, and before she could ask a question, his mouth was on hers, shielding her face from view as the dark figure walked past. His mouth tasted like mint and brandy, and she felt every muscle betray her as her mouth responded to his touch, his kiss. She let herself sink into it, her hands curling against his chest as every nerve ending flared to life. For one breathless instant, she forgot the surveillant, forgot the mission, forgot everything except the reckless thrum of wanting him. But just as she felt herself being pulled under by her desire, her rational mind surfaced. The move was precise, calculated cover. A couple kissing in the shadows was ordinary. Two operatives bolting from surveillance is what invited a tail. She *knew* this. She'd been trained by Frank to expect it.

Then, as suddenly as it had begun, he broke away and stepped back, his chest rising hard, his eyes avoiding hers as if he'd crossed a line. The man in front of her was no longer the one who had let his guard slip. That version had vanished. What remained was the operative—disciplined, distant, eyes fixed on some point beyond her.

"That was never part of your countersurveillance course," she said, her cheeks flaming as the surveillant continued down the narrow path.

Something dark, possibly fear or embarrassment, burned in his eyes. "Well, no," he admitted, running a hand through his hair. "We lost one, but I bet the other one is still circling."

Ava nodded, adrenaline still burning as they turned down the opposite end of the alleyway. "And what if they catch up to us?"

Ben inched the handle of his gun from his coat pocket. "Then we introduce him to American hospitality."

# CHAPTER

# 12

THE FROZEN WALKWAY stretched before Ava, a treacherous path veiled in moonlit snow. Behind her, an invisible weight pressed upon her, as if something—or someone—threatened to pull her back from her meeting with Konstantin. Frank had warned her what this career could cost her, a life in the shadows, never planting roots, never making friends. It had cost her mother everything, leaving Ava with only vague memories of a woman she barely remembered. And now Ava had entrenched herself in the same unending battle for America's security that would leave her stripped of the real, authentic life that she'd always longed for.

Rebellion whispered in her chest, a sudden searing urge to veer off the path before her, but to do so would be a betrayal of her country, her mission. If she could expose the Russian hand guiding the media platform Vibrantia—she could stop the turmoil inside her country; she could foster peace. And perhaps she could discover the truth about her mother.

She couldn't walk away now.

A low howl of wind snaked through the skeletal trees, pushing fresh snow to the ground as she trudged forward, her boots slipping on the slick walkway. It was too risky to meet Konstantin in the open, so they had settled on the outskirts of Moscow near the busy

Christmas market. A sharp crack echoed through the trees, an unseen branch snapping under the weight of snow. Ava froze mid-step and turned around, her fingers reaching under her coat for the pistol she'd tucked into the small of her back.

"Did I startle you?" Konstantin's voice drifted out from the darkness, amused. He unwrapped his scarf, revealing a face that was carved from long winters and the harsh realities of a life in the shadows. He seemed to have aged ten years since she'd seen him in Dubai.

"Yes," she answered coolly in Russian, stepping into view. "If you're trying to assert yourself as the more experienced intelligence officer," she added, not bothering to hide the annoyance in her voice, "you have succeeded. Now let's get on with it."

"Apologies, but I doubt that you scare so easily, *devushka*," Konstantin said, his breath fogging the air. "So, no time for pleasantries, da?" He chuckled. "I thought the Americans like to ease into business. You are different. Direct. I like that."

"Yes, I am," she said flatly. "Which means I don't have the patience for games. You said you had information. Let's hear it."

Konstantin sighed, folding his arms across his chest as he walked beside her. "Very well. At your dinner last night, I assume that Nathaniel Grey has told you that he is seeking *foreign* investment."

She felt a chill trace her spine. "So, SVR really does have eyes and ears everywhere."

"We wouldn't be very good at our jobs if we didn't," he said, his tone suddenly flat. "I assume you want to know about what your government calls 'foreign interference'." His lips curved slightly. "It's always amusing, this outrage. As if America does not do the same to others."

"Spare me the lecture," Ava said, her voice crisp. "We both know the Kremlin's goal: incite unrest, destabilize our institutions. We cannot allow that to happen."

"Then tell me what you need, Ms. Sloane."

"What I need from you is clarity: details on SVR's cyber command structure—where exactly inside Russia are these attacks originating? Our teams haven't been able to pinpoint the precise location of the coders. They're masking their locations with VPN equivalents." Her tone turned colder. "And Vibrantia—what proof can you get me that Grey is working on behalf of the Kremlin?"

"The movement was already there, simmering, waiting. SVR simply . . . gave it oxygen. A little funding. Some useful connections. Your country, it is fragile right now. A push in the right place"—he flicked his fingers—"and it crumbles."

Ava's pulse revved. "What kind of push?"

The wind picked up, sending icy tentacles scraping across her face. Konstantin's expression darkened, his smile fading. "This cyberattack—it is not just some protest. It is designed to send a message, to divide your country beyond repair."

Her breath hitched. "I need names, Konstantin."

"I will give you the only name you need." He sighed, a branch snapping under his weight.

"Dimitri Abramovich . . . he is the architect."

Ava pulled out her secure phone and looked at the intelligence report she'd found on Dimitri Abramovich when she'd learned about his connection to her mother. Together with a rogue nonstate actor named Sergei Volkov, Abramovich had launched Project Volk—a cyber campaign to hack state media and destabilize Putin's propaganda machine. In Russia, he had sparked a series of mysterious "leaks" implicating key Kremlin officials in treason while funding populist influencers and nationalist militias, setting the stage for unrest that he could alone control.

"Is this him?" she showed Konstantin the photograph.

Konstantin nodded. "Da. Powerful. Rich. Connected. And untouchable. But . . . he has weaknesses. Women. Money. His paranoia." He smiled faintly. "Perhaps you can find a crack in that armor, eh?"

She tucked the phone away. "Then I need to get close to him."

"You are learning how the game is played quite fast, *devushka*."

"Who says that I'm new at this?"

Konstantin chuckled. "I don't need to be a trained SVR assassin to guess that this is your first assignment inside Russia. Abramovich shouldn't be hard to find. He is hosting a grand holiday party tomorrow at his estate. Many important people . . . foreign ministers, oligarchs, and a sprinkling of other international 'friends.' Many secrets."

"And you're getting me in."

Humor returned to his eyes. "I can secure an invitation for you—and Alexei, if that's what he's calling himself these days."

"He's not my partner," Ava said sharply.

"I met Alexei when he first came to Moscow. Didn't he tell you?" Konstantin feigned surprise as the wind picked up the gray hair off his forehead. "We met years go. He was different then—less guarded. We even swapped stories about our divorces. I wonder why he neglected to mention it to you."

Ava felt a twist move through her at the revelation, but she didn't have time to process it. Not now. "If this is your attempt to rattle me, Konstantin, don't bother."

"I would never presume to do such a thing. Only a warning: Abramovich's estate is a viper's nest, and you'll be walking in with a blindfold on."

"Then tell me how to remove it," Ava shot back.

"I can get you in. but you will need more than a sharp tongue and a government-issued pistol. These people, they smell weakness." His gaze flicked over her puffy coat and boots. "You will need a proper dress, for starters." His voice softened, almost conspiratorial. "Go to a small boutique in town called Chloe—there is a seamstress there called Sophie that owes me a favor. She will help."

She raised a brow. "Am I running you, or have I been tricked into a relationship with SVR?"

Konstantin smiled broadly. "I prefer to call it a partnership."

"I want you to have this." Ava stopped walking and pulled out a wad of cash.

"I haven't earned this," Konstantin said cautiously.

"Take it anyway." She handed him the cash. "And let's not pretend that this is about gambling debts. I know that you don't lack personal wealth."

His smile faltered.

"Let's stop circling this," Ava said, stepping closer. "I need details. What's Grey planning? What is Abramovich really building? And how far does this go?"

Silence stretched between them before Konstantin exhaled, the humor draining from his face.

"You want answers," he said quietly. "Grey is more than just a businessman. He's a zealot. He believes in what he's doing. And Abramovich?" Konstantin's jaw bunched. "He's happy to let the fire spread until it devours everything . . . then he'll step in with the cure."

"Authoritarianism as a solution to chaos," she said.

He nodded. "And Grey thinks he's the one holding the match. But he's being used. He's the perfect face — polished, patriotic, dangerous. He draws people in without them ever realizing who's really pulling the strings."

"Then stop talking in metaphors and give me something I can use," she demanded. "Names. Routes. Strategy. Anything that connects them directly."

"I will," he said, lowering his voice. "But we're not alone."

A faint metallic click echoed through the trees. The sound froze the air between them.

Ava's hand flew to her pistol as she grabbed Konstantin's arm. "Enough talk. We need to move—now."

# CHAPTER

# 13

Dimitri Abramovich's estate was one of dark fairy tales, a sprawling palace with steep gabled roofs and intricate woodwork, barely visible through the thick curtain of snow-covered trees. But the silence of the trees wasn't peaceful. It was expectant. Surveillance cameras blinked from the pines like watchful eyes, and Ava couldn't shake the feeling that they were being catalogued, assessed by a legion of special forces guarding the compound.

As they eased toward the gate, an enormous iron structure emblazoned with the Abramovich family crest, Ava's heart gave a hard knock. Their driver flashed the invitation through the window, and she held her breath as the guard leaned forward with the bar code reader. Her mind ticked through contingencies. If it didn't scan . . . if the system flagged them . . . if the guard holding the scanner noticed something. One wrong move and the operation was over. Not just for Ben, but for the entire team. For Konstantin.

With a groan, the double wrought iron fence creaked open, revealing snow-dusted grounds manicured with precision. Ava spotted the guards immediately, AK-47s slung over their shoulders, their breath visible in the frigid air. They made their way up the driveway toward a lavish mansion that glimmered in the moonlight.

Ava's fingers tightened around the lapels of her white fur coat as the car crunched to a stop in the massive circular drive. She hated the coat. It made her feel ornamental, a trophy—when she wanted to feel sharp as she headed into the lion's den, the reassuring weight of her Glock at her side. But smuggling weapons into such a heavily fortified compound was out of the question.

Ava swung the car door open before the driver could do it, her heels hitting the packed snow with a delicate crunch. The air was so cold it caught in her throat. She forced her chin up, practiced elegance wrapped around tension as she passed a line of tuxedo-clad waiters carrying champagne flutes on silver trays. She felt Ben behind her, steady and close, gently lifting the satin train of her gown—effortless, instinctual. The quiet gesture of a romantic when no one was watching. To her, it was also a reminder that no matter how alone she felt in this moment, she wasn't.

"Careful," he murmured, the promising warmth of his breath on her ear.

She nodded, saying nothing, grateful for the moment of grounding. Her pulse always steadied under his touch, his voice. She glanced at him. He was dressed smartly in a Brioni tuxedo, the finest Italian fabric hugging his broad shoulders. The suit and dress were courtesy of Konstantin, who seemed to have "friends" everywhere in Moscow.

Inside, the warmth of the mansion hit her like a wave as she stepped beneath chandeliers that sparkled like jewels. A string orchestra played a Soviet-era romance song Ava recognized as "Moscow Nights," transporting her back to her childhood, where her mother had educated her on the beauty of Russian classical pieces. She had come here for answers. And yet the deeper she sank into the CIA's mission, the further away the truth seemed. She hadn't expected the mission to consume her life so completely; she'd thought she would be able to continue her search for her mother. But that illusion had shattered quickly. Her mission here required more time, more energy than she had anticipated. The adrenaline, the stakes, and the constant urgency had put her search on pause.

And the text message remained, archived, encrypted, and unanswered. She carried it like a splinter beneath her skin as she stepped inside the ballroom. The conflict within her must have been apparent as Ben's fingers gently brushed her elbow.

"Everything okay?" he asked, close enough to whisper in her ear.

"Fine." She inhaled deeply, steeling herself. "Let's find Roman."

With Konstantin's help, they had identified a young, disgruntled employee of Abramovich's named Roman and planned to confiscate his phone. On it, Ava hoped to find evidence that SVR was behind the cybersecurity attacks that threatened to pull America apart. She also planned to implant a recording device that could discover the location of the Vibrantia warehouse where the cyber hackers were stationed.

"Where should we look first?" she asked Ben.

His gaze slid toward the ballroom where men and women glided across the sleek marble with its gold-leaf accents.

"Our best vantage point is probably in there." He nodded at the ballroom.

"You want to dance?" she asked with a hint of playfulness, but her heart thumped heavily in her ears as she shrugged out of her coat and handed it to an attendant.

His eyes glimmered like a challenge. "Unless you have a better idea?"

Before she had time to argue, he reached for her hand and pulled her onto the dance floor.

"Plus"—he patted his pocket, where he carried a DarkFin, a small tool that could capture the IMSI, the International Mobile Subscriber Identity, associated with Roman's phone—"we have intel to collect."

Ava nodded slowly and allowed herself to be led. Ben's hand found her back, his fingers curving to the back of her ribcage. His grip steadied her, but when curious eyes fell on them, as the cold night whispered through the ballroom, it seemed more that he was claiming her. She could feel every one of his fingers through the thin silk of her gown as he took her into his arms. There was a part of her that knew she should pull away, but another part, a louder part, leaned into his touch, his warmth.

"You look incredible tonight," he said, his voice low and ragged in her ear.

She swallowed hard. "Focus," she said, barely above a whisper.

The orchestra surged, and Ava followed the rhythm with practiced ease. But dancing with Ben, the feel of his touch, the sound of violins rising and falling, made something within her flutter, unravel. Over the last three years, she had used her training, gliding through embassy events like a diplomat's daughter. But Ben had unsettled that confidence. He challenged her in ways that few others did. He questioned her assumptions, pushing her to think three steps ahead, and called her out when she leaned too hard on instinct without proof. And without even meaning to, he had reminded her why the work mattered in the first place. It wasn't just about revenge or ghosts from her past.

It was about preventing the future from falling apart.

Brass instruments soared, and her heart began to race, their sound full of hunger and something old, something unrelenting. His fingers tightened on hers, and their pace quickened, her silk dress whispering across the sleek marble floor. She fixed her eyes on his bowtie, unable to meet his face and acknowledge the aching within her. She was aware of every flicker of movement, every deep inhalation that raised his chest.

She refused to meet his eyes. If she did, she might fall into whatever this was between them. "How long do you think we have until the next cyberattack?" she said instead.

"Hard to say." His jaw was tight, his gaze flickering over Ava's shoulder as he continued to survey the room while leading her through the dance. "But we've seen this play before. Except Russia doesn't just infiltrate, they poison from within."

"And Vibrantia is their latest weapon," she added, shifting closer under the pretense of wanting to keep their conversation private. The smell of him, pine and something undeniably Ben, whispered along her senses. "Grey's Liberty Coalition isn't just rhetoric anymore. People are listening. They're angry."

Ben exhaled. "And Grey knows how to work the algorithms, and whether he realizes it or not, he's doing it for Russia."

"He *owns* the algorithms. He's feeding people a fantasy."

He lowered his eyes to her face. "We have to get ahead of this."

Ava nodded sharply, afraid to acknowledge the ember that glowed within her. Ben was all warmth and feeling, where Grey had looked at her like she was an object to be won, a means to an end.

"I won't let him tear our country apart," she whispered, more to herself than to Ben.

"*We* won't," he said, his green eyes darkening. "You're not in this alone."

The violins rose and fell like a breath between them. Ava's pulse quickened with the music as Ben's hand brushed the small of her back, steadying her as they turned. His touch left a trail of heat.

"You're distracted," he murmured.

"Maybe I'm multitasking," she replied lightly, though her breath hitched when his eyes searched hers.

"Multitasking gets people killed." A hint of a smile ghosted across his lips, softening the warning. "Especially when Konstantin's involved."

"You don't trust him."

"Should I?" Ben's brow lifted. "The man has more skeletons than Red Square has pigeons."

She stifled a laugh, stepping closer as the music swelled. "And yet, here we are—dancing."

His hands tightened almost imperceptibly at her waist, pulling her just a breath closer. The air between them thickened, charged. For a second, she forgot about Konstantin, about Moscow, about everything but the heat radiating off him. She shifted back, breaking the current before it dragged her under.

"Careful, Ben," she said, her voice steadier than she felt. "Keep looking at me like that, and someone might think you're enjoying yourself."

He exhaled a laugh, low, reluctant. "God forbid."

But his eyes didn't move from hers.

"I—" he said, his voice low, barely audible beneath the deep resonant hum of the cello.

She darted her eyes away, burying the rush of deep emotion beneath the layers she'd built. Her feelings for him were tangling within her, growing roots.

And that's when she saw him—Nathaniel Grey, lingering near the caviar display like a wolf at the edge of the wood. Her pulse quickened, and her fingers dug unconsciously into Ben's neck.

"Don't react," Ben murmured, sensing her shift in posture. "Just breathe."

But she could not. Not with Grey's eyes on her, narrowing like a blade. Ben's fingers tightened around hers. A warning. A goodbye.

# CHAPTER

# 14

"May I have this dance?" Grey's voice was smooth as he approached, but the weight behind his words felt more like he'd just challenged Ben to a duel.

The music seemed to stop, although Ava could hear a distant echo of it in her ears.

Ben's fingers tightened around hers—just for a moment—enough to send a warning and let go. If Grey suspected that she and Ben were up to anything, their operation would fail. She had a part to play, and so did Ben.

Grey's eyes slid over Ben without a flicker of recognition, and relief sparked within her. He didn't connect the man at her side with the stranger who had come to his apartment. Ben had been in disguise that night—another face, another identity. Tonight, he was just a shadow at her elbow, easily dismissed by a man like Grey.

She turned and forced a stiff smile at Grey. "Of course."

Ben's voice held an edge. "I need a drink anyway."

He turned abruptly, his shoulders tense as he disappeared into the crowd. She didn't watch him go. She couldn't afford to. Instead, she quickly smoothed her features, not wanting to admit even to herself what she'd felt in Ben's arms.

"What brings you here?" she asked Grey, her voice light.

He didn't answer. Instead, his hand gripped her waist, firm and possessive as he pulled her into the proper stance. He leaned in and whispered in her ear, "You and your friend seem close."

Her stomach hollowed as he led her effortlessly into the waltz. Ava lifted a brow. "You sound jealous."

Grey chuckled darkly, but the sharpness in his eyes remained. "Just observant."

She needed to move the conversation forward even as her skin crawled. "I was actually hoping that I would see you here."

Something dark flickered within his eyes. "Is that so?"

"You said you had big plans for Liberty Coalition. Something that would make Washington listen."

Grey smirked. "You're very curious."

She leaned in just slightly, determined to stroke his ego. Her hand brushed the edge of his lapel. "I like being ahead of the curve."

That did it.

His chest lifted a little, pride blooming like a weed. He wanted her to be impressed. He wanted her to admire him.

He twirled her, and when he pulled her close again, his breath brushed against her ear. "What if I told you that Washington is about to get a wake-up call? That by this time next week, people will finally understand that the federal government isn't as untouchable as they think?"

Her pulse hammered, but she kept her expression calm, neutral. "I'd say that sounds like a bold claim."

His fingers pressed into her lower back. "Not a claim. A promise."

Ava swallowed down the bile that rose in her throat. "And how exactly are you going to accomplish that?"

Grey's eyes held a challenge. "The best way to send a message is to hit the source of the problem."

He was leading her somewhere—carefully, deliberately—but she needed him to say it outright.

*He was close, too close.* But she needed specifics.

"You mean Congress? The White House?" She met his eyes, heavy with warning. He took hold of her wrist and led her out onto the veranda. Cold air hit her bare shoulders, but it did little to stop heat from rising to the surface of her skin. He pinned her with her back against the railing, one hand braced at her waist, the other went to her face. His fingers came to her chin, clenching it. Her pulse jumped, but she forced herself to remain still.

*Maintain cover*, she told herself.

"Too predictable," he said. "Besides, those places are just symbols. The real power is in the infrastructure. The agencies that enforce federal control. The places they think are untouchable."

His voice snaked in her thoughts until it clicked like a cipher unlocking. "SNS," she murmured, her voice hoarse, her heart racing.

Grey's eyes flashed with satisfaction. "Smart girl."

Ava felt her stomach twist. SNS, the Strategic National Stockpile, was the backbone of federal crisis response. If Russia took out a major SNS facility, it wouldn't just be an attack. It would be a statement—one that would leave the country vulnerable the next time disaster struck.

She forced herself to stay in character. "That's . . . ambitious."

His fingers moved from her chin to her waist, and his thumb pressed hard into her hipbone. "Necessary. The federal government controls people through fear—disasters, pandemics, economic crashes. SNS makes sure they stay dependent. But when people realize that Washington can't protect them? That's when they'll turn to us."

She had heard enough. She needed to get this intel to Frank. Now. But there was one more thing she had to confirm. "You must have powerful allies," she said carefully.

Grey's jaw tightened. "And why is that?"

She shrugged. "Because you built the Liberty Coalition on the idea of American sovereignty. But now you're taking money from Moscow?"

The light faded from his eyes. "You think I'm compromised?"

"I think you're too smart to be used by a foreign power," she said, her words laced with an equal measure of admiration and concern. "So either you're in control, or you're in over your head."

His long fingers clenched tight on her waist. "Moscow and I have shared a goal. They want Washington destabilized. Their money funds the operation, but make no mistake—I am the one pulling the strings."

That was it. *Confirmation*. The attack on SNS wasn't just about Liberty Coalition's ideology. It was about weakening the US government at the exact points where it mattered most. Russia had bought itself a homegrown insurgency, and Nathaniel Grey had sold his movement in exchange for their resources.

Her blood raced as her eyes drifted through the open double doors in search of Ben. Beyond the dance floor, next to the bar, she spotted his broad outline. Her stomach somersaulted, wanting to flee, wanting to find her way toward him. He turned as if he could sense her, hear her blood roaring in her ears.

Ben's eyes locked on hers, and she felt something burn within her as she realized that she was still locked within Grey's arms, a hand on either side of her, trapping her against the railing. She moved to push his hand away and smooth down the fabric of her dress.

"I could use a drink," she said, trying her best not to look in Ben's direction.

Grey caught her wrist before she could leave and spun her around. "You understand why America has to change, don't you?" Grey's voice was low, coaxing. Dread slithered into her veins. "This isn't just about politics. This is about survival. That's what the Liberty Coalition ensures, the future of the American people."

Ava forced a smile, yanking her wrist from his grasp. "I understand perfectly."

She reached the dance floor and nearly collided with Ben. His presence was a wall of tension, his eyes dark with something dangerous, something lethal.

"Sloane," Ben said, using her alias. But he didn't look at her. His gaze was locked on Grey, violence thrumming within him. Finally, he turned toward Ava, and she had the urge to back away from the two men as Ben's fingers curled at his sides. "The ambassador is asking for you."

Grey's jaw tightened, but he said nothing as Ava walked away next to Ben.

Ava's heart raced. She had the information they needed—intelligence on Russia's support for the Liberty Coalition—straight from the source. But now they had to stop what was coming before it was too late.

# CHAPTER

# 15

Ava closed the door quietly behind her and Ben as they made her way into an upstairs bedroom, her heart jackhammering. Ben's jaw was still clenched. He scanned the space with the calculated fury of someone seconds from snapping. An antique chandelier flickered above them, casting fractured light across the four-poster bed. Emerald green drapes stirred in the cold drafty room. A Christmas tree glittered with red and white lights in the corner, its soft glow at odds with the threat closing in around them.

"I'm going to fucking kill that guy," Ben said, anger radiating from him.

"Relax." She put a hand on his tense bicep, unsure for a moment if she wanted to soothe or feed the danger that pulsed within him. "I got what we came here for. How about you?" The sound of her heartbeat in her ears made it difficult to think. Her jaw still ached from where Grey's fingers had gripped her. But she swallowed down her anger, trying to focus on the threat that loomed.

Ben exhaled through his nose. "I think so, but I wanted to make sure I could get the DarkFin to upload." He dropped to one knee beside the device, all coiled energy and muscle. "It had to be at least ten feet within range to capture the necessary data, which I believe it was, but I got"—he paused and looked up at her; emotion danced briefly within his eyes, but he darted his eyes away—"distracted and moved away from the target."

Ava hovered in next to him, close enough that she could feel his body heat. He was breathing heavily like her. The DarkFin blinked, then went dark. But if it had done its job, extracting data from the target's phone, they now had tangible proof: evidence from Roman's device linking the Liberty Coalition and Vibrantia to Russia.

"Do you see an outlet anywhere?" Ben asked.

"There." She pointed under the lamp and began typing a classified email hurriedly into her secure phone to warn Frank of the upcoming attack, using the code name for Nathaniel Grey that had been randomly generated by the CIA.

**Subject: Urgent: Intelligence on Potential Attack on SNS**
**Frank,**
**Intelligence from TIBERIUS suggests imminent attack planning. I recommend immediate source verification and SNS coordination to secure critical infrastructure. Can escalate with CT team.**
**-Sloane**

Outside, voices and footsteps thumped heavily across the polished hardwood floors, sending a jolt of adrenaline through her.

"Konstantin said that he knew you," she said, trying to break the tension as they waited for the data to upload, "from your last deployment to Russia."

Ben froze and turned around to face her. "What did he tell you?"

"Only that you were married before and that you both bonded over your divorces."

"I met Konstantin seven years ago. Outside of Moscow. We were both drowning in our sorrows. It wasn't the best time for me." He gave a wry smile.

"How long were you married?" she asked.

He restarted the device, and it blinked white instead of dark. "A little under a year." He exhaled sharply as if the memory stung.

"What happened?" She regretted the question almost as soon as it slipped out, and she felt her cheeks flame.

He kept eyes focused on the device. "This life . . . it was too much for her. The constant moving. My trust issues. The isolation. By the time that I knew that she had enough, it was too late. She was pregnant—we wanted to do the right thing."

"So, you have kids." The revelation shocked her, not because he had a child, but because he'd never told her.

"A son. He's seven." His voice grew quiet, and a pained expression crossed his face.

Ava hesitated. "Why didn't you tell me?"

"Never came up." He turned back to the DarkFin and punched the button on the back of the device. "Dammit, if they gave me a faulty device, heads are going to roll." He was back to his all-business demeanor, not ready to let her in

"Why didn't you tell me that you had met Konstantin before?" she pressed.

"I didn't think it was necessary." He shifted slightly but still refused to meet her face. "It was random. A bar outside Moscow. Nothing operational."

"Not necessary?" Anger bubbled within her chest. "How could you not think that would be a useful piece of information?" Her voice sharpened. "You don't just meet people like Konstantin on the street."

He still didn't look at her. "I liked him too much to involve him in this line of work. I had no idea that he was SVR. He never tried to pitch me or anything like that. I'm telling you; it really was random. When I spoke to him about my divorce, he didn't judge or try to fix me, he just listened."

She inhaled deeply and let it out slowly. "I like him too, but this isn't going to work if you withhold information about my sources. We're supposed to be working together on this case."

Finally, Ben looked at her, really looked at her. "I agree."

Ava's throat suddenly went dry, and she swallowed. "I think you're right to be skeptical of Konstantin. Something tells me this isn't the first time he's walked a dangerous line."

He looked at her, his expression softening just before his eyes dropped. "Is that what you're doing with Grey? Walking a dangerous line?"

She hesitated to answer, and the weight of the silence seemed to thicken as the question hung in the air.

Ben shifted on the bed, his fingers tightening on the DarkFin as the data from the target's phone began to upload.

"I'm using him for information, that's it." She searched his face, trying to decipher his thoughts, but all she saw were walls. "Why would it matter anyway?" she asked.

He shifted toward her, the air crackling with what they did not say, what they could not, although his expression remained well guarded. "Promise me that you'll stay away from Nathaniel Grey." His voice betrayed him as it grew low, intense. "We'll find another way."

"I'm not sure there is one."

She couldn't help the pull of him, a magnet that was impossible to ignore. He had loosened his necktie, and the top two buttons of his shirt were undone. There was something terrifying in the way his eyes held hers, daring her to close the gap between them.

"I told you, I can handle myself," she said in a hoarse voice.

His gaze hardened, the air still fizzing between them. "I won't let him touch you again."

"I'm not yours to protect." The words felt raw on the back of her throat, rougher than she'd meant.

He darted his eyes away, his attention shifting back to the DarkFin as the data continued to upload from Roman's phone. The distance between them widened, although they hadn't moved, and she regretted her words.

"Let me see the DarkFin when you're done," she said, still trying to ignore the heat that rushed through every limb at his words: *I won't let him touch you again.* There was something fierce and possessive in his tone. She tried to steady herself against the feelings that rushed through her when he'd looked at her like she was his to protect. She wasn't, and yet . . .

Foreign voices spilled through the seams of the door, sharp and guttural, and Ava's pulse spiked. A thunderous pounding followed, then a barked order in Russian—"Otkroy!" *Open up.*

"Shit," Ava hissed.

Ben's gaze snapped to the door as he yanked the device from the outlet. "Move!" he shouted, already crossing the room. "Window. Now!"

He tore back the heavy drapes and unlatched the window with a practiced flick. "Go!" he urged, gesturing wildly. Beyond the glass, the manicured lawn lay cloaked in darkness, faintly haloed by the white lights strung through the evergreens lining the circular drive.

Ava's body moved before her mind caught up. Two strides, and she was gripping the iron railing, swinging a leg over into the icy night.

"Faster!" Ben's voice was clipped, commanding. He vaulted over beside her, already dropping toward the ground while she was still clinging to the ledge.

Cold air knifed through her thin dress but sweat pooled at the nape of her neck and trickled down her spine. Every second dragged like an hour. Her shoe slipped on the slick stone, and she cursed under her breath.

She kicked off her heels, barefoot now, toes scraping for purchase as she eased herself downward. A dog barked nearby. Too close. A harsh beam of light slashed across the lawn.

"Jump!" Ben's voice rose from below, raw and urgent.

She glanced back, her heartbeat thrashing within her ears. The distance to the ground seemed endless. She could hear the guards in the room above them, seconds away from leaning out and spotting her clinging to the façade like a trapped insect. A surge of panic seized her. She swallowed hard, shut her eyes, and let go of the brick. And then—nothing.

# CHAPTER

# 16

TWO HOURS LATER, Ava and Ben sat at the embassy, their anxious faces lit only by computer screens, their eyes locked on the cryptic data that flashed before them. The intensity of the night pressed down on Ava, her body still aching from her narrow escape at Abramovich's compound. She inhaled a shaky breath, her bruised ankle a painful reminder of how close they had gotten to getting caught. She adjusted the bag of ice Ben had brought for her injury and tried to ignore the throbbing in her ankle as she studied the geocoordinates.

"Don't you think you need a new one?" Ben asked, his eyes narrowed on the ice pack he'd forced on her earlier. She glanced down and saw that it had long since melted, but she hadn't bothered replacing it. There were more pressing concerns.

"I'm fine." She reached for her sweatshirt and pulled it over the t-shirt she wore with her jeans, refusing to acknowledge the ache that flared through her muscles.

Ben exhaled sharply but didn't press further. Instead, his gaze returned to the monitor. "Look at this."

His fingers tracked over the pinpoints on the computer screen where Roman had traveled within the last week. The geocoordinates all led to one point—a warehouse in the grim industrial zone in Moscow. Ava stood and leaned in, balancing on one leg. She used her index finger and thumb to zoom in on the classified imagery. The warehouse where the geocoordinates landed had a sleek metal exterior and blacked-out windows.

"Roman's been there almost every week." She hopped back over to her computer. Ben outstretched a hand to help her, but she used the back of her chair to steady herself.

She slumped down in her chair, and her fingers moved swiftly over the keyboard, pulling up financial transactions from Roman's phone. The list of purchases was staggering—advanced servers, AI-enabled workstations, networking equipment, and high-end security tools.

Her pulse pounded as the transactions scrolled before her. "Encryption tools, antivirus software, intrusion detection systems, firewalls . . . this isn't just some shady side business." Ava's breath hitched. "The Russians have spent millions of dollars on this. Abramovich isn't just running a cyber op—he's building a digital war machine."

The muscle in Ben's jaw flexed. "And he's testing it on the US." He tapped another screen, pulling up an unfamiliar program.

It wasn't just an attack plan. It was live. The cyber assault had already begun.

Ava's stomach dropped as Ben pulled up US security reports—data breaches, network anomalies, classified government sectors blinking red. "If they breach these firewalls, they could override financial systems, disrupt power grids . . ."

". . . or hijack classified defense networks." Ben's voice was grim. "We're looking at a total digital paralysis."

A chill crawled up Ava's spine. Her fingers flew across the keyboard as she logged into her secure computer and wrote to Frank to request a secure video teleconference. She needed answers, she needed clarity on what they had CIA's authorization to do to put a stop to Nathaniel Grey and Dimitri Abramovich, with no time to waste. Before she could send her message to Frank, his name flashed across the screen on her secure phone.

She answered the phone quickly, her chest still pounding from the weight of their discovery.

"Ava," Frank's voice was raw on the other end of the line. "Do you have any idea what's happening over here?"

"We just found evidence of—"

"No," Frank cut her off. "Turn on the news."

"Did you warn SNS?" she asked.

"Yes, all of that is taken care of—but Ava, just switch on the television." His voice was sharp with urgency.

Her ankle throbbed as she grabbed the remote, switching to Russian state media on the television above their computer terminals. Images of New York; Washington, DC; Miami; and Los Angeles flashed on the screen. Chaos. Violence. Unrest. Fires.

She couldn't breathe as she recognized the signs. This wasn't just a Liberty Coalition protest. It was a coordinated insurrection.

Liberty Coalition, a movement fueled by lies and manipulated information by Russian operatives, had ignited violence all over the country, and Vibrantia was their weapon. Curfews were in effect. Government buildings were fortified, and security forces deployed in full tactical gear. Armored vehicles rumbled through the streets of key cities, forming lines around federal institutions. Protesters had fractured—half demanding regional autonomy, others urging the preservation of national stability.

Ava felt her joints lock with fear as an image of Washington, DC, flashed on the television screen. The outside of the president's staff offices on Pennsylvania Avenue were riddled with bullet holes. Smoke billowed from nearby buildings.

"Everyone believes that the federal government is the enemy." Frank's voice was tense, his breathing rushed. "They think that we're withholding valuable information, but nothing could be further from the truth. And the worst part? We don't have enough time to prove them wrong."

An ache yanked through her. She wanted to reach through the screen, grab these people by the shoulders and shake them. They had no idea they were playing into Russia's hands, helping

Abramovich and Grey begin to drive the US to the brink of collapse. Cold fury rose in her chest.

This wasn't politics. Russia was causing war. Civil war.

"These messages on Vibrantia—we have to put a stop to this," Frank said. "The Liberty Coalition is going to tear this country apart."

"I'll call you back, Frank; I need a minute to think." She clicked off the secure video call, still staring at the TV while her head pounded. She wiped clammy hands on her pants.

After what Ava had seen on Roman's phone, there was no doubt that Abramovich was the architect of this chaos. While Grey was the revolutionary, it was Abramovich who was responsible for funding and coordinating the cyberattacks. How could they stop them before the country descended into further chaos?

She stared at the screen, feeling her chest tighten under the weight of the images. "Abramovich has bankrolled the movement, but Grey is the face." She turned toward Ben, her mind turning over a solution. "We need leverage." Realization struck her like a punch in the gut.

She needed someone on the inside, someone who could match Abramovich's wealth, power, and influence. But just as her mind settled on it, the one option that made sense—Nathaniel Grey—her heart argued against it. Her head pounded, her thoughts racing. Grey wasn't someone that she could trust—the minimal interactions they had had told her that much. Still, Grey was the only one who could rival Abramovich. And Abramovich was the only one who could stop Grey. If she could turn him, if she could expose the Russian manipulation . . .

The conclusion she had reached must have been apparent on her face as her eyes locked on Ben's.

"No," he said without preamble, his voice cutting through her thoughts. "I won't let them use you like this. You know what Grey wants, and you're not going to give it to him." He dragged a hand through his hair. "He won't take no for an answer."

Ava swallowed hard. She knew Grey wasn't just a businessman with misguided ideals—he was an opportunist. And men like Grey didn't play fair.

"If I could get him to see how Russia is manipulating him . . ."

Ben pushed off the desk and began pacing. "I think you're underestimating Grey's commitment to his own cause." His eyes were like steel. "We'll find another way."

Ava wanted to scream, yet she wanted to pull him closer. Ben was right in many ways, but she felt out of control, out of options—out of time.

Her frustration burned. "How do we stop this, Ben?" She gestured toward the television as the turmoil unfolded on the screen in real time. "How do we stop Russia from tearing our country apart? How do we shut down Vibrantia before this spirals further?"

Ben's voice was calm and firm, a direct contrast to the storm raging within her. "We fight them at their own game." He took a breath. "We find their weaknesses. We strike first. Let's see if Roman's phone has led us to the right location for where these cyberattacks are coming from. Perhaps if we can stop these hackers for a time, we can develop a more concrete plan to go after Grey and Abramovich."

Before Ava could respond, Ben's computer blinked with a new message. "Roman's on the move," he said. "And you won't like where he's going."

She shot Ben a look. *No more waiting. No more reacting.* "One word to Frank and I can have a special ops team here within twenty-four hours. We track down this warehouse and we wipe out everything—software, servers, and the cybercriminals, all of it."

"And what stops Abramovich from rebuilding?" Ben asked dryly.

Ava's pulse pounded as her eyes locked on Ben's. There was no getting around it. Nathaniel Grey was the key to unraveling this permanently, and they both knew it. A military raid would mean headlines, deniability issues, a trail leading back to the United States. Worse, Grey would go underground, along with his money and his reach. He could set up another network in weeks.

"The code is buried inside Vibrantia's servers," Ben pressed on. "Destroy the warehouse with a military strike and the world sees a smoking crater. But slip in quietly, take out the core with our own hands, and we cripple his network from the inside. No one traces it back to the United States, and Abramovich still thinks he's untouchable until the floor caves beneath him."

"Precisely," Ava agreed, "but you and I both know there's only one way."

Ben clenched his jaw, then the emotion disappeared from his face.

CHAPTER

# 17

Ava, Ben, Frank, and half a dozen of the CIA's SAD—Special Activities Division—officers sat in the Agency's black site high in the Caucasus mountains. The wind beat mercilessly against the steel compound walls, wailing as if in warning at what they were about to embark on. Ava let the cold settle like ice in her veins as she thought about everything that lay ahead—manipulating Grey, dismantling Russia's cyberattacks, preventing a catastrophe that could shatter her country. All of it made anxiety build within her chest.

But Ava let the cold settle in her bloodstream like steel. She needed to do more to manipulate the man who controlled the internet's narrative—Nathaniel Grey. The easiest course of action was to shut down Vibrantia completely. But the billions Grey had funneled into the US president's political campaign had ensured his immunity, and the president himself had agreed not to interfere with Grey's business, no matter how far it stretched.

Ava looked toward Frank, at the head of the room, his stance wide and hands clasped tight in front of him. The truth was apparent in the deep grooves of his face: Nathaniel Grey wasn't just dangerous, he was untouchable. *She was their only way in.*

She'd had two nights to make peace with that truth—nights spent lying awake in hotel rooms, staring at the only thing that kept her grounded when the mission felt like too much. Her mother's letter had always steadied her against the storms that raged inside her. The paper was soft from wear, the handwriting faded, but the hope in her mother's words were etched into Ava's mind. She'd memorized them so they could steady her when she'd felt alone: *Trust your instincts. Be cautious whom you follow, whom you love. And never let fear dictate your path.*

On the nights when she had nothing but mission briefings and surveillance footage for company, those words had been her refuge. But today there was no time for memory or reflection. Today, the stakes were clear, and she had no time to contemplate anything but the mission. If they failed, and if Abramovich and his network launched a new wave of cyberattacks, it would push the United States further toward civil war.

She looked toward the window, where the shadowy silhouettes of Marines guarding their meeting were barely visible against the wintery gray of early dawn. Their presence was a steady reminder that there was no cavalry coming. No reinforcements or safety net. Only the CIA officers inside that room stood between the United States and complete disaster. *They were it.*

"Nathaniel Grey is untouchable," Frank said, confirming what Ava already knew. "I'll need to remove some political hurdles before we can do anything against him or Vibrantia. US involvement needs to remain hidden in this operation. I don't want this to turn into an international incident. I want it done quietly, covertly."

"Until then," he continued, exhaustion edging his words, evidence of sleepless nights and impossible choices. "I think our best chance at preventing further cyberattacks is to eliminate Dimitri Abramovich and his network. But we need to lure him out of Russia. His security thins the moment he leaves the country. That's when we make our move."

Ben stood, the weight of his gun and ammunition shifting his stance. He was no longer the stoic, brainy intelligence officer Ava had first met, but a soldier preparing for battle.

"Killing him won't solve this. He's just the head. Cut it off and another will rise."

Frank nodded. "Ben is right. We need more than a targeted strike against Abramovich. We need to completely take out SVR's cyber infrastructure to deter future aggression, disrupt their operational capabilities. Just because Russia is raging a cyber war doesn't make it any less lethal."

Ava walked toward the table and sat down. "What if we insert ourselves in the SVR's cyber supply chain? Target their logistics? If we can disrupt their supplies, at least temporarily."

"It could work," Ben said, sitting down at the table. "It would at least delay their ability to launch further attacks."

Frank pressed his hands together in a prayer-like motion, the idea hanging in the air like a lit fuse. "You're talking about intercepting hundreds of servers," Frank said slowly. "Do we even know where they're manufactured?" His eyes ping-ponged around the room.

"One guess," Ben said.

The SAD team leader named Joe answered before anyone else could: "China." Joe was in his mid-thirties with brown hair graying slightly at the temples. He was unassuming the way most SAD officers were, but his eyes held an intensity, always calculating, always assessing.

Frank nodded grimly. "The Trans-Manchurian Railway."

"We've done it before," Joe added. "So have the Israelis—with mobile phones and pagers."

Ava met Frank's skeptical gaze. "We insert ourselves into the shipment, sabotage the hardware, and ensure the network collapses."

"We'll also need to insert explosives and a detonator," Joe added.

Frank scoffed. "You're talking about tampering with shipments from a country that could lock you all up for life."

"China's surveillance cameras are everywhere," Ben added, "not to mention the Chinese Ministry of State Security, MSS, agents. Diplomatic immunity won't mean a thing in Shenzhen."

"That's why we'll catch it while it's in transit," Ava said, her voice sharp as her eyes locked on Ben.

Frank's sharp laugh cut through the room. In transit? You want to land on a moving train going at speeds of up to a hundred and twenty miles per hour and break into a cargo car?"

She felt the muscles in her face twitch. At more than a hundred miles an hour, catching the train while it was underway would be nearly impossible.

Ben leaned forward. "What if we don't physically catch it? If we can get into the train-control system, we can slow it, force a delay."

Ava nodded. "The Beijing–Moscow run takes six to seven days with stops and border checks. There's time to work with, but the window is small."

Ben raised an eyebrow. "Even so, pulling that off will require serious prep."

"Then we start planning," she said, turning to Joe. "I need a full logistics manifest: route, scheduled stops, cargo manifests, and any declared servers or IT equipment."

Joe spread his large hands on the table. "Getting that level of intel means penetrating the MSS or the SVR, and either one is damn near impossible."

"Difficult," Ava countered, thinking of Konstantin. She exchanged a sharp look with Ben. "Not impossible. Leave that part to me."

Joe shook his head. "We'll have to intercept the operators' communications and hack the railway logistics so we can track it in real time."

"And map their surveillance," Ben added. "Any cameras, patrols, RF sweeps. We neutralize those before we board."

Ava's reply was steady. "We smuggle the explosives inside the servers bound for the SVR warehouse. Once the data center is verified, we detonate remotely and take out the hub."

Frank exhaled. "You've thought this through."

"What, you thought I wasn't paying attention at the Farm?" Ava shot back.

Frank shook his head. "No, it's not that. You just remind me of someone I used to work with."

Ava's stomach flipped as she did the math—*he couldn't have known her mother; he was too young . . . wasn't he?* Or was he just another man who'd read her file and assumed that he understood the weight of Ava's legacy? The CIA had made no secret of their unease during the recruitment process. Taking on Theresa Anderson's daughter had been a calculated risk, one that had raised more than a few eyebrows across the seventh floor. But Ava's skill set and her fluency in Russian—a mission-critical language that had grown more vital during an age of cyber warfare—had overridden their doubts.

She pushed the question aside. She couldn't afford to get distracted. "Won't the train have to stop at a security checkpoint between Russia and China?"

Ben nodded, catching on. "A much better opportunity to board the train."

"If we have the right cover," she added.

"I'll take care of that," Frank said.

She opened her mouth to ask for clarification when the door burst open and a CIA security officer strode in, his face pale.

"Dimitri Abramovich . . ." he gasped. "He knows you're coming."

# CHAPTER 18

PATCHES OF TWILIGHT bled through the gray clouds as Ava leveled a cold stare at Ben. Everyone had left, but the weight of doubt hung like a dense fog. The tension was suffocating. Frank clearly doubted their operation, doubted her, and that seemed to weigh more heavily on her than anything else. The plan was fragile; she knew that. Konstantin's access was a gamble, one that could easily collapse beneath them. If it did, she'd fall, just like her mother had. And Ben, what would he see in her then, if he uncovered the truth? That beneath the mission and the flag, what she'd really been chasing was the mystery of her mother's fate.

She stood, anxiety gnawing at her as she walked toward the window. The entire valley was covered in a thick blanket of snow. In the distance, the mountains were reduced to eerie outlines, obscured by snowflakes that swirled along a fuzzy gray horizon. The world felt empty, frozen.

It was Ava's voice that broke the silence. "We know that Abramovich is onto us . . . maybe this is doomed to fail." She felt as though she had swallowed glass, her voice still scratching as she went on, "Maybe Frank is right . . . perhaps this is a bad idea." The words tasted like defeat. Frank's doubt had burrowed deep, deeper than she wanted to admit.

Ben sighed. "We knew we were compromised the moment Abramovich's men found us at the party. And I'm not convinced Konstantin can get the intel we need." He raised a brow. "When Joe mentioned needing a penetration into the SVR, that's what you meant, right?"

"Konstantin's an experienced officer. If anyone can unearth train routes and cargo manifests, it's him." Ava turned to face him and exhaled, then let out a thin laugh. "But I worry about getting caught, same as everyone else."

His eyes were sharp, assessing, reading her too closely. "But you won't say that out loud."

She swallowed the truth; it burned in her throat. For all the complications that came with working for an organization that had quietly disowned her mother, she was still sorry to lie to them all. But the way Ben watched her, the way he read between her words, unnerved her. He saw too much. And yet, there was a part of her that wanted to tell him.

That her mother hadn't simply disappeared. That she'd been accused of treason—of turning on her country.

This Ava had never shared, mostly because no one at CIA had ever spoken of it—not even Frank. Although he likely knew—he had to. It was the kind of suspicion that never faded: It just lived in the shadows, waiting for her to stumble so that it could devour her too. Aside from that one notice her aunt had given her, an accusation that Ava had burned before anyone could see, it was hidden away in a file somewhere, locked beneath layers of restricted access. Just like all the secrets the CIA never wanted unearthed.

Ben drew a long steady breath and stepped closer, his presence warming the space between them.

"It's not just the op, is it?" he asked. She looked up, his eyes drawing her in, urging her on. "There's something else. Something you're not telling me."

Ava turned to face him, even as her heart thundered, even as the truth was on the tip of her tongue. She forced a roll of her eyes, then began typing a covert message to Konstantin on her secure phone. "I'm fine, Ben."

His silence stretched. "I know you are," he said finally. "But that's not what I asked."

She looked down at her hands and realized her knuckles had turned white from squeezing her secure phone. The warmth of his hand brushed against her arm, and her breath caught. It was a simple touch, barely there, but it sent a jolt through her. He made her feel something dangerous, something she couldn't afford.

Her pulse pounded. He was counterintelligence. It was his job to see what others didn't. She kept her eyes fixed on the phone, but her mind reeled with the truth that she suddenly desperately wanted him to know. He knew her mother had been Agency. He knew she had disappeared. But he didn't know the rest. He didn't know about the accusations—the potential of betrayal.

"What is it that you want to know?" she forced out.

"For one, why are you always acting like you need to prove yourself?" His tone was steady. "You're here for a reason. I can see why the CIA recruited you. You have the instincts, the drive. Yet, you doubt it . . ."

"I'm pretty sure I was driving Frank nuts," she said. "I have a habit of getting an idea in my head and just running with it."

The way Ben looked at her unsettled her, his eyes narrowing as if he could peel back her words and see what was beneath it. She had spent years covering her tracks, forging a new life through her adoptive parents. And yet, she still felt like she was running from a ghost. Today, staring out at the valley that was now a frozen expanse, stretching, expanding like a giant void, the truth about why she was really here in Moscow descended suddenly on her in an avalanche, making it difficult to breathe, to think.

Her aunt had been adamant that her mother's history should not affect them, and Ava had been thankful not to live in the shadow of her betrayal, but it was moments like this that it all felt too raw and unjust. While her superiors surely knew about her mother, it wasn't something that she had shared or discussed with anyone—and it was that lie that had kept her from getting close to anyone.

She looked at Ben, her heart slamming against her ribcage. She didn't want to keep the truth from him. She forced a smile. "Maybe I just like proving that people are wrong about me."

"Maybe." He smiled lazily at her—and there she saw a flicker of something that he had buried deep. "But that's not all of it, is it?"

*Did he already know?* The truth loomed between them. She knew this was part of his job. Perhaps he was pulling at threads, trying to unravel the truth from her. But the memory of the dance they shared, his lips on hers in the dark alley after her meeting with Grey, the way his hands had anchored her, still made her heart beat unsteadily. She had told herself that it had meant nothing, that it was all part of a game. But the reality was that he had shattered something within her, a tough exterior that she'd worked hard over the years to maintain.

Ben tilted his chin, studying her intently. "You're good at this, Ava. Almost too good. Like it's in your blood."

The question hit her like a slap, and she backed away from him, her pulse thundering. *He knows.*

His eyes didn't leave hers. "I learned about your mother a week ago."

Her blood froze. Before she could respond, he reached for her hand. She flinched but didn't pull away. His fingers curled gently around hers, grounding her, anchoring her to the moment.

"Before we go through with this, Ava," His voice was quiet, steady, but filled with something else. Not suspicion but something more.

She stared at him, her heart in her throat. She wanted to run, to bury the truth before it could surface. But standing there, looking into his eyes, she knew—there was nothing left to hide.

She blinked up at him, her voice sharp. "What are you talking about?" She twisted away from his grip, and Ben's full mouth drew tight. "My mother worked for the CIA," she said, her voice hard as she folded her arms across her chest. "I told you that."

"Yes," he nodded slowly as if she were something fragile. "You told me that she was CIA. That she went missing in Russia. But you didn't tell me *how* she died. What happened on that last mission . . . or why no one ever talks about her."

Sweat sprang on the back of her neck despite the chill in the air. Ava contemplated telling him the truth but couldn't possibly ask him to keep her secret. Ben was CIA counterintelligence—sworn to root out threats inside the Agency, trained to notice the tiniest fracture in someone's cover. To tell him would be to place a target squarely on herself.

Because one of her reasons for being here—her *real* reason—had nothing to do with the assignment in front of her. She hadn't joined the CIA just to serve. She had joined to uncover what really had happened to her mother. Her mother had been accused of treason, but the accusation had lived for years inside a restricted file buried deep within Langley's vaults, locked to all but a handful of the Agency's most senior officers. Ava had only learned of it when her aunt had pressed that letter into her hands.

But Ben was only now just putting it together, realizing that there was more to her story than she'd originally let on. As a counterintelligence official, Ben was one of the rare few who could access the file. Russia House's counterintelligence department had demanded it, and that meant that he had seen enough to know the official story. Enough to see the damning word "traitor" scrawled between the redacted lines.

Ben's gaze pressed harder, demanding answers. Inches away, she saw the suspicion within his eyes.

"I'm not like my mother," she said, fear and grief colliding within her. "I would never betray my country."

His usual stoic demeanor dropped, showing Ava just how vulnerable he was, how vulnerable they both were now. He stepped forward. "What happened to her, Ava?"

She hesitated. Then quietly, "The Agency thinks she betrayed them. But I don't believe it."

His expression hardened. "And you think it doesn't matter? That you can keep this kind of secret from the people you work with?"

"The higher-ups know, Frank knows, of course they know. But I didn't want anyone else to."

Ben's voice dropped to a whisper. "You should've told me."

"I wanted to. But I didn't know how you would take it. Or what you would think about me."

He flinched. "She didn't do it," she said, her voice faltering as she tried to hold back a wave of emotion. "She wasn't a traitor. It was set up. You didn't know my mother, Ben. She wouldn't. She couldn't." She swallowed a painful sob of emotion.

He placed his hands on both her arms, his touch was warm and solid, and she wanted to lean into it, into him. "What are you basing that on, Ava?"

"Emails," she whispered, coming up with that on the spur of the moment. "Between her and her Russian handler." It was a lie. So many lies. But how else could she push him off until she had proof that her mother wasn't guilty?

He exhaled sharply and dropped his hands to his sides. "Ava, it's probably just a matter of time before someone realizes how your past compromises the mission. They should have never sent you to Moscow in the first place."

Ava swallowed down the knot in her throat, catching his meaning. The fact that her mother was accused of spying on behalf of the Russians made Ava, in the CIA's eyes, a potential liability—and vulnerable to SVR recruitment, whether she liked it or not.

She exhaled slowly. "Look, I'm not asking you to do anything. I just need the chance to discover what they did to her."

"I believe you," he said finally. "I know that you'll do what's right."

She swallowed hard, her gaze unconsciously flickering toward his mouth. He had faith in her, and that meant more than she could say at that moment.

He stepped closer. "But when the time comes, please don't ask me to betray everything I've ever stood for. Don't put me in that position."

Ava could see the conflict raging within his eyes, and she tasted something sharp and bitter on her tongue. She hated that she was asking him to protect her. She was risking his career as well as hers now. Because they both knew that her past, her mother's potential betrayal, clouded her ability to serve the CIA objectively, especially in Moscow.

"I don't want you to betray anything. I want you to trust me."

Ben took a step towards her. His jaw flexed, his fingers curling as if he was holding something back. The distance between them shrank until she could feel the heat radiating off him. She couldn't tell if the pounding in her chest was from fear or because of the way he was looking at her.

He exhaled sharply. "Ava . . ." His voice was low, rough, a warning and a plea in one. For a heartbeat, she thought he might reach for her. The air between them went still, charged.

"We're walking a fine line here," he said finally, stepping back as if the space between them could save him. "And it's a line we can't afford to cross. Not with this mission. Not with everything on the line." His words were steady, but his eyes betrayed him, flicking to her mouth before hardening again. Then the agent was back. Cold. Controlled. Untouchable.

Snow beat against the window, wind pressing like something outside wanted in. Ava stood frozen, heat and frustration colliding in her chest. He'd just said what they'd both been denying, given shape to their feelings, only to wall it off again. His gaze lingered on her and then he turned and walked out, leaving her in the flickering light, breathless and furious at herself for wanting him to stay. Because they both knew the truth—the line wasn't ahead of them. They'd already crossed it.

# CHAPTER

# 19

Two weeks later, Ben guided them toward the Zabaikalsk–Manzhouli border crossing as the Trans-Manchurian Railway moaned in the distance, its low rumble bleeding through the truck frame. Cold wind sliced through the truck windows, and a shiver skipped across her breastbone. But it wasn't the cold that knotted her stomach. It was the secret that she'd asked Ben to carry that felt like a live wire between them.

Ava's stomach dropped as Ben downshifted and the truck descended. His jaw was tight, his eyes locked on the Far East mountains that clawed at the horizon, their jagged peaks backlit by the weak winter sun. To anyone else, he looked calm, focused. But Ava had learned to read him—the tense flick of his wrist at the wheel, the intensity of his eyes. He wasn't just thinking about the train they were about to intercept. He was thinking about her and the truth that they both now carried.

The fact that her mother was accused of spying on behalf of the Russians made Ava a potential liability whether she liked it or not. In the CIA's eyes she was a walking contradiction: An officer with a flawless track record but also a bloodline tainted by betrayal. No matter how many missions she completed or risks she took, the shadow of her mother lingered. And Ben knew. She didn't dare look at him, she didn't want to see the doubt or suspicion in his eyes. Their mission was too important, and time was running out.

It was, on paper, simple—smuggle the explosives onto the train, conceal them in cargo headed to the SVR's covert server warehouse, and once everything was in place, once the location of the data center was confirmed, they'd detonate remotely, taking out the hub of Russia's cyber operations in one decisive strike.

Ahead, the Amur Highway curved, its wide valleys stretching until Russia's and China's borders met. If their timing was right, they would have a moment to board the train while it stopped for inspection. She glanced behind her at the rest of the six-person team—all dressed as Red Cross field operators in gray uniforms, the Red Cross emblem displayed as a patch over their hearts, Ben's pulled tight across his broad chest. He was built more like a football player than the other CIA case officers she'd met—all marathon runners with sleek suits and impeccable manners.

She drew a long, shaky breath and fingered the edges of her tattered passport. She was traveling under commercial cover—disguised as a nurse. It was against the CIA's protocol to go disguised as an aide worker, but Frank had obtained special permission from the seventh floor given the importance of the mission. They weren't just smuggling explosives into one of the most surveilled border zones in the world, but also planning a huge strike against Vibrantia's infrastructure and Russia's covert influence campaign against America.

Beside her, Ben adjusted the radio volume, and static crackled before the team's comms bled through the radio. It was Joe, the SAD team lead, in the truck behind them. Ava leaned forward. In the mirror she caught a glimpse of Joe—gray uniform and grim face—in the driver seat of the truck behind them with the radio held up to his ear. Everyone looked the part.

Behind Ava and Ben, the medical kits held more than gauze and bandages. Hidden beneath layers of syringes and IV tubing were computer chips that contained C-4—dense and rubbery, almost like modeling clay. Joe had explained that on its own the explosive material was stable, able to be shaped and carried without fear of being ignited by accident. The danger came when it met the detonator, a sliver of steel and wire that held the promise of ignition. Once the two were joined, it became a powerful weapon.

When they breached the train, they'd have only minutes to embed the C-4 inside the servers and leave the train before it crossed into Heilongjiang province. They knew that each server was destined for the SVR's cyber command headquarters, the nerve center of Russia's digital war machine. If Ava and Ben embedded the C-4 explosives correctly, a remote detonation would wipe out not just the hardware but months of preloaded malware and infrastructure critical to their global cyber operations.

If they were caught now, everything would be lost and Konstantin compromised. He had given them the travel routes, the timing, everything they had needed to plan the op—and it would all be traced back to him, the best penetration they had of the Russian SVR and their best hope at ending the conflict in the United States.

"About to hit the checkpoint," Ben muttered, eyes flickering toward the sign in Russian and Mandarin stating that all vehicles needed to pull over for inspection.

Ava nodded sharply, her fingers tapping nervously on her passport. It would only take one slip up to shatter their cover. Everything hinged on this moment.

Joe's voice crackled in Ava's earpiece. "Stand by for diversion."

At the checkpoint, they groaned to a halt, gravel popping off the doors of the tattered truck like firecrackers. The smell of diesel fuel burned Ava's nostrils as Ben rolled down the window. A loudspeaker boomed in Russian and Chinese announcing a delay. In front of them, a border official barked a command, and the truck in front of them was ordered to unload its cargo for a secondary inspection. The driver's protests erupted into a yelling match, and Ava felt her pulse rev up.

Behind them, Joe and his team had pulled off the highway and onto a gravel track, where they would trigger small explosions to provide the diversion for Ava and Ben to board the train. Ben's voice cut through her thoughts. "How sure are you about Konstantin?"

"He confirmed everything a few hours ago." she said stiffly. "How much time do we have?"

"Five minutes until Joe triggers the first detonation. Maybe less. The train's already slowing for inspection."

She nodded, her fingers tapping against her thigh. "Then we move as soon as we're through."

Ben's grip tightened on the wheel. "If we get through."

She glanced at him. "We will."

"You really believe Konstantin's on our side?" he asked, his voice quiet but sharp.

"I have to."

"Do you?" he asked, his brow furrowed. "Because trusting a Russian spy, even one with a conscience, is a hell of a gamble."

She looked away, her heart hammering. "He got us Abramovich's location. He was right about Abramovich's compound, Vibrantia's ties to the SVR. How much more asset validation do you need?"

"And now you're trusting him to time a train intercept in one of the most surveilled regions in Asia while we haul C-4 dressed as humanitarian workers."

"Are you purposely trying to make me doubt this plan minutes before we enact it?"

"I just want you to think skeptically about Konstantin's information."

She didn't answer.

He looked at her, expecting an answer.

"I'm trusting me," she said finally, thinking of her mother's final letter. "My read. My instinct."

Silence stretched again. Outside, the checkpoint loomed closer. Cameras dotted the perimeter. A red light blinked ahead.

Ben exhaled. "I'm not questioning your instincts, Ava."

She turned to him. "You believe that my mom was a traitor. You believe that my judgement is flawed." Her words hung in the air between them, bare and dangerous.

"I didn't say that," Ben said. "But I worry that you're"—he paused, searching for the right word—"distracted. Distracted people make mistakes."

Ava's throat tightened. "When I told you about my mother, I didn't ask you to lie. I asked you to keep a secret."

He gave a bitter smile. "Same thing in this job."

A Russian guard stepped into the road, gloved hand raised. Ben eased off the gas. Another guard emerged from the fog and snow and moved to the passenger side. Ava straightened, sliding her gun into the glove compartment within easy reach. Her heart thudded as the guard barked in Russian. Ben answered smoothly, accent flawless, face unreadable. He handed over a forged manifest, the paper trembling only slightly between his fingers.

The guard's eyes flicked from the document to Ben, then to Ava. "I'll need to see both your passports," he said.

Ava forced a polite smile.

"Of course." Ben passed the passports.

The guard studied them in silence; seconds stretched until Ava could hear her own pulse. Snow hissed against the windshield. Finally, a sharp nod and the barrier lifted. Ben drove on without a word. Ava's breath escaped in a slow tremor as they cleared the checkpoint. She tucked her shaking hands under her thighs.

Then the world detonated. A blast ripped across the valley, lighting the horizon in a bloom of fire. Joe's diversion, an abandoned fuel truck wired with C-4, went up in perfect timing. Border agents shouted, sirens screamed.

The distraction bought them seconds. That was enough.

"Go!" Ava said.

Ben slammed the accelerator. Tires spat slush as they raced along the ridge. Ahead, the railway cut through the snow like a dark scar. Car seventeen waited somewhere in the line, with servers bound for the SVR's covert data center. Her plan repeated like a mantra: plant the charge, get off before the trainmoved. End the cyber war. End the lies.

"You don't have to come," she said over the roar.

He gave her a look that said she'd lost her mind.

"I'm serious," she added. "This op is mine. The risk is mine, along with the risk. I won't hold it against you if—"

He cut her off, eyes blazing. "Don't finish that sentence."

Ava wanted to reach for him, to force him to look, but the moment was gone. Words tangled in her throat. His jaw was set, knuckles white on the wheel. For a heartbeat she thought he might say something true, real, then the CIA operative took over again.

A crackle on the radio: "Command, perimeter. Movement in sector four. Three vehicles approaching. Not checkpoints."

Headlights flared in the rearview, bouncing off the snow.

Ben's grip tightened. "Hold on," he said.

The car fishtailed. He didn't look back. The convoy bore down, the train loomed, and whatever had flickered between them was swallowed by mission and snow.

"You asked me to keep your secret, Ava. You don't get to push me away now." Their eyes locked. A beat. Then another.

She reached for the latch on the glove compartment, retrieved her Glock, and placed it in her side holster. Anything to keep from leaning closer toward him. Anything to stop herself from doing what she wanted to do every time he looked at her like that, to let the ache between them bloom into something messy and real.

He watched her with a quiet intensity. She reached behind his seat for the medical kit containing the C-4.

"I'll carry it," he said, turning abruptly, reaching for the kit at the same time. Their fingers brushed, but he didn't move away. Instead, his fingers tightened on hers, and the current between them was electric.

"We do this together," he said, his thumb brushing the back of her hand. Her fingers curled reflexively into his.

"We move on my signal," she said. "No heroics."

He nodded once, his jaw working. "No heroics."

The train's whistle shrieked in the distance. It was time.

# CHAPTER

# 20

Ava inhaled sharply and stepped out into the icy wind. She moved toward the checkpoint with her breath tight in her throat. Ben flanked her, his medical kit slung over his shoulder—loaded with computer chips embedded with C-4 disguised within a blood pressure cuff that could level a city block. Behind them, Joe and his ops team had melted into the shadows. They were ghosts now, sent to unravel Russia's support for the Liberty Coalition's agenda.

"Stick close to me." Ben leaned in closer, his shoulders square despite the biting cold. "Let's not give them a reason to search."

Ahead, the train screeched to a halt, yanking Ava's attention to the platform. Nine border agents fanned out, each armed with handheld scanners and rifles. X-ray machines might be fooled. But if the border agents were using counterterrorism tech, they would be dead before they reached the train. Frank had warned them. They were gambling that the Russian and Chinese security services hadn't kept up with the West. If they were wrong, the entire op would fail. And their lives would be over.

Ava's fingers found the small signaling device in her pocket. A silent countdown. A precisely timed second explosion set up by Joe's team to let them slip onto the train. They moved in unison, their breathing puffing in the frigid air.

Thirty seconds later the first of Joe's diversions came—not a blast, but a jarring surge of motion and sound. The patrol guards rushed to see what had happened and found that a nearby fuel drum had tipped and clattered to the ground, its contents spilling in a loud whoosh. Moments later, flames exploded from the alley just off the platform. A plume of smoke climbed—dark, dense, and dramatic—but controlled. A car alarm blared behind them, shrill and insistent, followed by the distant shouts of bystanders.

Perfectly orchestrated chaos.

Guards ran with their weapons raised while others hesitated, uncertainty slowing their reaction. Two guards sprinted past Ava and Ben toward the alley, radios squawking.

Ben gripped Ava's arm tight.

"Show time," he whispered under his breath.

Ava and Ben moved through the crowd until they reached the train. Ben yanked the door open and gestured at Ava to follow.

The interior of the train was suffocating, like walking back in time to the black-and-white Soviet era with utilitarian design and heavy drapes. Narrow bunks lined either side of the interior of the passenger cart. But the car was eerily empty. The enclosed space, lined with patterned carpets and dark wood paneling, made Ava feel the walls tightening, closing like a grip in a trap. She swallowed hard, the smell of dust and mold heavy within her lungs.

The train lurched suddenly, and Ava's stomach did a somersault. With a hiss and a lurch, she felt the train push forward to a slow crawl. Her eyes snapped up to meet Ben's face.

"Fuck," they said in unison. They needed to reach cargo car seventeen and complete their task so they could get off before the train reached full speed.

They bolted through the passenger cart, their boots pounding on the carpeted floor. Ava stiffened and tried not to meet the faces of weary travelers slumped against worn cushions, their startled glances cutting through the musty air. The train's rhythmic clacking echoed Ava's pulse, thrumming with each step, each heartbeat as they neared cargo car seventeen.

The air between the train cars was sharp, biting with cold. The wind howled, whipping Ava's hair into streamers that danced around her face as she balanced on the ledge between the two cars. One misstep and she'd vanish beneath the train wheels.

With one long step Ben moved between cars sixteen and seventeen. He stopped on the ledge and outstretched his hand. "Jump!"

Ava inhaled deeply, kept her eyes fixed firmly on Ben's face, and leaped. He caught her with one arm hooked tightly around her waist.

Inside car seventeen, darkness swallowed them. Ava turned on her secure phone and flashed a beam of light across rows of servers—cold, humming machines strapped down like prisoners. Ava's pulse thundered. If they failed, disinformation would continue. The United States would shatter. Civil war wouldn't be abstract. A new world order would be written in ash and blood.

Ben turned toward her, his forehead beaded with sweat. Slices of pale sunlight filtered through the cracks in the train car, sparking through the darkness.

She glanced back at the servers. "Barcodes ending in 8448. Those are Abramovich's," she said sharply, her heart slamming against her ribcage as she scanned the front of the servers.

The train jerked again, and she stumbled. Ben's arm shot out, catching her waist and pulling her flush against him. His jaw was tight, his eyes locked on hers. Their faces were close enough that their breath mingled. He smelled like pine and something undeniably *Ben.* But the train was starting to gain speed, and she backed away. Then she spotted the servers they needed to dissemble, stacked neatly together. Ben unlatched the kit and began to remove the tools. With trembling hands, she ripped at the straps that secured the servers. One by one, Ben helped her gently slide them out of the neat stacks. With a screwdriver, Ava loosened the brackets and slid out the hard drive as sweat slicked her palms. Ben pried open the second server's casing and pulled out the hard drive. Then he cracked open his kit and handed her the first device: a thin, metallic chip housing C-4, made to latch seamlessly onto a hard drive.

"This better work," he muttered, sweat beading on his forehead as he used a glue-like substance to attach the computer chip onto the hard drive.

"We both know nothing is foolproof." Ava smeared glue across the second chip's back, pressed it firmly against the exposed hard drive, and held it as it set. One by one they worked, unscrewed server casings, slid out drives, attached the charges. Each chip glinted in the flashlight's beam before disappearing into the shadows of machinery. The train began to pick up speed, vibrations that traveled up through her bent knees into her torso. Her nerves grew taut like the strings of a guitar pulled too tight as they clicked the last server in place.

"How fast do you think we're going?" she asked, unable to meet his eyes for fear that he would hear the pounding in her chest.

"We're not at full speed yet. We can make it." Ben gestured toward the back of the swaying train car, his fingers tightening on the flashlight. "Come on, Joe's team will be there to retrieve us."

She nodded and started after him. Her eyes locked on his shoulders as the train jolted violently beneath their feet. The metallic screech of crashing metal rang out as if the train itself was warning them to go back. They both froze as Ben's flashlight hit something ahead—a hulking, elongated shape beneath a heavy tarp labeled "construction materials" in Russian.

"What the . . ." Ben's voice cracked, his usual cool demeanor faltering as he stepped forward. Ava latched onto his arm, her grip tightening with each step forward. The tarps rippled as the train vibrated. Ben walked slowly toward the dark objects clanking ominously together and yanked the tarp free.

Ava's breath hitched, her chest tightening at what stretched before them. Row after row of missiles gleamed. The confined space seemed to shrink, the walls of the train car slowly pressing in around her as the enormity of their discovery began to take root.

"Abramovich . . . he's buying missiles from the Chinese?" she asked, terror ringing in her ears.

He turned, his pulse visible in his throat. "It looks that way."

Ava's mind raced, fragments of intel slowly coming together with gut-wrenching clarity. "This must be the next stage of Abramovich's plan."

Ben stiffened, cataloguing the potential threat but showing no outward sign.

Ava glanced down at his watch, outfitted with the CIA's latest camera that could snap photographs clandestinely with a flick of his wrist. "Take pictures so we can see what kind of weapons we're dealing with."

Ben nodded sharply, the muscles of his jaw working as he snapped photographs. He looked up at her.

"We need to get off this train," he said. "Now."

# CHAPTER 21

THE TRAIN THUNDERED over the tracks, its roar vibrating through the air as they stepped out onto the narrow platform between the cars. Ava's breath caught in her throat as a blast of icy wind whipped her hair across her face. She pulled it back into a ponytail and scanned the earth below, searching for a soft place to land. Snow blanketed the ground. The landscape below was a deceptive sea of white, its softness obscuring rocks and jagged debris, ready to tear them apart upon impact.

"Is there a proper way to do this?" she asked, her lips and cheeks burning from the dry cold. "You remember that Frank insisted that jump training wasn't necessary for my mission."

Ben shot her a glance with one eyebrow lifted. "Don't hit anything hard."

"No shit, Sherlock." Ava snorted.

Ben stood beside her, his hand gripping her waist. It was as if an electric current moved from him, but he was all business when he spoke, his breath warm on her ear. "Angle your jump in the direction of the train to minimize the force of the impact," he instructed. "If you can, roll on your side to distribute the impact."

She gave a sharp inhale.

"Would it help if I told you that you'll be so cold you won't feel it?" he asked.

She turned briefly. Snow fluttered around him, covering his dark blond hair and thick stubble with tiny flakes.

She reached up to brush the snow from his beard. "Not really."

He cupped her face with both hands, and she felt warmth spread through every part of her body. It was a brief connection of truth before they dived off the train. "I won't let anything happen to you," he muttered.

She didn't have the words to respond, and they turned together to face the snow and trees that raced past them in a blur.

"Okay," she said, dread seizing her nerves. Wordlessly, Ben took her hand and squeezed it before letting go. "On the count of three."

"Ready?" she said, "One. Two . . . three."

Neither of them closed their eyes as they took a deep breath and leaped off the train. The earth spun until the ground rose up to meet Ava like shards of glass, snow stabbing into her. Ice exploded around her, every inch of her body screaming as she crashed down, the cold biting into every bone. Her breath caught, but there was no time to think, no time to adjust.

"Are you OK?" Ben's voice cracked through the fog of her disorientation as she lay staring up at the gray clouds.

She tried to speak, but a blinding pain flared in her ankle, making it impossible to form a coherent thought. Her chest tightened, "Where is Joe's team?"

Ben had his phone in his hand, and a burst of static crackled through Ava's earpiece.

"Falcon to Raven-1, do you copy?" He waited.

Nothing. A hiss of white noise. He tried again; his tone clipped. "Raven-1, this is Falcon. Report status. Over."

The comms answered with dead air.

Then a crack of gunfire split the silence. Bullets snapped past, too close. A sharp jolt of pain smacked the side of Ava's arm, and she hunched over, clutching at the sharp burn in her left shoulder. A cry caught in her throat. Ben was on her in an instant, blocking her body with his and returning fire at the guards shooting at them from the train.

Gunfire cracked behind them. With his arm locked around her waist, he dragged her toward the tree line. Snow burst at their feet, cold shards stinging her face. She stumbled, but his grip only tightened.

"Keep moving!" His breath came in short, visible bursts, the sound fierce against the roar in her ears.

Her legs burned. Every step sank deep into the snow, every breath scraped her throat raw. She didn't know if he was pulling her or if she was still moving on her own, but she didn't let go. She trusted that he knew the way, trusted him to get them out alive.

A flash flared to their right and he spun, firing back before shoving her forward again. The forest was close now, dark and swallowing, the only promise of cover in a world gone darker, dimmer.

"I think my ankle is sprained," she muttered through clenched teeth, her heart racing, nearly exploding. Her left shoulder burned. She used her right fingers to clutch her shoulder and something warm and thick pumped out. She lifted her hand to her face and saw the blood. "And I've been shot."

Alarm rose in his eyes, and in one fluid motion he lifted her off her feet as if she weighed nothing. His jaw was set, his focus unshakable as he carried her deeper into the forest.

"I'm perfectly capable of walking." She whispered, pain beckoning her to let it take hold. "You don't have to . . ."

But he ignored her protest and instead locked his arms tighter around her. "I think the time for you to walk has passed, but if you insist, I can drop you in the next snowdrift."

She resisted the temptation to smile through the pain. "A real gentleman."

"Only when it's convenient," he said dryly. "Besides, it's my turn to keep you from dying. You're welcome."

"Joe's team?" she asked in a hoarse voice.

"They're not coming," he answered, his expression grim. His hair and beard were covered in a thin layer of frost as he trudged through the snow that was up to his knees. "Either Joe and the team have been compromised or . . ."

The forest felt hostile as the distant sound of the train rattled the thin air. She clung to him, her thoughts clouded by pain and the growing dread that their operation to stop Abramovich was far from over. Pressing her face into his chest, she willed his warmth to crawl through every nerve until the pain was a faraway drum. Her heart hammered at the nearness of him, though her voice was barely a whisper.

"Then it's just us."

# CHAPTER 22

Ben carried Ava shivering through the darkness, into the thick snow, each step heavier than the last. They were miles from the railway, miles away from the nearest city. She was too exhausted to do anything. Her ankle was paining her, and she was losing blood from her gunshot wound. She was unconscious more time than not, mumbling about her mother, always about her mother.

He clenched his jaw, not wanting to think too deeply about the woman. Not now. Not when everything was falling apart and the Agency was probably already writing him up by association. The daughter of a traitor who had spied for the Russians. No wonder Frank had wanted him to keep such close tabs. And Ava—brilliant, guarded, unpredictable—was at the center of the CIA's most dangerous missions in decades—was at the center of it all.

If the CIA had truly abandoned her mother, who is to say that Ava wouldn't want revenge? Who is to say that she wasn't already questioning her loyalties?

The thought hit harder than expected. Not because he believed Ava was a threat. But because he knew that betrayal could twist even the most loyal of hearts. And if they had made her feel disposable, just like her mother, how long before the Russians made her feel seen? Valued?

The Russian SVR used the same tactics as the CIA to bend someone to their will—empathy as their weapon, validation as a hook, and loyalty earned through the illusion of being understood. And just because Ava understood these tactics, and had used them herself to turn Konstantin, didn't mean that she was immune. The SVR just had to wait until the CIA pushed her far enough. Until she was tired of proving she wasn't her mother.

And yet here he was—carrying her, bleeding, broken, through the woods like she was the most precious thing he'd ever held. His boots had long since filled with slush and blood from broken blisters. The cold had numbed him from the waist down, making it feel like he was moving through quicksand. But he had to set a grueling pace or risk being hunted down by the Russian border patrol guards, who he suspected were not far behind them.

By the time he spotted the jagged mouth of a cave carved into the hillside, he could barely feel his legs. But he pushed through, gritting his teeth and ducking inside. He hugged Ava tighter to steady her against the tremble of cold and shock.

Inside, the cave offered little in the way of warmth, but at least it gave them temporary shelter from the snow and frigid wind.

"We'll camp here until morning," he announced as he gently placed her onto the frozen floor of the cave.

Ava looked up, her gray eyes landing on his face as she slumped against the wall. The small cuts and dirt on her cheeks only made her fiercer, more beautiful. Her full lips were bloodless and cracked. And still—God help him—he wanted her. She was fierce and defiant, a walking contradiction. Just like the first day he had met her. She was everything he had always wanted. She was all strength, intellect, rare beauty—and dangerous.

But the CIA didn't know that Ava had come to Russia with more than duty on her mind. She was using the mission to unearth the truth about why her mother had died while in Russian captivity, even if that meant defying the very institution she served. And for Ben to keep that secret from the Agency, especially as a counterintelligence officer, would be seen as the ultimate form of betrayal. He had a responsibility to point out anything that could compromise their mission. And to shield her secret he would lose his job, lose his security clearance, everything. He'd built his life around duty, integrity, discipline. Yet he knew he would watch it all crumble if it meant protecting her.

He silently cursed himself, knowing that he was already in too deep. He turned away, choking on the ache in his chest, and began to rummage through the first aid kit, which still had some of the medical supplies.

"This might hurt a little," he said, taking out the gauze.

She nodded her consent, head rested against the cave wall, and gnashed her teeth together against the pain. He began wrapping the makeshift tourniquet above the gunshot on her upper arm while trying to count the miles that he'd likely walked from the train.

The wind roared, and a gust of icy wind seeped into the cave. His eyes met hers, and he felt that now familiar ache in his chest when he looked at her.

"I'm going to try to get us firewood," he said as the last of the evening light seeped out of the cave. "I need to be able to see what I'm doing when I stitch you up." He glanced down at his phone, which was still as good as a brick. "And also, so we don't freeze to death while we wait to get a phone signal."

"Don't you dare leave me here alone," she said through clenched teeth.

The truth was that he didn't want to leave her—not when darkness seemed to be closing in on them by the minute. But there were no sticks or loose rocks on the ground, nothing he could use to spark a fire. It was nearly dark, and they needed warmth if they were going to last much longer.

"Apply as much pressure as you can stand." He leaned down and squeezed her cold fingertips as he guided her hand upward. "You need to elevate your arm. Keep it higher than your heart to stop the blood flow."

"I'll be fine," she said, although her tone wavered.

"I'll be five minutes." He paused and turned around. There was a tortured feeling in her eyes, an unasked question on her lips. "Remember, pressure, keep it elevated. I won't be far."

The light from his phone bounced ahead of him as he disappeared into the storm. He kept busy gathering firewood, but his mind was all for her. And that kiss they had shared back in Moscow. He shouldn't have done it. He shouldn't have gotten that close to her. He had told himself that he had done it to dodge surveillance, that it was just an attempt to distract others with prying eyes. That it meant nothing. Except that it had meant everything and shattered his ability to think clearly when it came to her. *What the hell was he doing?*

He snapped a branch over his knee, the dry crack sharp in the evening twilight. His breath came out in puffs as he moved through the brush, his fingers stiff with cold. A splinter jabbed him as he reached for another branch, but the pain barely registered. It reminded him of camping trips with his brothers back in Montana—three boys piled into a two-man tent, daring each other to race barefoot in the snow just for bragging rights. Maybe it was Moscow. Maybe it was the snow, or maybe that carrying Ava through that storm had awakened something inside him, something primal, protective. Or maybe because this time, his older brothers weren't there to help him carry the load of what he now faced.

And the warheads.

Sleek. Lethal. Hidden beneath tarps and rail grease. If Abramovich handed those over to Nathaniel Grey and the Liberty Coalition, the fuse would be lit. Protests would become militias. Rhetoric would morph into action. And the Russians would be watching it all burn, standing ready to pick up the ashes, ready to take their place as the world's next superpower. He clenched his jaw. How could someone like Nathaniel Grey not see that he was dancing to Moscow's tune? Maybe he did. Maybe that was the cost of power these days.

Ben stood, cradling the firewood in his arms, and headed back. They had to get a message to Frank. Fast. Before this turned into a war that no one could walk away from.

In the cave, Ava asked drowsily, "Did you miss me?"

"Of course, it was almost quiet enough to hear my own thoughts." He smiled at her, dropped the wood, and got to work. The fire was small, but it sparked to life with a stubborn hiss.

"I've never been so freaking cold in my whole life." Her teeth chattered.

"Well, you look like a frozen corpse," he said, then dodged sideways when she threw a small stick in his direction.

"Jerk." She rummaged through one of the medical kits that sat beside her with one hand. "Any chance they'd have some kind of pain med in one of these?"

"Doubt it. If there was, they probably took it out when they smuggled in the C-4." He crouched beside her, glancing at her wound. "Time to clean this up. It's going to hurt."

She met his eyes and nodded once. the pain flashing across her face but not breaking her. She was still fighting, still here. And so was he.

For now.

# CHAPTER 23

*IT HURT. MY God, it hurt.*

Even with the bandage Ben had wrapped tightly around Ava's wound, blood seeped out. Panic clawed up her throat. They were miles from any city. With these weather conditions, it would be suicidal to leave the cave at night. She shifted, and despite the cold, felt a wave of heat, like a hot poker stick had been driven into her right shoulder. She tried not to think about the pain that shuddered down her arm or the deep terror at what they had discovered back on the train. The missiles weren't just weapons—they were promises of war.

Terror sang in her veins at the implications of what Abramovich was likely planning.

Perhaps Abramovich planned to smuggle them into the US, one warhead at a time. Or worse, maybe he'd strike Europe, fracture NATO, and force a weakened America to act. Or maybe, maybe Abramovich intended to hand them off to the Liberty Coalition and let the conflict start from within. An American civil war sparked by Russian hands.

The realization made her skin crawl.

She wanted to discuss her theories with Ben, but she had already shared too much with him. And Ben . . . he had barely flinched when they had discovered the arsenal, his reaction too measured, too controlled.

*Was there something he was not telling her? Had he already known what they would find?*

Ava swallowed down her question and studied the broad lines of his back as he silently arranged the sticks to build up the fire. The fire crackled to life, chasing out the worst of the cold.

As he moved to inspect her wound, she braced herself. "I'm not looking forward to this."

His eyes narrowed as he began to gingerly unwrap the bandage to inspect the wound. "My guess is that the bullet is lodged near the deltoid but didn't go through the trapezius."

"You seem to know a lot about the human body," she said hoarsely, trying to distract herself from the pain throbbing down her arm. "Was that part of your counterintelligence training?"

His lips twitched, but there was no hint of humor. "I was a medic in the military, before all this."

*Before all this.* It was difficult for her not to read more into his expression—the tight line of his mouth that seemed to tell a different story from the one he'd told her before. He had a secret to tell as well. His words hung in the air, making her want to ask him more about his past. But the pain in her arm dragged her firmly back to the present.

He reached for his medical kit. "It's not an exit wound, but the bullet must be lodged deep." He turned and took out the alcohol wipes to begin disinfecting his hands. "I need to remove the bullet, clean the wound, and stitch up. But we don't have anything for the pain. Do you want something to bite down on?" His voice was sharp, all business, but Ava could see something else lingering behind his eyes.

She pressed her forehead against her knees as he picked up a small scalpel. Another wave of pain bit into her shoulder, and she swallowed down the tears in her throat. "Just do it."

Ben delved into retrieve the bullet, and her body trembled at the tugging and tearing of her flesh. A sob tore from her lips as she clawed the frozen earth, dirt thickening beneath her fingernails. Her jaw locked, her mind teetering between the danger they were still in and the dark future that awaited. At some point, she passed out and awoke to find Ben's bloodied hands still steady on her arm, his eyes red-rimmed.

"The worst is over," he muttered, tying off the last stitch.

She forced her gaze from his hands and looked away as he disinfected the wound again. "Why did you agree to keep my secret?" she asked suddenly, anything to distract herself from the fire lancing down her arm.

His movements slowed. For a moment, he didn't answer, his attention fixed on the neat square of cloth he pressed into place. Her arm throbbed, but the silence was worse.

She thought he hadn't heard her question until his eyes lifted to meet hers. "You're a good officer," he said at last, his voice hoarse. "And I don't think that someone should be judged by the sins of their parents."

The words landed with more weight than she had expected, but before she could respond, he was up again and tending to the fire.

Flickering orange and yellow flames danced along the cave walls, illuminating the gold specks in Ben's eyes when he turned to look at her. But it was his presence—solid, unyielding—that suddenly chased the fear and regret from her heart.

She tilted her chin toward the fire. "Another trick you learned in the military, I presume?"

"I had an older brother who taught me survival tactics."

"Where are you from?" she asked as she watched the strong forearms twitch as he tended to the fire. "You seem outdoorsy. I'm guessing Colorado, or Wyoming."

Ben threw a look in her direction—wry, a little guarded. "Montana."

"Come on." She turned away from him, unable to look at him directly in the eyes. She didn't want him to know how badly her arm hurt when there was nowhere to go, nothing he could do. "I need something to distract me."

He exhaled slowly. "My brothers and I used to go camping a lot together. I had two older ones, Connor and Luke. They were bigger, louder, better at everything. But they looked out for me." He paused, his eyes resting on the flames. "Always did. Even when I didn't deserve it."

Ava's mind locked on what he had said, what he didn't. But she didn't push or pressure.

"Winters were brutal where I was from. We'd get snowed in for days. The power would go out." His eyes grew distant as he relieved the memory. "My mom would light every candle in the house and pretend like it was an adventure. My dad built us fire in a wood stove and made me and my brothers haul the wood in from outside in shifts. I hated it back then, but now . . ." His voice grew distant as he dragged a hand through his thick hair, eyes downcast.

"Now you're a guy who can start a fire in a cave with frozen fingers."

"Yeah, well, when I was ten, my brothers made me sleep outside once to prove that I could handle the cold. Scared the hell out of me. I swore I'd never forgive them." He glanced at her, the firelight catching the side of his face. "But when I woke up, they were both out there too. Just sitting under the trees with me, keeping watch. Never said a word about it."

The corner of his mouth twitched as he sat cross-legged in front of the fire. But there was something in his face—a tightness in his jaw, a flicker of hesitation—that unsettled her. Perhaps it was the same fear she felt tightening its grip on her, fear of what they had seen back on that train, fear of what it meant for the country if those weapons fell into the wrong hands.

A shudder of pain and cold rippled through her and her teeth knocked together.

"Come here," he said softly, gesturing for her to move closer to the fire, closer to him. When she hesitated, he sighed and crossed over to her, crouching behind her. "You're freezing." He came around her, careful not to brush her injured arm, and sat behind her. "Here," his breath warm on her ear. "Lean back on me."

She let herself ease against him, his arms a barricade of muscle and restraint.

"Any chance that you learned something about signaling for help during your survival training?" she asked.

"That would have been useful, wouldn't it?" he breathed into the top of her head. "If we weren't in the middle of a hostile territory."

She shifted, and a wave of pain yanked through her, cutting through her nerves like a blade. She wanted to scream, but instead she swallowed it down. "Tell me more about your brothers." She tried to keep her tone steady even as her pulse roared in her ears. "I want to know more about the person I'm trusting my career, my life with."

"You have nothing to fear from me." His breath was warm on her ear.

The flames danced up the sides of the cave, creating shadows, the ghosts of her past, of what was to come. "I couldn't trust my mother, the one person who is supposed to love and care for me no matter what."

He didn't respond right away. Instead, he hugged her closer, a quiet anchor against the storm within her.

"My brothers taught me that loving someone is always having someone's back," he said finally. "Even if they don't say it."

"Must've been nice," she said, her voice quiet. "Having someone look out for you like that."

A long silence passed between them. He wasn't trying to comfort her. He wasn't even trying to make her feel better about what she'd confessed about her mother. He was just letting her in, piece by piece. And it felt more intimate than anything she'd expected.

"Are we going to talk about what we saw back on the train?" she asked finally.

"I assume you mean the missiles."

"Yes, of course I mean the missiles." She pulled up the edge of her scarf with her right hand so that it covered her nose and mouth.

He hesitated. After several long minutes he answered. "Those were intercontinental ballistic missiles."

She turned to face him, terror ringing in her ears. "Abramovich is planning a nuclear war?"

"It seems that way."

Dread settled like a heavy stone in her stomach. "What if he's planning to arm one side of the US against the other?"

Ben grimaced, the lines around his mouth deepening like she had discovered a secret. Alarm rose in her throat. She tried to swallow it down, but it got caught, and her question came out hoarse.

"Ben, why don't you seem surprised by what we saw in that train car?"

"Counterintelligence is not my only specialty, Ava."

She had struck a nerve. He was hiding something—some shadow of himself and his mission that she knew nothing about. She knew she should pull away, protect what was left of her trust, her clarity. But she couldn't. His touch, his voice, the way he looked at her like she was both a mystery and a threat—it all tangled into this puzzle that she desperately wanted to solve.

She wanted to push further, wanted him to name the thing that haunted him. But something cold threaded through her veins. If those missiles were already in play, then chaos would ignite across her homeland.

The night pressed closer, and everything outside the cave felt too still, too cold. Their next move wasn't just survival. It was about millions of lives. What they did next could tip the world into a nuclear standoff—or stop it.

Fragile, fevered, fatigue pulling heavy on her eyelids, she leaned back into him. Now she needed him, and she hated how much that scared her.

* * *

For the past hour, Ava had drifted in and out of consciousness. And Ben—like the idiot he was—had kept her tethered. Held her tighter when her breath got shallow, just to keep her safe, from feeling too much of the danger. Even now, with her curled against him in the cave, her pulse faint beneath his fingertips. His mind raced, not with thoughts of his own career but with the fragile line she walked. The secret she carried. The future she could lose.

CIA security would never have approved her for this assignment had they known the whole truth. And if the seventh floor knew that she was using her post in Moscow to uncover what had happened to her mother, she'd be fired, immediately.

And yet . . . he'd kept it to himself. Why?

Because he understood, and because part of him, the most dangerous part, would never bring himself to betray her—even if it meant betraying everything else.

"Why did you leave the field?" she whispered, her voice almost swallowed by the crackling fire.

Ben closed his eyes. He hadn't expected the question. Hell, he didn't even know how she had the presence of mind to ask it. But it hit him like a punch to the gut. And maybe it was the pain in her voice, or the way she had trusted him enough to fall apart in his arms, but he didn't deflect. Not this time. He shifted, feeling the cold stones press into his spine and the weight of the memory settle over him. He knew he shouldn't tell her, shouldn't let her in. But he couldn't help himself, not when she was lying helpless in his arms.

"I was part of a CIA Special Activities Division team deployed to Kiev." His voice was strained as he watched the flames dance on the cave walls. "We had actionable intel about a GRU asset, a source within Russian military intelligence—someone who could pass high-value information about critical Russian battle plans in Ukraine to his handler near Kiev. My partner and I were tasked with intercepting the asset near the Belgorod Oblast border crossing before the handoff."

His head pounded, the memory flooding his senses like a nightmare. "The op was rushed. But Langley insisted that the intel was solid. We were on the Russian side, unsanctioned, and it was crawling with SVR surveillance. We should have pulled out the second we saw a second tail. But I called the play to move in."

He paused and scrubbed a hand over his face, feeling sick.

"I'd met with the source before," he continued. "Crimea would be in Russian hands if it wasn't for him. But Abramovich must have caught onto the meeting, onto our source, and the meeting was a trap. Abramovich somehow hacked the GRU asset's covert communication and fed us disinformation. They were waiting for us. My partner and I were grabbed, bags over our heads, thrown into a basement where no one could hear us. No diplomatic protection. No one to call."

Ava stiffened but didn't speak.

"They held us for nine days, insisting we were part of some larger intelligence operation to funnel information to the Ukrainians." His voice sounded like gravel now. "Dimitri Abramovich was a general in the GRU then, under Putin. Interrogations. Beatings. Sensory deprivation. Mock executions. We held our cover stories, but . . . it got close. Real close." His hand trembled more than he wanted as he rubbed it over his face. "When both of us refused to crack, it got worse. Abramovich decided to make an example of us to the other prisoners. It's personal with Abramovich—he blames me personally for any of his failings in Ukraine." He swallowed hard. "My buddy Jim didn't make it." The image of his partner's lifeless body still haunted him—eyes open, mouth bloodied.

He felt her still against him, listening, absorbing his words with her head heavy on his chest. It was a decision he replayed a thousand times. Every possible branch of the timeline. Every alternative outcome that could have saved Jim's life.

"My brothers were Army. Deployed just south of Kiev with a US military support unit assisting Ukrainian forces on the eastern front. I hadn't told them where I was going. I couldn't. But when I didn't make our scheduled exfil window, the best chance to escape enemy territory, they started pulling strings. Luke practically threatened to go rogue and cross the border himself. They were the ones who pressured Langley to get me out."

He paused, unsure if he could say the rest; the silence was filled only by the pop of fire.

"They were always like that," he said finally, feeling that now-familiar dull ache when he spoke about them. "I was the youngest, the reckless one. The one they'd have to pull out of rivers and drag off rooftops, talk out of dumb ideas. But I never thought that they'd go to war just to keep doing it."

He shifted, moving to pick up a log. He threw it onto the fire, watching the sparks jump. He hadn't meant to go this far, to unearth it all.

"Luke didn't come back." The words nearly caught in his throat. "Six weeks later, a drone hit his convoy. Russian interference."

"Oh, my God, Ben. I'm so sorry."

"I've done a lot of things I can't take back," he murmured. "Made calls that cost people their lives. But that one—"

He didn't finish the sentence. He couldn't. He finally looked at Ava and saw something between sorrow and disbelief written on her face. But he didn't want pity; he wanted her to understand.

"I know how it feels to carry the weight of something that wasn't supposed to be your fault—but is, anyway." He held her gaze, unflinching, honest. "That's why I'm keeping your secret. I don't know what really happened to your mother. But I know what it's like to have regrets. To live with the weight of them every day."

He studied her face, knowing now that there was nothing that she could say that could change his mind about the regret and shame he felt. He had to put the wall between them back in place. He hated himself for it. But it was safer this way. If he let her all the way in, there would be no turning back.

Her eyes roamed his face, searching for something. "Ben," she said softly.

He cut her off with a shake of his head. "Don't. We have a job to do, a mission. Let's stay focused on that." He saw the flicker of hurt on her face. But he couldn't fall deeper for her than he already had.

"Hey," she said, her voice shifting as she sat upright. "Source comms are routed over a separate drone than the encrypted phone.

There's no reason both should be down at once unless someone is targeting the system."

He blinked, thrown by the sudden shift, but grateful for it. "True," he said, cautious. "Although I'm not too sure what good it will do to communicate with our sources at the moment."

"Perhaps Konstantin can help."

"Not a bad idea, but how do you know that he wasn't behind that attack on the train? He could have warned someone."

"You said so yourself that I need medical attention—do we have a choice?"

No, not anymore. He cursed under his breath and locked his jaw as he lifted the phone, the screen scanning his irises before unlocking. He typed frantically into his phone, his chest expanding as he inhaled a deep breath. He could feel the heat of her fever through his shirt.

Finally, his phone buzzed. He looked down at his phone and let out a breath. "He has somewhere we can go. A safe house. It's not far from here."

"An SVR safe house? How do we know it's not been bugged?" She propped herself on one hand and winced.

"I'm sure it is," he said, already on his feet, "but I need to get you somewhere we can make a phone call and get you the medical attention you need. You have a fever."

He outstretched a hand, helping her to her feet. Her face was resolute, pained, but still determined. Still Ava. He wished she wasn't, wished she were someone that he could walk away from, report to Langley, move on. But she wasn't. Not even close. And now they were both running from their past.

He tightened his grip on her hand, just for a moment, and let go.

# CHAPTER

# 24

When Konstantin finally reached them, two hours later from his dacha in Zabaykalsk, he came into the cave grumbling like a yeti. His fur-lined coat was heavy with snow, his salt-and-pepper hair half-frozen to his temples as though he'd tracked over a glacier rather than a forest.

"You Americans," he huffed, exhaling cold steam as he ducked inside. "Always charging through the forest like you are characters in Marvel movie. I'm fifty-nine years old, but at least I know my limitations. You?" He raised a brow at Ben. "You look like a man who hasn't slept in two days but still thinks that he can outrun a train."

Ben didn't respond, but the corner of his mouth twitched despite the strain in his jaw. Konstantin's gaze landed on Ava, and he frowned. "And now she's bleeding and likely concussed. At least your story has that tragic feel Americans love in their movies."

He hooked an arm around Ava and pulled her up. "You do have a plan, right? Somewhere warm, safe, maybe with a decent bottle of vodka? Because I'm all out of brilliant ideas."

Ava found she could now put weight on her ankle, but groaned, slumping against Ben as pain flared white-hot through her arm. "Please," she muttered through clenched teeth. "Less talking. More antibiotics and pain relief."

"She speaks!" Konstantin said in a mock-reverent tone. "A fighter, even half-dead."

Ben went rigid beside Ava and shot Konstantin with a hard stare.

Konstantin held up both hands. "I forget how tightly wound you CIA types are. Just trying to lighten the mood in here." He waved a hand, motioning for Ava to exit the cave ahead of him.

Ben reached out to steady Ava as she limped toward the cave opening.

She exhaled through the pain and waved him away. "I'm OK."

Ben fell back beside Konstantin.

Konstantin stepped closer, his voice dropping so that only Ben could hear as they exited the cave. "You know, for someone with such impressive training, you're terrible at hiding how much you care about her."

Ben's head snapped around but Konstantin just grinned. "Come on," Ben said in a raised voice, moving a branch out of Ava's way.

"Your five-star accommodations await," Konstantin went on. "No room service but the rats are polite."

And with that, they followed Konstantin into the trees, toward whatever shelter an SVR agent considered safe.

Ben followed Konstantin through the snow, now carrying Ava in his arms. Every frosted surface sparkled silver in the moonlight. Pine trees dusted with fresh powder cast long, soft shadows. Ava could feel them sinking deeper with every step through the snow, but Ben never faltered, pulling her closer to shield her from the wind.

When they reached the safe house, the snow had stopped, but the tree branches still shuddered in the icy wind as Konstantin shouldered the door open. The house, though small and modest, radiated warmth. A fire crackled in the center like a lifeline, and Ava felt her nerve endings begin to come back to life, but also awakening to the pain.

She bit down hard on the inside of her cheek, refusing to show weakness. She still needed to discover who had leaked information that had led to their being discovered on the train. As Ben lowered her onto a leather couch beside the hearth, blinding agony flared in her shoulder and her vision swam. The room tilted—the hearth, the small kitchen, Konstantin's face, his brows furrowed.

"I need a doctor," Ben said, scanning every corner as if danger lurked in the flickering shadows. Konstantin was not just an SVR agent; he was an assassin, and their calling him was a signal of how desperate they both were. "I stitched up her gunshot wound, but she still needs antibiotics and her ankle braced."

"I've already thought of that," Konstantin said, his voice barely broke through the haze Ava was caught in. "I have a doctor; he ensures the ultimate discretion."

"We'll do fine with the US Embassy doctor, thanks," Ben said. Intensity seemed to leak out from every word, every gesture.

"I didn't walk through a snowstorm in the middle of the pitch black just to murder or poison you two if that's what you're thinking," Konstantin said coldly. "I would have at least waited until the morning."

Ava raised a brow. "How reassuring . . ."

Blood pounded in her ears, and her vision blurred, exhaustion and pain tearing at every muscle. She could feel the blood draining from her cheeks, and she wondered, quite calmly, if she had gone into shock.

"Look at her," Konstantin nodded in Ava's direction. "She's lost way too much blood. I'm surprised she hasn't passed out."

"Yeah, I noticed," Ben said, a flash of skepticism cutting through his easy tone.

"Stop talking like I'm not here!" she managed as her world faded into something dimmer, darker. "I'll take the doctor, now please."

"He's just in the other room." Konstantin held up a finger, worry suddenly etched across his weathered features. "One moment."

Ben's brows rose as Konstantin disappeared to fetch the doctor. "Convenient," Ben said as soon as Konstantin was out of earshot.

"He got a doctor," Ava said through clenched teeth, "I assume because you told him that I was injured. I don't think that's cause for concern."

"Perhaps," Ben said. "But I wouldn't put anything past the Russians. Don't drink anything, and don't take any pills he gives you."

She stared back at him. "You seriously think that he might poison me?"

Ben arched a brow. "Wouldn't be his first party trick. SVR and FSB have a whole cookbook of poisons, Ava."

"Don't be ridiculous. He wouldn't—he needs me, needs us both right now."

Ben gave a faint smirk. "Yeah, that's what every mark says before the tea kicks in."

Konstantin was no ordinary defector. For more than twenty years, he had served the SVR under a false name, Morozov, an alias so carefully constructed that even Moscow's own counterintelligence watchdogs had never uncovered his identity as Gallitzin. To maintain that deception for two decades was not just impressive, it was unfathomable.

Ben gave her a wary look as Konstantin walked back into the room followed by a man in his mid-fifties, with a salt-and-pepper beard and gold-rimmed spectacles.

"He doesn't speak any English," Konstantin said, casting a sideways glance at Ben. "Which will ensure his discretion. He's also married to my sister, so you can rest assured that he won't be telling anyone about this meeting."

Ben gave a dry grin. "Family business. Always works out great."

The doctor looked at Ava and said, "May I?" in Russian.

Ava nodded sharply as the doctor continued to speak. "Would you like something for the pain?"

Ava looked up at Ben, who hovered above them. His demeanor was calm, his lips pressed tight, and once again Ava regretted that she couldn't hide her emotions as well as he could. But when she touched his arm, he shook his head, and a somber look flashed in his eyes.

"No painkillers," she croaked, "but I will do some vodka. A lot of it."

Konstantin nodded and left the room, returning with a freezing bottle of vodka and two small glasses.

He looked at Ben and said, "I thought that you both could use a drink."

After Konstantin poured himself a glass and drank, to show it could be trusted, Ava took the glass of vodka and chugged it back in one grateful swallow. Ben met her eyes and did the same.

Konstantin refilled her glass twice; she chugged them down, then nodded at the doctor to proceed. The doctor's hands were steady as he irrigated the wound with saline and removed more of the damaged tissue. With each sharp, burning sensation Ava moved in and out of consciousness, but each time she awoke she was assured of Ben's calming presence beside her.

"Stay with me," she murmured, reaching for his left hand as the pain forced her eyes shut.

"I'm not going anywhere." His voice was steady as he gently squeezed her hand while the doctor administered antibiotic into the wound.

The vodka Konstantin provided dulled the pain, but not nearly enough. Ava's body still felt disconnected, heavy, numb, her mind circling the same impossible thought: someone had warned Abramovich. They'd known exactly when and where she and Ben would intercept the train. As the doctor left, carrying bloodied gauze and instruments, the questions kept spinning. Besides the CIA, only Konstantin had known their plans. Ben had warned her not to trust him completely. A knot formed in her stomach as dread uncoiled within her. And Joe was still missing. So was the rest of the ops team. Her vision blurred. She started to slump, but Ben caught her before she hit the floor.

"Easy," he murmured, saying something to Konstantin about a bed before scooping her up in one smooth motion. "Don't get used to this," he said quietly as he carried her upstairs, his tone light but his grip steady. "I charge extra for rescue missions and bedside service."

She managed the ghost of a smile, breathing in his familiar scent—pine and gun oil—trying to steady herself. When he lowered her onto the bed, she clutched his arm. The muscles beneath her hand tensed.

"You might've been right," she whispered, her voice faint. "About Konstantin. Someone tipped them off. We need to find out who."

"You need sleep," Ben said. The words were firm, but his voice softened at the edges. "I'll keep watch. Try not to dream about being wrong—it might kill you."

Her lips curved faintly, then her eyes drifted shut. The last thing she felt was the weight of the quilt over her and the warmth of Ben's lips brushing her forehead before the darkness took her.

# CHAPTER

# 25

Two days later, Ava and Ben watched in silence as the live video footage flickered on the screen. The CIA's Saint Petersburg Base was a cramped, dimly lit space overlooking the bustling city square. Shadows pressed like ghosts from Ava's past that refused to leave. Beyond the frosted windows, the iconic onion-shaped domes of the Church of the Savior on Spilled Blood glinted in the gray afternoon light. A place of beauty, absurdly calm in contrast to the atmosphere inside the base where they watched the chaos in Washington, DC, unfolding on the screen.

Ava sat still, her right fingers clenched tight to disguise their trembling, her left arm in a sling. The Capitol shooting played on the news like a looping nightmare—triggered by a lie. Lies spun from a server in the very Vibrantia warehouse that they were about to watch burn. The shooter had believed the federal government was coming for his land. His home. His rights.

He wasn't the first. He wouldn't be the last.

Beside her, Ben leaned forward, his jaw set and his focus narrowed on the news footage as though the world might tilt if he looked away. His nearness made her pulse thrum although he hadn't looked at her once. Since that night in the cave, he'd gone from steady, almost protective, to something sharper—cold and calculating—as if steeling himself against what he now knew. She had told him what only a few senior CIA leaders understood—that her mother had been accused of betraying her country. It was the one thing she'd sworn to bury so deep it could never see daylight, a condition of hiring, a price of entry into the CIA. Saying it out loud to him had been like unlocking a vault she never meant to open again. But in the cave, with his arms around her and his voice low in the dark, their confessions had felt dangerous and unshakably real. She had seen him lower his walls, felt the unguarded weight of him, and God help her, she had let him see her, too. She felt bound to him now, as though some unseen thread had wound itself around her ribs, tightening with every breath. It was beyond the mission, beyond anything she'd ever experienced. It frightened her with its intensity. He had no place in her life, yet she couldn't stop thinking about him.

Frank's voice cut through her thoughts as he paced relentlessly in front of the two television screens like a caged wolf. He turned to face the monitors, his stance wide, his arms folded across his chest. The somber voice of a news reporter narrated the shooting in DC, and each word drove a nail of dread into Ava's chest. They had to put a stop to Russia, to Abramovich's misinformation campaign, and to the Liberty Coalition's propaganda.

On the other television screen, classified imagery of the Vibrantia warehouse flickered into view. Cameras placed by the surveillance team showed hackers busily typing onto their computers, sowing discourse that would further destabilize the United States. The warehouse camera zoomed in on a man hunched over a computer, his fingers flying across the keyboard. Ava's breath hitched as she recognized Roman, one of Vibrantia's lead hackers, the man whose phone had let them to this point. Her gaze flicked to another corner of the screen where two other men busily typed, oblivious to what was coming.

The tension in the room coiled tighter as Frank glanced down at his watch. "Five more minutes until detonation."

Ava's left arm throbbed as she stole a heated glance with Ben. The night at the cave weighed heavily between them, something raw, something unresolved. She forced herself to focus back on the screen, heat flaming at her cheeks.

Tension crackled through the air. A sharp bang reverberated from the television. Ava's pulse jumped as everyone in the room sat silent. On the screen, one of the servers exploded into a fiery ball, hurling Roman backward. Smoke and debris filled the screen as shouts in Russian rang out. Another hacker, panicked but unharmed, ducked behind his desk. He shouted in Russian and placed his hands over his neck as shrapnel flew from a second server. Another man busily typing on his computer collapsed when the smoke burst from the third server. A fourth and fifth explosion sent a massive plume of smoke spiraling into the air. The screen trembled, went dark, then stabilized as hackers fled, their cries muffled by the roar of flames.

"Excellent work," Frank said, his tone sharp as he glanced at Ava.

Ava nodded, but a heavy, sick feeling filled her stomach. The adrenaline that had kept her sharp for the last forty-eight hours now left her feeling hollow, the weight of her actions pressing against her ribs. They had struck a critical blow to Vibrantia, but the battle was far from over.

If they didn't completely dismantle the SVR's network supporting the Liberty Coalition, it would only regroup and relaunch its attack against the US.

"Ava," Frank said, pulling her abruptly from her thoughts. "Can you get a message to Konstantin?"

"Yes," she said, throat constricting. She still wasn't sure how much she could trust Konstantin.

He had come to their rescue, but there were still many questions that had yet to be answered. Chief among them was whether the people who had shot at them from the train had been tipped off. And if so, by whom?

While Ava's thoughts danced over the possibility, Frank rattled off his demands. *Intel on SVR's cyber capabilities. Clarity on Abramovich's missile plans.* But Ava barely heard him; she was already calculating the layers of risk, measuring her instinct against the very real possibility that Konstantin could turn on them. She weighed Konstantin's story against the immediacy of their situation. Ben was right. Konstantin was too calm, too measured, his movements never wasted. That could be a sign of experience—or that he was already three moves ahead, playing a different game entirely.

"Sir," Ben cut in. "You realize that asking him about the missiles is basically waving a neon sign that says how much we know, right?"

"If there's an impending terrorist attack on the homeland, shouldn't we concentrate on learning their targets?" Frank snapped back.

"Sure," Ben said. "But Konstantin's not sitting in on Abramovich's evil-mastermind meetings. Push him too far and we lose the only guy crazy enough to feed us intel from inside SVR."

"I'm not interested in your theories, Ben. I'm interested in stopping an attack." Frank's tone was clipped as he turned toward Ava. "That should be everyone's concern right now."

Ava nodded again, her mind already racing through the logistics of arranging a meeting. "I can probably meet with him later today."

"Great," Frank said, his voice tight. "Show's over, let's get back to work." As Frank rose to leave, he turned toward Ava. "Update me as soon as you make contact with Konstantin, and I want a full countersurveillance team on your next meeting."

She nodded, sharing a pensive look with Ben. She knew he doubted Konstantin. Doubted his motivations. Perhaps doubted her, and she hated how much his approval meant to her.

After Frank and his secretary left, the room fell quiet, leaving just the two of them and the hum of tension still hanging in the air.

Ava pushed back her chair to leave, but Ben stepped in front of her, blocking the door. "Don't do this," he said, voice low, edged with something that sounded almost like worry.

"You heard Frank. I need to meet with Konstantin."

"There's something off about him," Ben said, his tone clipped. "You said it yourself at the safe house, he might've been the one who tipped off Abramovich about the train."

"Frank confirmed it was Abramovich who added the extra guards," she countered. "They were carrying missiles. Probably they had surveillance drones too. Konstantin likely had nothing to do with it."

Ben rubbed a hand across the back of his neck, frustration flickering behind his half-smile. "Yeah, or maybe he's just better at lying than the rest of us. Look, just be careful. You're walking a fine line with him."

"I know what I'm doing."

"I know you do," he said, trying for levity, but the words came out softer. "Just don't let Frank use you. I've seen that look in his eyes before."

She stiffened. "Like they used my mother?"

The words hit hard, and he froze. For a moment, the sarcasm slipped. Regret clouded his face. "Ava, I didn't mean—" His voice trailed off, rough now, the mask cracking just enough for her to see the truth behind it, the worry he'd been trying to hide.

"Don't," she whispered, her voice tight with barely contained emotion. "Don't bring her into this." But of course, every time Ava made a decision, she saw her mother's shadow before her. A woman who'd thought she was doing the right thing, who gave up everything for the CIA, only to end up in a prison cell, branded as a traitor. Ava had told herself that she was different, that she would never be blinded by anything but her mission. Never let anything or anyone in that could distract her.

Until Ben.

"I'm not like her," Ava said, colder than she felt. But her eyes stung, the burn of tears threatening to rise. "I won't make her same mistakes."

"I know," he looked down, his hand twitching. "I just—" he stopped himself, balling his hand into a tight fist.

*You just what?* She wanted to ask but didn't. *You just care but you can't afford to?*

Instead, she let the silence settle.

"What I need from Konstantin is intelligence that can be corroborated," she said finally. "Beyond that, the man is of no use to me. Once I have what we need on Vibrantia, and on the missiles, he's done."

Ben hesitated, then sighed. "Fine. But take the DarkFin. Swipe his phone the next time you guys meet. It should only take seconds. Make sure he's not playing both sides."

Ava stilled, her heart beating rapidly. She should have brushed past him. But his eyes, shadowed with doubt and something deeper, held her in place.

She forced herself to turn, to leave before she betrayed too much. Fear buzzed on the edges of her mind at the feelings she couldn't seem to cut off. She had always been good at guarding her emotions—keeping them safely tucked away was something she'd perfected in childhood, but with Ben standing close it felt impossible.

Something about Konstantin and his access felt deeply personal, but it was Ben's skepticism that cut deeper. He was right, especially with what they had discovered back on the train. The stakes were higher than ever. If Konstantin was playing her, it wouldn't just jeopardize the mission—it could bring the United States to its knees.

# CHAPTER

# 26

At the bar where Ava sat, there was a soft lull of conversation, dimming her inner voice until it went silent. She inhaled deeply and moved her hair to one side, letting the weak light wash her in an amber hue, exotic, deliberate. The movement still felt strange without the sling, her shoulder still tight but healing. She aimed for that elusive balance any female spy must master—someone a man wanted to impress but also someone who commanded respect. Outside, the wind howled against the snow-caked windows, but inside the bar it was warm, almost stifling. The smell of stale beer clung to the walls, so thick she could taste it, peeling plaster walls that spoke of late nights fueled by liquor and fists.

The bartender, a man with a barrel-sized chest, slid a vodka toward her. She smiled and sipped, aware of every look that drifted in her direction. In the corner, two men sat hunched over their beers, their gaze tense and their voices low. There was only one other woman at the bar. She glanced at Ava, a cigarette dangling from her thin lips. Ava's training had conditioned her to become more guarded, more watchful of her surroundings, but there was something within her that longed for the outside world to grow quieter, less important.

She shoved her hand into her coat pockets, her fingers brushing on the DarkFin device that would extract the contents of

Konstantin's phone once he arrived. She trusted that he wanted them to succeed—but training reminded her that instincts could be wrong, and loyalties could shift. If Konstantin decided his survival was best served by turning her over to the Kremlin, no Embassy intervention would save her or Ben.

Still, the question that kept her steady was the one that mattered most: what was Abramovich doing with an arsenal of missiles—and how did he plan to use them?

A haze of cigar smoke hung low over the bar as Konstantin entered, his gait confident but his eyes wary. He wore a black suit, a light blue scarf covering his mouth. When their eyes met, Ava offered a polite smile. His own smile creased at the corners, the warmth in it softening his usual restraint. Their exchanges had been brief, their banter light, but she hadn't forgotten the kindness he'd shown the night she was shot.

"I'm surprised you ventured this far into the country, *milaya*." His voice carried the old-world courtesy of a man born to formality. *Milaya*—darling. Strangely, she didn't mind. If it made him feel closer to her, more willing to take the risks they needed, she welcomed it.

"How's the arm?"

"Still sore," she said, "but better the longer I stay in the warmth."

"Good," he said. "I'd hate for you to blame me if you lost your right hook. Though I've heard your left was never impressive."

"I could still take you down in under thirty seconds."

He smirked. "Only if I were blindfolded—and drunk. I've been at this a long time, *milaya*."

She laughed softly. "You're lucky I don't test that theory. Especially since both seem possible in this place."

He coughed into his fist, smiling as he slid into the seat across from her. "I'm a gentleman, otherwise I might. I'm just glad your colleague called me when he did. Without antibiotics, your wound wouldn't have healed. And you both might've frozen to death in that cave."

She reached across the roughened bar table and touched his forearm. "I'm grateful you got to us when you did."

"We're partners, are we not? We help each other."

Her chest warmed at his words—but Ben's warning still drummed within her ears.

Konstantin cleared his throat and swallowed his vodka in one large gulp. "Now, tell me . . . what's so urgent that you'd risk frostbite and terrible vodka to meet with me?"

"I think you know what I'm going to ask . . . you must know what else was being transported on that train."

Konstantin hesitated, staring into the bottom of an empty glass. "I can give you a lot of information about the SVR—our tactics, our tradecraft. But don't ask for the impossible, *milaya*."

She straightened on the barstool. "I'm very grateful for the help that you provided us so far, but ours is a working relationship. When I ask questions, I need answers."

His thick white brows drew together. "Even at the risk of my own life?"

"Oh, don't be so dramatic. You've faced worse odds. Remember, I've read your file." She gestured toward his scarf. "And you made it here in the freezing cold with just a scarf and no overcoat, so you're practically indestructible."

Konstantin's lips twitched, but he didn't smile. "You're lucky I find your charm endearing. But I'll need another drink first."

"No stalling," Ava said, folding her arms across her chest.

"I'm negotiating, not stalling," he replied, his tone steady as he waved over the waitress. "And you will owe me after this"—he made his voice sound light. "Perhaps I'll ask you to teach me that famous right hook of yours."

One of the men playing chess waved Konstantin over, and Ava saw his jaw tighten in recognition. "I'm not certain this was a good idea," he muttered in a low voice. "Excuse me while I try and reassure this guy that there's nothing going on here. Be a good girl and pretend that you're my mistress."

"*Excuse me,*" Ava's voice rose slightly as he rose from the table. "I'm young enough to be your—"

But before she had the chance to say more, he was at the other table, leaving his phone behind. Ava looked at it. Her palms began to sweat as she considered what she was about to do. If he caught her going through his phone, their relationship would be crucially compromised. But too much was at stake—they were now talking about Russian missiles capable of reaching US territories. She had to do it.

She fixed her gaze on Konstantin as he spoke to the chess players, their laughter booming over the clink of beer mugs. This was her chance. She slipped the DarkFin device from her purse and placed it next to Konstantin's phone. Ten seconds to swipe the contents of his phone. *Ten Mississippi, nine Mississippi. . . .* Before she reached one Mississippi, Konstantin turned back.

His steps were deliberate. Ava's heart raced as she slid the device off the bar and back into her purse. She picked up her drink, trying to appear casual.

But as he sat down, his expression darkened. "*Milaya*," he said, his eyes glimmering with amusement. "You wouldn't happen to know why my phone just restarted itself, would you?"

Ava's eyes widened at Konstantin's abruptness, and she drew back slightly from the table, her right fingers curling tightly around the edges.

"I didn't touch your phone." And she hadn't.

Her pulse went staccato, thrumming with each heartbeat, each breath. A cold knot formed in her stomach. The air felt charged as she glanced at the two men at the chess table: FSB, likely—their presence here was too convenient, too coincidental.

"Let's go for a walk, shall we?" Konstantin held out his arm for her. There was steel in his eyes, but his voice was soft.

Ava hesitated, her instincts screaming to stay put. But she couldn't afford to draw more attention here, not with so many eyes already on them. Plus, she had an entire countersurveillance team watching and waiting outside the bar. They would intervene if things went wrong.

Sliding off the barstool, she smiled at Konstantin with a deliberate calm. "Let's go."

Snow crunched underfoot as they stepped out into the night. Wind sliced through her coat, her breath fogging up the air as she pulled up her fur-lined hood. Every car speeding past, every shadow lurking in the alleyway, sharpened her senses. They were exposed, vulnerable to the FSB now, and they both knew it.

Konstantin walked quickly beside her, his gloved hands clasped firmly in front of him. "Do you have photographs of these missiles?" he asked Ava quietly, as though the clouds themselves would betray them.

Ava kept her gaze forward, scanning the dimly lit street as she passed him the photographs that Ben had snapped.

Konstantin glanced at her, the deep lines on his face illuminated by the yellow streetlamps. "These missiles don't have to go far to reach Europe."

Ava's breath hitched, but she forced her expression to remain neutral. "I don't believe the Kremlin's problems lie with Europe," she said carefully.

"No," he said. "The unrest in the United States provides the perfect opportunity for the Kremlin to reassert themselves. Wouldn't you agree?"

The implication made her chest tighten. He glanced at her, watching, waiting, but Ava swallowed her next words. It had been only twenty-four hours since they had blown up Vibrantia's servers. Too soon to tell whether the operation had crippled SVR's ability to launch additional cyberattacks.

And the further she pushed Konstantin to deepen his access to SVR's plans, the more dangerous their mission would become.

She inhaled deeply, the icy air burning her lungs. "If Russia were to attack the United States"—she tried to keep her tone even—"where do you think they would go first?"

"I don't have a crystal ball." Konstantin shook his head and gave her a wry smile. "I cannot tell you what I do not know."

"Then tell me what you do know." Her voice carried an edge she didn't bother to hide.

He stopped suddenly and turned to face her. "Let me reach out to my contacts, see what I can find out."

"Who? Other SVR? I assume you have a division of your service that handles these sorts of things."

"I'm not going to reveal my subsource network if that's what you're asking." His tone held a warning, but Ava pushed forward.

"We're talking about attacks on my homeland that have the potential to spiral into full-scale war, I need to know that any information you provide is credible."

"Are you still worried about my credibility?" Konstantin's brow furrowed. "Did I not prove that to you during Abramovich's misinformation campaign?"

"You did," she agreed. "But you also have to understand that the intelligence I provide goes straight to senior policymakers, people who have the authority to wage wars. I have to be certain."

He studied her for a moment, then nodded and started walking again. "I don't think I've told you about my family," he began slowly.

"A little," she lied. She needed to know what his family meant to him.

"We are a family that can trace our lineage back centuries—all the way back to the Lithuanian dynasty of the thirteenth century. Members of my family have served as warlords, statesmen, diplomats, and admirals in the glory days of the Russian Empire." His eyes tilted heavenward. "But after the Romanovs were assassinated and aristocracy dismantled in the early 1900s, we disappeared into Europe's shadows. Yet our ties to Russia remain." He turned toward her, placing a hand gently on her shoulder. "Do you understand what I'm telling you?"

Ava's breath hitched as the pieces began to click into place. It wasn't the SVR that provided him with his intelligence, she realized. "You use your family as your subsource network," she said quietly.

He didn't acknowledge the truth aloud, but something flickered within his eyes—perhaps pride. "I cannot ever go into greater detail about their identity," he said quietly. "Please don't ask me to."

She gave a slow nod, her mind spiraling. His network, rooted in history and bloodlines, was unlike anything she'd suspected. It was more than his motivation. It was his access.

They passed by a kiosk's crumbling façade. Its rusted metal door bore Dimitri Abramovich's name in jagged black spray paint alongside a Soviet symbol. Ava's mother had once walked these same streets, hunting spies, chasing targets. These symbols and names were written into Russia's turbulent history. It made the past suddenly more real, more tangible. Konstantin's reach was more formidable than she'd guessed, and despite the risks, her estimation of his capabilities as a source deepened.

But so did the cost of trusting him.

Abramovich and her mother had crossed paths once—somewhere deep within Moscow's maze of secrets. And Konstantin, with his lineage and connections, might be her only link to what the Agency had spent years burying. Through his reach into Abramovich's world, she might finally uncover what she'd been searching for all along: the truth.

# CHAPTER 27

AVA KNEW SHE was being used as bait, and every instinct she had fought against it.

Across the dining room, Nathaniel Grey reclined in his chair as if it were a throne, his chin slightly lifted, his perfect aristocratic nose tilted upward as if he were in the company of lesser humans. Grey scanned the room with a cool attachment as if he expected the world to arrange itself around him. She'd seen this type before: men born to legacy, not burden. Men who never had to lie to survive.

Ava kept her posture open, the picture of ease, while her peripheral vision swept for exits, bodyguards, cameras. Reflections in the bar glassware gave her a wider view—the maître d' checking his watch, a server palming a folded note, a couple shifting their chairs just enough to block her sight to the kitchen.

Every conversation she had with Grey reminded her of how far she'd climbed, how many lies she'd told to escape the truth about her mother. And how Langley's mission was pulling her away from her own, the last few weeks dragging her in the opposite direction of what she wanted. But Konstantin's access was a flicker of hope in a battle she'd almost given up on.

*She's alive.* The text was the ember she couldn't stamp out. And the question remained: *how did Abramovich know her mother?* The question burned hotter than anything in this glittering room. She'd already mapped out her next move in her quest: Konstantin. He had the reach, the access, and perhaps the motivation to help her untangle the truth. The Agency had buried her mother's name in a classified file, labeling her as a traitor, a double agent. But Ava refused to let that be the final word, and she would use Konstantin to help her discover the truth. He had access to Abramovich, and that meant he had access to his past, potentially a history with her mother.

Her fingers toyed with the olives in her martini glass, a meaningless gesture to anyone watching, but for her, it was cover. She was measuring the distance to the service hallway, calculating the time it would take to vanish if Grey suspected her. She removed two of the blue cheese olives from their skewer and popped one into her mouth, relishing the salty taste until Grey's eyes settled on her. He looked at her like she was a fine wine to be sampled, stored.

Everything about Grey screamed that he was as predictable as the companies that he ran.

Eleven o'clock. His favorite restaurant, his favorite drink. But tonight, something was different, off. And even from here, she could tell that he was unraveling. His posture was rigid, his movements too sharp as he spoke heatedly with the two men seated across from him. She'd heard his fury firsthand when it had come through the secondary bug she'd planted in his apartment. The bombing at the Vibrantia warehouse had rattled him. His perfectly controlled empire had been breached—by her, although of course he didn't know that.

Something inside her beamed at the idea, but she kept her face perfectly neutral as he walked toward her. His gait was confident, but she noticed the wrinkles in his shirt, his tie undone. Nathaniel Grey, the picture of elegance, was crumbling. It should have pleased her, but instead she thought of Ben. He hated the idea of this meeting, the performance she had to put on. And he would be right. Grey was reckless, easily influenced by power and money, but they needed him—or rather, they needed his power and influence over Abramovich and the direction of the Liberty Coalition. They also needed to shut down Vibrantia for good.

"What a coincidence." His voice was smooth, hiding whatever storm brewed underneath.

She smiled at him. "Hopefully a happy one."

"Happy would be an understatement."

She ignored the flirtation, turning just enough to make her disinterest clear. She needed to get right to the point and leave. "I would ask you how your day has been," she said, motioning for him to sit down beside her, "but I think I can already tell."

"Just a minor setback in one of our warehouses, nothing we can't handle." His words were clipped as he waved the bartender over and ordered another glass of wine.

"Nothing at all? The way you were talking to those men over there makes that difficult to believe."

"Just bureaucratic overreach, the usual. The government wants all the data we collect from Vibrantia stored only on servers in the United States. Threatening shutdowns, citing national security. As if they won't just hoard the data for themselves."

She arched a brow. "Wouldn't the Russians just do the same thing? Why not take everything back to the US and cut your losses?"

Grey's gaze sharpened. "It's not that simple. Moving our operations back to the US would set us back years. Not to mention the Russian shareholders. . . ."

"Why do you care what they think?" She leaned in, her gaze sharpening. "You own eighty percent of the company. Buy them out. Cut their influence."

He stared down into his wine glass as if searching for answers and swirled it around. Finally, his lucid brown eyes met hers, and he muttered, "If only that were still true." He slugged back the wine, and Ava felt the muscles of her face start to twitch.

"What do you mean?" she asked.

He shook his head slowly and sighed. "I sold about half of my shares to Dimitri Abramovich six weeks ago."

Her blood ran cold as all the pieces began to click into place. Grey wasn't calling the shots at all. He was a pawn, just like everyone else. Vibrantia, the Liberty Coalition—all of it was under Russian control.

"Tell me something, Nathaniel—why Abramovich? Why him?" She forced her tone to remain even rather than accusatory.

He stared down at the merlot in his glass. "Because he made me an offer I couldn't refuse."

"That can't be all of it. You've built an empire, and you just handed over the keys?"

He hesitated, studying her. Ava let the silence stretch, then leaned in, lowering her voice so the bartender couldn't overhear. "You still have influence. You still have a voice—use it. Dimitri Abramovich's ideology isn't yours. You think he's your partner, but he's using you."

Grey's jaw tightened.

"I know you care about our country. But you're in bed with our enemies who don't share your ideology." Ava's phone buzzed in her pocket, but she ignored it, deciding instead to press on. "You want to preserve something real? Help us stop Abramovich before there's nothing left to save."

He frowned. "Us?"

She dropped her gaze, just for a moment. "You're not the only one who doesn't trust the government to get it right. But you can't fix this alone. And if Abramovich wins . . . then neither of us will have anything worth defending."

A pause, and something flickered within his eyes. Uncertainty? Regret?

Before she could respond, her phone buzzed again. This time, she glanced down. It was Ben, and he'd sent a single urgent text.

**Come back to the base. Now.**

Her pulse spiked. She glanced back up at Grey, who was eyeing her intently. "Everything OK?"

Ava forced a bitter smile. "Fine. Just work."

Her mind raced as she slipped her phone back into her pocket. The room felt unsteady, as if the floor had begun to tilt. He knew that she was at a source meeting with Nathaniel Grey. What was so urgent that Ben had asked her to return to base?

"I'm sorry," she began, and Grey straightened. "I'm not feeling that great."

He reached across the table and patted her hand. "Are you sure it's not this political discussion that's made you feel sick? I'm happy to change the subject."

"No." She waved him off, using it as an excuse to shake off his touch. Her phone buzzed again. She ignored it and stood, her chest tightening. "I'll text you later. Good night."

Outside, the sleet stung her face, cold and sharp like broken glass. She walked fast through the melting snow, nearly running. It was against every protocol to end an asset meeting so abruptly, particularly one that she was getting good intel from.

She texted Grey, trying to salvage the thread she'd begun weaving.

**Great to see you tonight. Sorry I had to take off.**

She'd made progress, Grey was teetering. But the urgency in Ben's message clawed at her. Something must be very wrong. Otherwise, he would never have pulled her out of that meeting. Her heart pulled her forward toward the base, demanding she get to Ben, no matter the cost.

# CHAPTER

# 28

When she arrived back at base, Ben's head was bent low, the dim light illuminating the sharp lines of his cheekbones and jaw. There was a part of her that wanted to rush and touch his stubbled face, kiss the fatigue away from his tired eyes. But the tension in his shoulders as he hunched over the conference room table told her something was terribly wrong.

"What is it?" she asked, her voice cracking with tension.

He shook his head, his eyes locked on the table in front of him. The report that sat in front of him was like an omen. Perhaps it was from CIA/Security demanding her resignation, she thought. She swallowed a breath that felt like a blade in her throat.

It had always been risky to employ the daughter of a woman once accused of spying for the Russians—a secret known only to a select few in CIA leadership. But Frank had insisted that the risk was manageable given her fluency in a mission-critical language. But now, with Ava embedded in one of the Agency's most classified operations in Moscow, perhaps they were rethinking that trust.

"Ben?" Her voice shook as she stepped further into the room. "What's going on? Is it Konstantin? Is he double-crossing me?"

"It's not that," he said in a low, tight voice, unable to meet her eyes. He was stalling, but why?

"My feelings won't be hurt." She forced a bitter laugh. "I half-expected it anyway. . . ."

But before she could finish, he stood abruptly and crossed the room in two long strides. His eyes were like two burning embers as he finally met her gaze.

He handed her the report. "Look for yourself."

She took the report from him, her fingers lightly brushing his, igniting the spark that existed between them, a cruel reminder of a connection she couldn't afford to dwell on.

"This is one of the photos we found on Konstantin's phone."

She stared down at the report, her palms suddenly clammy. The photograph hit her like a punch. Her mother, holding her as a young toddler, standing in front of their old apartment building in Pentagon City.

Ava's world tilted, her vision blurring slightly. "Why would this picture be on his phone?" she whispered.

"I was hoping you could tell me," Ben replied evenly, taking a step closer.

Heat surged to her face. "I have no idea. What game are you playing?" The paper she held shook as she tried to hand it back. "I assume that you know who both these people are since you're showing this to me."

"I had a pretty good idea; the resemblance is . . . striking." He ran a hand through his hair, making it stand up. "Then I ran the images through our biometric databases to confirm it. It didn't take long."

Her heart slammed against her ribcage. She met his eyes, searching for something—perhaps reassurance, an escape from the impossible, horrible truth taking shape in her mind.

"I don't know what you want me to say," she stammered. "I don't know why Konstantin would have a picture of my mother and me. Maybe he's studying me, gathering intelligence for the SVR, like we suspected." Even as she uttered the words, she knew they weren't true. Her heart twisted.

"Maybe," Ben said, his tone even, "but have you considered the most logical explanation?"

His question was like an armed bomb in the room. She wanted to flee, wanted to stop the truth from swallowing her whole. But his eyes were sharpened on her, forcing her to see the truth as it stared back at her. The woman in the photograph wasn't the mother Ava had remembered. This was a younger version, her features softer, still untouched by the pain and secrets that had lingered in the corners of her mother's mouth and eyes. Her mother's wavy, chestnut hair cascaded past her shoulders, just like Ava's did now. A chill crawled up her spine at the similarities, the memories. Since her mother's death she'd barely let herself look at old photographs. It was too painful.

"Konstantin was not my mother's Russian handler," she said as the possibility whispered past. "He couldn't have been. The dates don't match up. And why on earth would he have an interest in me?" She swallowed hard, the bitter taste of denial sharp on her tongue.

"I don't think that Konstantin is studying you as a potential SVR source."

"What are you trying to say?" she asked.

Ben's expression softened, just enough to make it worse. She didn't want his pity. "Ava . . . do you want me to say it?"

Her pulse roared in her ears as she turned away and began pacing the room.

Finally, she forced herself to look at Ben. She had to know the truth, no matter how devasting. "I'm going to see Konstantin."

# CHAPTER

# 29

VINTAGE CHANDELIERS DRIPPED amber light across the velvet shadows of The Cigar lounge nestled in the heart of Moscow's elite Arbat District. Konstantin sat in the corner in a deep leather armchair, his back pressed against the paneled oak, smoke curling in the air like unspoken confessions. He liked to think of himself as a man of typical Russian sensibilities—stoic and enduring, as most Russian men had to be to survive the harsh winters and tougher politics. He never drew attention to himself, never let on how Russian politics had punished him over the years. As a result, the SVR had molded him into something bold and relentless, until blending into the shadows was his natural state. He was used to surveying the world with an almost predatory patience, viewing people for how they could be manipulated instead of who they were. Until he met Ava.

When Konstantin had met her at the embassy, a faint glimmer of his buried humanity had surfaced. He was reminded of a different time, a different place, when his dreams had not been crushed by the grinding wheels of the state. Ava's face, a copy of her mother's, struck him with an ache that he could not shake. If he adhered to his years of operational experience, Konstantin would stay away from her—Ava was a constant reminder of the life that Theresa had left him for.

Now, as Ava entered the lounge, wearing a long dark wool coat and cream scarf that seemed to have been draped over her mahogany hair in a hurry, he recognized the absurd need to assure himself that she wasn't Theresa, was not some dream conjured by loneliness or too much vodka.

Tension gathered between his shoulders as Ava approached his table. "I must admit," he rose and said with the faintest bow. "I was surprised to see a meeting request so soon."

Her voice was low, as though she, too, recognized the danger of her words in this place.

"Have you discovered anything about the weapons?"

"China," he mouthed, "but I have yet to receive confirmation." He gave her a tight-lipped smile. "But I've hardly had the chance to send out the necessary inquiries. It's only been a few days."

"I see," she said sharply, pulling her gloves off and shoving them into her coat pockets. Her cheeks were red and chapped from the icy wind.

He studied her without meaning to, reading her posture for signs that she was under distress. He'd learned from Theresa that the CIA could be a difficult and controlling employer.

But Ava's hand trembled only when she reached into her purse and took out a photograph. The photo shook slightly in her hand as she held it up for him to see—a printout of a snapshot of Ava's mother and her as a baby from his phone, taken before a tragedy that had shattered him. The ache in his throat was heavy, merciless.

"I demand to know the truth." Ava shot him a direct look as if daring him to defy her.

"Of course you would collect off my phone." He shook his head and pinched the bridge of his nose. "Naïve of me to think otherwise."

"I expect answers, Konstantin. Did you know my mother?"

"Yes." His throat constricted, and he took a sip of his whisky, wanting it to burn away his regret, his lingering grief. He hadn't dreamed that it was possible that Theresa Anderson's daughter would show up on his doorstep one day. But here she was sitting in front of him, her eyes glittering with anger just the way her mother's had done. "I was her handler."

"Why didn't you say so before?" Her voice cracked with emotion. A waiter came over, but Konstantin waved him away with a flick of his wrist. He'd already ordered a vodka martini for Ava, up with a twist, just the way she'd ordered it last time they'd met.

"Because I wasn't sure." His words came out raw, each syllable threatening to demolish the walls he'd built over the years. It had been over twenty-five years since he'd last seen Theresa, but seeing Ava had made his grief feel fresh.

Her gray eyes flashed with anger, and she folded her arms tight across her chest. "And did you get her killed? Did you turn her in?"

The accusation gutted him. For a moment, the room blurred as the memories flooded— the desperate attempts to save Theresa, the helplessness as the FSB closed in, the anguish of losing her. It had been so many years, yet his feelings for Theresa had never changed, never dimmed.

"I did not." His chest tightened, grief roaring through him like fire catching dry grass. "I did everything in my power to save her."

Inside the club, a jazz trio began to play, swallowing the words between them.

Ava stared down at the picture as if the answers were hidden there. Konstantin knew that look well—she was consumed by her anger, her desperate need for answers.

When she finally looked up, he was caught in her gaze. She had Theresa's same cupid-bud lips, the almond shape of her eyes, the color . . .

"Do I need to remind you that I am paying you to give me information?" she said, abruptly. "I expect answers, just as I'm certain that you demanded them from my mother."

He almost smiled despite the knife in his chest. "Your mother and I were partners in our work. I never looked at her like an employee. I respected her, and everything that she fought for."

She placed her drink down and shook her head. "My mother was accused of betraying her country."

The words struck at him, and before reason intervened, he was gripping Ava's forearm from across the table. "That's not at all who your mother was!" He released her at once, horror at his own loss of control forcing him back in his chair.

Theresa had sacrificed everything for her country, her family. *How could her daughter not know this?*

Ava's gray eyes blazed. "Place one finger on me again, and I'll cut it off."

The fire within her broke through his sadness and he almost smiled, despite himself. *How had he not seen it before?* The resemblance to Theresa went beyond the physical.

"Forgive me." He raised his hands in surrender. "I let my emotions get the best of me. I only meant to say . . . you must have been very young when you lost her."

"Nine," she replied curtly. "Eleven when I learned she was dead."

"A very difficult age to lose a mother."

She narrowed her eyes at him. "Is there an easy one?"

He hesitated. Every word had felt like a misstep somehow, every truth a potential wound that he risked opening. Yet as he looked at her face—Theresa's face—he knew that he owed her something, even if it destroyed him.

"I will tell you what I can," he said at last, turning the unlit cigar between his fingers like a rosary bead. "Why she died. What she fought for. The truth that you were denied."

# CHAPTER

# 30

Ava felt light-headed from the smell of tobacco encircling her as she stared back at Konstantin, her pulse alive in the base of her throat. The room sparkled with gold-rimmed wine glasses and sculptures made of ice and butter, near a buffet of cold, smoked fish. She took another sip of her martini, hoping the burn would dull the ache in her chest. But the feeling refused to dissipate. It transported her to a different time, a different place—the day when she learned that her mother was dead.

The memory came unbidden, sharp as knife. She was eleven years old. The knock on her aunt's door had startled them both. Her aunt had opened it to reveal two somber-looking men, heavy with the weight of their mission. One of the men, named Tucker, seemed old, his glasses amplifying the purple bags beneath his eyes. The other, Phillipe, was leaner, his athletic frame at odds with the sadness etched into his face. The gun on his hip was a silent reminder of the world that her mother had lived in—and the work that had destroyed her.

With a jerk of her chin, her aunt had invited them in. She'd suggested tea or coffee as if it would soften whatever blow they were about to deliver. There were few instances in Ava's life that stood out as much as that day. And yet, she still remembered the smell of her aunt's attempt at making chocolate chip cookies. The kitchen smelled of burnt sugar and caramelized chocolate—and she didn't have the courage to tell her aunt that the cookies were burnt as she proudly served them on a tray alongside coffee for the men.

"What's this all about?" Her aunt's voice was steady despite the tension that coiled around them like a serpent.

Ava had sat stiffly on her aunt's deep leather couch, her fingers twisting at the hem of her oversized sweatshirt.

She remembered how the leather squeaked as Tucker had sat across from them in her aunt's favorite chair, his mouth set in a tight line. "Perhaps it's better that we speak alone first," he'd said to her aunt.

Her aunt had put an arm around Ava's shoulders. "My niece and I don't have secrets," she'd replied firmly. It was the only time Ava could remember her aunt hugging her.

Tucker had nodded and went on, removing a black baseball cap. "Very well. There's no easy way to say this." He paused, the words seemingly lodged in his throat. Finally, Tucker inhaled a deep breath and let it out slowly. "We've learned from our Russian contacts that Theresa Anderson died while being detained by the FSB."

The words had landed like a punch in Ava's throat, stealing the air from her lungs. The men said more, but the words washed over her as her vision had blurred, her mind scrambling to reject what she'd just heard. For two years, she'd clung to hope—fragile and flickering—that her mother would somehow return, that the woman who had taught her to fight, who taught her to be strong, hadn't vanished forever. This news had shattered that illusion. Her mother was gone. There would be no miraculous homecoming.

In the weeks that followed, Ava had buried herself in the details of her mother's life, trying to understand, trying to make sense of her choices. Choices that had left Ava alone and angry, a void that no answers would fill.

* * *

Now, in the dimly lit cigar bar, Konstantin's voice pulled her abruptly from the spiral of a memory that she'd rather forget.

Konstantin's voice was uncharacteristically soft. "Not a day goes by when I don't think of your mother or wonder what I could've done differently in order to save her."

Ava couldn't stop it—the grief that rose in her throat. She clenched her jaw until her molars ached, but another memory came anyway. Her mother's shampoo—that soft, floral scent as she leaned in for that last hug goodbye. The featherlight kiss on her forehead that was somehow grounding, anchoring her to something solid before disappearing again.

The memory shattered something, and her chest tightened. She wanted to hit something. No, she wanted to destroy. She wanted someone to feel that same pain—the gutting paralysis that made her whole world come crashing down. That girl, the one who had sobbed into a pillow, who'd stared at the ceiling searching for a shred of hope to cling to. But now, standing face to face with Konstantin, the center of it all, the truth pressed in, sharp and undeniable.

Ava's hands slammed the table before she even realized that she'd moved, rattling the crystal glasses. Several people glanced in their direction.

She didn't care.

"I know what you could have done," her voice trembled with rage. "You could have not convinced her to betray her country."

She shook her head in an effort to dislodge the pressure building between her eyes. "Do you have any idea what it was like to grow up wondering if she'd ever come home? To lose her and not even know why?"

Konstantin looked down. "Your mother . . . was a complicated woman. You must know that. She resented the CIA for the years they'd taken away from her. She wanted a way out."

"A way out?" Ava spat, her voice breaking. "She could have resigned. She didn't have to betray everything that she had fought for."

He shook his head and cleared his throat. "It wasn't that simple. At the time, the CIA required a ten-year commitment after the operational training. She felt trapped, and when she had you, her priorities changed. She wanted a fresh start, somewhere far away. She thought"—he hesitated, his voice dropping. "She thought she was doing it for you."

Ava's breath hitched. For her? The thought knotted in her chest with something sharp and bitter. "And yet here I am—sitting across from the man who helped destroy her."

Konstantin flinched but didn't look away. "I didn't kill her," he said quietly. "She refused to give up her colleagues. That was her line, and when she would not cross it, the FSB made sure she paid the price." He paused, eyes glinting beneath the dim light. "I traded everything I had to bring her out—the first time. My name. My freedom. My allegiance. I became theirs so she could walk free."

Ava swallowed hard. "And yet she still died." Her voice came out flat, scraped hollow. "And you're still here."

He exhaled, the whisky trembling slightly in his hand. "Later, they took her again—on German soil, traveling home. By then, she was already marked. I tried to reach her, but Dimitri Abramovich made certain she never left that cell."

The words sliced through her. Torture. Debriefings. Silence. Her stomach turned, and the air between them seemed to hum with the weight of everything unsaid. "How did she end up back in their hands?"

Konstantin's gaze drifted to the amber liquid in his glass. "She told me she was done with the CIA. She wanted to take you, disappear, start over. I believed her. But the SVR intercepted her route home. Abramovich ensured the rest." His tone hardened: resignation layered with something almost noble. "I gave them everything, Ava. It wasn't enough."

Her anger surged, cold and focused. "Then tell me everything. Names. Dates. Whoever was involved."

He nodded, his expression hollowed by guilt and memory. She leaned forward, voice low and lethal. "If you lie to me, or leave out one detail about my mother, I will make sure you regret it."

Konstantin met her stare, unflinching. "You sound just like her," he said softly, almost with reverence.

Ava rose. There was no time to process the grief that pressed against her chest. Not yet. There was still a battle to fight, and Dimitri Abramovich was her target.

# CHAPTER

# 31

THE HUM OF Air Force One's engines vibrated through the floor, a low, steady growl that moved through Ava's legs and into her chest. She sat rigid at the conference room table, her soul divided somewhere between memory and fury, reeling from the revelations of the past twenty-four hours. Finally, the truth had emerged in Konstantin's broken voice: Her mother had not simply disappeared, nor had she died quietly or peacefully. She'd been tortured: killed under duress in an SVR prison under Dimitri Abramovich's orders.

Ava's breath felt ragged in her throat. Her pain was more than grief; it was rage laced with guilt. All those years of unanswered questions she'd thought that perhaps her mother had chosen a different life, one without her in it. But she had been wrong, and Konstantin's deep feelings gave her a link to her mother's past, a way of discovering who she really was and what she had died for. And now the answer to how her mother had died stood in the spotlight: Dimitri Abramovich.

The man they were hunting now.

She forced herself to steady her breathing. She'd barely processed Konstantin's confession about her mother before she'd been thrust into this meeting, and exhaustion buzzed heavily on her already frayed nerves. The conference room was dim, the pink light of early dawn spilling through the oval windows, casting long shadows on the strained faces of the National Security Council, the president, Frank, and Ben. But the shadows did nothing to dim her need for revenge.

"Ava." Frank's jaw tightened as he leveled a cold stare in Ava's direction. "The president just asked you a question."

Her gaze bounced around the conference room table until it locked on Ben. He was watching her with an intensity that sent heat pooling in her belly. His presence tethered her, but it couldn't numb the fury building in her chest. She drew a sharp breath, trying to anchor herself.

"We have confirmation," she said, her voice tight, raw. "Dimitri Abramovich isn't just funding the chaos through Vibrantia. He's moved beyond cyber warfare. He's acquired a cache of Chinese nuclear warheads—ICBM-grade weapons—and intends to sell them to the Liberty Coalition as his proxy army. Their plan is to launch those missiles against the federal government."

The room stilled, the gravity of her words sucking the air from the space. Abramovich was notorious, an unpredictable international actor who had advised the Russian president for decades as well as served in the GRU and FSB. He'd never hidden his distaste for Americans.

Even the American president, a man nearly seventy years old with a white beard and a voice like molasses, a man who had weathered decades of political storms, inhaled sharply. He leaned forward, eyes like embers. "Are you telling me that Abramovich means to hand weapons to the Liberty Coalition—to let Americans fire on their own government?"

"He's been playing a long game for years," Ben interjected. "He's used his wealth, his cyberattacks, and his growing influence to position himself where no one expected. We always knew that he was behind Russia's misinformation campaigns. He's always been more than a disinformation strategist. He's a tactician. And now, he has the firepower to back himself up."

And it's more than that, she wanted to say. He tortured my mother to death, and now he's trying to finish what he started—with the entire West.

The president turned to Frank, his voice cutting through the tension. "I want eyes on those missiles. Satellite feeds, now." His gaze flickered toward the NSA director. "I also want all intercepted comms, anything that tells us about Abramovich's plans and targets. Every asset, every satellite, every resource needs to be focused on this."

The words fell heavy across the room, urgency crackling in the air.

"Sir." Ben leaned forward, his eyes flickering briefly toward Ava before settling on the president. "We need to assume those weapons are already en route. Abramovich won't hesitate to use the Liberty Coalition as their trigger finger. Either way, we're out of time."

Ava straightened, her voice steadier now. "Abramovich isn't afraid to make a statement. If he intends to use them himself, it's to show the world he holds power over the West. If he sells them to the Liberty Coalition, then he's betting on domestic insurrection to carry out his strike for him. That would shift the balance of power in ways we cannot afford."

The president exhaled slowly, his fingers tapping nervously on the table. "And Nathaniel Grey?"

"Grey's a puppet," Ava said. "Abramovich assumed near-total control of Vibrantia. Grey may wear the crown, but Abramovich pulls the strings."

Alan, the national security advisor, cleared his throat and leaned forward, pushing his glasses up the bridge of his nose. "So you're telling us that the Liberty Coalition—an American political group actively opposing the federal government—might soon control nuclear weapons." Ava met Frank's eyes from across the conference room table, trying to elicit silent approval to tell the president that his top advisor and the head of the political party that had gotten him elected could be involved. Frank gave her a soft nod, urging her to go on.

Ava and Ben nodded in unison.

The president's voice was steel. "Then we shut it down. Now. I want Liberty Coalition's top brass, including Grey, on a watchlist before this plane lands. We move on this, now."

Frank rose slowly, the weight of his office heavy on his shoulders. "Let's end this before the first warhead moves."

Ava's pulse pounded as the room snapped into action.

This was it.

The moment where everything she had worked so hard to uncover, every risk she had taken, every disappointment she had encountered, all coalesced into one truth: Her mother had paid the ultimate price, but Ava would be damned if Abramovich got to write the ending.

She met Ben's eyes once more, deep pools where she could simultaneously loose and find herself at the same time. No words were needed. They were already moving because failure was not an option. And Abramovich likely underestimated how many people were coming for him.

# CHAPTER

# 32

Dark winter clouds hovered as Konstantin sat at a café, sipping his coffee, watching people as they walked along the Russian Golden Mile, wondering how many ghosts would follow him home today. He always felt the weight of his past when he came to this part of the city. Here, among the meticulously restored nineteenth-century mansions, memories stalked him like old enemies. And none more persistent than that of Theresa.

In this part of Moscow, her presence was everywhere, memories so real that he could live within them. The nights they'd spent cooking together. The way she moved in his Knightsbridge apartment, barefoot and humming, filling the kitchen with the scent of ginger and honey as she baked pryanki and vatrushka. She'd clung to his grandmother's recipes like lifelines, losing herself in the ritual, trying to bake away the stress of her double life.

He drank in the cold air and tried not to think about Theresa, or the afternoons they'd stolen in his bed, the feel of her body against his, the way she used to look at him as if no other man existed. He thought he'd buried those memories long ago—until the night he had met Theresa's daughter.

Sixteen long years. That's how long he'd spent chasing Dimitri Abramovich.

Before he had met Theresa, the first half of his career had been marked by ruthlessness—spying, sabotage, and state-sanctioned killings across three continents. From Vienna to Tashkent, he had left behind a trail of silent exits and suspect disappearances. He was the SVR's death machine, the assassin they sent when the spy defected, when diplomacy failed. The kind of man who never existed in official files. But when he had met Theresa, everything had changed. He suddenly had something to live for.

Now the small, balding form of Yury Ushakov, his personal secretary at the SVR, emerged in the distance. Slight in build, Yury carried himself with an air of indifference, always impossible to read. Konstantin was thankful for the distraction. He couldn't let the ghosts of his past dictate his thoughts; thinking about Theresa again was too painful, too raw. But it made him more determined than ever to carry through with his mission: Dimitri Abramovich would finally die for what he did to her, and this time he'd have the American government behind him to help carry through with his mission.

Yury had always been sympathetic to that mission. Perhaps that was why Konstantin had trusted Yury with most of his secrets. Yuri was one of the few people who had been with him the day he'd learned that Abramovich had orchestrated Theresa's death. While the man had the personality of a doorknob, his discretion was paramount. And Konstantin had always felt that he was one of the few people that he could trust.

But today, something was different. Yury's face was pale, his jaw clenched. His scarf was impeccable, but his shoulders slouched as though he carried the weight of the world.

Konstantin smirked as Yury approached and flicked his cigarette into the ashtray. "That look on your face—I've seen it before. Tell me, is it my lucky day? Has the FSB finally decided to put me out of my misery?" His eyes darted to the gun Yury always had tucked in beneath his coat.

"My condolences." Yury sat down in the chair across from Konstantin, adjusting his cashmere scarf with meticulous precision. "Not today."

"Damn." Konstantin leaned back in his chair and patted his thick middle. "What does a man have to do to get fired?"

Yury sighed. "Considering you're the SVR's top assassin? I'd say it's a lifetime contract. Unless, of course, you prefer to leave in a coffin."

Konstantin let out a low chuckle, but the sound held no humor. "So, what is it then? Why are you here?"

Yury hesitated. Just for a second. And that hesitation made Konstantin's pulse spike.

"It's about the blood samples," he said finally. "The ones you had me take when we tended to Ms. Anderson after she was injured."

Konstantin's fingers tightened around his coffee cup. A slow, cold unease crept up his spine, "And?"

Yury met his eyes, his voice calm but absolute. "Well, sir . . . congratulations. It's a girl."

# CHAPTER

# 33

AVA OPENED THE door to her Moscow apartment, and Ben walked in without speaking. The silence between them was taut, like a bow sting pulled too tight. She motioned toward the main sitting room wrapped in the glow of twilight. Her apartment wasn't large, but it was perched high above the city with large windows that provided a view of the city's bruised skyline through sheer linen curtains. Outside, the sky deepened to lavender, bathing the Kremlin's domes in golden light. Far below, the wide avenue pulsed and hummed with traffic. Break lights beamed red against snow that had turned to slushy ice.

"I know what you're going to say," Ava said, her voice like steel as she motioned for him to follow her, then she whipped around. "And I'm going to say this slowly so that there can be no mistake about where I stand when it comes to you telling me what to do."

She knew that she was getting too close to Konstantin—that their relationship had blurred past the professional. Knowing what she did about Konstantin and her mother made it impossible for her to continue to be his CIA handler. Yet there was something within her that made walking away unmanageable. She had to know more about her mother's double life. And Konstantin was the key.

Ben wasn't just standing in her way—he was deliberately blocking her at every turn. She knew why. The photograph. He was the only one besides her who had seen it. God help her if it ever made its way back to CIA headquarters. It would ruin her because it revealed that she was running her mother's former SVR handler as her own asset.

She took a deep, deliberate breath to lessen the pressure building within her chest.

"I can't watch you ruin your life and risk your career," Ben said, his voice low and ragged. "I won't."

"You have to stop this." Her eyes flashed. "I am not some damsel in distress."

"No one could accuse you of that . . ." A muscle in his jaw ticked, the hard lines of his face softening to a point. "But Ava, this is madness. You have no idea what Konstantin is collecting on you, not really."

"Do you think you're my protector? That you need to keep me in line?"

"If that's what it takes."

The audacity of him stole her breath. Her hand twitched with the need to slap him. "How dare you," she seethed.

"I'll protect you, Ava." His tone softened, but his face was resolute. "Even if it means protecting you from yourself."

"You—" her words caught, heat pulsing through her veins, winding around her heart.

He had no right. No right to tell her what to do. No right to make her feel this way. Not when they were on the brink of a nuclear war. Her vision burned red, and she lifted her hand to strike him. But he was faster. His fingers caught her wrist in a firm, unyielding grip.

"Get your hands off me," she hissed, though her pulse roared in her ears at his touch, his nearness. "What are you going to do? Kiss me again? And this time you can't lie and say it's 'for cover' because there's no one else here."

And suddenly, they were too close. His body radiated heat, and the flicker within his eyes—a dark, almost primitive flicker—made her pulse skitter wildly. She froze, heat pooling in her belly. She should have stepped back, should have yanked her hand away. Should have remembered who she was.

But she didn't.

His touch wasn't just strong; it was claiming, an anchor in life where she'd been left adrift. Her family had peeled away from her until she learned not to reach back. Yet here Ben was, close enough for her to hear the thrum of his heart, feel the heat of his breath. The pull between them was stronger than her reason, stronger than any sense of self-preservation. She turned away, her breath shaky, the air thick enough between them to drown her.

"I don't need you to protect me," she ground out, yanking herself from his grip and stalking toward the door.

Her hand curled into a tight fist before her fingers fumbled to open the lock. Ben caught her elbow, not hard, just enough to her to face him. There was a near-madness glittering within his hazel eyes that made her want to lean into him, to collapse into the space he was offering. But her more rational side, the disciplined operative, whispered a warning.

"Ava." The way he said her name—hoarse, almost broken—sent a shiver down her spine. "Why didn't you tell me about Nathaniel? What he tried in his apartment?"

Shame flared hot in her chest, mixing with something far more dangerous—desire. She stepped back, her heart fluttering wildly against her ribcage like a wounded bird. "How did you know that?"

His lips twisted, but there was no amusement in it. "You bugged the room. A dozen other agents and I listened while you tried to brush him off."

"What does that matter?" she shot back, trying to feign indifference. She couldn't let him see how exposed she felt, how much it meant that he cared. "It's not like it was the first time I had to reject some dude's advances."

Their gaze locked, and something deep within her caught fire.

"Did he touch you?" His voice low, dark, and God help her, the way he was looking at her made her thighs clench. She inhaled a sharp breath, desire pulsing within her as if it were madness.

"Barely," she murmured.

The rage rolling off him was palpable, a storm breaking just behind his eyes. He closed the distance, his palms braced on either side of her face as she stood with her back against the door. His scent—clean, masculine, laced with something undeniably him—wrapped around her.

His chest rose and fell like he had just run miles, but his voice was barely above a whisper. "You think I don't notice? Every time you look at me?"

Her heart slammed so hard it ached. "I don't know what you're talking about."

"Yes, you do." His hand hovered an inch from her cheek, trembling with restraint. "You're under my skin, Ava. It's driving me insane."

Her throat tightened. She had never seen him like this—unguarded, almost desperate. It was the crack in his armor that she had always been waiting for.

"What do you want?" he asked, his voice tight. His question hung in the air, electric, thick as a storm.

She couldn't move, couldn't speak, but his words shattered whatever restraint she was still holding onto. And for once, she let herself let go of her reason, her need to control.

Her fingers reached up before she could stop herself; she was tracing the soft stubble on his jaw. He leaned into her touch like it was a confession. "You know what I want."

Their noses brushed, and she felt it, deep within her core—an unraveling. And in an instant, his mouth was on hers. Heat. Hunger. A storm breaking loose. Her tongue met his with a craving, a need she hadn't been fully aware of until this moment. Her hands tangled in his hair as his mouth devoured hers, desperate, deep. She kissed him back like it was oxygen, like it was purpose. His hands slipped to her waist, pulling her against the hard lines of his body. He groaned as her body molded to his.

She pressed against him and felt the strength of him through his jeans—dear God, he was hard, solid, unyielding. His lips dipped to her collarbone—caressing, teasing her with his open mouth. She wanted to feel all of him, and for every inch of him to cover her. His lips found her mouth again, stealing her breath and giving her life at the same time.

Her skirt rode up and his fingers found the hem, teasing along bare skin of her thigh. A silent question. She nodded and groaned against his mouth. He made a desperate sound against her lips. He lifted her skirt higher, pressing her back against the door, his body pinning hers. She lifted one leg and wrapped it around his waist. She tasted him more deeply, more wholly as he began to move against her, the strength of him stiffening against her with each rhythmic move.

His name slipped past her lips in a whisper, half-moan, half plea. "Ben."

"What the hell are you doing to me?" he murmured into her collarbone between kisses. His lips found hers again, teasing, tasting, pleading for more.

"If I didn't know better," she murmured against his mouth, breathless. "I might think that you wanted me too."

Ben growled, a low deep murmur through his chest, through her. "Ava." His fingers flexed against her hips, his body a branding iron against hers. "I've wanted you so badly since the day I met you, how can you not know that?"

She squeezed his biceps, her breasts pressing against his muscled chest. His breath was ragged as he inched his mouth away. "You fucking terrify me, Ava. What I would do for you . . . what I would sacrifice."

Her heart raced; the fog of the mission dimmed in hearing those words. His left hand moved through the tangle of her hair and clasped the back of her head. She leaned back, letting her head fall back as he dragged his lips along her jaw, the curve of her throat. He moved to cup her breasts as he showered kisses all over her cheeks and lips. Her fingers gripped his shirt, pulling at the fabric until it slipped over his head. She drank him in—muscle and strength, all of him bare before her.

In one swift motion he grasped both her buttocks and lifted her up. She wrapped her legs around his waist as he carried her toward the conference room table and sat her down gently. He positioned himself in between her legs, his eyes dark with desire. Her eyes raked over the strong lines of his muscled, tanned torso.

"You know this will change everything?" he murmured.

"Promise?" she asked, hands planted on the table behind her, bracing herself for what was about to happen next.

She moved to unclasp her bra, and he looked at her breasts, his restraint fraying. "You're unreal," he muttered. "I swear to God, Ava . . ."

She interlaced her hands tight around his neck and brought him toward her. His lips moved to her nipples and kissed her until she felt them stiffen under his tongue. His fingers skimmed the sensitive flesh between her legs, drawing slow circular movements over her panties that nearly undid her.

The world began to tilt as he continued to taste, and tease one nipple, then the other. His fingers stopped at the hem of her panties in a silent question. She answered him by moving her panties to the side so he could slide his fingers in her, coaxing her open with slow, precise movements. She gasped, her body clenching around the sensation, liquid heat pooling deep inside her.

She wanted him in her and reached for the buckle of his pants, sliding them over his hipbones. The sight of him stole her breath as she used her legs to draw him close. She could feel his heartbeat, furious and uneven like hers as he kissed her again, deeply this time as he filled her. Pleasure ripped through her, wild, desperate. A sharp cry escaped her lips, and he swallowed it with another kiss. She clutched at him, her body aching, needing more. His thumb pressed against her hip, anchoring them together.

"You're going to be my damnation, Ava," he whispered against her mouth. "But I don't care."

"Good," she gasped. "Because I'm not taking no for an answer."

In that moment, there was no mission, no secrets, only them. She felt a violent shudder rip through her, and suddenly there was no mission, no relentless pursuit for answers about her mother. She held on tight to Ben until the world around her narrowed into this single moment, steady and human in a life that had forgotten softness. And for once, she let herself stop running from it.

. . .

Later that night, Ava lay next to Ben in her apartment, allowing the passion she'd felt to settle deep into her bones, into the very core of her being. For a fleeting moment, she'd been free—free from her past, from the relentless need to prove herself to the CIA, from the suffocating weight of the mission, from the shame of being a daughter of a traitor.

With him, the weight of it had all disappeared. It terrified her, the power that he held over her emotions, and the willingness she felt to let it all fade away. He'd made her feel complete, wholly consumed and unable to see beyond their passion, and she feared that now, there was no going back.

She shifted closer, draping a leg over him, letting his warmth chase away the darkness creeping at her mind. Konstantin was her mother's handler. He'd been responsible for her mother's disappearance. Her death. And no matter what he claimed or what lies he spun on how he had tried to save her, she would never forgive him. He and Abramovich were the reason she'd grown up without her mother.

As if sensing her unease, Ben leaned down and pressed a lingering kiss on her temple. "Did you get any answers from Konstantin?"

Her throat tightened. "He admitted it. He was her handler. But there was something else. . . ." The words burned her throat, left her feeling raw. She took a deep, unsteady breath and forced herself to say it. "My mother . . ." A painful sob formed in her throat, and she swallowed hard. She lifted her head from his strong, bare chest and looked up. She felt the burn of tears prickling behind her eyes. "She didn't just disappear. They tortured her. To death."

His arms tightened around her. "Ava."

Her lip trembled as the first tear spilled down her cheek. Ben caught it with his thumb, his touch achingly gentle. "There was nothing Konstantin could do to save her?"

"He tried," she admitted, placing her head back on his chest, her nerves calmed by the gentle rise and fall of his breath, realizing now that she believed Konstantin on this. "The first time the FSB detained her, he got her out. He says he offered himself up in exchange for her freedom. But on another mission to Russia, on her way home to America, the SVR caught up with her on a connecting flight through Germany. They went back on their word. They chose to make an example out of her." She fought back the surge of grief that made her feel too empty, too vulnerable to go on.

Ben brushed the hair off her forehead. "At least he—"

"It wasn't enough." She shot up, her pulse quickening. She gathered the white sheet around her breasts. "She's dead."

Ben sat up, studying her. "I'm sorry."

Ava nodded, refusing to let grief capture her. She looked at Ben, really looked at him. There was an intensity in his eyes, his touch, that drew her in, and she wanted more of what had bloomed between them. But where there was desire, there was also fear. If she let him in, she could lose herself. And there was no room for softness now, not when there was too much on the line.

"My priority is getting through the next few weeks. The rest can wait." Her voice was tight. "Konstantin is the key to Abramovich's operational planning. He's our best lead. If I push hard enough, he'll give me what we need—where the missiles are headed, where they'll be deployed. Because they won't be launched from Russia."

Ben's jaw twitched. "Are we sure about that?" he asked.

Something cold unfurled within her at the look on his face.

She shoved the sheets aside, and flicked on the bedside lamp, scanning the floor for her clothes. "I need to meet with Konstantin. We were interrupted before, but he might have something new. He's our best shot at identifying which targets that Abramovich plans to hit first." She slid off the bed, the fabric whispering across her skin.

Ben's fingers closed around her wrist and she turned around to face him. His face was shadowed, stubble tracing his chin and jaw, his bare chest a landscape of strength and heat that she'd only traced in the dark.

"Not tonight," he said, his grip firm but gentle.

Her pulse thundered. "We don't have time—" she said, although longing filled her blood once more as he stood, bare-chested with muscles that reached all the way to his groin.

She should keep moving. She knew that. But his hands found her waist, steady and sure, and his breath brushed her cheek—warm, teasing, dangerous. God help her, she wanted this. Wanted him with a hunger that stripped away every ounce of discipline she'd ever learned.

"There's nothing you can do until morning," he murmured, his voice low and rough at the edges, threaded with that confident drawl she both hated and craved. "So maybe stop pretending you don't want to stay."

Her pulse kicked. "You're infuriating," she whispered, even as he drew her closer.

"Yeah," he said, a hint of a grin tugging at his mouth. "But I'm right."

She laughed softly, the sound dissolving as he turned her hand over and pressed his lips to the tender skin of her wrist. Heat unfurled through her body, every nerve awake.

"Then let's make a deal," he murmured, eyes meeting hers—equal parts mischief and sincerity. "For one night, we forget the world. No missions. No ghosts. Just us."

She smiled up at him, her heart thumping wildly in her chest. His lips found hers, his kiss was deep, consuming. She had spent her life chasing the truth, hunting ghosts, living in the darkness. But being with Ben had brought her to the surface of something perilously bright.

He paused, his face close enough that she could feel the scrape of his beard on her lips.

"I'm in love with you, Ava."

His words pierced through her doubt, her hesitation and she felt her chin tremble. "You don't. You can't."

He dragged a hand through his hair and looked up. "I do." His gaze didn't waver.

She couldn't believe him. Couldn't believe this. Her mother had walked away when she was little, and she had never known her father. The day she went to live with her adoptive parents, whatever fragile sense of self she'd had was stripped clean. Since then, love had always been something that left, something that turned its back on her. And yet, here was Ben—close enough for her to feel the heat of him, close enough to ruin her.

Emotion clawed at her throat. "You don't know who I am, not really." Yet, even as she said the words, she knew they were a lie.

He already knew the worst—the shadow that her mother's betrayal had cast over her life, the lines that she'd crossed in service to the CIA. And yet still, he stayed. Still, he wanted her.

Ben's hands framed her face. Warm. Steady. Anchoring her like no one ever had. "Nothing could ever change the way I feel about you."

She wanted to tell him that he was wrong, that if he truly understood, he'd run. Yet the inevitability of him pulled her forward, drew her under. She tasted the risk in the space between them and edged closer. If this was dangerous, if this was a mistake, she would make it with her whole body.

Tonight, she would let herself burn.

C H A P T E R

# 34

Ava walked along Mokhovaya Street, a snowy silver mist snapping along her skin. She welcomed the sting. Anything to clear her head before her meeting with Konstantin. Her face still buzzed with joy, the humming of Ben's words threading in her bloodstream. He loved her.

It still seemed unreal. Since as long as she could remember, love was something that had to be striven for, earned. Her aunt's approval was something that she had to work for—measured in chores and grades. But Ben's words felt steadying and destabilizing all at once. She no longer felt that Ben was her protector, but her ally in her mission, a strength that could steady her, that she could tap into. Someone who had chosen her despite the consequences.

The Kremlin's walls loomed beside her, a continent of stone, blocking the wind but not the weight on her chest. Ahead, the Kremlin's guards lingered near the wall, their cigarette lighters flaring in the wind before winking out, briefly illuminating hardened faces. The bells of the Kremlin rang out—a slow, iron heartbeat urging her forward.

Every unanswered question was another second Abramovich moved his pieces into place. She could almost hear ticking, each beat a warning, a reminder of what failure could cost. She needed to find a way to push Konstantin's access closer toward the edge, until she knew exactly where Abramovich planned to direct the missiles and how to stop him before they ever launched.

In her mind, she saw Dimitri Abramovich as clearly as if he were in the room with her. Before she'd left for her assignment in Moscow, she'd studied Abramovich, dissected his movements across continents, charted every business decision, analyzed his need for power, tracked the subtle tells in his body language. But after what he'd done to her mother, she wanted more than intelligence on him; she wanted proximity. She had slipped into the lion's den with Konstantin, with Grey. She'd do it again. Only now, she'd walk in armed not just with steeled nerves, but the intimate knowledge of his weaknesses.

She knew when Abramovich was most likely to drink too much, when his temper flared and when his arrogance led him to overplay his hand. She'd learned who he trusted, who he feared, and most importantly, who he underestimated.

She spotted Konstantin twenty feet ahead, snow threading into his gray hair. Too casual to be anything but deliberate. He'd seen her before she saw him. Of course he had. She came beside him, her pace matching his long strides through the melting snow.

"I'm still trying to wrap my head around why you insist on meeting in the open like this," Konstantin's voice was smooth, an attempt at levity that fell flat. "My club, it is warmer."

"I didn't feel like getting caught by the FSB today," she said in a low voice, her mind already working the angles of how to deepen his access to Abramovich.

Konstantin said nothing as they walked, although she could feel the weight of the unspoken words, the things that she wanted to ask about her mother. But the consequences of not fulfilling her mission first were too great. Questions about her mother would have to wait. She needed to focus on what mattered the most—stopping Dimitri Abramovich.

Finally, Konstantin exhaled, his breath curling within the cold air. "I have something for you."

"What?"

He hesitated, his thick grey brows pulling together. "Abramovich . . . he is not only moving weapons to fringe groups. He has already sold international continental ballistic missiles—Chinese made—to the Liberty Coalition. Their plan is to detonate them at one of America's own nuclear missile silos."

Ava felt a tremor shoot through her veins, her heart. Abramovich's plans weren't just catastrophic, they were diabolical; they could essentially destroy the United States. "It would cripple America's military power," she said, her voice thin. "It would look like a launch from within our own soil."

Konstantin gave a single grave nod. "It would shatter deterrence. And trigger . . . how you say . . . response."

Her fingers were already moving, typing a secure flash message to Frank and Ben:

ABRAMOVICH SELLING ICBMS—TARGETING US SILOS.

"When?" she asked, feeling as though the sidewalk beneath her had disappeared. "And how credible is this intel?"

"My sources do not have a date yet. But it is same network that led us to the Vibrantia warehouse."

She spun to face him, her breath fogging up the air between them. "We're talking about millions of lives. A global war."

He nodded solemnly.

"You need to give me something concrete—targets, launch points, names—" She felt the buildings around her begin to tilt.

A car pulled up beside them. Dark. Bulletproof. The kind of vehicle that swallowed sound, a vehicle from which there was no escape. Her pulse started going like a trip-hammer. She thumbed her watch to alert Ben and her countersurveillance team.

Konstantin looked at the car, then back at her. "I think it's time we take a trip."

"Have you lost your mind?" she asked. "I'm not going anywhere with you."

He raised a brow. "Still don't trust me?"

"Why the hell should I?" Her pulse thundered in her ears. "My mother trusted you, didn't she? And look where that got her."

Konstantin's face flickered—something subtle, but enough that Ava knew that she had hit a nerve.

"You're right," he said quietly. "I haven't been completely honest with you. But only because I have only just discovered the truth myself."

"What truth?" she asked, the world suddenly spinning.

Konstantin took a slow breath, exhaling like a man about to step off a ledge, and met her eyes, steady and unflinching. He looked like he was memorizing her face. "I am your father, Ava."

She stared at him, without words. He handed her two slips of paper, and she took them with trembling hands. The first bore the seal of the American Hospital of Moscow; the second, the European Medical Center. She scanned them quickly, almost frantically—they confirmed the truth that she had spent her life looking for.

Konstantin was her father.

The street, the people in the street, the car—all blurred, receding into darkness. She couldn't feel her hands. Her face. Only his words remained and the ice spreading through her veins.

She had known in the back of her mind that this had been a possibility. Memories she had buried long ago clawed their way to the surface: the father–daughter dance she had missed in the second grade, the time a boy on the school bus called her a bastard, the lies she'd told herself about her father being some American hero. Maybe even a CIA officer like her mother. In all the years since, she'd never imagined something like this. Never.

She whipped around, her pulse racing, nearly exploding.

"You are not my father," she snapped, clenching and unclenching her fists at her sides to ground herself. "You couldn't be." But shame coated her stomach. The idea that she was the product of some illicit affair made her feel dirty, like her identity crumbling before her eyes.

She didn't remember walking toward the car. Or opening the door. Or sitting down.

Later, when the forest blurred past her car window, tall pine trees frosted with snow. She couldn't remember how she'd got inside.

Dimly, she recalled stepping into the vehicle, but what had happened before—had she been drugged? Harmed? Her mind grasped fragments, but nothing made sense. Yet, when she glanced at Konstantin sitting beside her in the back seat of the speeding car, there was no evidence of a struggle. No pain, no bruises. And yet, everything felt . . . off. As if the very foundation of her reality had been pulled out beneath her.

She pressed her fingers against her temples, willing herself to think clearly. She'd fallen into a stunned trance since Konstantin had spoken those impossible words. *I am your father.*

For so many years, she'd imagined what it would have been like to have a father—to have that deep sense of belonging, to have someone who loved her unconditionally and wanted to keep her safe. She'd watched friends bask in that kind of quiet confidence, a security that she'd never known.

Her throat tightened as she turned away from Konstantin. A strange feeling was taking root in her chest—hope, fear, longing, and distrust, expanding with each breath.

"Did you really just say that you were my father?" Her throat was hoarse, barely above a whisper.

Konstantin exhaled slowly, rubbing a hand over his jaw as if he too were grappling with the weight of this revelation. "I know," he said finally, his voice low, tinged with regret. "It came as quite the surprise to me as well."

"But how?" Her pulse drummed painfully within her ears. "When?"

"When I first saw you at the embassy in Moscow, I thought I had seen a ghost. You look so much like Theresa. Then there were small things about you—mannerisms, the way you carry yourself—that reminded me of your mother. And when you told me your age. . . ." He trailed off, his expression unreadable. "I began to suspect. Perhaps . . . even hope."

Ava's stomach twisted. *Hope?* Had she ever truly let herself hope for this? A father? A family? She'd felt like an outsider since her mother disappeared—a burden that her aunt had carried reluctantly. She was far past the stage when she needed a father to help her grow up. She'd buried those desires long ago, turning the ache of abandonment into steel. But now, in the space between her disbelief and the terrible, impossible yearning in her chest, she felt something else: fear. This made her vulnerable, perhaps weakened her in some way.

She clenched her hands into tight fists. "How did you get evidence to prove this?" she asked, her tone colder than she had intended.

Konstantin nodded. "After you were shot, the doctor who treated you collected a DNA sample at my request."

Her chest tightened. "You had me tested without my consent?"

"I had to know," he said simply. "Had I known earlier, I would have never let you grow up without me." His voice was firm, but there was something raw and angry beneath it. "I knew about you, but Theresa told me you were from another relationship. Stupidly, I believed her. I thought it was her way of telling me that she had moved on, that she was truly done with me. But she wrote to me after you were born and told me about you. We maintained our friendship from a distance, but she knew I was still in love with her. She sent me a photo—the one you saw on my phone."

Ava's chest tightened, a sharp pang that cut into her chest. "She never married," she murmured. "At least, not that I'm aware of. Why would she keep me a secret from you?"

Konstantin looked out the window for a long moment before speaking. "Your mother never did anything without a reason. I assume she was trying to protect you. If the SVR and FSB had known about you, they would have used you for leverage against me. She must have known that. Had I known that you were my daughter, especially after learning that your mother had perished, there is no way that I would have let you grow up without either of your parents."

Ava stared back at him; her heart lodged in her throat.

The car banked right, the tires crunching over gravel as they began a long descent down a narrow road. Ava barely registered the towering pines giving way to a sprawling, gothic structure in the distance. A castle, dark and weathered, its turrets topped with Russian onion-shaped domes. Ivy climbed its enormous stone walls, partially obscuring intricate carvings—a gargoyle, a lion, the Virgin

Mary. Icicles clung to the roofline like daggers. The palace loomed large against the winter sky, resolute and foreboding.

Ava's fingers wrapped around the car door handle. "Why are you taking me here?"

"I think it's important that you understand where you come from. Who you are. And who I am." He gestured toward the front of the estate, where a family crest loomed above thick oak doors reinforced with iron studs. "But Ivanov will drive you home whenever you wish." He nodded at the driver. "You are not a prisoner."

Ava swallowed hard. Every operational instinct screamed at her to walk away. Konstantin was SVR. He had spent his life on the opposite side of everything she had fought for. Stepping through those doors would be the equivalent of walking into the lion's den. She could almost feel the hot breath of someone on the back of her neck, hidden eyes watching her. Any other mission and she would have already aborted. But this wasn't just an op; this was personal. She was too close to the truth she'd been chasing her whole life to turn back now. And yet—there was a part of her heart, an exhausted, desperate part, that wanted to believe him, to feel something other than alone.

# CHAPTER

# 35

THE CASTLE SWALLOWED Ava whole. Shadows clung like ghosts, the air steeped in the mingled scents of pine and lemon oil. Overhead, a domed ceiling stretched with mosaic tiles that glimmered with hints of colored light, battle scenes sprawled across them, warriors frozen mid-strike, eyes locked on enemies that she couldn't see.

A butler in a well-tailored coat emerged without a sound, his face unreadable as carved stone as he directed them into a library that seemed to breathe history. Bookshelves rose like sentinels into the vaulted ceiling. A massive fireplace roared at the far wall, its flames casting a restless light over the carved family crest above the mantle—an emblem that looked more like a warning than an a welcome.

"Our family." Konstantin walked beside her, his voice measured but edged with something colder. "It has a long history of walking in the shadows. Even after the fall of the Romanovs, the Gallitzin name still carried power." He glanced at her, then went on, more softly. "I don't expect your trust, Ava. All I want is your time."

She stopped abruptly. "Did my mother know about this place?"

Konstantin's gaze softened and for a moment, he didn't answer. "Yes," he said quietly. "She walked these halls. I never kept secrets from her."

Ava stared at him, her heart kicking against her ribs. She wanted to reject all of this, to call him a liar and walk away. But deep down, in the part of herself she had long kept hidden, something stirred. She had spent her whole life searching for truth. Now, she wasn't sure she was ready to hear it. She should leave. She should run, get back to the CIA's base. But instead, she stood in the firelight, her heart aching with the weight of every lie, every truth, every hope that she'd buried long ago. She needed to know more.

The butler approached Ava and Konstantin as they sat down in two Louis XVI chairs positioned in front of a roaring fire. The smell of woodsmoke and old books was thick in the air, clinging to the past like a whisper. Ava resisted the urge to rub her arms against a sudden chill that had nothing to do with the temperature. Instead, she glanced at her phone as it buzzed in her pocket.

**Ava, send the signal that you're okay or an entire SWAT team and me are coming to get you.**

She exhaled, thumbs flying across the screen. **I'm fine. Stand down.**

"May I offer you anything to drink?" The butler's voice cut into the moment. He set a cup of coffee on the polished table between them before turning to Ava expectantly.

"The same, please," she said. "No cream or sugar."

Konstantin smiled briefly at the small similarity, but Ava refused to acknowledge it. She had spent too long convincing herself that she didn't have a father. That not having one didn't matter. He might have just found out about her existence, but she still had a difficult time not blaming him for the years she'd spent alone, learning to live without knowing who her father was.

"I thought that you were broke," Ava said suddenly, eyes bouncing around the main hall where the interior was a blend of beautiful craftmanship and more modern, ornate pieces.

"Once I suspected you were Theresa's daughter, I had to find a way to orchestrate a meeting."

She took this in. "So, you really are running me, as much as I'm running you."

He smiled warmly in response but said nothing.

The door to the study suddenly flew open.

"Uncle! Uncle!" A small boy, aged three or four, came barreling up to Konstantin, a child-sized soccer ball held under his arm. His wild curls bounced with each step, his eyes alight with excitement.

Konstantin stood smiling, bracing himself against the chair as the boy latched onto his legs. "Mikhail, how is futbol going?"

"I got four goals the last game!"

"Excellent." He leaned down to ruffle the young boy's hair.

"Can we play, Uncle? Oh please!" Mikhail's excitement was boundless as he dropped the ball onto the floor and started kicking it with his tiny feet. Konstantin rose, and they began to pass the ball back and forth, improvising goals with the furniture. The ease of it, the warmth of Konstantin's expression, stirred something within Ava.

A woman entered, her silver-streaked hair in a neat bun at the nape of her neck. "Time to get back to your studies, Mikhail." Gold spectacles slid down the bridge of her nose as she carried an open book.

"But Uncle Konstantin is here!" Mikhail cried, darting past a makeshift goal.

"Well done, Mikhail!" Konstantin clapped the boy on the shoulder. Then his gaze lifted. "Hello, Anya."

"Welcome home, brother."

They exchanged kisses on each cheek before embracing in a hug. It was the sort of scene that would have made Ava envious when she was younger, but today it held a sincerity that made warmth spread within her. Her heart thundered with the question that she hadn't let herself consider until this moment. Could this be the family she had always longed for?

Konstantin hesitated, looking at Ava as if seeking permission. She nodded, though her stomach was clenched.

"Anya, this is my daughter, Ava Anderson."

The word *daughter* settled as a dull weight in her chest, heavy and immovable. So did her birthname, *Anderson.* Even after the adoption papers were signed, Ava had clung to her mother's last name like it was a covenant, a sacred promise. Not out loud. But in the silence, a beacon that her mother might follow if she could somehow return one day and call her home.

Anya's eyes widened, taking this in. "Ava Anderson, as in Theresa Anderson?"

So perhaps it was true. Konstantin had loved her mother. He had brought her here—to his family's home. Konstantin nodded.

"It's very nice to meet you, Ava," Anya said, offering a kind smile. "I hope that you will join us for dinner."

"I'd love that." The words left her lips before she could think better of it. She knew Ben would be worried, that the office would be on edge about her extended absence. But for the first time in years, something pulled at her stronger than duty.

Something unspoken passed between Konstantin and his sister, subtle but not lost on Ava. Anya placed a hand on her son's shoulder. "Come on, Mikhail. Let's give your uncle some time with Ms. Anderson. We'll see you both at dinner." She turned back at the door. "It was nice to meet you, Ava."

"You as well."

As they left, Ava took out her phone and texted Ben: **I'll be late tonight, don't wait up.**

"I can't stay long though," she said as she finished texting, although part of her wanted to stay within this domestic scene longer.

She stood abruptly, moving toward a portrait hanging near the fire. The man in the painting had aristocratic features—a refined, symmetrical face with defined cheekbones and a gaze that held secrets.

"This is Alexander Gallitzin, my uncle," Konstantin said as he stepped beside her. "During World War II, his command of English, Russian, French, and German made him a valuable asset to the Resistance. He used our family's connections to gather information on German troop movements."

Ava moved down the line of portraits, her gaze sharpening.

Konstantin continued, his voice measured. "This is his brother, Sergei—your grandfather's other brother. Sergei worked with the German Foreign Ministry and secretly passed information to an underground network aiding Jewish families and anti-Nazi dissidents."

Konstantin paused, watching her as he went on.

"In 1944, the Resistance intercepted intelligence about a high-ranking Soviet defector traveling through Berlin. British intelligence wanted him eliminated. Alexander volunteered for the mission, not knowing that his own brother, Sergei, had been assigned to oversee the defector's departure."

A muscle in Ava's face twitched.

"The night before, Sergei received an anonymous tip—an assassin was coming. He knew it could only be someone like himself, working in the shadows against the Nazis. And his suspicions were confirmed when he caught a glimpse of a man trailing the defector at a Berlin train station: Alexander. Sergei knew that if he raised the alarm, he would get his brother killed. Instead, he turned and walked away. Alexander eliminated the target. Most believe that Sergei died at the hands of the SS."

Konstantin exhaled, his gaze steady. "The Gallitzin family has always walked in the shadows, Ava. You come from a long line of people who have served their country, their causes, most in secret. The story of Alexander and Sergei is a story that demonstrates that Gallitzin family ties go beyond national loyalty. And I can tell you a dozen more like it."

Ava clenched her jaw. "I don't need a history lesson."

"No," he said. "I wouldn't think you do. But you need to understand that things are rarely black and white. And that your place in this world was decided long before you joined the CIA."

Ava was silent as she processed what he'd said. She wanted to tell him that he was wrong, that she had always carved her own path. But the truth was gnawing her, relentless and inescapable. She had always wanted a family. She hadn't wanted any of this life, the secrets, the half-muttered truths—but it had all been necessary to make a place for herself, to get the answers she sought about her mother.

She thought of the whisper network she could build across Europe—journalists, bankers, outcast diplomats, museum curators with buried loyalties. Perhaps this is what she'd been missing, not just a network, but a name. A name that still meant something to those who respected old blood lines and ancient codes.

"The Gallitzins walk in the shadows," Konstantin said. "You were born into this, Ava. Perhaps now you can use it."

She stiffened. "Our SIGNAL intelligence suggests that Abramovich could be just weeks, possibly days away from enacting his plan in the United States. I don't have time to build a network of spies."

"I've already begun building a network for you," he told her. "I've spoken with people who owe their freedom, their parents' freedom to this family. You can use your family name to unlock the old guard—the diplomats, the merchant families, the royal exiles throughout Europe. With our name, I'm confident you could unite them."

"There's not enough time," she said, her voice achingly desperate. "And to what end?"

"To stop what's coming." He leaned in. "I received intel that the Liberty Coalition has been funded through offshore accounts connected to Dimitri Abramovich's shipping conglomerate. They're planning to sabotage the US missile silos not from the outside, but from within. Domestic fingerprints."

"Civil war." Her voice was barely above a whisper as her blood ran cold. "That's not just terrorism, that's an engineered collapse."

"Exactly. And if the US fractures, NATO fractures and Europe will be next. The old guard have a vested interest in putting a stop to Dimitri Abramovich and his cause."

She turned toward the portraits again. Her ancestors had once fought tyrants under different names, different centuries. Perhaps this was her turn.

"I need access to Abramovich," she said slowly. "Not surveillance. Not second accounts. I need to be in the room with him."

Konstantin nodded. "Then we'll make it happen. But understand this—he's protected by more than money. He has dirt on half of the Kremlin and bodyguards trained by the GRU."

"I don't care." Ava's voice was low. "He ordered the hit on my mother. I'm not walking away from that." She inhaled deeply and let it out slowly. "I'm surprised you can."

"I've been after him for sixteen years, Ava." He reached for the poker and stirred the fire, partly, she thought, to mask his emotions. "Does this mean that you're ready to trust me?"

"It means I'm giving you one shot to prove whose side you're on." Her voice did not waver. "Help me take out Dimitri Abramovich, help me dismantle this plot against the United States. Then we'll talk about trust."

He smiled faintly. "Good. Because I've already begun assembling a team. There's someone I'm meeting with in Moscow. He controls Abramovich's logistic routes. If I can flip him, we can crack his entire network open."

Ava looked at him, really looked at him, and for the first time in her life, she didn't feel so alone. But whether she could truly trust this man was a different question.

# CHAPTER

# 36

After a long dinner of quail, borscht, and something Ava didn't recognize, she sat alone in a beautifully arranged bedroom. Her palm moved over the gold-threaded embroidery of the bedding, the loops and swirls catching beneath her fingertips like they'd been sewn in another century. She inhaled the sweet smell of freshly cut roses that filled a low crystal vase on the bedside table, and remembered the time her adoptive mother had planted flowers in the yard, only for the blooms to die in the salty air.

She had grown up on Disney fairytales—golden castles, true love's kiss, beautifully wrapped endings. But life had taught her better. Mothers left. Fathers vanished. Happily-ever-after belonged to other people. She had built her life on knowing that. And yet, as she sat in this ancient castle, in a bedroom fit for a princess, she felt the pull of something dangerous: the whisper that maybe, just maybe, she deserved a happy ending after all.

The fireplace cracked and popped with a newly lit fire, light shifting along the jewel-toned rug, wrapping the room in gold. She should want to leave, return to the cold, sterile familiarity of the job, the mission that had shaped her adult life. But she couldn't. Not yet.

Wind howled through the corridors, carrying whispers of the past—secrets of an ancient family to which she now belonged. She gazed up at the grand canopy bed draped with velvet, spilling down like a stage curtain, sealing her off from the rest of the world.

The Gallitzin family had exuded warmth, not just within the golden light of chandeliers, but in the way that they spoke to one another—the way they truly listened. Here, she had a family, a history, a place where she wasn't just a shadow slipping between missions. Tonight, she was deeply rooted within something ancient, something whole.

She closed her eyes, letting the moment sink into her bones, taking in the closeness, the comfort, the simple but powerful truth of being safe, and exhaled a breath she hadn't realized she was holding. This could be the home, the safety, that she desperately wanted to believe in. But her more rational side told her it was just a fantasy—a fragile, dangerous fantasy—and she would have to wake up.

During their meal together, Konstantin had been the first to notice the shift in her mood as little Mikhail had recounted a moment from his game, his voice animated, his energy boundless.

"You've been quiet," Konstantin had said, the remains of their meal scattered between them—a nearly empty dish of buttery potatoes, a basket of freshly baked bread. "Is everything okay?"

She'd hesitated. She had always been careful about what she shared, about keeping her aunt and her adoptive family at a safe distance from the darker corners of her world. But this was her father. Her family. At least they had claimed to be.

Konstantin had set his fork down and leaned in. "Whatever it is, you no longer have to carry it alone."

Ava had swallowed past the tightness in her throat. "I just—" She had had dreams similar to what she had experienced that night: a large family, laughter and chaos. She could still smell the homemade borscht they had had at dinner, the fragrant smell wrapping around her like an embrace from her mother.

Little Mikhail, who had not sat still the entire dinner, got up and wrapped his arms around her shoulders from behind. "We've got you, auntie."

A loud bang at the front door jolted Ava abruptly from the warm memory. She moved toward the window, her breath fogging the glass as she peered outside. A dark line of SUVs idled beneath the starlit sky, breathing clouds of heated breath. A cold wave of recognition washed over her. The same convoy Frank used. Or had she been wrong to believe in Konstantin, and this was the FSB to collect her?

A second knock, louder this time, followed by hurried footsteps. And then—

"Ava, Ava, it's me. Open the door."

Her heart rose in her throat. *Ben.*

"Ava," his voice was urgent, muffled by the thick wood. "Let me in, please." A pause. Then, lower, almost dryly, "Konstantin is looking at me like he wants to stab me."

She moved toward the door and yanked it open. Konstantin stood beside Ben, his jaw tight, his stance unreadable. Ben cast him a sidelong glance, something between irritation and amusement flickering within his green eyes.

"A little too late to play protective father, don't you think?" she asked Konstantin.

Konstantin stared, momentarily at a loss.

Ava exhaled sharply. "Thanks, Konstantin. I'll take it from here." She closed the door softly before turning to Ben.

Ben stood there, his hands shoved into his pockets, his gaze searching hers.

"Are you going to tell me why you're here?" she demanded.

He didn't answer right away. Instead, he studied her, his expression unreadable, the tension in his shoulders unmistakable. "I had to see you," he said finally. "To make sure that you were okay."

"You shouldn't have come," she said weakly. She wanted to tell him everything—how much she had craved this feeling that she belonged, that there was a family who could love her rather than see her as a burden. But she knew it was too soon. She needed to be cautious, rational, all the things the CIA had taught her to be.

The silence stretched between them, her chest continuing to expand at the sight of him.

His hair dripped with rain, and his clear green eyes were narrowed in worry. "You know how this works. The SVR—"

"I know exactly how it works," she cut in, her voice sharp. "But you coming here like this, do you have any idea what you're risking?"

"Do you?" His voice was rough-edged, and his eyes burned with something she couldn't quite name. "Because the CIA . . . Frank . . . they don't think that you're being honest with them. They think you're protecting Konstantin." He took a step closer, taking both of her hands. "They think you're a Russian spy, Ava."

The accusation slammed into her like a physical blow. Ava felt something inside her crack. They suspected what she had most feared—that she had betrayed the CIA and her country, just like her mother.

His throat bobbed. "I know that I said before that I didn't care what you had done. But I think now I must know for your safety as well as mine—are you?"

"A spy for the Russians—are you seriously asking me that?"

Ben stood very still, his gaze locked on hers. "You're not denying it?"

She let out a shaky breath. "You think I'm a traitor?"

"I don't want to think that."

She let out a hollow laugh, shaking her head. "Yet you do."

"Ava . . ." He reached for her, but she stepped back.

"And what if I were?" She began to pace. Her heart was pounding, nearly exploding from the significance of the last twenty-four hours. Everything had changed. She had a father, a family, a castle for God's sakes—it all began to descend upon her at once, and instead of pushing it down as she always did, she let it rise in her. Something about being with Ben made it impossible for her to keep the truth from him. "Of course, I can see why you would think that."

"Don't put words into my mouth."

"You have no idea what the last twenty-four hours have been for me," she said, her voice breaking.

"What's wrong?" he asked.

She looked up and saw something fierce, something protective in the tight line of his full mouth. "What did the bastard do?" he gritted out.

"Nothing," she choked on a fresh sob that she hadn't realized she'd been holding. "Konstantin . . . he's my father, Ben." She let out a long breath. "Konstantin is my father," she repeated, still having a difficult time reconciling herself to the truth.

Silence, but when she looked into Ben's eyes, she saw regret there, flaming.

"I spent my childhood alone, abandoned. And when my mother died . . . well, I was my aunt's responsibility, but she wanted nothing to do with me . . . bouncing around until I went into the foster system and was adopted." She felt the burn of her tears.

"When I was little"—her voice shook—"especially after my mother died, I used to dream about what it would be like to have a father come charging back into my life and claim me. Like any young girl, I wanted to pretend that I was a princess. And here I am." Her eyes moved around the room before settling on Ben. "Stupidly, I want to believe that it's real."

Ben's jaw clenched. "And what if it isn't?"

She let out a shaky breath, her vision blurring. "Then I lose everything, all over again."

Something in him stilled. "How long has he known? How long have you known?"

"Apparently the doctor who treated me at the safe house took a blood sample to do a DNA test." Her words sounded hollow.

Ben shifted, shook his head as if to clear it. He looked at her. "Christ, Ava, I wasn't expecting this."

Ava shook her head and wiped at her eyes. "Me either."

Her breath hitched, and suddenly Ben was there. Not with words, or questions. Just him. He wrapped his arms around her, strong and steady, pulling her against his chest. And she broke. The weight of everything, of doubt, of wanting desperately to belong—came crashing down, and she let herself fall into him. She buried her face into his shoulder and let the emotions spill out. He held her tightly as if to protect her from the revelation, and what it meant.

"I feel responsible," he whispered into the top of her head. "I should have found a way to have had you treated by the American Embassy by our doctors."

"Don't apologize." She sniffed and looked up, wiping at the tears that had dampened his shirt. "Do you know how long I've waited to find out who my father is?" she asked.

He looked at her, and the silence grew heavy. The rain outside began to thump quietly to the sound of her tired heart. In this moment she was tired of being strong, tired of playing the resolute spy.

"But I still don't know how to process this," she whispered into his shirt, unable to meet his face. "It's like . . . I've been drowning my whole life, and now—suddenly, there's land."

He brought her hand to his lips and kissed her fingers. "You're torn between two worlds now. You don't need me to tell you that you have a decision to make."

# CHAPTER

# 37

THE RAIN FELL steadily as Ava told Ben more about the day that she'd realized that her mother was never coming home, and how her mother's absence had followed her around like a shadow ever since. Outside, the wind moved in loud gusts, driving hard against the tall iron gates that guarded the castle grounds and enormous pine trees. She wasn't sure what she would face once she told Frank and the CIA about her newfound discovery about Konstantin. But Ben would stand beside her, and for now, that felt like enough.

After hours of talking and making love, Ava had fallen asleep, the piney rich smell of the room enveloping her like a cocoon, feeling something she hadn't felt in years—a fragile kind of peace. She awoke late the next morning to the hum of staff arranging breakfast in the main dining hall below. Ben had risen at dawn and kissed her before going downstairs for coffee. The room had grown warm from the lingering heat of their bodies, and Ava freed herself from the sheets. She dressed quickly, brushed her teeth, and pulled her hair into a loose ponytail before making her way downstairs. Partway down the stairs, she heard Ben speak.

"How do you plan to meet with Abramovich?" Ben's voice was sharp, protective.

Ava froze mid-step on the marble staircase, waiting within the shadows of the stairwell to hear the full context of their conversation.

Konstantin cleared his throat. "That was before—"

"Before what?" Ben demanded.

"Before my daughter wanted to meet him."

Ava's nerves fluttered. The words hung in the air, thick and heavy. *Daughter.* It stirred something fragile and unsteady inside her, and for a moment she was a child again, standing on stage at her first spelling bee, her mother's proud cheers ringing through the school gymnasium. The memory tightened around her chest. It had been years, decades, since anyone had spoken about her with pride.

"I will not place her in harm's way the moment I find her," Konstantin continued. "I intend to protect her as best as I can. If she needs information from Abramovich, I will retrieve it myself."

"So, you lied to her."

"Not lied, exactly," Konstantin said. "I prefer to say indulged."

A beat of silence. Then Ben spoke, his tone colder. "Can I give you a piece of fathering advice?"

"I didn't know you were a father."

Ben ignored the comment and leaned forward, his voice low and edged with warning. "I know Ava. Never lie to her again. Because if you do, you'll have both of us to deal with. And I'm not as forgiving as she is."

Ava smiled slightly at this. It made her more confident in her decision to let Ben in, to trust him more than she had trusted anyone before.

She stepped into view. "I don't appreciate being discussed like a child," she said coolly.

Both men looked toward her. Ben had the shadow of a beard that dusted his sharp jawline, and his eyes were lightly rimmed from a sleepless night. He wore the same white Oxford shirt as the night before, the top two buttons undone, showing a hint of chest hair. Konstantin was wearing a black sweater and matching trousers with white tennis shoes.

She crossed the room and sat down at the breakfast table, ignoring the way Konstantin studied her, as if searching for more signs of her mother, or perhaps himself. She poured herself a cup of coffee, deliberately adding two sugars in an act of quiet defiance. Konstantin still had a lot to prove—a DNA sample didn't prove that he had what it took to be a father. Not that she truly knew what a father should be.

"What exactly is the plan here?" she asked flatly.

Konstantin leaned back, his fingers steepled. "What do you expect to gain from this meeting with Abramovich? It's not like he's going to just hand over his operational plans. And I don't expect that you'll be able to convince him that he should reconsider his stance on the United States."

She lifted the coffee cup to her lips, meeting his gaze over the rim. "I don't plan to ask him anything. I plan to make him trust me. To draw him further into my web." She set the coffee cup down, her eyes flashing. "And when the time is right, I will strike."

"What makes you think that you can gain his trust?" Ben asked.

"He still leads Liberty Coalition," she said. The wheels in her mind turning, each piece of the plan slotting into place. "And Abramovich needs him. Needs his movement to fracture American influence from within."

"He sold his soul to Abramovich months ago." Ben's jaw tensed, hatred for Grey burning within him, deeper than Ava realized. "He's not going to suddenly grow a conscience."

"He doesn't have to. I just need him to think that I've grown disillusioned with the Agency. That I want to help his cause."

"This is a bad idea," Ben muttered, crossing his arms. "You don't have to do this."

Ava shot him a look. "We both know that Grey won't just talk to anyone.

Konstantin crossed to the window with a cigarette that he had yet to light, and he exhaled sharply. "He's right." He turned to Ava. "These men don't trust easily, and they don't forgive betrayal. If he suspects—"

"He won't," she interrupted, but softer this time. "I've studied him. He thrives on control, on being the smartest man in the room. I'll feed that. I'll feed him, and then, when the time is right . . ."

Neither man looked reassured as the butler entered and set down a silver tray with tea, rye bread, butter, and salami. A flicker of something unspoken passed between Konstantin and Ben. Ava knew they were right. But it didn't change what had to be done, what she had to risk.

"What's the end game with Abramovich?" Ben asked. "Assassination? Extraction? Arrest?"

"I obviously want to put a stop to this op he's planning targeting US missile silos." Ava's voice was ice. "But I don't want Abramovich arrested. I want him ruined. Publicly. Financially. Personally. I want him to watch everything he loves taken away—and I want him to know it was me who did it."

"I agree. Taking Abramovich out isn't enough," Ben said, casually tearing off a piece of bread and buttering it. "A little poison in his tea?" He gave a crooked half-smile. "Too civilized. I'd rather watch him realize he's losing."

"I want to destroy him," Ava said. "I want to strip away every illusion of power he's ever held. He must suffer—suffer the way my mother did."

Konstantin watched her carefully, a line forming between his thick grey brows. "You want justice." A pause as he exhaled smoke. "But revenge . . . revenge takes patience. It takes time to lay out such plans."

*Time.* The word lodged like a stone in her chest. She bit her bottom lip as realization descended upon her. The truth was that she didn't have the time or the resources to inflict the kind of pain she desperately wanted.

"You're right," she conceded, feeling as if the air deflated from her lungs. "I don't have years."

Amusement danced within Konstantin's gray eyes. "Ah, but I did."

"How?" Ben asked. "Abramovich's protected on every front—military, political, digital. And he's paranoid as hell."

Konstantin winked at Ava before returning to look at Ben. "It has been difficult, but not without pleasure. Working for the SVR, I've been able to adopt many identities over the years to collect the intelligence I need about Abramovich's life and business dealings. Slowly. Patiently. Every fake identity, every false friendship—it's been leading to this. I know his blind spots. I know where it will hurt him most."

Ava studied Konstantin—this man who was an SVR agent, her source, and now, unsettlingly, her father. She didn't trust him, but she believed in his hate. And for now, it was enough to be united in that common goal.

"We start by leaking intel," Konstantin began. "Hints that Western agencies are preparing sanctions on Abramovich's offshore accounts. That'll panic him. Make him shift his assets into crypto, gold—things we can trace."

"Yes," Ava interjected. "We set up the false accounts where he can transfer his money, but we control it. All of it. The transaction flows, the exit routes."

"Precisely," Konstantin said, turning toward Ben. "Is that something your people at Langley could pull off?"

Ben nodded. "If it gets greenlighted, yes. It'll need to go through cyber, counterintel, and a couple of legal loops, but it's doable."

Konstantin glanced back at Ava. "And about Nathaniel Grey… if we can get him back in control of Vibrantia—"

"We can expose the monster behind the curtain." Ava's tone was sharper now that a strategy was beginning to form.

"I have the footage, the data, the chat logs," Konstantin said. "All the evidence we need to peel Abramovich apart, bit by bit. We just need the reach."

*Vibrantia*—even the name was bitter in Ava's mouth. A breeding ground for the Liberty Coalition's radicalization, conspiracy, and algorithmic control. She'd watched as friends fell under its spell, her nation fracturing over the lies it amplified. Now, she would turn that same digital war machine against Abramovich.

"If you're serious about this," Ben said, his tone low but steady as he turned to her, "then we do it together." He leaned back, that hint of a smile tugging at his mouth. "You'll have eyes on you—mine included—trackers, surveillance, the whole nine yards. The

Agency's best tech watching your every move with Nathaniel Grey." He paused, the smile fading just enough to show he meant it. "You step into that fire; you're not doing it alone."

She hesitated, her fingers curling around her coffee cup as if anchoring herself. This is the part she hated most. Being managed. Being watched. She was used to operating in the shadows, but now she felt as though a spotlight had been directed onto her every move.

Meanwhile Konstantin remained silent, unreadable, as the staff cleared away the remnants of their breakfast, their movements practiced, efficient—background noise for the storm that was brewing. His silence was unnerving, like a wolf ready to pounce.

Konstantin snuffed out his cigarette and leaned forward.

"Then it begins," he said. "If it's redemption that you seek, Ava"—his voice was soft, almost gentle—"then that is what I will give you."

# CHAPTER 38

NATHANIEL GREY'S APARTMENT towered above the Moskva River, its floor-to-ceiling windows framing the dark waters below, where intermittent ice cracked and shifted in slow, deliberate movements. Ava stood at the window transfixed, mesmerized by the Moscow city lights reflecting off the black current like crushed gold. Grey's apartment in Moscow was what one would expect from a man who dealt in power—gleaming floors, vaulted ceilings, and dark leather furniture worn in a way that only expensive things were. The faint roar of traffic rumbled in the distance, and the smell of sandalwood and bergamot softened the smell of fresh paint.

Grey exhaled sharply, swirling amber liquid in his glass, a liquor that was likely older than him. "I admit, I didn't expect to hear from you again, not after I told you that I had sold everything to Abramovich." He hesitated before taking a long drink and setting down the crystal on the polished table. "You seemed to have lost interest in me."

She placed a hand on her chest, feigning offense as she leaned back in a dark leather armchair. She stared at the glass of white Burgundy sitting on a marble coaster that she hadn't touched yet.

"Do I really seem that shallow to you?" she asked.

"Not at all," he said, his voice slightly raised. "But you don't strike me as the type to entertain failure. Perhaps you think I'm weak for letting Dimitri Abramovich walk away with everything."

She studied him for a beat. "I don't think you're weak, Nathaniel." Of course, everything about Grey said that he was a man who needed the constant stroking that men with fragile egos required. It was what made him the perfect candidate for a recruitment operation—she could use his weakness, his constant need for validation.

"But I do think you should have come to me before selling your company to Russia," she said.

He let out a dry chuckle that made her nerves fizzle. "And why would I have done that? What could you have possibly done?"

Ava's lips curled slightly. "I'm an American diplomat. I hope you don't think the government is entirely useless."

Nathaniel scoffed. "No, of course not."

"Then it might surprise you to know that I have the ability to buy back the shares of Vibrantia that Abramovich purchased."

His eyes narrowed. "Since when does the American government bail out businessmen?"

"Since it serves our best interests." What she couldn't say, what she wouldn't, was that it wasn't the State Department that pulled those strings. The CIA had been buying silence, loyalty, and strategic leverage in Russia for decades.

"We can't afford to have our digital infrastructure compromised by foreign interests," she continued. "Social media is more than a business. It's a weapon."

Grey's fingers tightened around his glass, and a muscle jumped in his jaw. "That would have been useful information weeks ago."

Ava's gaze flickered toward the stacked boxes in the family room. Half of his furniture was gone, and his apartment walls had been repainted in a neutral cream. He was preparing to leave Russia, severing ties to a life that he no longer had control over. But she was here to hand him a way back in.

"What if I told you that I could help you buy back what you've lost?" she asked softly.

Grey's head snapped up, his eyes sharpening with curiosity. "Who says I'd want you to do that?"

"Because I've paid attention, and I can tell that you're someone who doesn't like to lose either."

His lips twitched. "No, I don't. But . . . what's your angle?"

"The US government would wire the funds," she said, careful to keep her tone even. "But there would be conditions," she added hastily. "First, you buy back your portion of Vibrantia. Second, you make me your business partner. I would own a significant share."

Grey leaned back, eyes gleaming with amusement. "Can't say that there's much of a downside to seeing you more often."

Ava's stomach clenched. But she ignored the feeling his comment evoked and smiled. This was about infiltration, disguise. The perfect cover to get close to Abramovich.

"I haven't told you the third condition." She paused for effect and added, "I want you to help me gain Dimitri Abramovich's trust."

Nathaniel tilted his head. "Why the sudden interest in Abramovich?"

Ava hesitated, her mind running through her next words. If she could maneuver Grey into being a willing source, she might be able to pry open the vault around Abramovich's plans, his targets. Perhaps Grey could be the key to unlocking the targeting data the CIA required—coordinates, timelines, launch protocols—the kind of intel that could stop what was coming before the United States became a wasteland.

She could hear Frank's voice in her mind: *No targeting data means no preventative measures. No way to protect the American people.*

Sources like Nathaniel Grey were always a gamble, especially when his motivations shifted like smoke, and she had seen men like Grey sell secrets to the highest bidder. She would have to rely on his love for the American dream, his claim to want to defend American freedoms. But Ava knew how deeply the Russians had manipulated him. And the question remained where his true loyalties lay.

Her fingers curled subtly around the edge of her chair, grounding herself against what she was about to reveal. Grey's patriotism wasn't enough. But if she could link his power and his wealth to the success of her mission—that would bend his will toward hers. If she played this right, she could save thousands of lives.

"We have reason to believe that he could be involved in planning a terrorist attack on the United States," she said evenly, but saying it out loud made her pulse race. "The details are still unclear."

Nathaniel's expression darkened. He sat down his glass with a deliberate clink. "I can clarify that for you right now."

Ava stilled. "Go on."

"Abramovich has devised a plan to target US ballistic silos." His voice dropped. "He wants to dismantle America's military power from the inside out."

Ava's heartbeat pounded hard enough to hurt. Finally—proof that Konstantin's intel was legitimate. She had to reach Frank immediately. Every missile site would need to be locked down.

"And you didn't think to alert Washington sooner?" she demanded.

"I didn't understand Abramovich's full plan until recently."

"And where exactly did this come from?" Ava steadied her voice even as adrenaline surged through her veins. One wrong move here could cost American lives.

Grey smiled. "I didn't become a billionaire by burying my head in the ground. My employees keep me informed. Even the janitors, the maids, the people in the background you never think to see. I make it my business to know everything about the people I work with."

He studied her for a moment, his gaze suddenly razor-sharp. "Which brings me to something I've been wondering about for some time now."

Ava swallowed. "What's that?"

He leaned forward. "Are you in the CIA?"

Silence stretched between them, and Ava felt her heart ram against her ribs. Ava held his gaze, measuring his words. She had been asked the question before, but not like this. Not with this much certainty. She took a sip of her wine. She knew the best lies were built on the truth. And she never let the truth slip beyond her control. She let the knowledge that a dozen of Frank's best protective detail were in the apartment below wash over her, calming the flutter inside her ribcage. She inhaled deeply and began to tell Nathaniel Grey her story, and what role she hoped that he would play.

At least part of it.

# CHAPTER

# 39

KONSTANTIN STRODE BETWEEN the massive Corinthian columns of the Bolshoi Theatre, the icy Moscow air curling around him. Konstantin strode between the massive Corinthian columns of the Bolshoi Theatre, the icy Moscow air curling around him. He had played many roles in his SVR career— diplomat, criminal, businessman— masks he could slip on and off with practiced ease. Today, he wore the mask of an executive from Dassault Aviation, along with a disguise so precise, a different jawline, hair darkened, posture slouched, that it erased his identity.

But he had never played the role of father, protector. And the role he played tonight would be his most challenging performance yet. Not only because Dimitri Abramovich, the man who'd ruined so many lives, sat across the box from him, but because for the first time since Theresa, he cared what someone thought of him. *Ava.*

Since meeting her, something had changed. A primal, unfamiliar instinct had taken over, a desire to be seen not just as a spy or shadow but as something good, a father worthy of her trust. Although the thought of disappointing her as a father terrified him more than the possibility of Abramovich seeing through his deception.

He moved through the opulent halls of the Bolshoi, past the gold-framed mirrors that had once reflected a younger man's ambition. He'd come here as a teenager with his grandmother, thrilled by the champagne bubbles on his tongue, the hauntingly beautiful voices that had stilled the night. He peered overhead at the scenes of classical mythology, depictions that had once stirred curiosity and intrigue. Once, the arts had meant something to him. But after years of wielding deals and recruiting spies beneath the gilded dome, now it was just another stage. Perhaps that's what a career of espionage did, stripped away the curiosity that made you hungry for each day and the beauty that came with art.

Now, the theater was just a place for masks and deception.

Inside, chandeliers blazed like frozen constellations, where Russia's elite gathered like kings. Tchaikovsky's symphony swelled, unfurling in an arc of passionate melodies that told of triumph and heartbreak. And for a moment, Konstantin let the music settle over him, changing shape of who he was. The knowledge that he was a father, that Theresa had given him a child, wrapped around his ribs like an embrace. Ava was the tether that he hadn't asked for, pulling him toward a life he had once forfeited, binding him to what he thought he'd lost long ago.

He took his seat in the Kremlin's box beside Ben, glancing down at the rows of oligarchs, ministers, and dealmakers. Among them sat the man he'd come to destroy.

*Dimitri Abramovich.* Salt-and-pepper beard, custom-tailored tuxedo, and a face that wore indulgence like armor. The glint of diamonds on his Patek Phillipe watch glinted under the low light and cufflinks was matched only by the smug amusement in his eyes. Every detail of his appearance was meticulously curated, a man who spent his entire life ensuring that he looked every bit the man with all the power. But those who wielded power were afraid to lose it—that was Abramovich's primary weakness. And Abramovich was a man who'd felt he was immune to consequence.

*Not for long,* Konstantin muttered to himself, shooting a knowing glance at Ben, who sat next to him on the velvet seats of the Kremlin's coveted box.

The curtain rose and a hush fell over the crowd of old-money aristocrats and Russian businessmen.

Across the box, Abramovich watched the ballet with a faint, detached amusement, savoring the turmoil onstage as if it were his own creation. Konstantin watched Abramovich, not the performance—tracking every subtle shift in posture, every whisper to his companions. He studied the man's circle: his confidants, his flatterers, his enforcers. Every glance, every gesture was cataloged, intel for later.

When the curtain dropped for intermission, Konstantin leaned forward, phone in hand, and let his voice carry over the velvet hush of the theater.

"How can the US claim to champion democracy?" he asked as he scrolled through a news article and turned toward Ben, his voice edged with the right amount of bitterness. "When they overthrow governments the moment it's convenient or it does not serve US interests? Iraq, Libya, Syria—they install their puppets, pretend it's liberation. And now they condemn Russia for doing the same?" It was bait. A well-placed barb designed to draw in a particular kind of predator.

Abramovich looked up from his phone, studying him now. "The United States doesn't want partners," he said, his voice like gravel laced with vodka. "They want subordinates. Russia will never kneel, nor should any country with dignity."

"With all due respect, sir," Konstantin said, letting his gaze linger a beat too long, just enough to suggest that he wasn't a man to be dismissed, "not all of us have the luxury of standing apart. Some of us are forced to do business with them."

Abramovich stood and reached Konstantin in four swift strides. He extended his hand. "I don't believe we've met."

"No," Konstantin said, taking his hand and shaking it firmly. "Nicolas Verdin."

Like Konstantin, Dimitri Abramovich was from the old Soviet guard that had made his way in modern Russia with unspoken threats, power clinging to him like a well-made suit. Except his path had never directly intercepted Konstantin's.

"I haven't seen you in our box before," Abramovich said, his voice slicing through every other conversation around them.

"I'm only in town for a night. Maybe two. I leave for London in the morning."

Abramovich's eyes narrowed. "Don't tell me that you're going in for the arms fair?"

Konstantin nodded slowly. Let Abramovich connect the dots himself. Let the bait dangle just enough to be tempting.

"The largest arms expo in the world," Abramovich mused with a sort of lethal quality acquired from years spent in the shadows. "You must be someone of consequence."

"I run Dassault Aviation," Konstantin said.

The trap was laid, and the lie was elegant, traceable, and believable. Dassault Aviation had agreed to backstop Konstantin's cover story—anything to get to the head of the Russian government.

Abramovich's lips parted slightly, his expression shifting. His neatly trimmed beard did little to hide a menacing smile. "Second only to Lockheed Martin."

Konstantin exhaled sharply. "Don't remind me."

Abramovich chuckled. "I heard they made you an offer last year."

Konstantin let out a dry laugh. "I've been bullied by the United States for years. I haven't bent the knee yet."

Abramovich's smirk lingered, but his eyes remained sharp. "No man, no country is perfect. But America believes it is untouchable."

Konstantin exhaled slowly, settling deeper into his seat. A game had begun, and he intended to win. "That is their mistake," he said in a calm voice, but something darker stirred within him.

It began years ago, in the dim light of the Paris metro station, when a trembling informant had pressed a bloodstained envelope in his hand. Inside, grainy photographs and the truth that had hollowed him from the inside out. Abramovich had ordered the hit on Theresa, the only woman Konstantin would ever love. Her smile, her voice, her very existence was erased because she had stood in the way of Abramovich's plans. That day Konstantin had buried the memory like acid, knowing that the moment he let it rise there would be no turning back.

Now seated beside him was the man who had ended the life of the woman he loved, and he let the rage rise, let it wash over him like a baptismal promise.

He would accept Abramovich's invitation when it came, because it would come. He would enter his inner circle, feign admiration, parrot his beliefs. And while Abramovich basked in the glow of his ego being stroked, then Konstantin would peel back the layers: the shell companies, the laundering routes, the names of his fixers and financiers. He would dine at Abramovich's tables, laugh at all his jokes, toast all his victories. All the while cataloguing his weaknesses, his doubts—all his vulnerabilities that could be used against him.

And when the time was right, he'd become the very force that unraveled Abramovich, with patience, precision. His vengeance on Theresa's killer would be slow and exquisite, served cold beneath the crystal chandeliers of Moscow's elite.

# CHAPTER

# 40

Ava walked into the meeting with the CIA Security feeling as though she were wading through quicksand. The air inside the outer vault was still, but she could feel the weight of the situation pressing down on her chest. Every breath felt heavier, every thought dragged her deeper into the reality she'd been trying to outrun.

Nathaniel Grey had made her. The words still rang in her head, sharp as a knife's edge. *Are you really CIA?* His voice was too knowing, too casual. The moment he'd asked, the ground beneath her had shifted. It didn't matter that she had denied it. The damage was done. Frank had overheard everything, thanks to the listening device that Ava had planted in Nathaniel's apartment herself. The irony made her stomach tighten. She'd been undone by her own surveillance. She'd laugh if the weight of it wasn't so damn irritating.

With a heavy click and a mechanical thump, the vault door hissed open. Cold air brushed past her, skimming across her skin as if the room itself were sizing her up. Inside, two figures sat behind a long conference table, etched dark in the fading light—one man, one woman, both clad in crisp black suits, the unspoken uniform of the Agency's security staff. Fresh from Langley, flown in just for her.

A bead of sweat slid down her spine, making her white button-down cling uncomfortably to her skin. The last time she'd sat across from CIA Security, she'd felt the same intrusive scrutiny, the same tightrope walk between self-preservation and honesty. They would twist her words. They'd take what she said and reshape it until she wanted to contradict herself. Then they'd pull the thread until she unraveled. The Farm had trained her for interrogations like this.

It didn't make them any easier.

The man spoke first, his voice smooth but edged with calculation. He wore a slim black tie, his dark hair slicked back with the same precision of a man who never left anything undone.

"Ava," he said, gesturing toward the chair opposite them. "Please, sit. I hope the fact that we've called you in here hasn't alarmed you."

Ava pulled back the chair, the metal legs scraping against the floor. She let a smirk ghost across her lips, even as unease curled low in her stomach.

"Not at all," she said lightly. "I love a good chat with CIA Security. Do I have the pleasure of being hooked up to the polygraph today?"

The woman across the table, her blond hair an unflattering shade from years of drugstore dye, sniffed, unimpressed with Ava's sarcasm.

Ava felt the shudder roll down her spine. This one was playing the bad cop—and was the kind of woman who followed the letter of the law and enjoyed making others suffer for stepping out of line.

"There will be no polygraphs unless we deem it necessary," the man replied smoothly.

Ava didn't allow herself to exhale. She knew they didn't need a machine to catch a lie. They would baseline her first, then start to prod and see what topics made her squirm.

"The first thing we'd like to discuss," the woman said, sliding a grainy surveillance photograph across the table, "is your relationship with Konstantin."

Ava kept her expression perfectly still, but her pulse thumped hard between her eyes. "I believe you already know that he's my source," she said evenly. "I've reported him in several cables to headquarters."

"I'm not sure that you understand the question." The woman leaned forward, hands clasped in front of her, her eyes unblinking.

"What is the nature of your relationship?" Does it extend beyond the normal handler-asset dynamic?"

Ava's breath caught, but she forced her shoulders to stay loose. *They think I slept with him.* She could feel the accusation hanging in the air, the way they were waiting for her to falter, eventually break under the scrutiny.

"I hope you're not implying that I have a romantic relationship with Konstantin," she said, her voice sharp despite the knob of uneasiness tightening within her stomach. "Because I can assure you—"

She stopped herself. Nausea curled in her stomach. *Don't get defensive. Don't give them anything to work with.*

"You've achieved the highest penetration of the SVR in two decades, so naturally we're concerned," the man said.

"And why, exactly are you concerned? Because I'm a second-tour case officer or because I'm a woman?" She sniffed. "I'm pretty certain you would not have come out all this way if I were a man."

The two security officers shared a glance, and Ava felt her eye twitch. These CIA officers had never worked with clandestine sources in the field. They didn't understand how fragile recruitment operations were, just how much trust it took to convince someone to betray their country. It wasn't just manipulation; it was a relationship. And that relationship had nothing to do with sex. *They think we turn sources like flipping a switch. They don't understand what it takes to hold someone's life in your hands.*

"I don't use sex as a ploy to get my sources to trust me," she said finally, "if that's what you're insinuating."

The woman pulled out a second photograph and slid it across the table. A satellite image of the Gallitzin family compound. Another shot—her entering with Konstantin.

Ava's hands clenched beneath the conference room table. *Of course, they were watching.*

"I don't need to explain to you how serious it would be to your employment at the CIA if you were caught in an inappropriate relationship with your source," the woman said coolly.

Ava gritted her teeth. "I did stay overnight, but it's not what you think."

"Oh? What should we think?"

"You shouldn't think anything," she snapped before forcing herself to take a slow breath. "I had too much wine. I stayed in a guest room. End of story."

"Not our business?" The woman tilted her head. "You must not have worked at the CIA very long."

Ava's nails dug into her palm under the table.

The man cleared his throat. "What my colleague is trying to say," he said, in that diplomatic patronizing way men at Langley spoke, "is that we understand the pressure you're under to deepen your access to Konstantin, given his proximity to the Kremlin. But there's a fine line between access and . . . familiarity. We know this is one of your first cases, and that you're still early in your career, but it's important to keep things strictly professional. Otherwise, things become . . . complicated when it's time to sever ties."

Ava nodded once, but inside she was raging. They had no idea how far off base they were.

The man leaned back, shifting the conversation. "The second issue is your cover. Nathaniel Grey has made you. Do you believe he'll reveal your identity to others?"

"I don't," Ava said. "But I do feel compelled to inform you that Nathaniel has demonstrated an interest in taking our relationship beyond the normal parameters of a handler-asset relationship."

The woman raised a brow. "Then make sure that he understands that's not an option."

"Though maintaining access is critical," the man added. "We need to keep eyes on the Liberty Coalition."

"And CIA Security does support your proposal for Nathaniel to buy back his shares of Vibrantia," the woman added. "As much control as we can maintain over that platform, the better."

Ava nodded. "Is there anything else?" she asked, voice smooth. "Or can I get back to my job?"

The man's lips quirked slightly, but his voice remained serious. "One last thing, Ava. Be careful with Konstantin. He's been SVR for a long time."

The woman met Ava's gaze, something unreadable in her expression. "I'd hate to see you caught up in one of his lies."

Ava gave a sharp nod, but her legs felt weak, nausea rising.

*They know.* They knew Konstantin was more than her source. Although they hadn't yet suspected the truth—that he was her father. They were either waiting for her to slip up enough to fire her or they were using her, playing their own game with her access. She swallowed hard, forcing a neutral expression. *They think they're pulling the strings.* But Ava wasn't about to let herself become anyone's pawn.

As Ava rose from the chair, the woman spoke again, her voice quieter now, almost conversational. "Oh—and one more thing," she said, reaching into a thin manila folder and sliding a final photograph across the table.

Ava turned and stared down at it, her breathing uneven. It wasn't Konstantin. It wasn't Nathaniel.

It was a grainy surveillance still—her mother.

Alive. In Moscow. Her face marked by twenty extra years, the silver in her hair catching the light like frost. Ava's chest tightened like she couldn't draw enough air.

"We'd appreciate it," the man said, his voice as casual as ever, "if you told us exactly what you know about her."

# CHAPTER

# 41

Snow was swirling under a slate-colored sky as Ava left the embassy. Ben sat on a bench outside, his black wool coat stretched taut across his broad shoulders as he sat hunched over, absorbed by something on his phone. The Russian Foreign Ministry's Stalinist-era skyscraper loomed in front of him, cold, immovable. At the sound of her boots crunching in the snow, he turned slowly and stood, his gloved hands clenched into tight fists at his sides, his hair dusted with snow.

"I've been working with the cyber team," he said in a low voice, his eyes flicking behind her. "They're slowly going to begin releasing footage of the atrocities Abramovich has committed over the years—assassinations, child trafficking deals, mass public surveillance. The defamation campaign against him won't be pretty, but it'll be effective."

Ava nodded, though her thoughts were still on her conversation with CIA Security. The surveillance photo of her mother tugged mercilessly at her insides. The one that the CIA had thrown on the table like a live grenade. It looked decades old, yet eerily fresh, as if time itself had bent. Her mother's face was lined with more than twenty years of age, but Ava knew how easily a photograph could be altered. She'd seen artificial intelligence transform faces before. She'd even done it herself.

"Good," she said finally, though her chest ached. "The more we can do to cause Abramovich's inner circle to implode, the better."

"Once those closest to him defect, the generals will follow." Ben stepped toward her, close enough that their heated breath mingled in the cold air, but not close enough to embrace.

She felt the threat of what loomed ahead, the unanswered questions about her mother that were still a blot on her thoughts. She wanted to feel his arms around her, to feel his breath on her ear as he held her close, but she knew it was impossible. There were cameras posted at every angle around the embassy. And while he wasn't her source, their relationship was still a risk—both to their careers and the mission. The CIA saw attachments as liabilities, distractions that could compromise judgement.

"How did it go with Security?" he asked.

"Exactly as you'd expect."

"That bad?"

"Worse. They think I'm sleeping with Konstantin."

Ben let out a sharp snort of laughter. "Christ, he's old enough to be—well, he . . ." He stopped himself and glanced up at the high-security fencing and guard posted behind her.

Ava stepped closer, instinct pulling her toward him. It all felt like too much, and she wanted to rest, wanted to collapse into the feeling of safety she'd felt back at the Gallitzin family castle.

"Are you hungry?" he asked.

"Starving," she said. "I don't know about you, but I could use a glass of red wine and something warm and hearty. Maybe a soup of some sort?"

"Sounds great." The minute they turned the corner and were out of view of the embassy, Ben took her hand and brought it into the crook of his elbow. "I know a place."

They walked in silence, the snow dampening their footprints. "How was the opera?" she asked.

"Promising. It appears Abramovich took the bait. Konstantin played into his ideology. He seems eager for someone with Konstantin's access to arms dealers and ex-military types." Ben hesitated, his eyes downcast. There was more.

"What else?" she prompted.

He exhaled, his voice measured. "After I got back from the opera with Konstantin, I spoke with Frank. He's starting to suspect that something is off with you, Ava. Not only that maybe you've been compromised, potentially even working as a double agent for the SVR, but that your relationship with Konstantin has crossed a line."

Ava bit the inside of her cheek. No wonder the CIA's Security staff had grilled her. This wasn't just standard paranoia. It was Frank's suspicion. And Frank was supposed to be her protector, her mentor, her friend. But in the CIA, loyalty was conditional. Everyone worked toward their own objectives, even if that meant sacrificing someone else's career.

"He asked me if you're hiding anything," Ben said.

Ava felt the blow even before he had stopped speaking. "What did you say?" She could hardly get the words out. She felt sick.

He clasped her hands, smile flickering. "Hey, I said I'd keep your secret. And I meant it." His gaze hardened, the grin fading. "But Frank's got me on a short leash. If you're playing me, I've gotta report it. Don't make me be that guy."

Ava swallowed hard. She could see the strain on his face, the conflict raging in his eyes. He was doing this for her—shielding her, risking everything. And the weight of it crushed her. She was making him a traitor in the eyes of the Agency. He knew that her source, Konstantin, was her father.

As she lifted her gaze to Ben's, tracing the hard cut of his jaw and the warmth buried in his eyes, a fierce ache rose in her chest. She wanted to close the space between them, to fold herself into his arms and let the truth spill out: the meeting with security, the photograph of her mother. But she couldn't. Not when every secret she'd already asked was a weight of its own. She couldn't ask him to keep another—that the CIA Security team was now asking her questions about her mother.

"I'm going to tell Frank the truth about Konstantin," she said suddenly. "Maybe he can help navigate some of this. I've built something with Konstantin that no one else at the CIA could. They can't replace me with just any other case officer. And besides, he's getting us close to Abramovich, right?"

Ben nodded slowly but Ava saw the muscle in his jaw twitch. "I think he made progress at the opera," he said. "Konstantin latched onto Abramovich's political ideology almost immediately."

They turned down the next street, the quiet pressing in around them as they walked hand in hand. Ava felt the presence before she saw it, a shadow moving just out of sight. Instinct kicked in, and she tapped his forearm with her index finger. A silent signal, just like he had taught her.

They had a tail.

Ben pulled her closer, his voice calm and measured as he continued speaking, but Ava barely caught his words. Her thoughts were on their pursuer, on Ben's steady presence at her side. On what Ben was risking. On what she was asking of him. On the photograph of her mother that haunted each breath, each thought. Even with all her training, all her experience, she still didn't know how to make sense of all of it.

"I think you're making a mistake, Ben." Her voice felt small, her chest tight. "I can't let you do this."

He frowned. "Do what?"

"Risk everything for me." Her throat ached. "I won't let you."

His jaw tensed, but before he could respond, a figure stepped from the shadows. *Frank.*

He wore a long dark overcoat and a fedora like he had stepped out of a black-and-white film from the 1950s. The pressure grew steadily between her eyes as she stared at what looked like a ghost of the Cold War era. This had to be about her debriefing with CIA Security.

"You're both not as invisible as you think," Frank said softly, his voice almost hesitant.

"Why are you trailing us in the first place?" Ava asked. "We thought you were FSB."

"I tried to catch you before you left the embassy." Frank's gaze flicked to Ben, lingered, then returned to her. "You've been recalled to the United States. I'm so sorry."

Ava's pulse skittered as her gaze darted from Frank to Ben and back again, searching their expressions for any sign that this was some kind of sick joke.

"Back . . . now?" Her voice came out sharper than intended, but she couldn't tamp down the dread curling within her gut.

Frank's silence was all the answer that she needed.

Her gaze snapped to Ben, and he flinched. "You told him." The words were dry in her mouth. "You told him about my father."

Ben edged closer. "Ava," he said, his tone a plea, "it's the safest thing. You're going to get detained, or worse."

"I can't go back," she said, trying to inject venom in her words, anything to mask the feeling of the ground shifting beneath her. "You both know that." Her breathing turned shallow. "Konstantin won't work with anyone else. And we're so close to learning about Abramovich's intended targets."

Frank stepped in, his voice smooth. "Ben will take over. We need continuity with Konstantin. The operation can't afford to stall."

Her stomach twisted violently. She wanted to vomit. "Did you know about this?" she demanded, her voice barely above a whisper as she met Ben's eyes.

The tightening of his lips was confirmation, and she felt something inside her break.

Sensing the shift, Frank turned his back and began to walk away while typing into his phone, his silhouette receding into the dim corridor.

"You knew," she said to Ben, her voice barely audible as the pieces clicked into place. "You *knew* who he was to me before I did. That Konstantin was my father."

Ben's jaw clenched, and his eyes filled with torment. "They told me before the ball," he admitted, his voice low and jagged. "The photo . . . the blood work. I wasn't supposed to tell you until the operation was over. I've seen operations like this before—manufactured leverage, psychological pressure. They doctored a photo of your mother because they want you tethered to the op, desperate for answers. Motivated."

Ava's breath caught, a sharp stab to the ribs. Her knees nearly buckled. "So, I was just . . . a tool." Her breath hitched. "An unwitting bridge to Konstantin, to get to Dimitri Abramovich."

Her stomach lurched and rage rose in her throat. "So all of this, the text message, the photograph, this assignment…my entire life turned into a trap. A leash."

"No, Ava." He reached for her, desperate, but she slapped his hand away. "You were never just a tool. I didn't plan to feel anything but I—"

"Don't," she said, her voice suddenly calm, deadly calm.

His jaw tightened, eyes gleaming with the weight of the words he had yet to say. Ava kept her gaze fixed on Frank's back fading into the shadows as Ben went on, his voice distant.

His face pinched with pain. "I didn't want to tell you like this."

"No," she snapped, her voice as sharp as a whip. "You wanted me pliant. Focused. A little pawn for Langley."

"I never thought I was at risk of falling in love with you," Ben admitted, his voice raw. "I knew you would never forgive me once you discovered the truth. But I couldn't walk away. I couldn't stop from getting close."

A bitter laugh escaped her. "So, you fell in love with me against your better judgment? Is that what you're saying?" Rage rippled through her like a storm. Before she could stop herself, she slapped him hard. The sharp crack echoed within the eerie walkway. "And all this time you were warning me about Nathaniel Grey," she hissed, "when you turned out to be the real manipulator."

"Ava, you have to believe me." His hands twitched as though to reach out to her. "You're in way over your head with Konstantin. You don't know what he's capable of, what the Gallitzin family is planning." Ben pinched the bridge of his nose.

"What do you know that I don't?" she asked.

He hesitated and finally said in a low voice only meant for her. "They want to overthrow the Kremlin; they want to restore the old aristocracy."

She stood there stunned, her tongue felt like sandpaper. *The Gallitzin family could easily throw the world into chaos.*

"And now that it's out that you're with the CIA," he continued, "you'll be seen as an accomplice to any plot against the current Russian leadership. I can't let you wait around until the FSB detains you." There was determination in the set of his jaw, the intensity of his eyes.

"You don't get to decide what risks I take, Ben," she shot back, her voice sharp even as a chill ran through her. "We all signed up for this, knowing damn well it could end with a bullet or a prison cell. That's the price of doing what we do."

"This is different, and you know it. Nathaniel Grey has placed a target on your back. You must leave. Now."

She hated that he was right. Hated that the logical choice, the safe choice, was to walk away. To go back to the United States and let someone else untangle the mess she'd uncovered. But logic had never solely dictated her choices. Not when her mother's fate was still a mystery. Not when her father's past held more questions than answers. If she left now, she would never forgive herself.

"I'm staying." Her pulse hammered in her throat as she stepped toward Ben. "You, Frank, CIA Security—you can all go to hell." Ava saw a flicker of warning in Ben's eyes. But it was too late. She had made her choice. "And one other thing," her voice was like ice. "I want all the details about that photograph that CIA Security showed me of my mother, or you can kiss access to Konstantin goodbye."

# CHAPTER

# 42

THE WIND KNIFED across the Moskva River, its dark waters groaning like old bones beneath sheets of fractured ice. Ava shivered and pulled her coat tighter, but nothing could shield her from the cold that traveled through her or the weight of what had unraveled that afternoon. She walked in silence next to Konstantin, their footsteps muffled by the freshly fallen snow. Gold-domed cathedrals loomed in the distance, their color dulled by Moscow's gray, wintery breath. The Kremlin's towers stood watchful, a fortress of deception that could close on her at any time. She was caught there, between the echoes of her mother's past and the uncertain shadows of her future.

"I had my people check out that photo of your mother on the streets of Moscow," Konstantin said. "It's AI generated."

She'd known that was the truth all along, but it still hollowed her out. That glimmer of hope was extinguished. The CIA had dangled her mother's ghost to pull her deeper into their game.

Ava's pulse thundered against her skull. The CIA had known that Konstantin was her father, yet they had kept it from her. *Frank* had known. Had he been playing with her this entire time? And Ben. *Oh God, Ben.* The knowledge of his betrayal slammed into her chest so hard the edges of her vision blurred.

Beside her, Konstantin exhaled a plume of smoke into the icy air; his eyes were distant as if retreating into a memory too difficult to carry. They passed a street vendor, the scent of sizzling blini and woodsmoke cutting through the cold, and suddenly she was back in that cave with Ben, the memory as sharp as broken glass. The heat of his body beside her, keeping her warm and safe. His voice, low and steady, anchoring her through the pain. And later, when he'd listened—not just heard but listened—when she told him at the Gallitzin family castle how alone she'd felt all her life. How had she not seen the signs that he'd been in on the CIA's deception?

Had everything between them been part of the lie? Had they used her just like they had used her mother? She had bled in front of Ben, trusted him with pieces of herself no one else had ever seen. Her heart fought its way up her throat, and she forced it back down. All that mattered now was what had brought her to Russia in the first place.

Her mother's absence had been a wound that never healed, an ache that had carved her into the woman she was. What had truly kept her mother in Russia? How much of what she had been told was true, and how much was a lattice of lies?

She felt like a fool. A fool for not seeing past Ben's lies, the CIA's manipulation.

She turned to Konstantin, her voice sharp as ice. "When the CIA found out about my mother's imprisonment, what did they do?"

Konstantin stopped, mid-step. Overhead, a lone crow cawed above them, its black wings slicing through the ashen sky. When Konstantin finally looked at her, his expression was tired, lined with years of knowing too much. "I didn't think you needed to ask me that question," he said quietly.

Ava swallowed hard, her pulse a wild staccato against her ribs. "What was my mother working on when they discovered her?" Her voice cracked; she cleared her throat, tried again. "When she was detained, I mean."

Konstantin's gaze drifted toward the river, as if searching for answers that were lost long ago. Ava could see the grief written in the lines around his eyes. "Twenty years ago, Russia was... coming apart," Konstantin began, his voice low, heavy with memory. "The economy was in ruins—empty shelves, prices climbing, soldiers dying in wars no one even believed in." He gave a short, mirthless laugh. "Then came Dimitri Abramovich. He offered... how do you say—an escape. Promised to make Russia great again, to rebuild strength, stability, opportunity." His lips curled with disdain. "But dreams, they do not come cheap. He needed a partner."

Ava's stomach twisted. "Vibrantia. But Nathaniel Grey is my age—too young to—"

He nodded, already following her thought. "Da. Back then, the company belonged to his father, Timothy Grey. A proud man. He wanted nothing to do with Russia. Thought we were a nest of corruption." His mouth tilted in a humorless smile. "He was not wrong. But at the time, your American president, he pushed for cooperation. Trade. Friendship."

Konstantin's eyes darkened, his words slowing. "Your mother came to Moscow with that delegation for defense talks. In truth, she was CIA. She had lived here before. She knew the game." He exhaled, voice edged with regret. "She warned them the Russians would never honor the deal. That the talks were only cover—to study American weapons systems."

He shook his head. "They overheard. And because the president controls your CIA . . . " He hesitated, a shadow crossing his weathered face. "He made sure nothing was done when she was taken by the FSB."

Ava staggered back, the cobblestones tilting beneath her. The gray buildings, the gold domes, all blurred together. Her throat burned as she fought back tears.

Konstantin's tone softened. "Yes. Your mother was a double agent, but not as they told you. Through me, she fed Moscow lies, disinformation. All while bringing truth back to Langley. She walked a very dangerous line." His voice dropped to a whisper. "But her loyalty? It never once wavered."

The words hit her like shrapnel. *And the CIA had let her mother rot in a Russian prison.*

Ava's face and hands burned from the dry, cold, icy rage building inside her. The betrayal she felt over the CIA's deception about knowing Konstantin was her father paled in comparison to the fury she felt within her now. They hadn't just lied to her. They had abandoned her mother, branded her a traitor, and let her die for a story they didn't bother to verify.

The wind howled through the streets, scattering the snow like ash. Ava pulled her coat tighter, but the cold had already burrowed deep, past skin and bone, and into that hollow space where her trust had lived. Ava felt truly untethered. She could trust no one—not the Agency that shaped her, not the man she loved. The memory of Ben, the warmth of him, the illusion of safety, seared through her like an old wound reopening. He had been the only person she had let in, the only person she had thought understood what she'd been through.

She gripped a railing as they made their way up a set of stairs to the road, her knuckles white as she tried to ground herself against Konstantin's revelations.

The city around her blurred, like images smearing ink in water. Pieces of her past, her mother's laughter, reassurances from her aunt, the certainty that she belonged, fractured and scattered, carried off by the wind.

Nothing was certain anymore. Nothing solid. Not anymore.

CHAPTER

# 43

As they walked through the cold, Ava tried to find the words to tell Konstantin about her childhood. But her memories caught somewhere between her heart and her throat. Instead, a flicker of her aunt's narrow eyes flashed within her mind, how her aunt's brow furrowed when Ava entered the room and never quite fell on her face. Ava shivered, both from the cold and the chill of the memory: the house they'd shared, the stiff antique furniture, the doors that were always closed.

They moved along the river in a silence that felt less like peace and more like an open bruise. Snow hissed on the overpass, an ever-shifting line of dark cars blinking red in the snow. She wanted, needed to talk about Ben, but her emotions felt like ash in her mouth. How stupid she'd been, letting him in, giving him pieces of herself that she couldn't get back. But it wasn't him, nor her childhood, that had her stomach twisting in knots.

It was her mother and how she'd died that hollowed Ava out. The CIA had abandoned her, and FSB had broken her. Shame and fury braided itself within Ava's chest, slow and merciless.

The wind picked up, catching the edge of her scarf as they continued side by side. Konstantin stopped without warning and stepped cautiously forward, and for a heartbeat, Ava feared that he might try to hug her. She couldn't stand the idea of anyone offering her comfort right now. He must have known, and instead reached into his coat and handed her a thick leather case with both hands.

She opened it with hands that felt not entirely hers. "What's this?" she asked, seeing a small handheld computer inside.

"I've waited for years for justice," Konstantin said with the bluntness of someone who had turned his grief into machinery, "and now I'll watch Dimitri Abramovich unravel alongside my daughter."

"Justice died with her." She opened the computer and looked down, her heart climbing her throat. "I just want him to suffer."

"The password is 7-1-1983," Konstantin said, his voice suddenly softer.

She looked up, her eyes burning with tears. "Mom's birthday."

Her emotion surged, and she blinked hard, pushing it down. Not here. Not now.

She tapped in the digits, her fingers steady despite the drum inside her chest, and watched as file after file opened: a blueprint of economic instruction with cryptocurrency exchanges, intercepted emails, and doctored intelligence reports. A step-by-step plan to disassemble Abramovich and ruin all he'd worked for. *Slowly. Publicly. Irrevocably.*

Ava clicked another folder, and a surveillance video of Abramovich appeared. "But how—" The amount of detail Konstantin had compiled was staggering. This wasn't just a plan; it was a public execution. The breath that had been packed inside her ribs loosened.

Konstantin's voice came from behind her, low and resolute. "First, we'll start with fear and let doctored intel reports whisper of NATO sanctions. Once it reaches the Kremlin, Abramovich will transfer his money out of his accounts. Only he'll be moving it unknowingly into our hands." Ava brought up a diagram that showed how every fund was rerouted into crypto networks as he continued, "Every transfer hacked."

"We're going to bankrupt him?" she asked.

"No, we're going to hand him the rope to let him hang himself."

Her fingers ran over the screen as he outlined the rest of the operation. Something fierce, close to retribution began to whisper along her veins.

"Then we should hit the markets. False intelligence about a cyberattack on a huge oil reserve. He'll panic and offload his energy reserves."

Ava stared at the plan, her pulse humming beneath her skin. "But you'll have already shorted the markets." She could see it now: a world watching as Abramovich unraveled, not knowing who had pulled the strings.

"Exactly. Public collapse, private ruin. And the best part is, it's already begun. Videos of Abramovich ordering mass assassinations, child trafficking . . . it's all being spread by hackers onto Vibrantia. Turns out we don't need access to Nathaniel Grey's algorithm to ruin Abramovich's reputation."

"How long will the financial piece take?" she asked.

"Also already begun. I have an intel report circulating now about a false cyberattack. Abramovich has already begun dumping his country's energy reserves to stabilize the ruble. The Russian ruble is already crashing. It won't be long until Abramovich hemorrhages billions. Publicly."

Something electric pumped through her veins. "And when he runs?"

Konstantin clicked on the last file on the encrypted folder using a biometric scan of his index finger. It was imagery of a secluded estate on the Black Sea. "We'll be waiting for him."

Ava's breath caught, an echo of her mother's scream emanating from deep insider her. She had no right to feel relief. She had only the right to act. Her eyes snapped up to meet Konstantin's. "How did you do all this?"

And then—

Tires screamed against wet pavement. Ava spun, burning rubber hitting her nostrils just as a black van fishtailed into view. Two men in ski masks leaned out the windows, M4s flashing. The night exploded with the clatter of gunfire, bullets sparking off concrete. *Clack. Clack. Clack.*

"Move!" Konstantin's shout was raw, hoarse.

Her heart slammed against her ribs so hard she could feel it in her ears. No drills. No do-overs. This was it. She bolted after him, boots hammering the slick street, lungs clawing for air as the two of them dove under the underpass. The van's engine roared above them, echoing through the concrete like a beast closing in. Ava yanked her Beretta free, flicked the top lever, slammed a fresh mag into place. Footsteps pounded closer.

Ben's voice flashed in her mind. *Precision. Consistency. Speed.*

She swung out from behind the pillar and fired—once, twice. The nearest gunman jerked, collapsing against the van with a guttural cry. The other assailant fired and the bullet sliced past her ear so close it scorched the air. Konstantin fired back and the gunfire ricocheted off the overpass, sharp and deafening. Her heart hammered as she frantically tried to embody the lessons she'd been taught. *Slow is smooth. Smooth is fast.*

But her nerves were electric, her palms slick with sweat as the attackers closed in. Konstantin's hand clamped around her arm.

"Go!" he barked, shoving her behind him as another van screamed to a stop up ahead.

She turned, willing her legs to push forward, to flee. But the metallic clacking of gunfire sliced at her nerves. A flash. A shout. Muzzle fire painted the night in bursts of white heat. A figure in black charged straight for her, weapon raised. Konstantin lunged past her in a blur. His fist cracked against the man's jaw. Bone crunched. The attacker stumbled back, but another came from behind. The rifle butt slammed into Konstantin's skull with a sickening crack. Blood ran down his temple as he crumpled to the pavement.

She had lost her father in the space of a heartbeat. The grief was so immediate it tasted metallic. It crawled along her nerves and settled beneath her skin.

The van's door smacked open and shut like a tomb sealing. Grief attacked every nerve. It had to be the FSB who had caught up to them. The thought of it made her mouth go dry. Even the memory of her mother, once her compass, vanished. Where there had been a stubborn flicker—a belief that somehow the story might right itself—now it collapsed within her. And her plan to take down Dimitri Abramovich would die with Konstantin.

The van juddered into motion. She had been abandoned by her mother, her father, then the Agency by silence and betrayal. But she had survived it, and that endurance didn't just make her strong, it made her dangerous. She let the shadows gather around her, and she willed something colder, more ruthless to take root—a plan without mercy.

# CHAPTER

# 44

A rope bit into Ava's wrists, the fibers fraying her already raw skin as they bound her to the back of a rusted metal chair. Her bare feet were numb from the steel floor where they were chained. A sodden towel had been shoved into her mouth, heavy with the rank taste of mildew and sweat. A blindfold crushed her eyelashes against her skin. She tilted her chin downward, her breaths ragged against the gag.

She heard it before she felt it, the slosh of water above her, a moment of silence, then a deluge. A wall of ice-cold water crashed down, forcing its way through her nose, her mouth. It stole her breath, flooded her lungs. Her body convulsed in the chair, fighting the primal urge to inhale even as panic clawed at her cracked ribs.

Her heartbeat pounded behind her eyes, each pulse a drumbeat of survival, but the water kept coming, drowning out the sound of her choked gasps. When it finally stopped, she slumped forward, and coughed violently, her throat burning as she gagged on the remnants of the water lodged inside her.

A voice, low and measured, slithered into her ear. "Name the men you're working for, and I can make this all go away."

The voice was familiar now. She heard it in the darkness between beatings, behind the blindfold. A voice that carried patience, amusement even, as if the man speaking had already decided the outcome. She forced herself to steady her breathing, to suppress the instinctual whimper clawing at the back of her throat.

"Who's your boss?" he asked again, each syllable coated with the remnants of countless cigarettes.

Never. She could never give up Frank or Ben, nor anyone else she had worked with while at the CIA. It didn't matter what they did to her, or what secrets they had kept. She would never betray her country, her mission.

He yanked the towel from her mouth.

"Go to hell," she rasped, her voice shredded from hours of interrogation.

There was a long pause, then a soft chuckle, devoid of humor.

Her stomach twisted violently. But she wouldn't let him see her fear. *Who was this man, this monster?*

"Name the men you're working for, and I can make this all go away." The whispers in her ear grew heavy within her head, her heart.

"I don't know what you're talking about. I am a foreign service officer who works at the US Embassy in Moscow."

Another wave of water came fast and hard, stealing the air from her lungs before she could brace for it. She thrashed against the restraints, her body screaming for oxygen, but it was useless. Darkness tugged at the edges of her mind, a whisper of death that crept steadily forward.

"You're a spy," the scratchy Russian voice said.

"I'm not. I review visa applications."

"Liar."

Ava braced herself for another deluge. But it stopped as suddenly as it came. She sagged against the chair, wheezing, sucking in what little air she could through her nose. The towel was yanked from her mouth. She coughed up water, her throat raw, but before she could find relief, a fist buried itself in her ribs. Pain erupted in her side, sharp and unforgiving. Fingers gripped her jaw, forcing her head upward. Her eyes watered as the blindfold was ripped away. She squinted against the blinding, fluorescent light.

Dimitri Abramovich stood above her.

His face was more severe in person—a hawkish nose, steely eyes, and severe cheekbones. He was older than he had looked in reconnaissance photos, mid-sixties maybe, but he radiated authority, the kind that came from decades of control and unchecked power. His clothes were simple—black button-down shirt and dark trousers—and his hair was slicked back, showing a receding hairline. He was the architect of her nightmare, the unraveling of America's defenses.

Ava swallowed hard, forcing herself to focus. She knew what he was planning—targeting US missile silos, crippling America's military capabilities and its ability to retaliate against a foreign threat. They had spent the last months dismantling Abramovich's financial streams, intercepting his communications, and disrupting his network. And now she was caught in the trap she had worked to set for him.

Abramovich smiled as if he could read her thoughts. "Why don't we skip all the pleasantries? We both know who you are, what you do." He sat across from her in a metal chair, one leg draped across the other. "I don't want to mince words with you, or make you believe that your life will somehow be saved if you give me all the answers, because it will not. There is no amount of whimpering that can keep you from your fate."

He blinked, but his eyes held no flicker of mercy, only the quiet promise of pain. "What you can do is hasten your death. And we can give you a clean, simple ending. The question is, how much pain it will take before you tell me what I need to know?"

Ava shuddered, not from fear but a deep, unrelenting need to pummel Abramovich to death. But she could see that he was endlessly patient, a man who enjoyed these types of games.

"My boss is the US ambassador," she said, "you can easily look him up."

A short beard did little to disguise a smirk tugging at the corner of his mouth. "Still pretending, even now? Let's make this simpler. Tell me where all my money has gone."

She pinched her lips together. She could lie, feed him false company names, but Abramovich wasn't stupid. He would verify every name, every detail. If she gave him the wrong intel, he would know. Then what would he do?

He leaned closer, his breath laced with smoke and something metallic, something rotten. "What do you know about Vibrantia's social media campaign to destroy my reputation?" His voice was softer now, almost coaxing, as if he were asking her casual questions over dinner. "What else do you have on me, and who gave it to you?"

He was fishing, testing how much she had uncovered. If he thought she knew everything, he would kill her immediately. But if he believed she was still piecing it together, he might keep her alive—at least long enough for an extraction team to find her.

Ava lifted her chin, forcing herself to meet his gaze. "I have no idea what you're talking about. I stamp passports all day."

Abramovich exhaled through his nose, his amusement waning. Then he nodded to someone behind her. Boots shuffled forward on the sleek metal floors, followed immediately by the sickening scent of gasoline. A hand gripped the collar of her shirt, yanking it forward, and then she felt the cold splash of fuel trickling down her chest, soaking her clothes. Panic overcame her as she tried to pull in air and relieve herself from the horrible ringing inside her head.

They were going to burn her alive.

She inhaled deeply and tried to separate herself from the terror that wracked her weakened body. She could flee only mentally; she would need to retreat into the deep recesses of her mind. She needed to find a place where she no longer felt pain, nor the threat of what was to come. And for her that was in Ben's arms—the only place she had ever truly felt safe. But that sense of safety had been ripped away the moment he confessed, shattering the illusion she had clung to like oxygen.

Abramovich tilted his head, watching her with something akin to curiosity. "This can end one of two ways, Ava. You tell me what I want to know, and I will make this easy for you. Or . . ."

A flick of his wrist. A match struck against the rough sole of his boot. The tiny flame danced in the air, hungry, waiting. "What? You'll do what you did to my mother?"

Abramovich stared at her, the corner of his mouth twisting into a knowing smile. "You think I didn't know who you were? I knew from the beginning, *devushka*. Your mother—Theresa Anderson—the infamous "American Red." His eyes gleamed, predatory, enjoying the shock that flickered across her face.

"My mother wasn't a traitor." She spat the words, her voice shaking with fury.

"The evidence was quite damning if I remember correctly, encrypted messages traced to her laptop, an unexplained bank account, meetings with a known SVR handler—" Abramovich paused and let the accusations settle over her. "Wait a second, I heard that she had an affair with her SVR handler."

Ava swallowed down what she truly wanted to say. Konstantin had told her the truth—that Dimitri Abramovich was complicit in her mother's plans all those years ago and had sold her out. Grief licked the edges of her mind once more, but she inhaled deeply, resolved to push it away and stay locked firmly on the present. On what her chances were to escape.

Ava forced a smile, her lips cracked and bleeding, the memory of her mother in the forefront of her mind. "Go to hell."

Abramovich sighed, letting the match burn down between his fingers before extinguishing it with a slow, deliberate pinch. He slapped her, and she spit in his face.

"You first," he murmured. "But not yet. First, you're going to tell me all the details of Langley's little plan."

# CHAPTER

# 45

Ava fought to keep herself awake, but unconsciousness clawed at her, threatening to take her under. Abramovich had left, giving her time to "contemplate her cooperation." She stiffened, the smell of gasoline thick in her nostrils. She had escaped death, for now, but once Abramovich realized that she'd given him fake names, there would be no alternatives. Every cell of her body screamed for rest, for relief, but something deep inside of her resisted, an instinct woven into her very core. She had to keep fighting—even as fear lapped mercilessly at her, even as terror clamped down, she had to press forward.

It was what her mother would have done.

Footsteps erupted on the other side of the locked door, and Ava willed a sliver of hope to crack through her despair. Frank and Ben had to be looking for her. *They must be.*

It was standard procedure that Ava, along with the other CIA case officers, would return to the embassy after their source meetings, no matter how late. They had to have noticed when she didn't return last night. And when they realized that she'd been kidnapped, Ben would insist that the CIA mount a rescue operation. But a new unsettling thought took hold—perhaps Ben would not be with them. Not after the way they had left things.

She was never supposed to remain in Russia. The plan had been simple: Meet with Konstantin, turn him over to Ben. Yet she'd stayed despite Ben's warnings, regardless of Frank and the CIA's orders to return to the United States. She'd convinced herself that she could finish what she'd started—and they weren't going to physically force her onto a plane. But that defiance cost her everything.

The taste of failure felt bitter on her tongue. Her father was dead, and their plan to expose Abramovich's market manipulation and dismantle his reputation had died with him. The full weight of it had yet to settle deep within her bones—but when it did, she knew it would crush her. If only she'd listened. If only she'd not been so stubborn. Konstantin might still be alive, their plan might still be in play.

Would Frank and Ben still see through her plan for Vibrantia? Surely, they'd know that without dismantling Russia's misinformation machine, taking down Abramovich would mean nothing. The Liberty Coalition's political chaos would keep spreading, poisoning America from within. And if Nathaniel Grey was the one who sold her out to the FSB, she would make him pay—for what he had done to her, and to Konstantin. .

The thought of Konstantin—of her father—was a jagged thing inside her chest. She'd only just learned who he was, but she'd begun to recognize the parts of herself that she never fully understood: the quick, instinctive way her mind worked under pressure, the steel she carried in her voice when she refused to back down. Traits she'd always thought were accidents of her own making but now seemed inherited, perhaps traits of the Gallitzin family legacy that she'd never fully know. It was a revelation and a wound, leaving her raw and untethered once more.

She didn't have childhood memories to console herself with, nothing to lean on; all she had was a glimpse of a man that she'd longed to know all her life. And a glimpse was all she'd ever have.

The harsh, erratic ping of automatic fire made her head snap upward. Boots pounded against the concrete floor, and the door slammed open. Four shadows moved into the room, figures in tactical gear moving with deadly precision. Her heart leaped at the sound of English.

"Stay calm, ma'am. We're here to get you out of here." It was a tall man Ava recognized as one of the US Marine guards at the embassy. Her heart seized as she scanned the men, searching for what she already knew to be true. Ben wasn't there.

Her heart plummeted until a tall, broad form broke through the chaos, hazel eyes locking onto hers that sent a jolt rippling through her body—Ben.

Relief crashed into her with a force that nearly stole her breath. She choked on a fresh sob as he moved swiftly to cut her free, his hands warm against her icy skin. The relief she felt at his touch was overwhelming, like she had been waiting to draw breath.

"Ava," Ben rasped, his voice raw as he used his thumbs to wipe away her tears. His face was covered with blood and sweat like some Celtic warrior resurrected from battle. "What did they do to you?" he asked.

She couldn't speak. Words dissolved in her throat. Instead, she clung to him, burying her face in his shoulder, letting herself go for the first time in twenty-four hours. His scent—leather, pine, and something unmistakably Ben—wrapped around her like armor, shielding her from the horrors she had endured. For a fleeting moment, she forgave him for the lies. Not because he deserved it, but because she needed to. Because the warmth of him, the safety and solidness of his arms was the only thing strong enough to keep her from splintering apart.

He tilted her face upward, his touch firm yet reverent as though he was afraid that she might vanish. "Forgive me."

Then his lips were on hers, desperate, aching, breathing life back into her. He tasted of her salty tears and his sweat, and of something dark and unrelenting, perhaps his rage. Her body sagged against his, exhaustion flooding her now that safety was within reach, the fragile pulse of forgiveness that she wasn't ready to name.

Gently he inched her away, his eyes roaming all over her body. Rage filled his eyes at the sight of her, bloodied and battered.

"Where is he?" Ben said through clenched teeth, nearly shaking with fury. But the moment was shattered as a guttural shout rang out behind them. "Where's Abramovich?"

The door slammed open and chaos detonated. A guard stumbled in, rifle half-raised. Ben didn't hesitate. One shot, clean and final, dropped the man before he hit the ground. Six more flooded the doorway, weapons blazing. The room erupted in flashes and smoke. Ben and his team moved as one—fluid, silent, deadly—years of training distilled into motion. Each shot landed true. Each breath counted. Bodies hit the floor in brutal rhythm.

Ava ducked low behind an overturned table, heart pounding. A seventh guard charged at Ben, a hulking figure with a machine gun. Ben met him head-on—fast, controlled. Steel flashed as Ben slammed his knife deep into the man's throat before the gun could fire. Blood sprayed the wall. The body collapsed, thudding onto the ground.

Another shadow cut through the smoke. A guard with a serrated blade lunged from Ben's blind side. Ava didn't think. She moved, her fingers finding a pistol on the floor, cold metal biting her palm. She raised it and fired. The gunshot cracked like thunder that vibrated through her bones. The guard's eyes went wide, the knife slipping from his hand as he crumpled to the concrete.

Ben spun toward her, chest heaving. "Ava."

The air was thick—smoke, gunpowder, blood. Her hands shook. The gun wavered. She'd saved him. She wasn't broken. Not by Abramovich. Not by any of this. Before either of them could speak, another burst of gunfire tore through the hall. Ben shifted instantly, stepping in front of her, shielding her with his body as the rest of the team moved in, firing in controlled bursts.

Somewhere nearby, something exploded. Heat rolled through the doorway; flames licked the edges of the smoke. Ava coughed, eyes stinging.

"A decoy," Ben said, voice rough. "They're trying to flush us out. You okay to move?"

Pain shot down her leg, but she forced herself upright. "I'm fine." Her gaze caught the blood seeping down his arm. "You're not."

He gave her a crooked grin. "Just a scratch. Come on."

Together they pushed through the haze, into the next fight—alive, side by side, still standing.

# CHAPTER

# 46

WHEN THEY RETURNED to Ben's apartment, he turned on the shower and let steam roll through the space as he filled the bathtub. The embassy doctor had checked Ava over—broken ribs, a split lip, bruises that would fade. But no words or medical exams could assess the deeper damage. The kind that likely wouldn't heal with time.

She wanted to feel safe. But she couldn't. Not while Abramovich was still alive.

Across the room, Ben sat on the edge of a claw-foot tub, his face turned away as he shook lavender-smelling bath salts into the hot water. Her whole body ached as she stood in the doorway, pulling a terrycloth robe around her body. But nothing she did would keep the cold away.

The chaos of being detained, the violent torture, the threats—none of it compared to the image she couldn't erase, of Abramovich's face as he'd taunted her with her mother's death. Ava clenched her hands into tight fists, fingernails biting into her palms. She wanted to face Abramovich again. She wanted to make him suffer.

"Do you want to talk about it?" Ben's voice was quiet, careful, his face still turned away.

She shook her head. "Not yet."

The silence told her that he understood, or at least he was trying.

Finally, he looked at her, his blue eyes wrecked with exhaustion, with guilt, and perhaps something close to longing. "Ava, I . . ."

She knew what he wanted to say, how sorry he was about what he'd kept from her about Konstantin, about her bloodline. And maybe someday, she'd let him apologize. But not now, not when she felt like the ground beneath her was still shifting.

"Do you want anything to drink?" Ben asked. "I could make you some chamomile tea. A glass of wine?"

"Perhaps something a bit stronger." She tried to smile but only managed a twitch of her lips.

He turned off the water, the sound tapering into a silence that almost seemed sacred after the chaos of the last twenty-four hours. At the doorway, Ben paused and planted a soft kiss on her forehead. She wanted him to touch her; she wanted to bury her face into his chest, inhale the scent of him. But something stopped her. He hesitated, for just a moment, the silence heavy between them, a longing that she couldn't name. He nodded as if sensing her fragility, her confusion, and left the bathroom, closing the door behind him to trap in the heat.

When he left, Ava sunk down next to the bathtub, hugging her knees to her chest. Warmth wrapped around her, but her body still trembled from exhaustion and adrenaline. She closed her eyes and willed the heat to smooth her frayed nerves, her tired heart. But her mind was fixed on the nightmare still unfolding outside these walls. Abramovich still had plans—plans that threatened US military silos, strategic launch sites that, if compromised, could cripple America's ability to defend itself in an attack.

The implications were catastrophic. The kind of scenario the CIA ran war games over, hoping never to see it play out in reality. And right now, they were three moves behind, and here she was, sitting on the bathroom floor, the world pressing against her.

Ben creaked the door open with a quiet thump, a glass of scotch in his hand. He crouched beside her and offered it wordlessly. She took it and drank, the liquor burning its way through her chest like a small defiance against the cold uncertainty pressing against her ribs. "I didn't tell Abramovich anything," she said, her eyes fixed on the bathroom tile as she cradled the glass with both hands. "If that's what you're wondering."

"I know," he said. "If you had, the plan wouldn't have worked so well."

Her head snapped up. "What do you mean?"

He gave her a tired smile. "It worked, Ava. All Abramovich's offshore accounts have been flagged. The Swiss and Emiratis have frozen all his assets. He lost billions."

She blinked. "But when he questioned me, I just assumed he was onto us. That he was baiting me."

"He suspected. But he didn't act fast enough. He waited, moved millions into his private accounts, ones that we seeded through CIA fronts. And then *click*. Gone. He lost everything."

She stared at him and saw that his eyes were shadowed by sleepless nights. The scope of what they had done together, and with Konstantin's help, sinking in.

"We actually pulled it off," she said, her voice thick with emotion.

"We did."

She sniffed loudly, thinking of Konstantin, thinking of everything he had sacrificed to get them to this moment—all the years of surveillance and false identities that had finally paid off.

"Konstantin, he—" She drew in a shallow breath. Her chest ached. She felt like it might split open from the pressure building that had nothing to do with her injuries.

"He would be proud," he said.

The silence that followed was thick with a grief that threaded through them both. Ava took another sip, her fingers trembling around the glass.

"But Abramovich's still planning the attack."

Ben's face darkened as she took a long gulp of the scotch. "NSA picked up some chatter this morning. He's moving faster than expected with all this bad press. We may not have much time"

Her pulse quickened. "We need to go home." The word home caught in her throat. It wasn't a place she longed for—it was the man whose touch she could still feel like fire on her skin.

His fingers barely grazed her arm, and heat bloomed where he had touched. "When I learned that they had detained you," he said, voice raw, "I thought I'd never see you again. And that I'd never have the chance to tell you how sorry I am, that I should've told you about Konstantin the moment I found out."

Ava searched his face, the shadows cast by the flickering light tracing the bruises that hadn't fully healed. He looked older somehow, worn by guilt and sleepless nights. This wasn't the defiant operative who always met danger with a smirk. This was a man stripped bare.

He took her hand in his. She wanted to turn away, to protect the part of herself that had hardened since the betrayal. But the memories flooded in—the cell, the sound of fists against flesh, the echo of his grunt when he took the hit meant for her. The way he had looked at her, blood dripping down his temple, telling her to run.

He had fought for her. Bled for her. And when everything fell apart, he'd still come back.

He looked at her now with that same quiet intensity, the kind that pulled at something deep inside her. It wasn't words that made her believe him—it was the way his hand trembled as it found hers, the way his eyes never left her face as if memorizing her all over again. Her heart still ached with the fracture between them, with the lie that had nearly undone her. But maybe forgiveness wasn't something spoken, it was something proven. In the way he'd shielded her when the bullets fell. In the way he stayed, even when it could cost him everything. And in that moment, despite the chaos still raging, she made her choice. She let his hand stay in hers.

"Will you hold me?" she asked, her hands still trembling as she placed the glass tumbler down with a quiet clink.

He pulled her into his arms, and they sat there in silence on the bathroom floor, their bodies stiff at first, then melting together. He smoothed her hair down her back, his warmth grounding her, her face pressed against his chest, the memory of Abramovich's violence still burning fresh in her mind. She wanted to find a way to fight through the terror, the deep aching inside her chest.

She pulled away slightly and untied the robe. She lifted her arms in a silent request. Ben understood and gently stripped off her bloodied shirt. She unclasped her bra and let it fall. She wanted him to wipe out all the terror, remove any trace of Abramovich and what had happened to her in that room.

He reached around the back of her head and slid off her hair tie, letting her hair fall around her bruised shoulders.

"You're so beautiful," he said in a raspy voice.

"Liar."

"I'm serious, Ava. There's nothing that you could do, or that could happen, that would make you less beautiful to me."

"I have a feeling you say this to all half-naked women in your apartment."

He smiled at her, his desire flaming within his eyes. "I mean it."

She didn't respond. She just looked at him—really looked. She stood and unbuttoned her pants. He slid them down, as if she were breakable. There was just the quiet, desperate need to be cared for. To feel something other than rage, pain, and exhaustion. He knelt and pressed soft kisses against her ribs, his mouth trailing over the bruises as if he could take away her pain. She put her arms on his shoulders, urging him upward. His mouth met hers, and he kissed her deeply, reminding her that she was still here, that she was still alive. And she let herself forget everything for the next few hours, letting him tend to her as if she were the most fragile, loved thing in the world.

Afterward, she laid on Ben's strong, bare chest, staring up into the steam. She tried not to think of her mother, of Konstantin. The millions of lives that hung in the balance. But after ten minutes, her mind took over, and she gripped the side of the tub to sit up.

"I want Konstantin buried next to my mother."

Ben frowned. "She's here?"

"The CIA refused to fly her body home after the FBI branded her a traitor." Her voice wavered as she stared down into the soapy water. She looked up, her red-rimmed eyes full. "But she wasn't, Ben, I know she wasn't."

Ben took her hand and threaded his fingers through hers. "Ava . . . there's something that you need to know."

She stiffened as he stood beside her. "More secrets?"

"No more lies, I swear." He inhaled through his nose and kissed her swiftly. "Konstantin asked me to look into some things for him before he died. The money the FBI discovered in your mother's account."

She tightened her grip on his hand. "The payments they accused her of taking from the Russians."

Ben nodded. "It wasn't Russia's money. It was CIA slush funds—used to finance covert operations. And those meetings she had with Konstantin? She wasn't feeding intelligence to the Russians. She was feeding them disinformation. And in return, she was gathering intel on their weapon programs."

Ava's pulse pounded. "How do you know this?"

"I went through her old emails to Langley. Buried deep in the records—codes, signals, messages Konstantin knew to look for. She wasn't a traitor, Ava."

Konstantin had told her the same, swearing that her mother had remained loyal to the CIA. But words were not proof, and part of her feared that it was born out of his love for her, not truth. But Ben's evidence left no room for doubt about her mother's allegiance.

Ava's hands trembled so violently she had to curl them into fists on her lap. For years, the question had lived inside her like shrapnel, corroding every memory she had of her mother's voice, her laughter. The shame that had haunted her, that shadowed every mission. Now, with Ben's quiet words laying out the proof—signals, codes, a hidden loyalty woven through deception—the doubt she'd held for so long about her mother worked its way free.

Her mother had not abandoned her. She had not betrayed her country. She had not died with her honor in question. At last, Ava could believe it. Tears blurred her vision, softening the outline of Ben as he leaned closer. He kissed her hand, grounding her against the tidal wave of relief.

A lump formed in her throat. “She was a patriot.” Ava lifted her chin slowly, her voice steady despite the pounding of her heart. “And only in death will she reclaim her name.”

“Let’s get you home so that you can bury your mother properly.”

She nodded and swallowed a painful sob that rose in her throat. “Only if I can bury my father with her.”

# CHAPTER

# 47

Seventy-two hours later, Ava and Ben led the way through skeletal trees, their boots crunching through packed snow as they made their way down the narrow pathway. The cemetery lay quiet beneath a heavy Arlington sky, a dull pewter sea pressing low over the city. Half-moon gravestones peaked through thick snow drifts; their curved edges softened by the night's relentless snowfall. Trees lined the route like blackened sentinels, their gnarled limbs brittle from ice.

A bitter wind knifed through Ava's coat, threading icy needles through the seams and burrowing itself deep within her bones. She curled her fingers into a tight fist, but the frost bit deep, even with gloves, until Ben's hand found hers. He shifted his body to shield her from the worst of the cold and tucked her hand into the crook of his elbow, ignoring Frank's discerning gaze beside them. Ben had risked it all for her, his career, his standing as one of the CIA's most senior counterintelligence officers. He had done it all for her.

Ahead, a gathering of Konstantin's family stood in somber silence at the cemetery—Gallitzin relatives who had crossed continents to say their farewell. The weight of grief hung thick in the frozen air. Konstantin had been more than an SVR operative. He had been a man who had risked everything to save the woman he loved. He had given his soul over to the SVR in a desperate plea that the FSB would spare her. But still, Theresa Anderson had died. And now Konstantin was dead as well.

Ava swallowed her tears as she looked down at her mother's grave, the marble slick with ice. The truth had finally surfaced, and it was Ben who had secured the intel that finally cleared Theresa Anderson. A mole inside the FBI had wanted her mother dead, and they had succeeded, but *why* remained a mystery.

Frustration coiled within Ava, a slow, simmering rage. She knew who her mother was. A woman who had bled for her country. A woman who had given her life over to protect the people that she loved. And as payment for her sacrifice, she had been marked a traitor and buried in Russian soil for fourteen years.

Ava clenched her jaw, feeling the burn of unleashed tears. Somewhere deep inside, she had always known, even before Konstantin had told her, before Ben had quietly intervened. Theresa Anderson came from a long line of warriors. Her mother's father was a veteran of Afghanistan, her great-grandfather a soldier in Vietnam. Her grandmother had worn the crisp uniform of a US Navy captain. Duty was in her blood. In Ava's blood.

She knelt, pressing a folded flag onto the headstone. The stark white stars against the deep navy fabric were a gift from the Moscow Chief of Station. Ben's research had surfaced at least three major Russian assassination campaigns targeting US diplomats that Konstantin's intelligence had thwarted, giving Ava the ammunition she needed to argue for her father's burial alongside her mother. And with Frank and Ben's help, she had even secured an official pardon for her mother.

For Ava, it felt like she was mending something that had been torn in two long before she was born. They would rest peacefully now, side by side under the same earth, no longer forced to live a lie.

The sharp crack of rifle fire echoed across the field. The seven-member firing party stood rigid, their navy-blue dress uniforms crisp against the stark white snow, their movements precise as they fired. Smoke curled from the barrels of their rifles, dissolving in the frozen air as three volleys rang out in measured succession. The Marine embassy guards moved in solemn formation, bearing a casket draped with an American flag.

When Ava gave the signal, the flag was removed and folded with practiced precision. Each motion was deliberate. Controlled. She remembered the day her mother had taught her about the thirteen-folds flag. She'd been no older than seven, standing beside her mother in a quiet room, staring at the glass cases filled with medals and faded photographs of the men and women who had served before them.

"The process is highly precise," her mother had said, her hand warm on Ava's shoulder. "Each fold represents something—honor, remembrance, duty."

Snow swirled around Ava now, mixing with rain that had turned into icy fists of hail. Black umbrellas dotted the cemetery in endless waves, a silent sea watching, waiting. A Marine in full dress uniform stepped forward and kneeled before Ava. His face was solemn as he extended the folded flag with both hands.

His voice was steady, but his words crashed over her like a wave. She tightened her grip on Ben's hand. "On behalf of the United States, the US Marine Corps, and a grateful nation, please accept this flag as a symbol of our appreciation of your loved one's honorable and faithful service."

Ava's throat constricted as she let go of Ben's hand. Her fingers, raw from the cold, closed around the fabric. Ben's arm curled around her waist, anchoring her as she clutched the fabric to her chest, feeling the weight of all she had learned—about her mother, about the sacrifices she had made, about the love she had never spoken about aloud.

Ava had found letters that had hidden away in an old prison archive, unread for years.

Her mother's voice had survived, etched onto brittle pages that Ava now carried with her, tucked safely inside her purse for the last two days. Only now did she feel as though she had the right to read the letters as she stood over their graves.

She reached for one now, fingers trembling as she unfolded the worn paper, her breath catching at the familiar, looping script. The ink had bled in places, smudged by tears or time.

*Dear Konstantin,*

*I don't expect that this letter will reach you, but I must try. These will be my last days, and there is something you must know.*

*You have been deceived.*

*I have loved you always. I have never stopped. I made up the story that Ava was from another relationship to keep her safe, but it was never true. She is yours. She has always been yours.*

*I will love you always,*
*Theresa*

Ava's chest ached, and she inhaled a deep breath to lessen the building pressure. Ben rubbed a hand up and down her back. Her mother never betrayed her country, or the man she had loved. Of course not. Ben stared at her mother's tombstone. It bore only six words that told the truth at last: "Theresa Anderson—A Patriot Until Death."

After the funeral, Ava stood inside her Watergate hotel room staring out at the Potomac River, moving slow and gray. The room was dim, lit only by the glow of a single lamp. Ava stood near the window, arms crossed as if she to hold herself together as she stared out at the trees along the tidal basin, their buds still tightly closed, the promise of bloom not yet spent. Everything felt suspended, like spring wasn't sure it was safe to come.

Ben stood behind her, his silence thick and coiled. He hadn't touched her since they got back, not since the funeral—not a hand on her back, not a look that lingered. Just deliberate distance. She could feel him pulling away from her since the heated glance from Frank; it had landed between them like a warning shot. And when the CIA director had looked at them, it was with the full weight of the Agency's judgment.

Finally, Ben spoke in a rough voice. "We should end this. Before we go into headquarters tomorrow."

Her breath hitched, but she didn't turn around. Not yet. She stared out at the river as if it offered an answer, or at least, a delay. When she turned, she saw what she had feared—the walls were back up. The softness in his eyes was gone, and that distance that he held everyone else that had crept back in.

"It's not just the optics, Ava. It's my job, it's yours. We both can't afford distractions right now."

The word *distraction* hit her like a slap, and she could feel the heat flaming behind her eyes. "Have you thought about how awkward it will be if we end things?" she asked, her voice sharp with disbelief, with anger. "We work in the same building. The same vault. On the same operation."

There'd been moments when she'd felt like it was a dream with Ben, and she'd almost forgotten what her job required of her—detachment, mission, and duty over everything else. A part of her desperately wanted to remain within that dream, but Ben's words were a sharp jolt back to reality. He'd risked his entire career to clear her mother's name, but he had a duty to uphold his part of this mission. As a senior counterintelligence official, he had to pull away. Even as the rational side of her knew that was the truth, her heart fought against it.

"How do you see this playing out?" Ben asked, his voice cold. "You're in operations. I'm in counterintelligence, questioning every move you make, every source you run, every report you file. That's what counterintelligence does." There was a pained expression in his eyes as he undid his necktie with an angry jerk. "That's what I was supposed to be doing in Moscow."

She stared at him, her breath caught in her chest. "You're doing this now?"

"I should have done it months ago."

She stepped toward him, her hand twitching with the need to slap him. She needed him to feel the same way she was feeling. "Don't stand there and say this is about protocol," she said, anger pumping hot through her veins. "You're pulling away because you're scared. You're scared because you think this ends the same way it did for you before. That if you care about someone, you fall apart. That you fail again."

Ben's jaw clenched. "You're not thinking clearly. You're blinded by this rage against Abramovich, and believe me, when I get the chance, I'll kill him slowly for what he did to you. But right now, think about what's at stake. It's not just you and me; it's America's security on the line now."

She jabbed him in the chest with her index finger. "Don't you dare hide behind patriotism. You knew the stakes from the beginning. That didn't stop you then. So, what is it really?"

He looked away, unable to meet her eyes. And for a long excruciating moment, she thought he might walk out without a word.

"I missed it," he said, eyes finally locking with hers. "When the SVR set the trap for you and Konstantin. When they tracked you both down to that meeting. I saw it too late. I was too focused on *us*. On you. I should have been able to see it, to stop it before you were ever within reach of him."

"That's not fair. You're blaming yourself for something that neither of us could have predicted. It's the risk of operations. The risk of what we do."

"I'm trained to see threats," he said, stepping closer, taking both her hands in his. "But I didn't—because *I* was compromised."

"You weren't compromised," she said, her voice cracking. "You were human."

And for a second, so was she. A woman, not a CIA officer. Someone who wanted to be loved more than she wanted to be safe.

He shook his head. "That's the problem, Ava."

Silence stretched between them, dry and brittle, like a broken tree branch ready to snap.

"I know the cost," she whispered. "I chose this career, this life. I knew what it could take from me."

Ben's jaw worked, his eyes searching her face as if trying to memorize every detail.

"I can't be the reason it takes anymore."

Ava turned away from him, because if she looked at him one second longer, she'd let herself focus on the tension between his brows, the unspoken plea in his eyes. She might slap him again just to keep him close. Or worse, she'd beg him to stay. And that would break her worse than anything else. She straightened as if that could arm herself against the next moments.

Her reflection stared back at her from the window—haunted, tired, someone she barely recognized. "Then what are you waiting for?" she said, her voice like glass. "Go."

# CHAPTER

# 48

RAIN PATTERED STEADILY against Ava's windshield, the rhythmic thumping matching the pace of her heart as she made her way toward the CIA's headquarters in Langley, Virginia. A reporter's warnings crackled through the car radio: *Mass protests . . . federal overreach . . . state sovereignty at risk.*

It was late March, and cherry blossoms would soon be blooming along the Potomac River, but Ava felt the same oppressive Moscow clouds pressing in on her. If she was too late—if Russian agents already had access to the US military base—thousands of lives and American nuclear deterrence would be lost in a single strike.

Konstantin had told her about the power of the Gallitzin family, the network of spies that she could tap into now that she was one of them. But it wasn't until hours after his funeral that she had received an anonymous note ensuring the Gallitzin family's support and the intelligence that made the threat clear: Russian deep-cover operatives, disguised as military contractors, were preparing to infiltrate F.E. Warren Air Force Base. Their forged badges would pass routine checks, but biometrics would expose them.

It was a masterstroke—Russian agents already in deep cover, hidden in plain sight. The US military wouldn't even know what hit them. This kind of covert sabotage likely would set off a chain reaction, one that would further destabilize the already fragile geopolitical situation in the United States between the Liberty Coalition and those who opposed it. And once the attack occurred, there was nothing that the CIA could do to bring the country back from the brink of civil war.

At the entrance to CIA headquarters, Ava rolled down her window, and the chill of the damp morning air rushed in as she offered her badge to the guards to have it scanned. Pulling past the security gate, she looked at the main headquarters building, shrouded in a thin veil of rain that blurred the building's sharper edges. It was as if the building could fade into the world around it, just like the people who worked there, just like her mother had.

Ava parked in one of the thousands of spaces and exited the car, her rain boots sloshing along the wet asphalt from the ever-expanding parking lot as she walked the half mile to the New Headquarters Building, NHB. The cold sent a fine mist against her skin, as if the world itself was reminding her of what she had lost, what was at stake: Russia's destruction of America's intercontinental ballistic missiles would mean all-out war, the loss of thousands, possibly millions of lives.

Inside, at the head of a long table, sat the CIA director, Cain Stuart, a man who'd spent most of his years in the CIA's analytical unit rather than out in the field. But he was still a towering figure within the Agency, with silver-streaked hair and steely eyes that had always conveyed authority. But there was something else today, something in his sharp gaze that conveyed skepticism that Ava had never seen before.

When she entered the room, Director Stuart stood along with the others in unison, their eyes raking over her as if they could somehow see signs that she had been compromised by her newfound Russian roots. At the head of the table, Cain pulled out a chair next to him and motioned for her to sit. At least a dozen other officers were there, including the FBI director—a reminder that they'd need the Bureau's help if the Russian operatives, who'd been within the United States for decades, were now US citizens. It wasn't the first time Russia's deep-cover agents had seamlessly blended into American society and vanished without a trace.

Sitting along the back wall with the other analysts was Ben. His posture was rigid, his gaze focused on the table, avoiding any chance of eye contact with Ava. She recognized the pull before she saw him, the tension that was always there between them. But today felt different—heavier, more complicated.

In Moscow, they had crossed lines they couldn't uncross, and with each day it had become increasingly apparent that her feelings for him were evolving into something deeper and more permanent. But she couldn't afford to process it now. Not here. Not with the clock ticking. Within the sterile coldness of the conference room, they were back to being colleagues, or at least pretending to be. Their roles were clear: She would track down the Russian agents targeting the US military base, while he would make sure that the CIA's movements remained undetected by Moscow's watchful eye. He was right. They couldn't afford to be distracted by what had happened between them, not now, possibly not ever. They were on the same side, but on opposite ends of the mission. And that was the way it had to be.

"Ms. Anderson," Cain said, his voice cutting through the silence. "Take us through this one."

Ava nodded sharply, her fingers pressing hard into the edges of the table as Jeremy, a young analyst with a post-doctorate in Russian studies, distributed red folders labeled RESTRICTED HANDLING.

Ava laid out the intelligence of a high probability infiltration attempt, a Russian-sponsored operation targeting a US military facility that held nuclear weapons. The words on the page were stark, clinical, yet chillingly familiar to the ones Director Cain had likely seen before. Except this time, they were from the CIA's best penetration of the SVR in decades—her father, code name Excalibur.

Silence followed as the gravity of the report settled over the room. After several long minutes the director looked up, sighed heavily, and pushed his glasses further up onto the bridge of his nose before shifting his focus onto Ava. "And the source of this report is—?"

"Excalibur. And his subsource network," Ava answered.

Cain's eyes sharpened as he looked toward Frank, now director of Russia House. "He's passed asset validation?"

Frank nodded. "Polygraph and a psych eval. He was responsible for helping us dismantle Russia's last disinformation campaign utilizing Vibrantia, and his intelligence has been corroborated by Tiberius."

Cain turned to the NSA director. "Any signals intelligence?"

"We've picked up some chatter on Abramovich's phones. He's planning something big, but the details are still vague."

Cain exhaled sharply and fixed his gaze on Ava. "And Excalibur, he died in that gunfight you were involved in on the streets of Moscow?"

Ava swallowed down a lump. *It hadn't just been another operation.* It had been an execution, and Konstantin had died because of the risks he'd taken for her.

"And I know he was your father," Cain added. "But what other assurances can you give me that Excalibur wasn't feeding us disinformation?"

She hesitated, then finally admitted, "Because I trusted him." The words surprised her. She had never said them out loud before. Trust was never a currency she'd spent freely.

A flicker of something unreadable passed over Cain's face. He nodded and turned to the FBI director, who pushed a thick dossier across the table. "I took the liberty of drawing up all the foreign contractors working on US military installations who have entered the country within the last six months."

"These men have likely been here for years," Ava countered.

Cain cleared his throat and turned to address the secretary of defense. "I want all contractor access to be subject to secondary biometric verification on base. Any discrepancies result in immediate detainment and interrogation. Lock down all nonessential contractor movement until the threat window has passed."

Ava felt the moment shift. The weight of command settling over the room. The urgency. The responsibility. The expectation that she and the others in the room would act without question. But her questions still lingered. About her mother when she was detained by the Russians. About how no one in this room had lifted a finger. And why, after years of service, loyalty still felt like a one-sided contract. At one time, she'd believed in the Agency's mission without hesitation, believed in preserving America's security at all costs. But what was the cost of serving an entity that would willingly abandon their own?

"I want all explosive ordnance disposal teams placed on high alert," the secretary of defense interjected, "with rapid-response units stationed near all key personnel and infrastructure."

Cain turned to Ava. "I want you and your team to conduct immediate background checks on all contractor entries in the past thirty days. Run them through every database we've got."

She nodded automatically, even as doubt gnawed at the edges of her resolve. This organization had abandoned *her mother.*

"Ben," Cain continued, "make sure that none of this catches the Kremlin's attention. I don't want them shifting tactics or targets at the last minute."

Ben barely glanced at Ava before nodding, but she saw it. The flicker of concern he tried to hide. *He knew.* He understood that every mission she took part in now carried the ghost of her mother. Knew that every choice she made was a battle between duty and the betrayal she could never forget.

Beneath the table, her fingers curled into a fist, nails pressing into crescent moons into the skin until the pain steadied her. There was no room for personal grievances. Not now. Maybe not ever. The pounding in her chest reminded her that she was still alive, still tethered to purpose. Everything was on the line—her credibility, her family's legacy, and the survival of America's nuclear arsenal.

Yet beneath her armor of discipline, a quiet ache lingered: Was she still fighting to protect what America stood for? Or was she fighting to prove that her mother's sacrifice had not been in vain?

# CHAPTER

# 49

Ava's fingers raced across the keyboard as intelligence reports and classified intercepts flashed on the screen in front of her. The glow of the computer screen illuminated the exhaustion written on her face—every keystroke fueled by the gnawing dread that they were already too late. She desperately needed an operational lead—a photograph, a phone number, an email address—any scrap of intel that could be used to track down the Russian operatives. But the hours bled past midnight, and time blurred. The outside world felt increasingly distant, the windowless vault adding to Ava's feeling that time was closing in.

No one spoke; there was no need. The silence carried the same urgency Ava felt with every hour they failed to find a lead. The constant pressure was something she'd grown used to—knowing she was at the center of something larger than herself. But tonight the stakes felt greater than ever: One misstep and the United States's nuclear deterrent could vanish into Russian hands.

Ben sat next to her, the quiet murmur of his keystrokes a gentle reminder that she wasn't alone. She didn't look at him, but she could feel the weight of him beside her, ready to flag an operational lead that was too risky.

"What about sending messages out to the five-eyes?" Ava asked Ben. 'Perhaps they've heard whispers of the attack. MI5 usually has someone we can talk to."

"Too risky," Ben said, his jaw tight.

Ava exhaled through her nose, although she knew he was right. An inquiry through MI5, British intelligence, and its intelligence partners—the "five eyes"—would likely get back to Abramovich. And if he knew the CIA was onto him, he could change targets and tactics—and they would find themselves five steps behind.

Ava glanced up at the screen that hovered above their workstations. Images showed protests erupting in Omsk, Molotov cocktails arching through the night in Rostov. "Looks like Abramovich's hold on power is slipping," Ava said.

"Slipping, yes," Ben countered, his eyes grim. "But a man like Abramovich does not fall quietly."

Before she could reply, Derick from NSA marched over, a report clutched tightly in his hand. "Intercepted chatter—a burner phone tied to Abramovich's security detail." He dropped the paper onto their desks. "Details are vague, but the tone is clear. His plans are already in motion."

"Even if we oust him tomorrow, it might not matter." Ben scanned the lines of the report. "His war machine is already warmed up."

The mood shifted, energy pulsing throughout the room. Chairs scraped back, phones shrieked, voices dropped to clipped whispers, energy drinks were cracked open. The SCIF was alive with the urgency of a war room, and yet beneath it all was a drum beat of dread.

By the time half the team staggered off for food and more caffeine, Ava and Ben were alone in the painful silence of the SCIF.

Ben cleared his throat but kept his eyes fixed on the screen, the blue hue casting shadows beneath his eyes. "I know that you don't want to believe this, but I'm on your side, Ava. Always have been. Always will be."

She refused to look at him, although the need for him still burned inside her chest. All her life she'd wanted the kind of intimacy she'd felt with Ben. She hadn't known it fully until the night after she'd made it out of Abramovich's jail. But her entire life she'd been lied to, and her greatest fear was giving over her heart and later realizing that it had been a mistake.

She bent her head and pinched the bridge of her nose as her latest search results began to populate. Clicking into the CIA's travel database, she started cross-referencing the NSA's flagged phone numbers for Dimitri Abramovich. Another window opened on the second monitor, feeding the data into a phone-tracing database, mapping second- and third-tier connections like a spider web of digital footprints. The threads were faint, but they were there. She just needed one that led to somewhere real.

Ava clicked on the latest search results on her computer and scrolled past the dead ends, the burner phones, the disconnected lines—until a result populated on her screen. *A name. A face.*

Sergei Volkov, DOB August 8, 1982. She entered the name in a third database that ran a search against all the intelligence reports available—and a chill ran down her spine.

"Ben." Her voice barely broke through the steady hum of the air filtration system, but he heard her. She felt him shift beside her, leaning in. She didn't take her eyes off the screen as he read the dossier from the Danish Secret Service along with her.

*Sergei Anatolyevich Volkov.*

Former GRU officer. Ruthless private military strategist. Shadow operative. A mercenary with blood on his hands. A ghost who moved between war zones, leaving nothing but whispers and bodies behind.

Ava scanned the report, her heart thrashing. *This is it.*

After serving in Chechnya and Ukraine, Volkov became disillusioned with official Kremlin politics and carved his own path as a mercenary warlord, forming the Volkov Group—a covert paramilitary force specializing in assassinations, sabotage, and hybrid warfare. His operations were funded through black-market arms deals, cyber heists, and contracts with rogue states—and Dimitri Abramovich.

Seven years ago, he'd entered the US through the John F. Kennedy International Airport.

Ben exhaled sharply. "I'll call Frank."

Two hours later the director's conference room buzzed with the weight of what Ava had uncovered. The overhead florescent lights were harsh, but the brightness cut through the exhaustion that clawed relentlessly at the edges of Ava's mind. She stood next to Ben, the adrenaline of her discovery still burning through her system. The room was full—Frank, Director Cain, half a dozen senior analysts and operations officers—but all eyes were on them.

"Sir, the discovery of the warheads on the Trans-Siberian freight line was never the win we thought it was." Ava slid a photo across the table: the train, charred and split open, warheads half-buried in the snow. "Those ICBMs weren't meant to be launched from Russia. They were bait. Decoys. The entire seizure was engineered by the GRU to misdirect us."

"The warheads were sold off to the fringe buyers under Abramovich's direction," Ben interjected. "Their movement across the black market was meant to flood our intelligence channels—make us chase false signals and scramble our surveillance assets. Meanwhile, the GRU's real operation was already in motion."

She clicked the remote and the map displayed at the front of the room zoomed westward—across the Atlantic, into the United States. "The real threat isn't overseas, sir. It's inside our own borders." She pointed to a schematic of the Minuteman III command structure, Next, America's ICBM silos displayed on the screen—Wyoming, Montana, North Dakota.

The room went still.

"If they succeed," Ben said. "It won't be Russian missiles hitting American soil. It'll be ours, launched from within, under the illusion of a system malfunction or rogue retaliation."

"You're saying Abramovich intends to weaponize our own arsenal against us?"

"Orlov Strategic Solutions, OSS." Ben ran a hand through his hair. "Publicly it's a logistics and security company. But in reality, it's a front for a covert paramilitary force advancing Russian interests under the guise of private contracts."

Ava picked up where he left off, flipping open a briefing packet with damp palms. "Based in Saint Petersburg, Russia. Founded by

Sergei Anatolyevich Volkov, a former GRU Spetsnaz colonel who served alongside Dimitri Abramovich in the Russian military. Staffed with ex-FSB, Russian Airborne Troops—battle hardened and loyal. They started securing Russian energy infrastructure in Central Asia, but by 2014, they were in Ukraine, embedded with separatists, training, fighting, eliminating targets under the cover of civilian security advisors."

Frank crossed his arms, a bead of sweat visible on his furrowed brow.

Director Cain leaned forward; his shirt was rumpled, signaling that he'd gotten as little sleep as Ava and the rest of the team. "What else do we know?"

Ava didn't hesitate. "They call him the Wolf of Moscow."

"Trained in covert tactics, psychological warfare, cyber espionage," Ben said. "He served in Chechnya, then Ukraine, before breaking off from official Kremlin oversight. That's when he formed the Volkov Group—a paramilitary force specializing in assassinations, sabotage, and hybrid warfare."

Ava's gaze swept the room. "Intelligence now indicates there's been a security breech at the missile base in Wyoming—and we believe he's connected."

Frank swore under his breath as he turned toward Ben. "Run additional background checks on everyone with access—personnel, contractors, missileers. Anyone showing signs of resentment, financial trouble, or instability. Someone inside that base has been compromised or soon will be. I'm sure they're looking for access codes, security procedures—any weaknesses that they could use to their advantage."

The air in the conference room seemed to constrict, heavy with the realization that the breach might not be digital at all—but human.

"You're telling me Volkov, the Wolf of Moscow, could be coming to the US?" Cain leaned back in his chair with steepled fingers, his eyes dark. "And he's targeting our nuclear arsenal?"

Ava's voice didn't waiver. "Not could be. Not maybe." She locked eyes with him, her chest hammering with uncertainty and fear. "He's already here."

# CHAPTER

# 50

Ben leaned against the cool glass of the airplane window, pretending not to notice Ava, a few rows away. But every few seconds, his gaze flicked to her reflection—her brows narrowed in concentration, her face bathed in the pale blue of the computer screen. Even now, buried in classified satellite imagery and grid coordinates, she radiated a fierce, relentless energy that tugged at him like a gravitational pull. He should be thinking about the target, about Volkov, but he was still wracked with guilt over what had happened to Ava in Moscow. How he'd missed the signs, and Abramovich and his men had come for her. He would never forgive himself. It was like Ukraine all over again.

He couldn't forget the moment the call came in about Ava—Frank's hoarse voice informing him that Ava had not returned to Moscow Station after her meeting with Konstantin. Initially, he'd told himself that it was a glitch. That she was late. That she would find her way back like she always did. But hours had stretched on, and when the surveillance footage surfaced—grainy but brutal, showing her being dragged into an unmarked van, he'd felt his heart drop out of his chest. Then he'd ignored Frank, gone against the Moscow Station chief, and torn the city apart to find her. They'd pleaded with him for patience, to wait for the Delta hostage rescue team to arrive from Germany. But he'd gone anyway, assembled a team himself. And while he'd found her and rescued her, he would never forgive himself for what Abramovich had done to her. They'd killed her father, tortured her, nearly broken her—and knowing that he hadn't prevented it gutted him.

And now he had to keep his distance. It was the only way to remain objective, to keep her safe, to spot the threats lingering around every corner. He'd do whatever it took to ensure that what happened to her in Moscow never happened to her again. Even if it cut him to the bone to keep his distance, to act as if he didn't love her.

He rubbed the back of his neck, trying to exorcise the memory of her—the way she'd looked in his apartment in Moscow, strong yet vulnerable, letting him cradle her against him. The way her face looked when they made love, when the line between emotion and mission had blurred. He hadn't meant to fall for her. He'd told himself for months that it wasn't happening. But when it came to Ava, logic had failed him. It always had. And yet, that same logic now screamed at him to keep his distance. It was the best way he could stay clear-minded and detect any threats, the best way to keep her safe. That and the mission were all that mattered.

He shifted his gaze back to his laptop, trying to review encrypted data feeds, but his guilt clung to him as he typed commands into the system. He stared at the latest surveillance maps of F.E. Warren Air Force Base on his computer screen. The base unfolded in neat rows, with cul-de-sacs and green spaces. He knew its isolation was not an afterthought. The base's position, surrounded by miles of open terrain, served its purpose—deterrence and defense at its purest form. Unlike the sprawling air bases with roaring fighter jets and endless runways he had visited while in the military, the power of F.E. Warren remained hidden underground, its launch silos capable of reaching over six thousand miles at Mach 23—*fifteen thousand* miles per hour—without reliance on GPS, making it resistant to jamming and cyber threats.

Ben felt a band tightening around his chest. Even with all the base's defenses—armed patrols, intrusion censors, reinforced latches—the possibility of Sergei Volkov breaching this fortress gnawed at him. It should be impossible, but Ben had learned the hard way that nothing was impossible for someone with Volkov's background.

He began typing strings of code to trace digital footprints that didn't belong—ghosts left behind by GRU cyber operatives. But no matter how many threats he neutralized, no matter how many operations they won, the guilt he felt over Ava's capture would never disappear.

He heard her shift in her seat several rows away, could feel her watching him. She always looked at him as if she could see right through his shields. And a part of him wanted her to keep looking, wanted her to see the parts of himself that he had buried.

"I think we have it." Ava's voice was low but firm. "Cyber traced the activity. GRU hackers are planning a coordinated attack in two days. They'll spoof alerts of a missile fuel leak at a different site."

He nodded, jaw tight. He should have just kept going, focused on the data, the strategy, the facts. But his eyes drifted back to her—because, dammit, he couldn't help it.

He rolled his neck like he was trying to shake something loose. "We still need to identify who Volkov has working on his side at the base."

Ava straightened, already running through the possibilities. "Let's have Treasury run the entire maintenance team's financials. Someone's bound to be drowning in gambling debts." She paused. "I also think we need to counter trace. I'll request a list from Swedish intel—any accounts with untraceable deposits over three million within the last six months."

Ben shifted. "Do we really want to highlight this to Swedish intel?"

"It's not like they're super chummy with the Russians."

"No, but they share intel with China, who is."

"Fine," she said, "you'd have sign off on any request anyway as the CI lead."

"I'm not saying don't do it." He exhaled slowly, eyes still on her. "I just want you to be aware of the trickle effects."

"I'm aware," she said decisively.

He looked away, back at his screen, forcing himself into the grid and data. But his thoughts stayed with her, making him question what he was doing, making it harder to remember to keep his distance.

From the corner of the cabin, the FBI attaché cleared his throat. "I've flagged local law enforcement. Cheyenne PD and Wyoming Highway Patrol are watching for anything unusual."

Ben's eyes drifted toward Ava, the way she stared at the base below like she could already see the breach—like she knew what was coming. The pieces were moving. The board shifting. Volkov and his operatives would make their move. He wished that he could prevent Ava from becoming one of those pieces. But she didn't need saving now. She needed backup. And he sure as hell wasn't going to fail her again. He would burn the world down before letting her get hurt.

And when the time came, he knew there would be no more distance, no more lies between them.

# CHAPTER

# 51

In a dim hotel in downtown Cheyenne, Ava stood by the bed, the stench of musty carpet and cheap cleaning solution colliding in the air, making her head swim. She unpacked her clothes without thought, her fingers moving on autopilot as she laid out her black yoga pants, long-sleeve black shirt, and Glock 9mm on the nightstand. Tomorrow, before the first hint of dawn, they would head to the Air Force base.

A sudden knock at the door shattered the silence, and she inhaled a sharp breath. It was nearly midnight, and anyone who wasn't Ben or Frank had no reason to disturb her at this hour. But Frank had been left behind at Langley with Director Cain, so that left only one option. She could feel her pulse quicken in her throat, an odd mixture of relief and anxiety settling deep within her chest.

"Ava." Ben's voice came through the door, rough and familiar in a way that made her chest tighten. "I have an update."

Her hand hovered on the doorknob as the weight of exhaustion pressed down on her. Every muscle ached from too many sleepless nights, too much loss, too much pretending she didn't care. But it wasn't just fatigue, it was him. Ben, always too close and yet somehow unreachable.

She hated that part of her still wanted to fall into his arms, to forget everything for just one breath. But reason and the damn mission wouldn't let her. She knew the breakup had been the logical call, the smart move. And yet the knowledge did nothing to dull the sting.

She drew in a slow breath and opened the door. He stood there, looking as wrecked as she felt, eyes shadowed, and shirt creased. What hit her hardest wasn't how he looked, but the quiet desperation behind his gaze.

"Don't worry," he said, his voice rough. "I'm not here to talk about us." His words were clipped, and she felt a pang of disappointment despite herself.

"The Swedes sent over the name just over thirty minutes ago. This has to be the first time I've seen them respond this quickly. Usually they're more likely to hide a terrorist of interest than help us stop them." A hollow chuckle escaped his lips. "You were right," he said, running a hand through his hair. "I'll admit it when you're right."

He reached into a diplomatic pouch and pulled out the report. He handed it to her, his fingers lightly brushing hers, and for a split second, the heat between them felt raw, alive. But it was fleeting, gone as soon as it came, as he began detailing the intel. "Our man is a disgruntled maintenance officer named Captain Richard Holloway. Orlov Strategic Solutions appears to have deposited $5 million in a Swiss account three months ago. He's got gambling debts and resentment about being repeatedly passed over for promotion."

The words barely registered in her mind. What mattered right now was how his voice cracked slightly when he spoke, like he was on the edge of something more than just the traitor who would help Russia destroy the world.

She forced herself to focus, her mind grabbing onto the data. "Wow, that's more money than I thought," she said. "The Russian oil market must be doing better than I originally suspected."

"The Air Force should be taking him into custody as we speak. Debriefings will begin in about an hour."

She reached for her gun on the nightstand. "Well, who needs sleep anyway?"

"No. Sleep, Ava." Ben's voice softened, and she caught concern in his eyes. "You're going to need it if we're as close as I think we are to Abramovich enacting his plan."

Her stomach churned at the thought. There was no way that she could sleep knowing that they had Holloway in custody. "Not a chance. I want to be there as soon as he starts to talk. Are they going to allow us to view the debriefings over CCTV?"

"Yeah, but the Air Force will take the lead on this, since he's one of theirs. "

Ava nodded. "Is that all?" Her voice was sharper than she meant it to be, betraying the frustration she felt clawing at her. She wanted to collapse into his arms, but the distance between them felt miles wide. The mission had to come first, yet she longed for a moment of peace, normalcy, with Ben before the entire world came falling down around them.

"There's something else." Ben's voice dropped lower, his gaze flickering toward his phone. His fingers hesitated over the screen, and then, with a quiet sigh, he pressed a button. Before she could respond, there was another knock at the door. "But before I share it, I want you to understand that it was necessary that this be kept as a secret, not only for his safety, but for yours as well."

"His?" The weight of his words hit her like a hammer to her chest, squeezing the air from her lungs.

She walked slowly toward the door, her hand gripping the doorknob. The cold metal sent a chill up her arm as she desperately tried not to hope, not to pray. She creaked the door open and standing in the doorway—was Konstantin.

He was smaller than she remembered. Not frail, just stripped down. As if the violence had carved away anything unnecessary, leaving only what was essential. His pants hung loose on his frame, and his usually pristinely ironed shirt was wrinkled. She knew what Abramovich and his men were capable of—what they had likely done to her father. But it was his eyes that stole her breath from her lungs.

Gray. The same shade of gray as her eyes.

She had grieved for him. And yet, he was here. He was—alive. The weight of the days she'd spent believing his death was her fault crashed into her, an unbearable mix of regret and guilt that had pummeled at her insides. But here was her hope, a second chance, staring at her. She felt her face tremble, betraying the flood of emotion she could no longer contain.

"Why?" It was all she could manage as she swallowed her tears.

"I gave you what you needed, what you came for." Konstantin's voice cracked, an unfamiliar vulnerability slipping through. "It was time for me to let you go."

Her breath hitched in her throat. "So you faked your own death?"

"I've done it before."

"Who the hell did they bury then?" she asked.

He shrugged. "One of Abramovich's thugs. He won't be missed."

Ava's chest tightened, her mind still a whirlwind of anger and disbelief. "How did you get out?"

"Your good friend here." He nodded at Ben, who had a somber look on his face. "If that's still what you're calling one another these days."

She turned toward Ben, her pulse thundering in her ears. "You had no right to keep this from me."

"How else were you supposed to show that level of emotion at his funeral?"

"I'm a better actress than you think." The words slipped out, but they didn't bring the satisfaction she'd hoped for. "Plus, my mother—"

"I'm sorry." Ben's gaze softened, though the hurt behind his eyes lingered, impossible to miss. "It was necessary to keep this from you. The exfil wasn't easy, but one of the conditions was that the truth be kept from you until he was safely back in America."

Her anger simmered, but a bitter laugh escaped her lips. "Keeping things from me for the betterment of the op seems to be a convenient answer these days." She turned toward her father, the weight of their situation pressing on her. "Now what?"

Konstantin met her gaze, the steel in his eyes softened by something unspoken, something too hard to name. "Now I settle down as a cattle rancher in Wyoming and have the life I've always dreamed of."

"You want to be a cowboy?" Her voice betrayed her, an unbidden laugh almost escaping. She couldn't tell him how desperately sad his death had made her, how saying goodbye made her feel as though she'd been robbed once more of a family, a sense of belonging.

"Among other things." His smile was small but genuine. "I first and foremost would like to be your father, if you will let me."

# CHAPTER

# 52

AVA'S HOPE WAS like an anchor in her chest as she looked out at the stars, sharp above the expansive plains of Wyoming's wild country, their cold light reflecting off patches of lingering snow. The April wind was brutal as she and Ben arrived at F.E. Warren Air Force Base, rattling the nearby chain-link fence that surrounded the facility and cutting through her newly issued Air Force jacket. The air carried the scent of jet fuel like a warning, a reminder that she wasn't playing a role, and this wasn't a training exercise. The stakes were real and rising by the second.

Their objective was clear: intercept the Russian GRU operatives before they infiltrated a Minuteman III ICBM silo. They now knew that the warheads discovered on the train had only been a diversion—the missiles themselves weren't the real threat, but the cover for a larger operation aimed at hijacking America's own nuclear arsenal from within. The GRU didn't launch their weapons; they needed people inside the silos who could override safeguards and reroute launch commands at the source. But with Captain Holloway holding back critical information during his debriefing with the Air Force, they were no closer to Sergei Volkov or stopping whatever nightmare he was about to unleash.

What they were up against felt small when she thought about what Ben had done. He'd risked everything again—his career, his life—to reunite Ava with her father, the man she thought was dead. The realization landed hard. She wanted to reach for him, to say something real, to stop burying her feelings for him. Every moment with him felt like she was standing on the edge of her own undoing.

"How did you get Konstantin out of Russia?" She glanced at Ben, her footsteps uneasy on the frozen ground. "That can't have been easy."

Ben turned slightly, his face half shadowed by the dim security lights. He hadn't shaved in days, and his beard had grown out slightly, flecked with auburn highlights.

"The Gallitzin family," he said after a moment, his voice low, "your family, is more connected than you realize."

"Was it wise to involve them?" she asked. "Surely, the CIA wouldn't be thrilled about you working with . . . outsiders to smuggle Russian SVR agents in and out of the country."

"That's why I worked with the FBI," he said, his gaze locked on the looming outline of the SCIF building. "They weren't in the dark about Konstantin's help over the years. How do you think I found the emails proving your mother's innocence?"

"FBI had them? All this time?"

"They were part of a restricted handling case. Apparently, only a small number of people knew about the operations that your mother and Konstantin were running back then."

"If that's the case, why didn't any of those people come forward?"

Ben's jaw worked. "Dead," he said flatly. "All of them."

The word hit her like ice water, a chill uncoiling at the base of her spine and crawling upward, wrapping around her ribs until it was hard to breathe.

"This case seems to be getting shadier by the minute," she said, but the words felt too small, too frail for the truth that laid between them.

He'd risked everything for her—his career, maybe even his freedom—to give her what she'd longed for all these years. A father. A family. And though she tried to hold them back, the words tore out of her chest before she could help it. "Why?" she asked, her voice cracking.

He stopped and looked at her with an intensity that pinned her in place, and for an instant the mask slipped, and she saw the truth burning in his eyes. "You know why."

Her pulse was a dull roar in her ears when they reached the entrance to the SCIF, drowning out everything else. The squat, windowless structure loomed like a bunker meant to bury secrets. Ben scanned his badge, and the scanner's red light swept over his credentials, then prompted biometric identification. Ava forced herself to mirror his detachment, his focus, knowing that it was useless.

The scanner hummed as it analyzed her irises. A soft beep. Authorization granted. The vault door clicked open, revealing the steel-gray elevator door that would take them to the secure facility. Ava stepped inside, her heart slamming against her ribcage. Not just because of the mission ahead, but because of the man beside her—a man who would sacrifice everything for her but still wouldn't let her fully in. And she wasn't sure how much longer she could pretend that didn't break her a little more every day.

Inside the SCIF, the air thrummed with quiet urgency as a dozen Air Force personnel sat at their workstations, the blue glow of their monitors casting halos on their faces as they monitored real-time surveillance of the ISBM silos. The air smelled of recycled oxygen and stale coffee, an atmosphere that Ava had become accustomed to in recent weeks.

Ben talked quietly with one of the officers, asking about the most recent updates while stealing glances at the front of the vault, where a closed-circuit television showed an Air Force officer feeding questions to Captain Richard Holloway in clipped, controlled tones. Holloway's head was bent, his features hidden from the camera.

Ava approached Lieutenant Colonel Kareem, the ranking Air Force officer observing Holloway's debrief with his arms folded, his stance wide. Kareem's deeply lined face was neutral, but the tension in his shoulders betrayed him, telling Ava that the colonel was growing impatient with the lack of progress with the interrogation.

"Mind if I take a stab at it, Colonel?" she asked in a low voice.

He exhaled a sharp breath through his nose. "Be my guest. Washington's breathing down my neck."

Ava entered the interrogation vault alone, the low hum of the air conditioning unit the only sound. She'd quickly looked over Holloway's service record—two decades specializing in missile defense with the US Air Force, and a clearance level that granted him access to some of the United States's most sensitive programs. But there had been an alarming uptick in suspicious financial activity on Holloway's bank accounts during his last periodic reinvestigation.

When Department of Defense security had questioned Holloway, he'd said he inherited the extra funds in his bank account from a recently deceased aunt—but no obituary or will was found. It didn't take a seasoned intel operative to see the markings of a traitor. And if Ava's instincts were correct, he had been feeding information to the Russians about the US missile defense program for some time.

Holloway's chair let out a small creak as Ava approached, his gaze darting from her to the door and back again. He was in his mid-fifties, with gray hair that had begun to whiten at the temples. His uniform was neatly pressed, but the slight twitching of his legs, the tapping of his fingers on the table, made clear that he was nervous or hiding something. Or both.

"Captain Holloway," Ava said, sitting across from him and propping her elbows up on the metal table between them. "You're in a difficult position. You know that, right?" Her voice was slow, deliberate. She wanted him to feel his predicament.

His Adam's apple bobbed as he swallowed. Silence.

Ava offered a slow, cold smile. "You've been compromised. We have records of your communications with Sergei Anatolyevich Volkov." It was a lie. But she needed the cutout, the intermediary who was feeding Holloway's information back to Volkov and Abramovich. Holloway couldn't have been working alone.

His face remained blank, but a flicker of something—panic, maybe—darkened his eyes. "I have no idea who Sergei Volkov is."

"That's not what your call records indicate."

His jaw tightened, but he said nothing. The tension thickened between them—a storm cloud ready to break.

She folded her arms, her voice calm, but with an edge. "We know about the money transfers. And, most importantly, we know the Russians are targeting US missile silos. You're feeding them critical information—intelligence that could tip the world into the next world war."

His breath hitched, barely perceptible, but enough.

She pressed forward. "Why, Captain? Is it just about the money? Or is it something more?"

A muscle jumped in his jaw, and he shifted uncomfortably in his seat. He looked away, his fingers curling into tight fists. "You wouldn't understand."

"Try me." She softened her voice just enough, weaving sympathy into her words. "I know what it's like to be overlooked. To feel like no one values your sacrifices."

His eyes snapped to meet hers.

"What are you?" he scoffed. "Twenty-two? You have no idea how difficult this job has been on me and my family. The military takes and takes, and when you ask for more, they tell you to be grateful and shut up."

Ava nodded, her expression carefully neutral. "Listen, I get it." She softened her voice. "But was selling secrets really the answer?"

"I didn't sell anything," he hissed, his voice rising. "I'm not a traitor."

Ava waited, letting the silence press in, trying to gauge his next move. Holloway's twitching movements became more pronounced, and sweat pebbled on his upper lip.

"I could hook you up to a lie detector," Ava said slowly, "but I think you believe your lies."

"I told you," he said through clenched teeth. "I'm not a liar."

"Then tell me who recruited you. Volkov is not working alone."

Holloway's gaze darted toward the door, and Ava's stomach clenched. He was protecting someone. Someone powerful. He was fighting, but not for himself.

She needed to press harder.

Ava tapped her fingers on the table, the cold metal biting into her fingertips.

"Captain Holloway, you have a wife, children. What do you think your family would do if they discovered what you were doing? The consequences of your actions aren't just going to affect you. Your job with the US military is over." She leaned forward and clasped her hands on the table in front of her. "But there are certain things that I can do to make sure that your treachery isn't made public."

Finally, he looked at her, fear blazing within his eyes. "I didn't sell out. I'm not like them."

Ava stood and leaned over the table. "Who's *them*? Who's pulling the strings? Volkov didn't recruit just you. You're part of a larger operation."

"You have to make them understand," Holloway said in a strained voice. "It wasn't supposed to be like this. I—I didn't think it would go this far."

Ava's pulse quickened. This was the break she needed. "Who, Captain?" she asked, her voice firm. "Who recruited you?"

Holloway's hands clenched into a tight fist on the table, his knuckles turning white. He exhaled sharply, eyes clouded by regret and fear. Finally, he spoke. "I thought I was helping. But now, I—"

Before he could finish, the door to the interrogation room slammed open, cutting him off. Ava turned sharply, her hand instinctively going to the 9mm in her side holster.

It was Ben, his voice serious, his eyes flickering between her and Holloway. "Ava, there's been a development."

She hesitated, then turned, throwing Holloway one last glance before she exited the room, her eyes hard and unyielding. "We'll finish this later."

Back in the common area, the air was tight with tension, as if the walls themselves held their breath. Ava sank down into a chair next to Ben, eyes narrowing at the screen. GRU unit 29155—an elite team of cyber warfare experts—was active.

"Look at this," Ben pointed at Splunk, the CIA's dark web monitoring software that tracked where cyber criminals operated. "Someone is disguising their activity as routine Air Force maintenance. But the coding is too sophisticated for common hackers. Looks to me to be an anomaly."

"I agree," Ava said. "This has GRU fingerprints all over it. Export the report to Langley."

But before she could escalate the report, a second Air Force analyst waved her over.

"It's a second flag." The analyst pointed at her screen, which was showing Recorded Future and Threat Connect, a second tool used to highlight real-time intelligence for emerging cyber threats. "A maintenance override request. Site K-12."

"Time to move," Ben said, his voice like steel.

Ava didn't hesitate. This was it.

# CHAPTER

# 53

"WE'VE GOT RUSSIANS inside one of our silos." Colonel Kareem's voice cracked through the vault like a thunderclap. "THREATCON. Everybody moves, *now*!"

Ava and Ben bolted toward the elevator, Colonel Kareem's heavy boots hammering on the floor behind them as he barked orders into his secure satellite phone. The air in the vault was thick with the smell of stale coffee and sweat. It suddenly felt suffocating, and Ava felt desperate to be above ground.

Kareem raised a secure radio to his mouth as they stepped into the elevator shaft. "Control, this is MAF Delta, we have a security event at Echo-4, confirm?"

Static. Then a clipped, tense response. "Confirmed. Stand by for the TRF deployment."

Ava's pulse slammed against her ribs as she stole a glance at Ben. His jaw was tight. "This is real," she murmured under her breath. She had seen events like these unfold within the movies. Never had she imagined that she'd be a part of one.

Ben nodded. "Yeah," he whispered, as Kareem continued to bark orders into his phone. "It's real." Ava saw Ben's fingers twitch against his side as the elevator doors groaned shut.

A heavy, sick feeling entered her stomach. Somewhere, far above her clearance level, men with hardened faces in dark suits sat in a steel enforced room, red phones flashing, readying themselves for the unimaginable.

The moment when the world imploded.

When the doors hissed open above ground, the world had already shifted. A klaxon siren wailed, cutting through the icy dawn like a blade. Missile Security Forces and the Quick Reaction Force, QRF, swarmed the base, boots clacking against the asphalt. Under a low, gray sky, Air Force personnel scrambled into their CBRN suits—protection from chemical, biological, radiological, and nuclear threats. Federal agents and local police swarmed. Her nostrils filled with the acrid smell of jet fuel, and her stomach lurched. If the Russian operatives had compromised the US nuclear arsenal, World War III would ensue.

The wind tore through her hair, flinging loose pieces of asphalt against her face until her eyes burned. Ava knew they were behind. If the Russians had breached Site K-12, this wasn't just an infiltration—it was an act of war. Ava and Ben rushed toward a UH-60 Black Hawk, its rotors chopping the air into currents that rippled outward. Beside her, Ben and five paramilitary officers moved, faces carved in total concentration. Ava's breath was ragged, her chest tight as she ran toward the helicopter.

"I want all access roads blocked." Kareem shouted over the chaos to his second-in-command. "All airspace restricted. Assume the intruders are hostile."

The young lieutenant faltered for only a moment. "Rules of engagement?"

Kareem's answer was cold and absolute. "Neutralize the threat."

The lieutenant nodded sharply and rushed to the area where the TRF, Tactical Response Force, was already moving. Ten men in full military fatigues sprinted to their armored Humvees with their M4 rifles locked and loaded. They didn't need to speak. The air itself seemed to pulse with a grim awareness of the duty, the danger, and the unspoken truth that not all of them would return.

A woman in fatigues rushed toward Kareem carrying a handheld computer, her hair tied haphazardly into a messy bun. "I've elevated the Force Protection Condition to Delta and notified the secretary of defense. He's asking if you deem retaliatory measures necessary."

Kareem's eyes flicked toward Ava and Ben. Something unreadable passing through his heavy gaze. "You sure about this?" His voice was low, almost personal, like he'd just asked if they were ready, not just if the intel was solid.

Ava swallowed hard. "Yes."

Ben didn't hesitate. "Given what we know about Sergei Volkov, absolutely."

The colonel inclined his head toward a UH-60 Black Hawk helicopter. "He'll take you to the K-12 site. The TRF will be right behind you."

Minutes later, Ava and Ben were airborne, the thumping of rotary blades vibrating through her bones. Below them, the base shrank, melting into an island of asphalt and frozen plains as they made their way toward the silo. Ava tried to lock her fear away and focus on the mission before them: to secure America's nuclear arsenal. But the stakes were far too high.

Ava gripped the side rail, scanning the ground below, her 9mm a reassuring weight at her side. The wind whipped her hair across her face. She squinted at the scene below. A long wire fence topped with barbed wire had been clawed open. Gates twisted where the locks and entry points had once been. The roads that led to the silo were empty, except for the deep tracks of heavy tires made by the men who had come to seize what was never theirs.

She brushed the hair out of her face and pressed the radio to her lips. "TRF, be advised—attackers have breached the facility. Possible sabotage attempt."

The helicopter touched down with a violent lurch, its skids biting into the gravel. Ben and a dozen paramilitary officers fanned outward with their weapons drawn. Moving toward the guard house, Ava's boots crunched against shattered glass. Despite the morning chill, sweat was pouring down her sides, making her T-shirt stick to her skin.

Inside the guard house, the scene was eerily still. A radio hissed with static. A coffee cup laid overturned, its contents seeping into a keyboard blinking with an error message. No bodies. No alarms. The surveillance feed was dark. A sinking feeling pooled in her gut—the site had been taken swiftly, silently.

With his finger hovering over his trigger, Ben darted a quick side glance at Ava and held her gaze for a moment too long. Something heavy and unspoken passed between them. There were too many unsaid things between them, and they knew that today would likely end in bloodshed.

A voice crackled over the comms. "Any sign of the intruders?" Colonel Kareem asked.

Ben exhaled. "Most likely inside the silo," An armored Humvee roared to a halt near the silo's entrance, tires spitting gravel. The TRF spilled out, moving in tight formation with their M4 rifles raised as they scanned the area for intruders.

Ben quirked a brow at Ava. "Ready?"

Ava nodded sharply, her heartbeat drumming in sync with the howling wind. She gripped her sidearm as they moved toward the silo in unison. The prairie grass bent in the wind, whispering warnings that no one would heed. Beneath their boots, the missile slumbered in its steel tomb, humming with cold and the kind of silence that carried power that could end a city in a blink.

Inside the silo, the heavy, metallic smell of blood made Ava's stomach lurch. She turned the corner to see a young Air Force security officer bleeding from a chest wound. She swiped a sweaty palm on her pants and crouched next to the dying officer.

"They went below," the officer gasped. Every word, every breath was a struggle. "Two teams. One to the silo. One to the control room."

Above them, the launch shaft loomed, a massive blast door, an unmovable beast of reinforced steel, smelling of machine oil and cold iron, its edges slick with decades of sweat and desperation, designed to open once and only once.

Ava exchanged a look with Ben, the meaning unspoken but understood.

"We need to split up," Ava told Ben as a medic rushed in. "You cover the silo. I'm going to the launch control room."

His hand brushed against her arm—a fleeting touch, almost nothing, but she felt the intensity of it. "Don't do anything reckless," he said, his voice low.

She almost laughed, but something about the moment stopped her.

He looked at her, and an ache pressed hard against her ribs. If this was the last time—

Ben moved fast, like he'd already lost too much time. His mouth crashed against hers, rough and desperate, a collision of fear and something deeper. Her chest tightened, fearing this could be the last time she felt his touch, tasted his mouth. His hand lingered at her wrist, fingers tightening for a fraction of a second as if holding her in place against him. Slowly, painfully, he inched himself away. "I love you."

"Don't die," she said. The words tumbled out, raw and unpolished.

He smiled at her, but before she had time to breathe or even think, he whipped around and raced down a large metal staircase, deeper into the silo until it swallowed him whole.

Ava heard a steady thumping as the rest of the TRF team followed her down to the launch control center. The deeper they descended, the thicker the air became with the metallic smell of ozone and old electricity. Red emergency lights bled in shadows down the steel walls, and the ventilation system thrummed—a mechanical heartbeat too steady for what was coming.

When they reached the bottom of the stairs, the sharp, acrid smell of hydraulic fluid burned her nostrils. It was stifling, thick and suffocating from the weight of recycled air. The corridor ahead stretched into darkness, lit only by the flickering emergency lights casting eerie shadows along the steel walls. Each footstep echoed, a ghostly reminder of the silence pressing around them, above them.

Captain Sam Novak, the TRF team lead, moved swiftly and silently beside her, his breath even despite the tension thickening in the air. Ava spotted the control room ahead. Captain Novak and the rest of the TRF stacked up along the wall beside the door with their weapons primed. Novak signaled their positions: breacher, point man, entry personnel. A fifth man braced himself behind a ballistic shield, ready for whatever resistance they would face behind the door.

Novak nodded at the breacher who jiggled the door handle. Locked. Sergeant Ethan "Cipher" Vance slid a fibric-optic camera beneath the door to check for threats. The grainy footage flickered on his small screen: empty chairs, blinking monitors. No bodies.

Ava's stomach twisted. *Where the hell were they?*

Novak gave the go-ahead. The breacher fired four rapid shotgun blasts, each impact reverberating through Ava's body. The steel door clacked open, and the point man surged forward, rifle raised, sweeping the room in calculated arcs. The others followed in a seamless flow, securing corners for hostiles, searching for planted explosives, waiting.

Empty.

Ava's heartbeat was a heavy, dull ache as she took in the launch control room. Abandoned consoles. No sign of a struggle. Then—

"Unauthorized launch sequence initiated." The robotic voice of the system's artificial intelligence cut through the stillness like a knife, mechanical and detached, but the weight of the message vibrated along Ava's spinal cord.

Vance rushed forward, fingers flying over the keyboard, his breath shallow as he began to type, trying to override the sequence. Seconds stretched like hours as Ava's heart raced. Finally, he looked up from the monitor, sweat glistening at his temple. "They've uploaded malware into the missile's guidance system."

Ava's throat constricted. "What does that mean?"

Vance's eyes flicked to Novak before answering, his voice barely above a whisper. "It can cause any launch to fail."

She felt the ground beneath her shift. "Can you reverse it?'

"I'll do my best."

"Or can we just shut everything down?" she pressed, desperation ringing in her ears.

Her stomach twisted, tightening with each breath, each heartbeat. If the Russians had disabled their retaliation capabilities against a nuclear threat, the US was vulnerable to any attack.

"Let me try to see if I can override things," Vance muttered. "If they send one more burst of malware, even remotely, we're finished and so is everyone. And everything within a five-mile radius."

Ava felt cold, though sweat slicked her spine beneath the body armor. Every fear she'd ever buried converged in this single, breathless instant. The control room shuddered with the low hum of dying power; the overhead fluorescents sputtered and dimmed, barely holding on as red warning strobes bathed the walls in an ominous glow.

Boots shuffled against metal. Ava's pulse jumped, and she spun around, her breath snagging in her throat.

A shadow lurked in the darkness. A faceless figure all in black, a ski mask concealing any trace of humanity. No insignia. Gunfire cracked, and she hit the floor in a roll, the impact from the ground rattling up her spine. Her gun was up before she had to think. Breath steady, her finger tightened on the trigger. Then she heard it.

A familiar voice saying her name.

# CHAPTER

# 54

"AVA, WHAT ON earth?" The man removed his ski mask, his rifle hanging loosely at his side.

Nathaniel Grey's eyes bore into hers—cold, unreadable. The radio slipped from her fingers, clattering onto the steel floor with a sharp, metallic clang. But her grip on her rifle tightened.

"I might ask you the same thing."

Grey exhaled, his stance rigid. "You know my beliefs. The federal government has been undermining state autonomy for the last century—ruling from Washington with unchecked power."

"So, you officially sold out to the Russians? And I thought you wanted to protect American freedoms." She held back a laugh as the realization clicked into place—*Grey was the mole, the double agent.* "The irony is staggering."

Grey's jaw flexed, but he didn't deny it. So he was the cutout between Sergei Volkov, Abramovich, and their new detainee, Richard. The one who had corrupted US service members, convincing them they were patriots—when all along, they were pawns in Russia's game. Richard Holloway had no idea he was helping the Russians.

"For a billionaire, you really aren't very smart. You answer to Dimitri Abramovich, an international war criminal. You're not fighting for America. You're helping the enemy burn it to the ground."

Grey shook his head, though his jaw ticked. "What is America anymore? Surveillance. Censorship. The federal government has been putting pressure on Vibrantia to censor its political viewpoints for years."

Ava felt her trigger finger twitch. But she hesitated. He truly believed what he was saying. Was it possible that he didn't know what he'd really done? Was he a traitor or just a fool who thought he was a patriot?

She studied him. Grey wasn't pleading. He was standing his ground, conviction radiating from him. *Government overreach. Free speech suppression. Decentralization.* He had clung to those ideals so hard that he'd missed what they were doing to him.

"Spare me the speech," Ava snapped, her voice sharp as a blade. "You've been played. They fed you just enough truth to blind you to the bigger lie. They want to create division. They want to make America weak."

Behind her the missile control system whined, making the stakes clear. This wasn't about Grey and his treachery; this was about stopping a catastrophe. The countdown continued, code strings cascading down the screen. The Russian malware had embedded itself deep into the silo's systems, arming sequence partially activated. Overhead, a digital clock blinked.

**00:12:43**

Vance's override was still in process, while Grey was stalling. But he wasn't trying to save his life. He was trying to cost them theirs.

"Bullshit." Grey growled and lifted his SIG pistol. "It's tyranny in disguise!"

Novak tensed beside her, muscles coiling. "Drop your weapon!" he barked, his voice cutting through the room like a gunshot.

Grey didn't move. Instead, his eyes darted between the team and Ava, calculating. Ava's heart thudded. She didn't want to kill an American, her source. Not because he didn't deserve it, but because part of her understood his misguided motivation.

He was a pawn in their game that he hadn't even realized he was playing. But was ignorance an excuse when American lives were on the line?

The override attempt was still in progress. Grey held firm, his fingers coiled tight around the gun pointed at Ava.

"Last chance," she said.

Then, in a split second, he moved. Panic tightened like a band around her ribs, but her instinct took over, and in a single mechanical movement, she pulled the trigger of her M4.

*Crack.*

Grey's head snapped backward, and a red mist filled the air. His body collapsed before her rifle even finished swinging upward. He let out a single cry, more surprise than pain, and crumpled, his limbs twisting and twitching unnaturally on the floor in a final protest. The air reeked like burnt circuits and blood, death clinging to the back of her throat like smoke.

She exhaled slowly, lowering her M4 and blinking hard. The world was silent except for the ringing in her ears and the sudden, terrible stillness of the body in front of her. She'd killed before, from ten thousand feet above, but never at close range. She tried to breathe, but her lungs would not open.

*She had done this.*

She knew she should feel something—guilt, relief, possibly triumph. But there was only the cold certainty that it had been necessary to prevent war. She hadn't wanted to kill her source. But she had to make peace with the truth. He hadn't just failed his country, he'd willingly helped its enemies, those who would threaten its survival.

"You good?" Vance asked.

She nodded tightly, although her face and hand hummed with cold.

Vance was already at the next terminal, fingers racing across the keyboard to stop the countdown. “He almost locked us out.” His voice was tight, focused. “I need five more minutes.”

Ava’s earpiece crackled, Colonel Kareem’s voice sliced through the static, sharp and raw.

“Ava, they’ve taken Ben.”

The comms went dead mid-transmission, the last words drowned by gunfire.

# CHAPTER

# 55

THE WORLD AROUND Ava froze. Her heart sank as cold reality crashed into her. The price for her work was far steeper than she'd ever imagined. Clenching her M4 tighter, Ava stared at the scene—Vance typing furiously on the mainboard, trying to stop the Russians from instigating the next American civil war.

Everything was now in the background to the devastating news of Ben. He had risked everything for her, his career, his reputation, his life. He'd done it all to make her happy, to give her what she'd always wanted, and she hadn't been able to tell him how deeply she cared for him, loved him. And now the Russians had him.

Somewhere in the concrete maze above them, Ben was pinned down, bleeding—or worse.

Panic clawed at her throat, but she forced it down, forced herself to think. If the Russians knew about her and Ben, and they likely did, they may have captured him for leverage against her and the team who was trying to prevent nuclear chaos.

Ava leaned against the wall, her gun suddenly trembling in her right hand. Before she had time to move, a shadow shifted behind Sam Novak—a tall figure, a body carved of muscle and violence. Sergei Volkov.

Ava barely had time to react before a hiss of gas filled the room. "Get out! Gas!"

White fog emanated from the vents, stinging her eyes. She hacked and coughed, covering her mouth and nose with her collar. Her limbs became heavy and limp. Her eyes stung, and her vision blurred. She staggered toward Vance, intending to drag him toward the exit, but her knees gave out. Shapes loomed in the mist—boots pounding, dark figures with their weapons drawn.

"Ambush!" Novak roared, before a muzzle cracked into his skull and dropped him cold.

Ava squinted against the fog and lifted her M4, which felt like lead in her hands. Sergei Volkov emerged from the cloud of white smoke and wrenched it from her. A boot kicked into her ribs, and she choked from the pain. Another blow to her face made her jaw snap. White-hot pain flamed through her skull as Volkov pinned her wrists behind her back.

Everything blurred until she saw him—Dimitri Abramovich.

Over six feet tall, wearing a bespoke black tactical coat and a predator's smile, his angular face bore a deep scar that ran from his left temple down to his jawline. His glacial blue eyes locked on Ava as he stepped into the light.

It was as if she were numb from the neck down. All the terror from inside the Russian prison began to descend on her. The pain that came from being waterboarded, the violent spasms that racked her body until she had no idea who or what she was. The memory sharpened and she tasted bile as Abramovich moved with terrifying precision, every step measured and controlled.

"You . . ." It was all Ava could say as cold rage rippled over her. She could not move. Her anger had her locked in place.

"*Dobryy vecher,*" he murmured. "Miss Anderson. Still so reckless."

Ava struggled upright, blood dripping from her mouth. "What have you done with Ben?" she asked in Russian.

Abramovich's brow twitched in fleeting recognition, but he only smirked—a slow, cruel twist of his lips. "Alive," he said coolly.

"For now," Volkov added. "Depends on how well he holds up this time."

Her heart stuttered. *This time.*

Ava's blood turned to ice. Her mind reeled over what had happened the last time she and Ben had slept together. He awoke soaked with sweat in her bed, whispering fragments of an operation in Ukraine that had gone terribly wrong. She remembered parts of the story that he'd told her inside the cave—how he'd been detained after a failed intercept of a GRU asset near Ukraine. How only he had walked out, but his colleague didn't make it. He'd never shared all the details. But Ava had seen the scars, heard the emotion in his voice when he spoke about his friend who'd died, knew he held himself responsible for that death. And knew he still mourned the death of his older brother who had tried to save him.

Abramovich tilted his head, studying her reaction. "You want him back?" he murmured. "You know the price. Call off your little computer nerd and perhaps I'll give him back to you . . . if there's anything left."

Novak grunted on the floor as a guard kicked him in the gut. "Don't listen to this bastard," Novak coughed, "he's trying to—"

Abramovich silenced him with a backhand.

Vance twitched at his console. "The malware . . . it's spread," he said, panicked, a gun now pressed to his skull. "This will cripple our entire missile defense grid—permanently." A bead of sweat pebbled along his hairline.

Abramovich straightened; his voice was cool, triumphant. "We'll give America the war it's been aching for. But not with Russia. No. No. We'll do just what Nathaniel Grey and his little followers never expected, we'll launch a nuclear war, not on America's enemies, but on itself. We'll let your own people destroy themselves. One launch command, one well-timed 'glitch.'"

*Civil war.*

The muscles of Ava's face trembled as she now saw Abramovich's plan crystal clear—he planned to pit America against itself by turning the federal government against the states. He planned to enact a civil war from which the United States would likely never recover. If the federal government launched nuclear weapons on the American people, no one would ever trust the feds again. Russia would achieve its goal and emerge as the superpower. It was the ultimate play: missiles fired not at enemies but at their own people. It would shatter the country.

Ava felt like she was going to be sick, the realization of what was at stake like shrapnel in her mind. She had to stop this.

"Your life is over." Ava's gritted out. "What you did to Ben, what you're planning, I'll make you pay for it."

Abramovich smirked. "What I did to him? My dear Ava, I broke him. There will be no coming back from it."

She lunged forward, only for another guard to kick her legs out from underneath her. She hit the floor hard, her knees slamming against the concrete with a crack, pain jolting up her spine.

"What do you want?" she screamed, her voice raw, hoarse.

Abramovich stepped toward her and flicked a damp hair from her forehead. "What I want," he said, "is the location of Konstantin Gallitzin."

Her heart stopped. *They knew about Konstantin.* They knew about her father. She tried to school her face into stillness, but Abramovich smiled like a shark, sensing blood.

"Did you really think that you would be able to sneak out him out of Russia without the Kremlin noticing?" he taunted. "Foolish girl."

Volkov stepped toward Vance, pressing the gun harder into his temple and looking up at Ava, his eyes glimmering with hatred. "You decide, girl. Your country or your man." He held back a laugh. "Although I can't guarantee what kind of condition Ben will be in."

Ava's mind reeled. This wasn't just about secrets, stolen data, or the threat of nuclear war. It was about the people she loved. About those she could not lose, she would not lose. Slowly, painfully she forced herself to her feet, wiped the blood from her mouth, and lifted her chin. "No deal."

She straightened, fighting down her fear. "Where is he?" she ground out. "Tell me."

Abramovich just stared back at her, amusement dancing in his eyes.

Then she swiped her M4 off the floor and hurled it at the overhead alarm switch in one quick motion, shattering the glass. Glass rained and sirens shrieked. Emergency lights bathed the control room in a bloody red. In the chaos, Novak and Vance moved swiftly, pulling their weapons and mowing down the other men in the room. Then Vance dove back to his terminal and began furiously typing to override the launch sequence.

Abramovich lunged toward the main console, but Ava was quicker. She leveled a rifle at his chest. "Tell me where he is, dammit!"

He froze. On the console behind him, the launch sequence blinked on the screen, counting down toward annihilation.

"Abort the sequence!" Ava's voice cracked like a whip as she jabbed Abramovich in the chest hard enough that he winced. "Now!"

"You won't kill me," he said, voice dripping with disdain, eyes flashing with anger. "Not when you need me. Not when you still need to know how to stop it. Not when you still don't know where Ben is.

"What you did to me will look like child's play when I'm done with you." She fired two shots inches from his feet. He flinched, backing away, but he saw her lethal resolve. Something had shifted within her since her captivity, a resolve that had little room for mercy. She aimed the gun at Abramovich's head while Vance fastened his wrists behind his back. "I won't ask again."

The digital clock froze.

**00:02:37**.

Vance let out a ragged breath and looked at Ava. "We've got control back."

Ava lowered the rifle, though her muscles tightened. Novak was dragging Abramovich away, cursing in Russian. It was over. For now. But she still couldn't breathe. Not yet. Somewhere below, within the concrete belly of the silo, Ben was hurt, possibly fighting for his life. She sprinted toward the door, her chest heaving, her T-shirt soaked with blood and sweat.

"Hold on." Her voice cracked as she ran—a plea, a prayer. "I'm coming for you."

# CHAPTER

# 56

AVA SAW HIM before he saw her.

The air inside the silo was thick as iron, a scent that clung to the back of her throat. Shadows flickered on the curved steel walls, and in the center of it all, Ben was on his knees, his arms bound behind him with a plastic zip tie. A strip of silver duct tape covered his mouth. Blood had soaked through his shirt, close to his collarbone, and there was a dark red gash on his forehead.

One of Abramovich's men stood over Ben, gun drawn. Another stood next to him, staring down at his phone.

Ava stood on the stairwell above, out of sight. Her pulse roared in her ears, but she didn't wait. She fired two shots.

The first man dropped before he even knew he was dead. One shot—clean, efficient—and his body folded in on itself, the gun clattering against the concrete with a hollow metallic clack. Ava moved before the echo faded. She ran for Ben, whose head hung low, shadow cutting across his face. The second man turned, eyes narrowing, but she was already on him—an instinct honed by training and something deeper, older, raw.

Her knee drove into his ribs with the force of fury contained too long. The air left his lungs in a strangled plea. She tore the weapon from his grasp, reversed her hold, and brought the steel butt down across his jaw. Bone split. His knees gave way, the world narrowing to the sound of her own pulse. She fired two final shots.

The silence that followed felt heavier than the gun in her hand and relief hit her like a blow—sharp, unsteady, almost painful. She lowered the gun, her arms trembling. Around them, the stillness felt wrong, the kind that hummed before danger found its voice again.

"Are you hurt?" she asked, voice rough.

Her heart plummeted as she reached for him. "Ben!" She ripped the duct tape from his mouth, desperate to see his eyes, to hear him breathe.

He lifted his head, dazed, the faintest recognition flashing across his face. She pressed her lips to his.

"You're late," he rasped, trying to smile through the pain, his eyes still closed.

"Traffic," she said, her voice cracking.

Her hands were already on him, assessing his wounds, cutting his restraints. She moved his shirt to examine his body. The gash near his collarbone was inflamed but not life-threatening. Her eyes roamed over his shoulders and marred arms, searching for gunshot wounds. She breathed more easily, finding no signs of anything fatal.

"Ava!" Finally, his eyes shot open. His face blanched as if he only just realized that she wasn't a mirage. "How did you—you have to get out of here, now!"

"Don't be ridiculous." Her pulse throbbed in her ears as she hooked both arms beneath his armpits, urging him upward. "Come on. They won't be far behind."

But he didn't budge.

Terror attacked every muscle. He was shackled to the floor. The chains were industrial thick, bolted through the concrete, biting into his swollen ankles. His left leg twisted at an unnatural angle, the skin mottled and dark with bruises. Her rage choked her, tearing at her throat. It felt like her lungs had been scraped raw.

"What happened?" The words came out fractured, though she already knew. She had her own scars—memories of being at the mercy of men like Dimitri Abramovich. The sickness rose fast, a metallic taste flooding her mouth as she fought it back.

"He took a crowbar to my leg." Ben's voice was hoarse, agony flittered across his face. He drew in a shallow breath. "Ava..." His gaze lifted to hers, fevered and unsteady. "You need to go. You'll never make it out with me like this."

Nausea stirred below her ribcage. He was right. There was no way that she could move him, not without the use of an elevator. And even with US forces back in control of the facility, their comms were still down. They had no back up. No help.

She stiffened, reaching for his hand, temporarily grounding herself with the feel of his skin as her chest ached. "We'll find another way," she said, though her voice broke.

"Ava . . . help isn't coming. And you can't carry me."

Her eyes burned as their eyes locked. He reached up, lifting a trembling hand to touch her face. "Don't cry, Gallitzin," he said, his voice frayed but steady where it mattered. "You'll ruin your cover."

Her heart raced, though something deep within her core had steadied. The name still sounded foreign, like a passport she hadn't earned. But it was hers now whether she liked it or not. "I'm absolutely not leaving you without you."

Heavy footsteps came from outside the door; she reached for her M4. Then a familiar voice called out.

"Step aside, *dochka*."

Ava's heart stopped. It was Konstantin.

He emerged from the corridor, his long dark coat sweeping behind him like a shadow unfurling. Gray eyes sharpened on her. A pistol in each hand. The glint of a blade at his hip. Her father, once a ghost, now someone she could cling to, perhaps, depend on.

"You followed me?" she whispered.

"Never stopped," he said simply, "although the fighting going on above between your federal agents and local police didn't make it easy." His gaze flicked to Ben. "We'll get him out."

"Konstantin," Ben murmured, dazed.

"Save your strength." Konstantin crouched on the ground, examining the locks binding Ben to the floor. "Old Soviet make," he muttered, pulling a slim tool from his coat. "Apparently Abramovich is traveling with his own torture tools, the bastard."

He inserted the tool with practiced precision, sliding it between the locking mechanism and the ratchet arm. The lock gave with a metallic click, and the shackles fell from Ben's ankles. Ava blinked back hot tears. How many times had she prayed for backup like this? For someone to just show up.

But just as Konstantin and Ava came on either side of Ben to ease him off the floor, the heavy blast door behind them groaned open. A rush of cold air swept in, carrying the scent of oil and metal. Dimitri Abramovich stepped through as if he owned the room, his face impassive. Beside him loomed a broad-shouldered man in a pit-stained white T-shirt, his eyes flat and waiting.

Ava's pulse froze, and her hand went to her holster, but Abramovich was faster. His henchman's weapon was already raised, the black barrel glinting under sterile lights.

"Well, well, what do we have here?" He took in the sight of Konstantin standing next to the broken shackles. "I didn't expect a family reunion."

His eyes narrowed on Konstantin. "You should have stayed dead." Abramovich glared at Ava. "And you, I cannot seem to get rid of."

"Let Ben go," she seethed. "You only have yourself to blame for your failures."

"I'm not done with your boyfriend yet. We have a score to settle, me and him. I lost Crimea because of him."

"Like hell you do." She cursed and rose to her feet, ready to launch herself at Abramovich.

"Would you like me to arrange to have both you and your father detained next to him?" Abramovich asked. "I'm a very accommodating host."

She gritted her teeth. "What happened to Novak?"

"He tried to kill me." Abramovich made a bowing gesture, like he was announcing himself at court. "But as you can see, I'm still very much alive. I sought assistance, and your Liberty Coalition compatriots were only too happy to oblige."

Ava felt sick. He'd used Liberty Coalition, just like he'd used Nathaniel Grey.

Konstantin rolled his shoulders backward. "I can see that you brought reinforcements," he nodded to the large man who stood in the corner awaiting orders. "You never could handle the dirty work on your own."

The large man lunged, swinging a fist toward Konstantin's ribs. But Konstantin moved swiftly, one swift duck, a quick pivot, and he put an elbow to the man's throat. The henchman collapsed, gagging.

Abramovich drew his pistol. "You think you can kill me and walk out of here?"

"I'm not going anywhere." Konstantin raised his own weapon. "I'm here to end this."

Abramovich advanced, a predator savoring the cornered prey. Ava's pulse spiked, the world narrowing to the gleam of the knife at his hip and the sound of his boots scraping the concrete.

But in a flash of motion, Ben was on him. Bloodied, battered, but burning with fury, he lunged and caught Abramovich by the throat. The force drove Abramovich backward, the sound of impact echoing off the walls. Ben's face was a mask of exhaustion and rage, but his voice was pure steel.

"You really thought this would end any other way?" he snarled. "You've failed every mission you've ever touched, Abramovich. Moscow's done with you. Your money's gone, your friends have vanished—and after tonight, so will you."

Abramovich choked, clawing at Ben's grip as Konstantin stepped in, weapon raised and steady, the barrel inches from Abramovich's skull.

No one saw the brute rising from the shadows, hulking and silent, clamping his hand around Ava's arm before she could turn. As he slammed her against the wall, the air left her chest. Cold metal kissed her throat—a knife, trembling from his own adrenaline. Her fingers twitched toward her weapon, but the pressure at her neck deepened. The world constricted to the thrum of her pulse and the sound of Ben's breath—ragged, furious, ready to explode.

Ben backed away from Abramovich, his chest heaving with rage, and Konstantin lowered his weapon. "You harm one hair on her head, and I will end you." She could barely hear Ben's voice as her pulse flooded her ears.

Her vision swam, white sparks clouding her vision.

Abramovich laughed. "You still don't get it, do you? I hold the cards. Not you." He nodded at the huge man, who dug the tip of his knife into Ava's neck. "Neither of you do. Even when I am gone, my movement will continue through the Liberty Coalition. America will never be safe."

The knife drew blood and Ava yelped, her fists clenched tight at her sides as she eyed her M4 on the floor.

Ben was waiting—for an opening, a distraction, anything. He glanced up at the countdown clock that remained frozen and back at Abramovich. Blood dripped down from Ben's forehead into his eye, but he didn't wipe it away. "You've already lost," he said.

Abramovich chuckled. "You think I care about outcomes? I live for the chaos. This is only the beginning."

Ben took one slow step forward, his eyes flicking to where the large man still held the knife to Ava's throat. "Then die in it."

Ben moved with precision, muscle memory overriding pain from his injuries, and in one swift motion grabbed the blade from the man holding Ava, twisted the knife from his grip and plunged it deep into the man's chest. Ava swiped her M4 up off the floor and spun around. She fired once, twice, and Abramovich's shoulder exploded in red.

Abramovich staggered back, and Konstantin closed in like a storm. "You don't get to hide behind your chaos anymore," he said, his voice low though it shook with fury. "You didn't just betray her, you orchestrated it. You fed the Agency false intelligence, made them believe Theresa was working for you. You turned her into a traitor in their eyes so they'd look away when she was taken."

The words hit Ava in the chest like shrapnel. Memories she'd tried to bury resurfaced—the official denials, her mother's story redacted from Agency files. All this time she'd believed that the CIA's silence was bureaucratic indifference, when it had been deception engineered by the man standing before her. The room seemed to narrow around them, the hum of the silo fading to a distant roar.

Abramovich clutched his bleeding shoulder and spit blood, grinning. "She was a means to an end. You both were. You of all people should understand that."

Konstantin's face twisted—quieter, deeper than rage. He lunged, burying his knife into Abramovich's chest, twisting until the man gasped, his face blooming with shock and fear. "For Theresa," Ava's father whispered. "You will burn in hell for what you did to her."

Abramovich gasped, blood bubbling from his lips, but Konstantin held him upright. Ava stood frozen, the words her father had spoken—*for Theresa*—ringing in her head. She saw it then, not just grief, not just rage: a man haunted by all he had lost. A man trying to give her mother the justice he never could give her in life. Konstantin was no longer the spy, the ghost; he was her mother's reckoning. And hers too.

Ava fired one final round between Abramovich's eyes, and then she saw her mother. Not Abramovich crumpling to the floor. Not the gun slipping from his limp hand. But her mother's eyes, green, wide, and soft, misting with pride. Not real, just a memory. But Ava felt it, deep within the marrow of her bone. A presence. A peace.

She was eight again. Her mother's hand brushing hair from her cheek after her piano recital. The smell of garlic and fresh basil in the air at her favorite Italian restaurant. A crooked smile as her mother wiped the pizza sauce from her face. A single napkin torn in two.

"It's over, Mama," she whispered.

Now her knees nearly gave out, all the pain and terror rushing out of her at once. The air felt too thin, her vision swimming. She closed her eyes and reached out, fingers searching for something solid, but only found the cold concrete beneath her palm.

"Ava." The voice was distant, raw like sound carried through water. "Open your eyes."

Ben was next to her, pale but awake, blood smeared across his face like war paint. She leaned into his arms, dizzy with relief, her body suddenly aware of every bruise, every breath. For a moment, neither of them spoke. The silence between them felt sacred as she looked up and brushed the damp hair away from his forehead, her fingers trembling.

For years, she'd believed herself untouchable, living her life on the fringes of attachment only so that she didn't have to feel the pain that came from loving someone, then losing them. But now, staring at Ben, she knew she'd been wrong. It was worth the potential heartache to feel the way she did about him.

"Ava." His hand cupped her face, his thumb brushing away a tear. "Now do you believe me? What I'd do for you—the lengths I'd go?"

"I thought you wanted us to stop seeing each other." She smiled faintly through her tears.

He gave a half-smirk, the kind that used to drive her crazy. "Yeah, well. Turns out I'm an idiot. I thought I could keep my distance, stay focused on the mission. But the truth is..." His eyes locked with hers, steady, unflinching. "You're the only thing that's ever felt real. Everything else—intel, ops, orders—it's all noise."

Her throat tightened. She'd spent years building walls, convincing herself that love was a liability. But now she saw it—the bravado, the teasing deflections had always been his way of protecting her. Of protecting himself from feeling too much. And she'd done the exact same thing.

"I love you," she said softly.

Konstantin stepped back, folding into the shadows.

Then Ben's mouth was on hers, aching and breathless and fierce—making her feel tethered, known, and undone all at the same time.

Boots pounded down the hall. "Clear!" someone shouted as the two of them inched away from one another, fingers still intertwined.

Medics rushed to Ben, their voices clipped, efficient, but Ben's eyes never left hers as they tended to his wounds.

Ava glanced over her shoulder. Two medics were crouched over Ben, wrapping the deep split along his ankle. Blood soaked through the bandage, but he waved them off, muttering something about being fine. Typical Ben—bleeding out and still trying to look invincible.

The air throbbed with noise—rotor blades chopping overhead, radios spitting static, agents barking orders as they hauled prisoners from the wreckage. Floodlights cut through the smoke, slicing across the steel walls of the silo. What had once been a vault of secrets now buzzed with the raw pulse of revelation.

A shadow moved through the haze. Konstantin. He walked toward her, his face carved with exhaustion and ash. His coat hung open, streaked with dust and blood, but his eyes, those familiar, haunted eyes, never left hers.

"You came," she said.

He stopped in front of her, smoke curling between them.

"You are—" His throat tightened. He forced the words out, raw and uneven. "—my daughter."

The pain she'd felt as a girl had lived inside her veins as long as she could remember. But now, for the first time in her life, she wasn't fighting alone.

She exhaled, the breath shuddering out of her as something inside her finally broke free. Around her, the world roared back to life. Orders shouted. Helicopters landing above them. But beneath it all, she felt the quiet truth settle deep in her chest.

Outside, helicopters circled overhead as Ava, Ben, and Konstantin emerged from the silo. Emergency floodlights flashed against the compounds that, until minutes ago, had been the epicenter of a quiet civil war—a war fueled by Russia. And yet, despite the devastation and confusion, something had changed, a new peace had settled across the open plains of America's backcountry.

Dawn began to spread its wings across the open plains, warm and effortless as state troopers and paramedics working side by side with the federal agents and military personnel. And in that moment, with the sun breaking over the horizon, the remnants of a war deterred smoking behind them, Ava understood why it had all mattered—why the betrayals, lies, and violence had all been worth it. That if they hadn't stepped in, if they hadn't fought back, America might had fallen to the chaos. She had seen what Russian influence could do, how it spread rot beneath the surface, eroding truth, turning neighbors against each other.

Her mother had died believing no one would come for her; died forgotten by the very system she had served, fighting the war no one had seen or acknowledged. Ava had carried that weight with her for years. But today she felt something close to peace. And that was why, despite everything it cost her, she would do it again. So no one else's mother would be abandoned, nor their cause lost or forgotten. She would do it for the country that her mother had believed in, even as it failed her. Because America was worth saving—from the outside and from within.

"They counted on us turning against each other," she whispered as Ben's hand tightened in hers. "We didn't."

Konstantin stood behind them, silent as ever. He reached out and placed a hand on her shoulder without agenda or words. Just there. And that was all she'd ever longed for, everything she had ever needed.

# Epilogue

**Six months later**

THE TRAIN STATION in Prague smelled like wet stone and blooming chestnuts. Ava stood near the departure board wearing a tan trench coat, her collar turned up against the rain and the world. The ceiling arched high above her, a ribcage of steel blackened by steam and age. Pigeons clattered somewhere under the rafters like restless ghosts, and the Vltava train brakes came heavy, hissing and tired. Though the war had gone quiet, it wasn't over. She would need to take these next months to prepare.

Frank had said, "Build a network, quietly."

He made it sound so simple, so easy. Yet Ava knew better. Nothing was ever simple in this line of work, especially when it was tied to blood. It wasn't as if she had a calling card with her name printed on it that said she was from the powerful Gallitzin family. She would need to study her targets, gather intelligence on how they operated, and ultimately what made them tick. That would take time, patience. She would start in Prague and build out from there—Berlin, Warsaw, possibly Tallinn. Cities with old roots but new money, fresh in from Russia and its oligarchs.

Ava kept her eyes on the platform, travelers with distant gazes who moved quickly past her, like they had somewhere important to be. The train from Vienna screeched in late, brakes screaming like a dying god. From the train, a man wearing a fedora stepped off with a folded newspaper tucked under his arm.

Konstantin didn't look at her, but he didn't need to. He'd spotted her long before the train had stopped. They walked together without speaking, two shadows moving toward a café that had likely not changed since the wall came down. They took a table near the rear, their backs to the wall, where they would get the first look at any potential threat.

"How was it?" she asked.

Konstantin sat across from Ava, stirring his espresso, not adding sugar, never looking up. Outside, the rain clinked against the metal roof, the only sound breaking the silence once the trains stopped. After six long months in Vienna without word, Ava had started to think the worst. Maybe the Gallitzin family never intended to help her. Perhaps they'd abandoned the idea of challenging the regime, choosing the safety of a quieter life, one that didn't involve upsetting the status quo.

After a long pause Konstantin looked up, eyes moving like he was trying to memorize her face—perhaps especially the features that belonged to her mother.

"I told them you might reach out," he said finally in Russian. "Some are willing. Others . . . they remember too much."

Ava didn't blink. "I only need the ones with the access—the people who haven't forgotten what we're fighting for." If the old Russia were allowed to rise again, she knew they'd unleash another wave of lies, poisoning the truth, tearing at the seams of a country trying to heal.

"They want a better Russia, a truer one. One that is not written by thieves and liars. So, *da*, most are willing to help, if it means a new government, a new Russia. Yes, I believe they will help." He sat his spoon down and leaned forward. "But they are my family, our family. The CIA must follow through on their promise. Otherwise, they will pay with their lives."

Ava nodded and sat back in her chair, her pulse thrumming hot through her head, her heart. He was right. The Agency had a habit of breaking its promises, of leaving people behind. "My family, my mission, they are the same now," she said.

"Careful," her father said, his expression darkening. "That is precisely the kind of thinking that got your mother into trouble. Your family should always come first, and if there's ever a day when you must choose between them, choose wisely, or you could lose them both."

Outside, the rain turned to mist that flitted within the café like dew settling.

A beat of silence stretched between them before Konstantin reached into his coat pocket and slid a phone across the table wrapped in a cloth napkin. "This has everything—phone numbers, emails, addresses—everything you should need. You have cousins in Brussels, Riga, Lyon. My godchildren. One priest. Some are clean, most are not. You'll have to decide who you can trust—or who's loyal to whatever they've been surviving on since the Gallitzin family was exiled from their homeland."

"How will they know me?"

"They'll know your eyes," he said. "They're mine."

Ava looked at him, into the eyes so like her own. She quietly tucked the phone into her purse before she spoke. "Why help me now? I know how dangerous this must be for you."

He paused and looked out at the platform then back at her. "Because. You're not working for the CIA right now. You're working for something much older. Your homeland. Your family." He stood and leaned down, pressing a soft kiss on her forehead. "And because I want my daughter to come home."

The train rocked gently as it pulled away from Prague, the outside blurring past like pastel watercolors left out in the rain. Ava sat alone in her compartment. Her coat was folded neatly beside her. In her lap was the phone from her father, her inheritance, with all the data she needed. Her mind was already in Brussels, developing cover stories, assessing potential targets for recruitment. The mission demanded clarity, but her thoughts kept straying, reeling back to Ben, back to the day they had said goodbye in DC.

She wanted to cry, she wanted to pound her fists into something. She'd lost so much. This job had stripped so much from her. Yet she couldn't walk away. Not now. Konstantin believed that a constitutional monarch could bring Russia back from the brink. She believed it too: a constitutional monarch could serve as a unifying figure—one that could restore national pride and cultural identity. And if the family that ruled was her family, she could help ensure that the Russian government remained loyal to the United States.

Cyberattacks and misinformation campaigns would become things of the past, and America would finally be left to heal.

Ava didn't hear the compartment door slide open. She felt it, a subtle shift in the air. Instinct pricked down her arms.

"Is this seat taken?"

She looked up, her eyes blurred, and her throat thick. "You came."

Ben was travel worn, and it looked like he hadn't shaven in days, but his eyes stayed sharp, stayed steady, like a lighthouse in a storm. "Always."

Ava blinked, the heat behind her eyes refusing to fall, torn between fury and relief. "What are you doing here?"

He gave her a crooked smile. "Couldn't let you run around Europe all alone."

"So, you're stalking me now," she said, although the truth settled deep within her chest.

For as long as she could remember, all she could think about since she was eleven, her dream had been uncovering what had really happened to her mother. The unanswered questions had festered into a bitterness, fueling her relentless desire for revenge. But now, after finding Konstantin—her father, her family—something inside her had shifted. For the first time, she had a purpose that wasn't driven by loss.

And there was Ben. He sat down across from her like he had every right to be there, that familiar spark in his eyes. "You see, we have these travel databases."

Ava shot up from her seat, hand clamping over his mouth. His breath was warm on her fingertips. She dropped her hand, and he seized her waist, pulling her down onto his lap, her knees on either side of his hips.

"Still," she said, fighting her own breath, "Langley will not be pleased."

"Technically, I'm here on their orders."

Ben's voice carried that familiar drawl—half-truth, half dare. He reached up, cupping her face with a rough hand. Ava couldn't deny the magnetic pull toward him. Logic didn't stand a chance.

She laughed under her breath. "Since when did you start taking orders?"

A smirk tugged at his mouth. "I don't. I just ignore the ones I don't like."

Silence stretched between them, thick with everything they weren't saying. She pushed herself off him, breaking eye contact.

"Nothing has changed," she said, her voice steadier than she felt. "My mind is made up. This isn't a game. These people—this network—it's personal."

"I know." His tone shifted, low and certain. "That's why I'm here."

She wanted to tell him she didn't need him. That she could handle it. But the words caught in her throat. She did need him—just not in the way Langley had written into the op plan.

Ben leaned forward, elbows resting on his knees, the corner of his mouth still curved like he knew it. "Then tell me what you've got."

She handed him the phone. Their fingers brushed, and for a moment the whole train seemed to hum with that same dangerous electricity that always sparked between them.

"This is… my family," she said, the words jagged in her throat.

He sat beside her, studying her face before glancing at the screen. "Family, huh? That's one hell of a complication for a clean op."

"I believe in what we're trying to accomplish," she said. "But I don't want anything to happen to them."

Ben exhaled, then looked at her with that wry, knowing grin. "What kind of intel are we after—the helpful kind, or the kind that gets you shot crossing a border?"

"Both," she said.

He nodded once, the grin still ghosting at the edge of his mouth. "Figures."

Outside, the lights of the city blurred past the window, flickering across their faces as the train thundered on —two operatives caught between duty and something far more dangerous.

Perhaps Ben would change his mind about helping her. She could feel his hesitation, the moment he realized what she was asking. Not a favor but help with a revolution, an enormous change in Russia. She could see it in the clenching of his jaw, his knuckles gone white as he held her phone. She was dragging him into something irreversible. Blood would spill. She knew it. He knew it. But she could not step away. Not when her family's future and the future of her country—and her father's country—was on the line.

"I know what you're thinking," she said, her voice low. "I know what it could cost you, us both."

Ben lifted his eyes, his gaze fierce and unwavering. "Abramovich is dead," he said finally, his voice low. He reached out, his palm warm against her jaw. "The only life I see ahead for me is at your side. If I have that"—his thumb brushed her cheekbone—"I have everything. My future is yours now and what we do now together."

Her heart leaped, then soared as the train picked up speed. The gray Czech countryside blurred to a wild green, and for the first time in a long time, Ava let herself believe in a future, and let herself breathe.

# ACKNOWLEDGMENTS

THIS BOOK HAS been with me for a long time, longer than the pages suggest. It was shaped by memory, by loss, by love, and by a career that taught me how much of ourselves we carry quietly. I did not write it alone.

First, to my family, thank you for being my constant and my safe harbor. To my husband, Matt, thank you for believing in this story even when it demanded patience, late nights, early mornings and more emotional distance than either of us would have preferred. You carried more than your share so I could finish this book, and your steadiness made it possible. To my boys, you are the reason this story exists. You remind me every day why truth matters, why courage matters, and why the women who came before us deserve to be remembered.

To my mother, who inspired Theresa, this book is, in many ways, a tribute to you. You showed me what quiet strength looks like, how to carry fear without letting it define you, and how to love fiercely while shouldering heavy things. The heart of this story belongs to you.

I want to honor the memory of my father, Tom. His absence is one I still feel deeply. Writing the character of Konstantin allowed me, in ways I didn't anticipate, to revisit a father–daughter relationship I miss—the sense of being known, protected, challenged, and loved. Through him, I was able to explore the complicated bonds between parents and children, and to sit, briefly, with the grief and gratitude that coexist when someone you love is gone.

To my colleagues from the intelligence community, this book exists because of what I learned beside you. Thank you for the professionalism, loyalty, gallows humor, and humanity you bring to work that often requires silence. While this story is fiction, many of the emotional truths within it are not.

I am deeply grateful to my manager, Jim Strader, for championing me and this book from the very beginning. Your belief in my voice and your guidance helped carry this story to the page. To my agent at CAA, Tia Ikemento, thank you for your fierce advocacy and for trusting this story and its ambition. To my editor, Sara Henry, thank you for your insight, care, and steady editorial vision. And to Matthew Martz and the entire team at Crooked Lane Books, thank you for giving *The Patriot's Daughter* a home. This opportunity is one I do not take lightly.

Finally, to the readers: thank you for trusting me with this story. *The Patriot's Daughter* is about legacy—what we inherit, what we question, and what we choose to protect. I hope it stays with you long after the last page.

—Brittany Butler Jennings